FREEDOM'S
CHILD

FREEDOM'S
CHILD

A NOVEL

JAX MILLER

B \ D \ W \ Y
BROADWAY BOOKS
NEW YORK

Copyright © 2015 by Jax Miller Limited

Published in the United States by Broadway Books, an imprint of the Crown Publishing Group, a division of Penguin Random House LLC, New York.
www.crownpublishing.com

Broadway Books and its logo, B \ D \ W \ Y, are trademarks of Penguin Random House LLC.

Originally published in hardcover in the United States by Crown Publishers, an imprint of the Crown Publishing Group, a division of Penguin Random House LLC, New York, in 2015.

Library of Congress Cataloging-in-Publication Data

Miller, Jax, author.
 Freedom's child : a novel / Jax Miller. —First edition.
 pages cm
 I. Title.
 PS3613.I5374F74 2015
 813'.6—dc23
 2014036455

ISBN 978-0-553-44687-6
eBook ISBN 978-0-8041-8681-0

Printed in the United States of America

Book design by Elina Nudelman
Cover design by Michael Morris
Cover photography: Hero Images/Getty Images

10 9 8 7 6 5 4 3 2 1

First Paperback Edition

FOR BABCHI AND THE BOSS OF THE CITY.
AND TO PAT RAIA, THE ROBIN TO MY GOTHAM.

FREEDOM'S
CHILD

PROLOGUE

My name is Freedom Oliver and I killed my daughter. It's surreal, honestly, and I'm not sure what feels more like a dream, her death or her existence. I'm guilty of both.

It wasn't long ago that this field would ripple and rustle with a warm breeze, gold dancing under the blazes of a high noon sun. The Thoroughbreds, a staple of Goshen, would canter along the edges of Whistler's Field. If you listen close enough, you can almost hear the laughter of farmers' children still lace through the grain, a harvest full of innocent secrets of the youthful who needed an escape but didn't have anywhere else to go. Like my Rebekah, my daughter. My God, she must have been beautiful.

But a couple weeks is a long time when you're on a journey like mine. It could almost constitute something magnificent. Almost.

I catch my breath when I remember. Somewhere in this field, my daughter is scattered in pieces.

Goshen, named after the Land of Goshen from the Book of Genesis, somewhere between Kentucky's famous bourbon trails in America's Bible Belt. The gallops of Thoroughbreds that haunt this dead pasture are replaced with the hammering in my rib cage. The mud cracks below me as I cross the frostbitten field, steps ripping the earth with each fleeting memory. The skies are that certain shade of silver you see right before a snowstorm; now, the color of my filthy fucking soul.

I'm reminded of the sheriff behind me with an itchy finger and a Remington aimed between my shoulder blades. I'm reminded of my own white-knuckled grip on my pistol.

Call me what you will: a murderer, a cop killer, a fugitive, a drunk. You think that means anything to me now? In this moment? The frost pangs my lungs in such a way that I think I might vomit. I don't. Still out of breath, I use the dirty robe to wipe blood from my face. I don't even know if it's mine. There's enough adrenaline surging through my veins that I can't feel pain if it is.

"This is it, Freedom," the sheriff calls out in his familiar southern drawl. The tears make warm streaks over my cold skin. The cries numb my face, my lips made of pins and needles. There's a lump in my throat I can't breathe past. *What have I done? How the hell did I end up here? What did I do so wrong in life that God deemed me so fucking unworthy of anything good?* I'm not sure. I've always been the one with the questions, never the answers.

PART I

1
FREEDOM AND THE WHIPPERSNAPPERS

TWO WEEKS AGO

My name is Freedom, and it's a typical night at the bar. There's a new girl, a blonde, maybe sixteen. Her eyes are still full of color; she hasn't been in the business long enough. Give it time. Looks like she can use something to eat, use some meat on her bones. I know she's new because her teeth are white, a nice smile. In a month or two, her gums will shelve black rubble, and she'll be nothing but bone shrink-wrapped in skin. That's what happens in that line of work. The perks of being young are destroyed by the lurid desires of men and the enslavement of drug addiction. Such is life.

A biker has her by her golden locks, heading for the parking lot. The place is too busy, nobody notices. He blends in with the other leather vests and greasy ponytails, the crowd crammed from entrance to exit. But I notice. I see her. And she sees me, eyes glassed over with pleading, a glint of innocence that may very well survive if I do something. But I have to do something now.

"Watch the bar," I yell to no one in particular. I'm surprised by my own agility as I jump over the bar and into the horde, pushing, elbowing, kicking, yelling. I find them, a trail of perfume behind the young girl. I take the red cap of the Tabasco sauce off with my teeth and spit it out. The biker can't see me coming up behind him as he tries to leave the bar; he towers over me by a good foot and a half. I cup my palm and make a pool of hot sauce.

███

I still own the clothes I was raped in. What can I say? I'm a glutton for punishment. My name is Freedom, though seldom do I feel free. Those were the terms I made with the whippersnappers; if I did what they wanted, I could change my name to Freedom. Freedom McFly, though I never got to keep the McFly part. They said it sounded too Burger King–ish. Too '80s. Fucking whippersnappers.

Freedom Oliver it is.

I live in Painter, Oregon, a small town showered in grit, rain, and crystal meth, where I tend a rock pub called the Whammy Bar. My regulars are fatties from the West Coast biker gangs like the Hells Angels, the Free Souls, and the Gypsy Jokers, who pinch my husky, tattooed flesh and cop their feels.

"Let me get a piece of that ass."

"Let me give you a ride on my bike."

"How 'bout I give you freedom from those pants?"

I hide my disgust behind a smile that convinces the crowd and stick my chest out a little more; it brings in the tips, even if it makes me shudder. They ask where my accent's from and I tell them Secaucus, New Jersey. Truth be told, it's from a shady area on Long Island, New York, called Mastic Beach. It's not like the peckerwoods can tell the difference.

I tear out my umbrella in the early morning after my shift is over and the bar is closed. I squint through the October rains and the smoke of a Pall Mall. I swear to God, it's rained every day since I was born. To my left, adjacent to the Whammy Bar, is Hotel Painter. The neon letters drone through the rain, where some key letters are knocked out so the sign spells HOT PIE. Appropriate, given that it's one of those lease-by-the-hour roach motels that offer ramshackle shelter to anyone wanting to rent cheap pussy. The ladies huddle under the marquee of the reception desk to hide from the rain and yell their good-byes my way. I wave back. Goldilocks isn't there. *Good*. Looks like the night's slowed down.

Fuck this umbrella if it doesn't want to close. I chuck it to the dirt lot and climb into the rusty hooptie of a station wagon. I remove my nose ring and put the smoke out in an overflowing ashtray.

"Jesus Harry Christ," I scream, alarmed by a knock on the window. I can't see through the condensation and open it a crack to find a couple suits. "Whippersnapping jack holes." They look at me like I'm nuts, but I'm pretty sure they expect it. People have a hard time trying to understand what I say most of the time. "Isn't it late for you guys?"

"Well, you keep making us come out here like this," says one of them.

"It was an accident." I shrug as I get out of the car.

"Trying to blind a man with Tabasco sauce was an accident?"

"Semantics, Gumm," I say as I fiddle with the keys. "Guy got rough with one of the girls, so I slapped him on the cheek. Only I missed his cheek and got his eyes. I only just so happened to have Tabasco sauce spill in my hand not a moment before. Besides, he's not pressing charges, so I'm sorry you guys had to make the trip from Portland."

"You're walking on thin ice," says Howe.

"Tabasco won't blind you." I shake the rain from my hair. "Just hurts like fuck and keeps you awake."

"Well, he was mad enough to call the cops. If it weren't for us, you'd be sitting in jail right now," says Gumm.

"Besides, an eye patch suits him." I lead them into the closed pub, turn on the power, and grab three Budweisers. They eyeball the beverages. "Relax. I won't tell," I offer.

The lights are dim, borderline interrogational, above the island bar in the middle of a large, old wooden floor furnished with the occasional pool table. The scent of stale smoke hangs heavy, etched in the wood's grooves like a song impressed on a vinyl record. The music turns on to Lynyrd Skynyrd. U.S. Marshals Gumm and Howe each flip a stool down from the bar and sit.

"You know how it goes," says Agent Gumm, with his salt-and-pepper hair, handlebar mustache, and sagged jowls. He doesn't want to be here, I can tell. I don't want him here either. Court-mandated. Fuck the system. Let's get this over with. We'll fill out the forms, I'll get a lecture. *Consider this a warning.* Yeah, yeah, it's always considered. To Gumm's side is Agent Howe, who does a quick read over the files in their manila envelopes. "How's this job treating you, Freedom?"

"I'd come up with a clever remark, but I'm too tired for the bullshit." I wipe my leather jacket with a bar towel. "Just slap me on my wrist and we can all be on our way, why don't you?"

"Was just asking about the job, is all," says Howe, a handsome man in his early forties with jet-black hair and green eyes. I'd bang him. Well, maybe if he wasn't such an asshole. Though I doubt that'd stop me anyway.

"Let's cut the shit. You two didn't come all the way here from Portland to get on my ass about a tiny bar scuffle."

They twirl their bottles between their palms. Gumm uses his sleeve to wipe the sweat from his beer off the wood. They look at each other with those raised eyebrows, the kind of look that says, *Are you going to tell her or should I?*

"Will ya just spit it out?" I roll my eyes and hop onto the bar in front of them. I pull their envelopes from under me and sit Indian-style, their eyes level with my knees.

"Freedom, Matthew was released from prison two days ago. He was granted an appeal and won." Gumm pretends to cough with the words. Well, isn't that just dandy? I rest my elbows on my knees, chin on my fists. Which facial expression shall I feign? I go for ignorance, as if I have no idea who this Matthew is that they're talking about. But I do. It's why I am a protected witness. In the Witness Protection Program. WPP. Whips. Whippersnappers. But lucky me, I was dismissed with prejudice, meaning I cannot be charged for the same crime twice. Thank God for small favors.

"And?" I don't want them to know that my heart is pounding and I'm starting to sweat.

Gumm leans in closer. "For a time to be determined, we are heightening your protection. We'll have one of ours come see you on a weekly basis. Keep a low profile."

"You mean lower than a biker bar in the middle of nowhere?"

"A small cross to bear for killing a cop, Freedom." And there are those nasty looks and curled lips from these guys that I know all too well. "C'mon, you've got nothing to lose if you admit it already. I mean, you can't be tried again for it. We know you did it."

"Good luck proving it. And nice of you assholes to give me a heads-up." I chug my beer and aim my chin at the door. "Be careful driving back to the big city in that rain. Don't want you two dying in some terrible accident." I finish the beer. "That'd just be terrible."

At least they take the hint. Sometimes they don't. Sometimes they overstay their welcome. Sometimes they do it on purpose just to piss me off. "By the way." Howe rises from his stool and closes his coat. "I have to ask. Procedure, you know . . ." He speaks through his teeth like he has thorns in his ass.

I'll save him the trouble, if only to get them the hell out of here faster. Their files stick to my wet boots as I bounce from the bar. I grab the soggy pages from under me and hand them over. "Don't worry, I'm still on my meds," but this is a blatant lie. And I think they know it's a lie but don't care. "No need to ask."

■ ■ ■

I think about Matthew, released from prison after eighteen years; eighteen years of his imprisonment that secured my eighteen years of freedom.

Alone in the shitty apartment, I crawl out of wet clothes and dry my naked body against the cushions of a musty tweed couch. Alone I cry. Alone I look at an old picture of my dead husband, Mark, the one photo that survived an incident with a sink and a book of matches a couple decades ago. Alone I open a bottle of whiskey. Alone I whisper two names in the dark.

"Ethan."

"Layla."

Alone. Fucking whippersnappers.

2

MASON AND VIOLET

I am a boy. This woman's arms protect me from the vastness of the ocean, blue as far as the eye can see until it forms a gray line dotted with ships. I bury my face in her neck; her laughter moves my small body. But I don't know who she is. I look up at the sky through her red hair; pockets of sunshine flash spellbindingly through wet locks. Her body, warmer than anything I've ever known, a blanket in the coolness of the waves. Her skin smells of coconut and lime. The sounds of seagulls roll in my ears, and I know I love this woman, I just don't know who the hell she is. "Who are you?" I ask. She never answers in these dreams, just a straight row of blinding white from her mouth. I can't wake up and I'm not so sure that I want to. She turns so the waves crash into her back, screams of delight in my neck. I wrap my legs tighter around her waist. And during the stillness between the wallops, I trace the tattoos on her shoulders, pick grains of sand from the ends of her hair, and tell her I love her.

"Where is your sister?" she asks.

■ ■ ■

Mason Paul wakes, shivering in his own sweat, the air still thick even hours after making love, her taste still on his lips. What makes this recurring dream a nightmare, he doesn't know. He uses his thumb and index finger to gently grab the bones of Violet's wrist, moving her arm from his stomach. Mason grabs a pack of cigarettes hidden in his sock drawer and sneaks outside, his movement delicate so as not to wake her.

Still too warm for an October night in Louisville, Kentucky, Mason stands naked at the double doors of his balcony, unsure whether his shoulders are an inch higher because of the satisfaction she left with him or with trepidation from the dream. Behind him, Violet snores, sprawled on top of silk sheets the color of her name. He pulls on the Marlboro and watches the stars that glow orange to correlate with the nearing of All Saints' Day. He pours a bourbon Manhattan with a splash of butterscotch schnapps. It smells like candy corn. It smells like Halloween. *These dreams, you'd think I'm some damn mental case.* He clears the phlegm of a mild hangover from his throat.

The branches of black willows swing in the large backyard of the Victorian home, a Queen Anne architecture of ivory with black fringes, one that probably housed masters and slaves more than a century ago. He brings his silver necklace to his lips, warming the cross with his breath, but it's just habit. In recent years, Mason decided it might be less disappointing to consider God as a loosely thrown noun instead of something profound. But it reminds him of his younger sister, Rebekah, the only member of his family who hasn't shunned him. He misses her greatly. The bourbon doesn't help.

The home was born of old southern money from Cavendish tobacco fields that line the property's edges, well-to-do bankers who made lucrative investments when the American economy was at its golden peaks. And now Mason, a promising twenty-four-year-old with a possible future in one day becoming the state's most successful defense attorney after sticking his foot in the door of one of the most profitable law firms in Kentucky only weeks after acing the bar exam. Impressive at his age, but not entirely unheard of. Currently an associate at the firm, rumors of him being the next senior associ-

FREEDOM'S CHILD

13

ate attorney swirled around the offices, which would make him the
fastest to reach such a position. The result of a lot of interning, many
many hours, and being smart as a whip. He flicks the cigarette down
to the grass when he hears Violet turn in her sleep and pretends not
to notice her.

A moment later, she wraps her lanky arms around his bare chest
from behind. "You've been smoking, haven't you?" Mason hears her
smile bleed into the question. *I always knew I'd end up with one of my
coworkers. Of course, she'd be a corporate lawyer embroiled in the campaign
against big tobacco companies.*

Cicadas shrill in the distance and bullfrogs croak in the nearby
swamps and weeping willows. Mason smirks. "Who, me?" The
Manhattan glistens in the moonlight as he places his hand on hers,
his gaze still in the backyard.

She squeezes him and breathes onto his back. "I can feel your
heart racing with my lips." She kisses between his shoulder blades.

"Another dream . . ." He takes a long draw from the martini glass.

"It'll be OK," but she worries her attempts at comfort fall on deaf
ears.

Mason walks out of her arms and into the bedroom, sitting
down on the ottoman with his bottle of Maker's Mark, his laptop,
and papers on the floor around his feet. He goes to his fake Facebook account, Louisa Horn. Thoughts of his sister Rebekah swim
through the furrows of his brain. No word in days is odd for her.
Hope she finally got the sense to get out of that place. Mason tries to distract himself with the pile of papers that form a cyclone around
him. He shuffles through the work, breathing the vapors of bourbon between each page. He feels bad that he can't make love to his
girlfriend because of the distractions of his sister not writing and
the rape case finally about to end tomorrow. It's always that kind of
stuff that gets to him. Who could get a hard-on with siblings and
court trials on the brain?

"You're *still* working on the Becker case?"

"Just double-checking that all my ducks are in a row for tomorrow, is all." He looks up at her and smiles. "Otherwise, you can forget about Turks and Caicos."

"Not a chance in hell." Violet stretches and yawns.

He studies the photos from Saint Mary's Hospital, the victim's rape exam. Tender patches colored eggplant branded under her eyes and between her thighs stir something that merits another sip. Behind him, Violet looks down at the same thing.

"How many times do you have to look at those?" she asks.

"Believe me, I don't like it any more than you do." He traces the edges of the paper with his fingertips. He sometimes wishes he could become desensitized, lose all sympathy toward the victim like some of his colleagues. "It's just until I can become senior at the firm, love. Maybe partner, in a few years."

"Sell your soul to the devil?"

"More like renting it out." From an envelope, he pulls out a photo and hands it to Violet. He speaks low onto the rim of his glass. It was the only opening in a good firm back then. It was where he was needed. But he wants to get into a different area of practice soon enough, maybe white-collar or real estate, something like that.

She examines the picture. "Where the hell did you get this?"

"An anonymous tip." He takes the photo from her and examines it. "This is what's going to win the case. This is what's going to make me partner at the firm."

"Paint the victim as a whore . . ." She trails off.

"I know." Mason takes a deep breath and rubs his brow.

"It's perfect." Violet kisses the top of Mason's head and walks off. "You're going to be a fucking star."

He watches her walk out into the hall, enjoying the way the naked skin of her backside rocks before him, something akin to the artwork painted on the inside of a virtuoso's dream. As she disappears down the staircase, he washes the image down with another sip. His eyes wander back to the photos, the one Violet approved of: the victim, topless and laughing on his client's lap the night of the rape in question. The Maker's Mark gives him confidence, a little more hope than he might have if he were sober: if he can just win this case, he can move into any area of law he wants and never again have to defend another scumbag criminal.

"Where is your sister?" The question of the redheaded stranger from his dream reverberates between his ears.

"That's a damn good question, lady," he answers to himself as he goes back to the laptop. "Hopefully as far away from Goshen as someone like her can get."

It doesn't sit with him well, Rebekah not contacting him. He knows she's naive, a bit gullible, traits that can be confused for being slow, but can be chalked up to southern hospitality. Mason clicks to her Facebook page. The inactivity is out of character—she usually posts devotional scripture daily. The last post reads: *Galatians 5:19–21.*

After years of having it shoved down his throat, Mason still knows the quote without having to look it up. *"Now the works of the flesh are manifest, which are these; Adultery, fornication, uncleanness, lasciviousness, idolatry, witchcraft, hatred, variance, emulations, wrath, strife, seditions, heresies, envyings, murders, drunkenness, revellings and such like: of the which I tell you before, as I have also told you in time past, that they which do such things shall not inherit the kingdom of God."*

Below the scripture is a photo of Rebekah and their little sister, Magdalene. But Mason never met Magdalene—his mother was just pregnant with her at the time he was shunned from their church, disowned by the family.

Mason created a fake Facebook account, Louisa Horn, to stay in touch with his sister. He wonders if his parents finally worked out that Rebekah was in contact with him behind their backs. From what he understands, Rebekah was able to keep their father's suspicions at bay by telling him that Louisa Horn was merely somebody interested in their church. Mason knew of the church's newly added techniques of preaching in front of department stores and such, trying to lead the lost into salvation, notches in the Bible belts . . . and the fictional Louisa Horn was just another prospect.

Had Mason known that wanting to become a lawyer, even the mere thought of leaving home, would warrant a sudden severing of contact, he would have been more cautious. But over the years, the wiring in his dad's brain seemed to shift and loosen from that of a normal-enough evangelistic preacher into something else, something more fanatical. None of the rumors credible, Mason could just laugh them off. But with his father's transition only developing when Mason was a teenager, and the four-year age gap between him and Rebekah, the fervent dogmas of his father were mostly in hindsight, changes progressing after Mason left home and his family chose to have nothing to do with him.

Mason sits back, rubs his chin, and squinches his brow. He white-knuckles the neck of Maker's Mark. The red wax coating that covers the glass makes it look like his hands are bleeding. *Stigmata*, he thinks, remembering an elderly lady in the community who went to his father once for guidance, convinced that she bore the wounds of Christ. But that was a long time ago, back in Goshen. Never a shortage of religious zealots there. Mason rereads the Galatians scripture from his laptop once more. He gets a shiver and thinks to himself, *Run, Rebekah, run.*

3

THE COCKROACH

My name is Freedom and my eyelids are heavy. Through the hangover, I stretch my nakedness across the unkempt bed. My mouth tastes like death, the whiskey seeps grossly from my pores, cheekbones soggy with rye. 11:30 a.m. Not bad. My thighs, sore from hip bones; I know the feeling well. I turn over to Cal on his stomach, his naked ass in the air as he lies stiff in a dead man's pose.

"You cockroach," I yap as I kick him right off the bed. He takes the tangled sheets with him. "Who the hell said you could come over and fuck me?"

"You called me in the middle of the night and threw yourself at me," he yells up from the floor. I have no reason to disbelieve him, it's not the first time. Cal's a cowboy, and that's the best way to describe him. Five years my junior and looking even five years younger, Cal's the rare sort who can pull off long blond hair and cowboy boots. I, of course, will never admit it out loud, but he has the body of a god and is hung even better than Christ himself.

I throw his white tee at him and slip into a CBGB extra-large T-shirt and stumble into the kitchen. I don't know whose shirt this is. Could be anybody's. It's mine now.

I find a clean dish among a pile of ones I plan to wash someday.

I pour dry farina into a chipped bowl and drown it in spiced rum. I sigh. "Was I at least good?" I tend to black out during my romps in the hay. He comes up behind me, turns me around. He picks me up and I wrap my legs around him on the dirty sink.

"As always, Free-free." He smiles. I'm too hungover for his smile. I push him away.

"Careful, cowboy." I take a shot from the rum, just to bite the hair of the dog. The cap's been MIA for days now. There's a silence that some would regard as awkward, but it isn't, not to me. In fact, I like quiet. Quiet is good. He gulps orange juice from the carton in front of an open refrigerator. He breathes the tang from his cheeks like a fire-breathing dragon.

"Who is Mason?" He doesn't care. He reads the ingredients of the juice. He likes the organic shit. Hippie.

"Who?" I observe the filthy kitchen. I just don't have the energy to clean it. I haven't had the energy in a long time.

"After you passed out," he speaks into the pathetically empty fridge. "You were having a nightmare and kept on yelling *Mason.*" I play dumb, an act I play well. What can I say? I live in a world surrounded by incompetent retards, including Cal. But his skills in the sack compensate for a head full of rocks.

"I never met no Mason." It's a double negative, therefore I still tell the truth. A simple manipulation of words to sneak past Cal. "I probably just heard it on TV or something." The phone rings and I rummage through the kitchen cabinets for it. I put it there when the headaches come. Cal looks at me like most people do: confused. I follow the cord to where the phone sits on a few cans of peas in the back. "Yeah?" I answer. "Yellow? Hello?" I hold the receiver tight against my jaw. I pretend to end the call, covering the hang-up with my hand. "It was the wrong number. Those good-for-nothing salesmen or something." I'm not telling the truth.

"Your face says otherwise, Free-free."

I hate when he calls me Free-free. It reminds me of a kid's pet hamster. The carton of orange juice is back to his lips for seconds. Must be the gin I added to it the other day. And with that stupid grin and those washboard abs, I pretend to watch a commercial ad for Tropicana. I think of their slogan: *Tropicana's got the taste that shows on your face.* Sure, if dumb is a flavor.

"I gotta shower." I untangle the phone cord and walk for the bathroom. "Please be gone by the time I'm out."

4
HOME TO MA

THREE DAYS AGO

Matthew Delaney sits on the lidless metal commode in a solitary cell. Ossining, New York, home to Sing Sing prison. He holds a small stack of papers on his bare thighs as he wipes himself.

"Let's do this, Delaney," says Jimmy Doyle, the correctional officer. Matthew smiles politely and requests just another minute to finish. The officer looks away. The officers always look away. One by one, he tears each page into tiny pieces and flushes them with his piss and shit.

He kisses one last inch-long square, cut perfect with nail clippers he had snuck in more than a year ago. The scrap reads "Nessa Delaney."

"Nessa, Nessa, Nessa," he whispers to the wall of his six-foot-by-eight-foot cell, an old photograph with her eyes scratched out taped above his cot. "I don't know which I might enjoy more. When I made love to you all those years ago . . ."

"Time to go, Delaney." Doyle opens the steel door.

But Matthew takes one more moment to speak to Nessa. "Or when I find you and cut your arms off before drinking the blood?" He feels his guts lift with excitement, the idea of her death akin to the feeling of falling in love. The hatred and yearning for her have blended into one single emotion over the years, one he could neither resist nor fully grasp.

A smirk crawls across his face as he walks down the C-block. Toward the north end is med-sec, medium security, where, as opposed to the solitary confinement that Matthew was so accustomed to, these were shared cells with bars.

Matthew swings his bag filled with his personal belongings over his shoulder as he follows the officer, one he was well acquainted with. The inmates of the north end holler and cheer at his departure, rattling their tin cups against the bars and turning their soap wrappers into confetti, as such celebrations are afforded after a man's time is served. At the last cell, before entering another passage of security, an inmate sporting ink of the Aryan race throws his shoe at the side of Matthew's head.

And the smirk becomes teeth grinding.

In a swift movement that resembles something choreographed, Matthew lets his bag fall, reaching into the cell with both arms and pulling the prisoner backward against the bars. He uses his left hand to pull on his right wrist, arm wrapped around his neck and pulling tighter. "Do we have a fucking problem?" He seethes at the man, whose lips start to lose their pigment. He cannot answer, his voice constricted by Matthew's elbow.

"Cut it out, Delaney." The guard grabs his biceps. "You're two steps away from freedom. You gonna throw it away because of this asshole?"

"Freedom . . ." He releases the man.

"Now, c'mon." Doyle keys in a code. "Your family's waiting."

When they pass security and have a minute alone, Matthew sighs, the blood returning from his face and back to the rest of his body. He shakes the guard's shoulder. "I can't thank you enough for all you've done while I've been stuck in here, Jimmy."

"I've known you since we were kids, Matty." But Matthew knows the help came only because his mother was the guard's go-to dealer for good cocaine and the occasional supper. Matthew couldn't care less, as long as he could get the information his little heart so desired, information pertaining to Nessa Delaney, now known, if his information is correct, as Freedom Oliver. "I'll come by the house and see you guys soon, gotta visit my mom down there, anyway," he tells Matthew.

When met by other officers, the guard nudges Matthew in the back. "Let's move it, Delaney."

∎∎∎

Mastic Beach, New York: once a hidden gem on the south shores of Long Island, adorned with summer homes and bungalows for Manhattanites getting away for beach holidays during the warmer months. In recent enough memory, it was a safe haven where everybody knew everybody and the streets were lined with crisp, white fencing. Mastic Beach had color and clear skies and everyone loved to listen to the elders speak about the place when the roads were still made of dirt and of pastoral lands before the invention of the automobile. Small businesses were family-owned and -operated, with scents of baked bread that permeated in and through Neighborhood Road. Marinas flooded with beautiful sails that poked from Moriches Bay and rose to the heavens.

But then heroin trickled its way through the sewers of Brooklyn and emptied into the streets of Mastic Beach, and before long, crime rose to astronomical levels. Where people used to smile in passing, now they keep their heads down in fear of being jumped and beaten. Stabbings are as common as visits to the Handy Pantry. The elderly are robbed and the children of Mastic grow up way too fast. *Thirteen and pregnant? Congrat-u-fucking-lations.* And chances are, if you actually have a grassy patch big enough to be considered a yard, then more than once you've seen the lights of a police helicopter looking for a suspect on foot. And in those instances, your brain runs through every troublemaker that you know from your block until you have an idea of who it is they're looking for.

Today, Mastic Beach is the dumping ground for Section 8 government housing and every perv, creep, and sicko on the Sex Offender Registry list. The town glows red on maps because of them. Every week, the residents get letters in the mail, mandated by Megan's Law, telling them of rapists and child molesters living only a few houses down. Small businesses have become enclaves of illegal Arabs. And the gangs have colonized the area: the Bloods, the Crips, MS-13. The whites are the minority these days. Except for the Delaneys. They're their own gang, a whole other species.

■■■

Peter doesn't have to count how many boxes of wine it takes to get Lynn Delaney drunk. The answer is two, the equivalent of six bottles. But it's no wonder, when the mother of the Delaney brothers weighed in at six hundred–plus pounds.

Lynn becomes out of breath with every lift and swig of the wineglass. The cabernet stains the crevices of her smile, a smile hard to see past the quarter-ton of lard melting over the king-size bed that has to be supported by cinder blocks instead of the standard brass legs. It's the first time Peter can remember his mother making an effort to improve her appearance, the purple lipstick stuck to her gray and hollow teeth, a result of too many root canals from years ago when she actually gave a shit about her grin.

"Luke!" she shouts across the house.

"What," Luke whines from the kitchen.

"Grab me my hair spray off the dresser here." The yells cause her to be out of breath.

"Get Peter to do it. He's closer to you."

"Peter can't do it. Peter's retarded." Peter eyeballs his mother's grotesqueness from his wheelchair. Lynn continues, "Just get me the fucking hair spray, goddamn it."

"Fuck sake, Ma." Luke storms up the hall to her bedroom and tosses the hair spray that was sitting only three feet away from her.

The fat under her arms jiggles as she uses the ol' Aqua Net, the lighter fluid with a shelf life of ten thousand years, in her nappy gray curls. From the kitchen, John and Luke scream together at the Yankees game, the cracking of Heineken cans from the freezer. Peter smells the fish off his two brothers after they had spent the day down at Cranberry Dock.

It wasn't uncommon: grown men living with their mothers in these parts. Could be blamed on a shitty economy, but it's usually overbearing mothers who need house funding and/or lazy men, and there was a shortage of neither in Mastic Beach.

"Ungrateful little bastard," Lynn says behind Luke's back.

"Hey, Ma, Matthew's pulling up!" John screams.

"I'm fucking coming." She pumps the last of the generic wine from the box and sifts through a pillowcase full of prescription pills until she finds a Xanax to chew on. She plucks the clumps of mascara from her blue eyes, rubs her lavender nightgown straight, and burps as she turns off one of her reality judge shows.

She totters and flounders to climb aboard Mr. Mobility, the poor scooter that carries her overflowing body down the hall. Peter follows in his wheelchair. She rolls down, past the crucifixes and photos of the boys when they were actually still boys. At the end of the hall next to the entrance of the living room, a small table that serves as a shrine to her dead son, Mark: a framed photo of him in his NYPD blues, smiling around burned-out tea-light candles. She kisses her hand and touches the picture of his face. She worships the dead. Many in that dirty town do. They pour the first sips of all their drinks to the ground, they get married with speeches of the greatness of lost loved ones, even if they were scum. That's just the way it is. Praise the dead, turn the scumbags into heroes. Beside Mark's photo are three red candles, one for each of Lynn's miscarriages. And though she lost them before their genders could be determined, she knew, she just knew, they were all daughters and named each one, respectively, Catherine, Mary, and Josephine.

An Irish Catholic, Lynn's made a lucrative living abusing the welfare system and five sons with as many different fathers who took her name instead of Uncle Sam's. Delaney, a name attached to trouble and whiskey tolerance. It's a joke around the neighborhood that even the mailman gives the Delaneys' mail to the cops, since they're bound to be there sooner or later. As the car pulls in the driveway, Peter watches Lynn inspect her sons lined up by the front door.

First is the youngest brother, Luke, the most charming and promiscuous of the Delaneys. Even when all the girls knew he was responsible for spreading chlamydia to some of the locals, he was still irresistible to them. With blond hair and green eyes that can pierce holes into yours, and rumors of having a porn-star-size cock, he toyed with the idea of becoming a model a few years back. But he never went anywhere with it and opted to hang drywall for a living instead and spread his seed all over Long Island. Six kids that he knows of, at least. Peter curls his upper lip at the overwhelming stench of his cologne attempting unsuccessfully to cover the smell of fluke fish and sweat.

Next is John, a stout man with all the recessive genes: green eyes, red hair, and a temper that can make the streets shake. He has a silver cap for a front tooth and a face full of red hair. He speaks very little, always has, and always seems to dress in heavy clothes, even flannels in the summer. Known as Mastic's loan shark, John goes nowhere without his baseball bat. If you can pay him back, he's the best there is. And if you can't, just change your name and skip town. While everyone knows that he's not a mute, not one person outside of his family can recall one time they ever heard him speak. Lynn scratches his beard. "Why must you always hide this pretty face?"

Peter is the one in the wheelchair with cerebral palsy, who everyone assumes is mentally retarded, even his own mother sometimes. Peter is Lynn's excuse to collect a disability check from social services. Unlike his brothers, Peter prefers to stay in his room with pirated movies and books online, staying out of trouble, so to speak.

Peter hates his mother. She talks to him like he's a child, makes him eat the things she knows he can't stand, and always steals the money he's entitled to from the government, instead opting to spend it on stuffing her own face while Peter gets the scraps like a junkyard dog. And the term *junkyard* is fitting, given that the home is kept like a hoarder's paradise.

His mother smooths out his loose Spider-Man tee, uses her spit to fix his black hair, and pretends not to notice when he jerks away from her. He tells her to fuck off, but no one hears him, or they don't want to.

In one uniform motion, as if the dam breaks, they all go out to the porch to meet with Matthew. Matthew screams with a smile into his brothers' arms as he steps out of an old Buick, a clear plastic "personal belongings" bag trailing him. Headlocks and punches in the arms and thighs are the traditional greeting of the Delaneys. And, of course, what kind of reunion would this be without the stares of the nosy neighbors, the same ones who call the police every time the Delaney household gets a little too loud in the middle of the night? Luke is the first to break out the beer.

"Let's take it in the house," Lynn shouts from the doorway.

Matthew holds the beer up against the light of an overcast sky. "Christ, eighteen years in the joint, this is certainly overdue."

"What's it like not getting laid for eighteen years?" Luke jokes on the way into the house. Lynn smacks him on the arm.

"Almost worth it, after tonight." Matthew laughs. "Sorry, Ma."

Inside, Metallica plays in the background as they spend the morning catching up. But the time's come to talk about the very topic that has brought such a cloud over the family for so long: Nessa Delaney.

Find her.

Find her kids.

Bring them home.

Make the family complete once again.

▪ ▪ ▪

The spines of the other Delaney brothers surge with currents of electricity when around Matthew and their mother. With the back doors open, leading to a small backyard, the kitchen smells of wet autumn leaves and marijuana. It's impossible to tell where the October fog begins and the smoke ends.

"Eighteen years is a lot of time to think. To collect. To dream," says Matthew, between sips of his Heineken. He tilts his head to the side. "I'd be lying if I said I didn't want the cunt dead," his voice always smooth and velvety, like a song at a funeral. As he says the words, he swears he can detect Nessa's scent. How could he possibly explain his love for her to his family? Who would understand? And despite being caged like an animal for nearly half his life, his eyes always smile, like he's dying to tell the world all the secrets of the universe. The rest of the guys fidget in their seats around the kitchen table. They nod and pretend to understand, out of fear.

"She murders Mark. Your brother. My son," Lynn begins, stoned on her Xanax-and-cabernet cocktail. "She takes my grandchildren and hides them away so that we can never see them. The children of Mark." She absently picks the red nail polish from her fingernails. She feels the blood in her body start to curdle. She feels her feet start to swell, start to retain water from not being back in bed, decides it's because she needs sugar and proceeds to stuff an orange Hostess cupcake into her cheek. "And then she frames you, my innocent Matthew, and sends you to prison for eighteen motherfucking years." Lynn shakes her head with a smile, citrusy crumbs falling in the folds of her neck. She crosses her hands, those fat little sausages with red tips like she's ripped through someone's flesh. "Nessa Delaney." She sticks her tongue out and cringes, resents the fact that they once shared the same last name. "The audacity of the cunt. She must pay." Lynn begins to sweat with the efforts of chewing and swallowing. "And we must find her children. After all, isn't that what family's all about?" Her sons recognize that gleam, the flames behind her eyes starting to ignite with ingenious plotting, often seen right before she shoplifts or rips a guy off from Craigslist or sends her sons to get something she wants but can't have. "I wish we did this twenty years ago."

"Yes, Ma, but it's my revenge too," Matthew says as he puts his hands on hers. "As much mine as yours."

"They should make a saint out of me for waiting so fucking long."

"Yes, Ma. And you waiting for me to get out so this revenge could be mine means more to me than you'll ever know." Lynn bats her eyes at his appreciation.

Peter starts to object but stutters over his own words. Matthew shoots him a glare so ferocious and hateful that it paralyzes him in his own wheelchair. With a flat, soulless tone he says, "And we're all in this together."

Peter gets his first good look at Matthew. He notices the thin threads of white at the edges of his black hair only make him look more monstrous than before, like a mane beginning to ice over. His blue eyes are still too light to match the rest of his face, those eyes that nearly turn to white when he's doing something evil. He looks more like Lynn than ever, except he's lean and hard. Prison hard.

"But how the hell are we supposed to find her and the kids? We know she's been a protected witness since she killed Mark," says Luke as he rolls another joint.

"O ye of little faith. In prison, everything is accessible for a price. Information is no exception." Matthew taps his finger on his temple. "Everything you need to know about Nessa Delaney is in here." He looks over to Lynn and smiles.

Lynn Delaney has never been prouder of her sons in all her years. At the sight of Matthew, the long wait almost seems worth it. In this way, her Matthew can guide the rest, be Lynn's eyes and ears on their journey to kill her ex-daughter-in-law. "I only ask that you do things to Nessa that no mother would want to hear about until she begs to die. And I don't need to tell you to be sure none of it gets back to this family, do I?" She sighs. "And as for your niece and your nephew, just . . . break the news slowly to them. Show them love. Tell them Grandmother has waited patiently for twenty years and looks forward to hugging them." She takes a cigarette from Luke and puffs away. Her teeth are burned.

"She goes by Freedom Oliver these days," says Matthew.

"Freedom?" Lynn scoffs. "Fucking clever."

"Let's leave in the morning, then." Luke smiles at the thought of bloodshed.

"Fuck that." Lynn kicks the bottom of the refrigerator from the motor scooter. "I'm not waiting any longer." The steam seems to rise from her, liable to ignite the Aqua Net if she gets too angry. She brushes black cat hair from her sleeves, composes herself with a wheezing from the throat, and puts her cigarette out on the kitchen counter, no ashtray or anything. "My boys, my boys . . ." From her sleeve, she pulls out two fifty-dollar bags of cocaine and cuts five lines with her driver's license in front of them, a driver's license long expired since she hasn't left the house in more than three years. The boys' spines become a little more erect. When she's done, she licks the edge of the card before turning a twenty-dollar bill into a straw. Peter can't help but wonder how a habitual coke addict could be such a morbid size. "You don't want to keep your mother waiting, do you?" She inhales a line through her left nostril before handing the twenty-dollar bill to Matthew. Her jaw sways back and forth, her pinkies twitch with the mechanical taste.

Matthew stares straight ahead before he snorts the next line. "No, you never have to wait for us, Mother." The others nod, agreeing with anything to get a turn at the coke. They watch as her nose starts to bleed, as it usually does, down her face and landing on the remaining orange cupcake, the white drizzle of frosting now spotted with crimson. But Lynn doesn't mind her warm blood falling down on her dessert, and she stuffs it in her gob anyway. She stares each one of her sons in the eyes. "Let John drive." Lynn throws a set of keys on the table. "The plates are fake and the E-ZPass is stolen, so tolls for the bridges and turnpikes are free. You guys better head off to avoid rush hour."

With their hearts racing with drugs, anticipation, and obedience, they leave.

Lynn watches Matthew, Luke, and John take off from the window. *This is payback for Mark, you stupid bitch,* she says to her reflection. She is a queen, releasing her wolves into the wild, on the hunt. As the car leaves the driveway, she sees the next-door neighbor. An old man from Puerto Rico, he paces in circles in an old and ragged green dress with black polka dots. His daughter's mentioned before that he was showing signs of dementia. *Is anyone normal anymore?*

She licks the blood from her lips, hears the creak of Peter's wheelchair turning toward her. He stammers, as if his vocal cords are trying to disconnect from his body.

"Yu, yu, you're . . . a . . . f-f-fucking ba-ba-bitch," Peter says.

Lynn uses the back of her hand to wipe the blood across her face, up her cheeks like war paint. She leers and says, "And here I was thinking you my-my-my-might want to eat ta-ta-ta-today . . ."

5

THE NEED TO KNOW

My name is Freedom and I hate this woman's looks. Yeah, it's an antipsychotic, just give it here so I can go. Walkers Pharmacy, the Botox bitch, I call her. Too much collagen in the lips. Maybe she's not giving me a dirty look after all. That might just be her face.

Seeing a psychiatrist is not my idea. Whippersnappers make me do it. Every week for the past eighteen years. That's 936 hours. What good has it done? I grab my prescription and leave.

▮▮▮

My name is Freedom and I'll be happy the day I never have to hear ZZ Top again. As always, I leave myself about half an hour to hang out in the back before my shift starts. I sit in the office where we keep the safes, computers, security cameras, accounting and inventory records, cluttered manuals, and magazines. It's where I take advantage of the Internet, being that I don't actually own a computer and the service on my cell phone sucks like an eager Vietnamese prostitute.

Carrie stands behind me, but she isn't the nosy type at all, just eyeballs the office.

"What are you doing?" I ask. I already know the answer and say it with her: *I'm moving things with my mind.* She's always rearranging something. Carrie's my boss, but a good boss. A husky lesbian, she's one of my only friends here in Oregon. She's rough around the edges but has a huge heart and never makes a pass at me, aside from the occasional "If you were a lesbian, my God!" She's the gay pride–ish type, too, with tats of rainbows and naked pinup girls all over her thick arms.

I return to the computer screen and open three windows after I log in to Facebook. On one page is Mason Paul, attorney-at-law. On the second is Rebekah Paul. The third is a young girl named Louisa Horn, but I suspect it's a fake profile: one friend, and the only activity is random posts on Rebekah's wall. My money is on Mason, since he and his sister aren't Facebook friends. On Facebook maps, Louisa's locations match Mason's. And by the looks of things, Mason has little, if any, connection anymore with his adoptive family, with the church.

I look up Galatians 5:19–21 in another tab. Above it, from yesterday, is a post from Louisa Horn that reads: "My sister in Christ, where have you been? I miss you." It's been a couple days since she's posted anything or there's been any activity from her account. It's unlike her. "She hasn't posted anything in a while," I say to Carrie. I'm not supposed to talk to anyone of my past life, my life before I was Freedom Oliver. But I do. She knows who I am, who I was, who I'm looking at. I trust her. Nothing I disclose to her goes anywhere else. She even knows the things I can't disclose to the whippersnappers.

"You know how those young'uns are." Carrie arranges magazines that don't need to be arranged in the first place.

"No, something's wrong." I don't look away from the computer.

"You don't know that, Freedom." She focuses on me.

"I can feel it." It's true, something just isn't right. "I hate that name, Rebekah." I tap my nail on the screen. "Her fucking Amish Walton parents."

"They're not Amish."

"No, but they might as well be." We both smile a little as she leaves for her shift.

I browse through her photos. There's a certain purity about Rebekah, and I don't think this just because she's my biological daughter. And while I'll throw a heap of sarcasm at how she was brought up, I'm happy with her upbringing. She was raised by a good family, raised in the church. I sift through her photos: long, curly hair of ginger with spots of rust across the bridge of her nose. She has a million-dollar smile that stretches between those cute dimples, the only radiance from very conservative attire: long denim skirts over old white Keds, frilly long-sleeved button-downs.

As for Mason, it's clear he'd found his own way, beyond the graces of God. Girls, bars, smoking, a form of rebellion that wouldn't do too much harm, typical youth crap. With a full head of brown hair, Mason is incredibly handsome, as seen in the photos tagged to his page through Violet. Trips to Gatlinburg's Smoky Mountains, tequila sunrises, washboard abs. Christ Almighty, he's the spitting image of his father, that piece of shit.

Mason and Rebekah were raised by an esteemed reverend in Goshen, Kentucky, Virgil Paul and his ever-so-obedient wife, Carol. I've seen him preach via the Internet: a very charismatic man with a smile that makes it look like he's in excruciating pain. He always sweats and huffs his way through his sermons in his deep southern drawl. He's average-sized, with black hair and a square head. Tan compared to the pale children and wife he stands with after the service, to bid farewell to the born-agains and thankfuls and the newly restored. But goddamn it, it beats the hell out of the life they'd have had with me, had I tried to get them back. Then again, I don't think I'd be in this state if I hadn't had them in the first place.

Rebekah usually posts every evening, 7:00 p.m. on the dot. Always scripture. Always links to her family's church's website. And lucky me, I'm one of the most faithful online followers of the Third-Day Adventists' webcast. My username is FreedomInJesus, and every Sunday, without fail, I follow the sermons. On several occasions, and I attribute this to being one of the oldest online members, I've gotten to speak through Skype with Virgil and Carol Paul, *a real fucking honor to meet you nutjobs; I'm your biggest fan.* I spill my heart over forgiveness and obedience and mercy and this, that, and the other. *Spreading the gospel in Or-ree-gan, praise Jesus.* Anything for a possible glimpse of Mason and Rebekah.

A few weeks ago I wrote letters to both of them. In fact, I have a massive pile of letters to them I keep at the house, but I never before had the heart to send them. I'll send them one day, when the time is right, I suppose. They just seemed so happy, so blissfully unaware, I didn't want to be the tornado to rip through their precious existence. The first time I wrote to them, I brought the letters to work and kept forgetting to take them home. When I did, I must have accidentally mixed them up with my bills. Of course.

As soon as the mailman collected them, I realized my mistake. I even chased after him, nearly mowing him down with my car to get those letters back. I ripped the mailbag from him and spilled it all over the street out of mere frustration. I knew my apartment complex was early enough in his route that there'd be a good chance I'd find them. When the mailman yelled and tried to stop me, I barked at him. Literally, I barked and growled like a dog with rabies. When he started to call the cops, I dared him. "Go ahead, call the fucking cops, see if I care!" But when the witnesses started looking out their windows, I left with a fleeting "Fuck you, man" and went on my way.

Working at the Whammy Bar, large brawls between bikers tweeking on meth aren't all that uncommon. In those instances, I stand on the bar and pull firecrackers from my boots and throw them at the biggest guys I see.

I found the mailman again nine blocks later.

I could make him out in long socks and shorts up Lindsey Street with his bag of mail. I snuck into the back of his truck through the front and rummaged in an infinite amount of letters, but nothing was organized, none of it made sense. I looked up every few minutes to check if the nerd was coming back. And he was. But I hadn't found the letters. And there was no way he wouldn't see me, as the only way out was climbing over the driver's seat, which was on the passenger side. Time to do it. Just run faster than him. Shouldn't be too hard. Just move.

I pulled the firecrackers from my boots, where I always kept them, and lit the fuses. I usually cut them, so they explode within seconds, but I left the fuses long, to buy us time. I lit three strings, twenty firecrackers on each, and threw them in the back of the truck as I booked it. I nearly busted my ass as my foot got caught in his seat belt. He saw me. He ran. I can't remember how many backyards I ran through.

When I reached my street, I breathed a little easier with a cigarette as I caught my breath. I squatted down and leaned against a tree on the side of the road, when lo and behold, guess who sped around the corner ... and by speeding, I mean about thirty-five miles per hour, but fast enough that the mail truck's engine sounded exhausted from the reckless speed. But I didn't move. I smiled as he throttled in my direction. I waved. *You stubborn asshole.*

The truck swerved all over the street with the loud pops of firecrackers going off in the back. And for a second I imagined a scene from some kind of old Prohibition-era film. Smoke poured from the front and back, a gray that matched the layers of fog that hovered over Painter.

The only problem with this was that I probably just broke a million federal laws.

Took a lot of paperwork on the whippersnappers' part and a thousand angry lectures from them to get out of it. It was nothing a little fake crying and a push-up bra couldn't fix, but I got the warning.

Later that afternoon, after they'd removed the smoldering remains of the mail truck, I walked by with a bottle of Johnnie Walker to head to Sovereign Shore, my favorite place to hide. On the way, I found a stray envelope on the street. I grabbed Mason's letter from a puddle and tucked it in my bra.

I never got Rebekah's letter back. But I'd signed the letters Nessa Delaney instead of Freedom Oliver and addressed them to the Paul household so that if they never made it to Rebekah and Mason, the parents couldn't suspect their faithful servant FreedomInJesus.

At the Whammy Bar, I crack my neck and think about how I should have done more to keep my children, how I didn't try hard enough. But it's better this way, at least for them. That's what I keep telling myself. But the grief still makes me sick to my stomach, even twenty years later. All the milestones I missed out on. At least someone else got those opportunities, to watch two great kids grow up before their eyes. I guess.

6
THE MUSIC OF THE DEVIL

TWO NIGHTS AGO

Darkness fills the restroom of the truckstop outside Goshen, Kentucky, where Rebekah Paul cries into a dirty mirror with each chunk of hair that falls into the sink. Her own heavy-handed snips of the scissors send whimpers echoing through the greasy, dim stalls behind her. *"God, be with me,"* she repeats over and over again, the muffled roars of the truck engines outside rolling in her ears. The sounds of hair slicing are loud near her cheeks; her heart races like it will break through her sternum.

The yellowed lamps over her head buzz with the dying insects they devour at two in the morning. She doesn't recognize her own reflection, her hair bleached and chopped to the scalp. In the shadows of the restroom, the spots of blood on her collar seem black, similar to the spots on her diary back at home when the pens would leak ink. She looks down, uncomfortable in jeans and a white, tight-fitted Jack Daniel's tee. She kisses the cross around her neck for the last time with a split lip and tucks it under her shirt so no one can see it. She grabs her backpack. *"Lord, forgive me."*

The cool air feels good on her eyes as she walks out to the parking lot; the smells of autumn leaves and oil surround her. At the corner of the lot, Rebekah makes her way toward the Bluegrass bar, an old and grungy pub, as a few big rigs thunder past. She doesn't recognize the music, something bluesy with guitars, tunes she was forbidden to listen to, the music of the devil.

She has to use both arms to pull open the wooden doors to the pub and is met by a wall of stale cigarette smoke and dirty sinners. Bearded men in suspenders with frothy mugs all turn to stare at the skinny girl, her head down, feeling the cross on her chest through her shirt. She looks around, finds an empty table in the back corner, and goes straight to it, her head aimed at her shoelaces the entire way. She can hear the whispers already, undertones of unspeakable acts they want to do to her, words that shame the Lord and secure them seats in hell right next to Satan himself. She uses her short sleeve to dab the tears from her face, the cotton painful on her skin.

"I know that hurts worse than what it looks," says an unfamiliar voice. Rebekah looks up to see a thin and ragged man with a nicotine-stained beard and mustache and long, oily hair tucked behind a New Orleans Saints cap, black with a gold fleur-de-lis. "Here, sweetie pie, this oughtta help." He places a tall glass of beer in front of her.

Rebekah sniffs it. "I'm not allowed to drink," she says to the glass. "Drinking is against God." She doesn't even realize that it's illegal to drink before twenty-one years of age; the subject was just never brought up at home.

"Naw, sweetie pie, you ain't gotta worry 'bout that." He sits close to her in the booth so that she has to move over. "Fact is, God sent me here to look out for ya. A prophecy, ya know?" It isn't uncommon to hear such talk around Goshen.

She smells the alcohol on his breath and shifts in discomfort but listens anyway. "You're a prophet?"

"Yes, ma'am," he says with an incomplete smile. "Our Savior told me that you'd be here, 'n that I needed to com'n getcha outta here and help ya turn from yer evil ways and turn back to the righteous path of God. That's what He said."

"He did?"

"Yes'm." He looks back over his shoulder. "Why are you running away from home? God told me you was running away." She looks at him in astonishment—perhaps he really was sent by God. But then she looks down and doesn't answer. "Where are ya tryna go, sweetie pie?"

"The West Coast."

"Why, hell, that's where I'm goin' too." He keeps tonguing the sockets of missing teeth in his grin. "I can give ya a ride if you want."

Rebekah gets a bad feeling and looks around the bar. The man leans in close, pressing the front of his body against her side, and breathes heavy enough to make her ear wet. He rubs her knee. "Come with me, sweetie pie."

She turns her head but can't get away as he starts kissing her neck, the fog of liquor about to make her sick. *God, if you want to send someone, send someone else. Please, God,* she thinks to herself. "You're too close, mister." She tries to push him away, but she's too weak against his weight.

"Hey," a second man yells behind him. She breathes easier when he's pulled away from her. "You best just leave her alone." Rebekah sees a young man in a soiled apron that's supposed to be white, in a stance that says he's ready to fight. "Now, I ain't messin', Joe, you just get on out of here, ya hear?"

"It ain't like that, me 'n the girl was just talkin', is all." He puts his hands up.

"I've seen enough of what you call talkin'." The cook takes the man's hat and throws it hard into his chest. "Now I suggest you be on your way, I ain't playing around."

"Fine, fine. I'm leaving," he says as he grabs his cap and drags his feet. Rebekah watches a few men from the bar start to gather around the cook. "But you ain't seen the last of me, kid." Eyeballed by almost a dozen other truckers who show signs of backing the cook up, the man leaves. When he's out the door, the men go back to their spirits. Rebekah finds herself crying again, alone with the tall glass of beer he left behind. She doesn't know what comes over her, but she puts the foam to her lips to taste it. The bitterness of it makes her cheeks water. *Forgive me, Lord.* She throws her head back and chugs the first beer of her life, breathing only out of her mouth in between swallows so as not to taste it. It runs down the side of her face and neck before she slams the glass on the table. She uses her sleeve once more to pat away the ale, with heavy gasps to catch her breath. She stands up and the room spins under her feet. She looks around for the man in the apron, but he isn't there. She can't explain what possesses her, the need to chase after this stranger. Perhaps this is who God sent.

"Have you seen that cook with the dirty apron?" Rebekah asks a bartender.

"Your hero just went to the back for a smoke," she answers with a smirk as she dries mugs.

Using too much strength, Rebekah nearly falls through the screen door of the kitchen that leads to the back alley. Outside, the cook sits on top of a few red milk crates near full trash bags, smoking. The vents of the kitchen hum above them. "Thank you," she blurts out. Suddenly, she feels awkward, with intervals of clearheadedness between the bouts of dizziness.

"It was nothing." He smiles at her. She feels a flutter to her stomach, unsure if it's the beer or the fact that she's never before talked to such a handsome guy in all her life. He takes a crate and places it in front of him, waving her over to sit. "Where are you heading, anyway?"

She crosses her arms, too bashful to look into his eyes. "West Coast. Or as far as I can get."

"Away from whoever did this to you?" He points to her face.

She clears her throat and looks down. "I had it coming."

"No woman has it coming." He winces with anger. "You don't deserve that."

"No, I did." Rebekah looks to him for a moment. "Because I sinned."

"Everyone sins." His cigarette goes out and he relights it. "Doesn't make it right, though."

"I'm Rebekah." She holds her arms tight, unsuccessfully trying to hide her body in the snug clothes.

"Gabriel." He holds his hand out to her.

She stares at it with hesitation for a moment. "Like the archangel." She puts her hand in his.

"Sure." He sucks hard on his cigarette. "Like the archangel."

Rebekah watches him shake his hair from the hairnet, a full head of black and soft locks over jade eyes. He unties his apron to reveal a white undershirt and sleeves of tattoos. "So you're a cook?"

"Part-time. I help my ol' man do drywall on the weekends. Helps me pay for tuition at U of L and my rent."

"My brother went to the University of Louisville!" she squeals. "Did you know Mason Paul? He's a big-time lawyer now."

"Never met a Mason Paul, but it's an awfully big school. Name sounds familiar, though. Oh, wait, sure, I know who he is. He's the one defending the Becker case all over the TV. That Becker, sure gonna be one hell of a linebacker, I'd say. I knew the name Mason Paul sounded familiar."

"What is school like?"

"You've never been to school?" She shakes her head. Suddenly, Gabriel realizes what kind of girl she is. Must be a Mormon or something like it, the sheltered kind. And now she's running away, rebelling, naive. Those types come a dime a dozen back at the university. "You're not missing much." Her purity attracts him and he doesn't want to stop staring at her. He can see that her frail bones and soft skin have never been touched in a way that they should have by her age. It's like looking at the sands of a shore that's never been discovered by the ocean. But he fears she will drown out there, out in the real world, away from her shielded existence. "You shouldn't be trying to hitch rides cross-country with truckers. It's dangerous for girls like you."

"It's my only way out." She rubs the toes of her shoes on the dirt. "Do you believe in God?"

"I believe in something . . ." He looks away, not wanting to appear strange when he sees her shy away from his gaze. "When was the last time you ate something?"

"Yesterday, I think." He puts his finger up and walks back to the kitchen. He returns with a burger and fries in a foam container.

"I can't afford it."

"Don't worry about money." He watches her inspect the food as if she's never seen anything quite like it. "You need to eat." She uses both hands at once to shovel the food into her mouth. "Why don't you let me take you out one day? Like a proper date, before you head off to the West Coast, I mean."

She looks at him wide-eyed. "I'm not allowed to date boys."

"How old are you?"

"Twenty."

"You're old enough to make up your own mind and stop doing what your parents ask of you."

"I do what God asks of me." She continues to shove the food in her face. Gabriel takes his apron and goes to use it on her arm, where some ketchup spilled. But she pulls away, fearful, like an injured bird, broken in the sun and being circled by vultures.

Gabriel stares at her with wonder, and though she's spoken only a few words, he's fascinated by the mystery that surrounds her. He wants to know her more, he *has* to know her more. He could see her vulnerability from a mile away and feels the need to wrap her innocence in a blanket and keep it away from the cruelty of a world that wants to take it from her. "I'll take you to the West Coast." And as he says the words, he surprises himself. But she's a reason, the excuse he's been looking for to drop everything around him and see the world. "I know you don't know me, but you can trust me." For some reason, he expected more of a joyous reaction.

"Thank you," she says, with her eyes down and half a cheese-burger in her cheek.

"Let me take you home. We can leave in the morning." Really, his intentions are good. "You can have my bed and I'll sleep on the couch. OK?"

"All right." She believes this is her prayer come true, that God sent Gabriel to save her from the man who rubbed against her and wanted to take her away. She shows a glimpse of a smile as he takes his apron and throws it in the Dumpster behind him.

"Let's go." He leads her through the alley and toward the truck-yard. "I'm parked right over there." He seems to almost skip in his pace. He stretches his arms over his head and looks up to the night. "Share this moment with me."

"What?"

Gabriel paces around her and tastes what may very well be free-dom for the first time in his life. "Make a memory."

Rebekah scurries to catch up to him, her french fries shaking in the container. "What are you talking about?" The smile aches her cheeks.

He stops her in her tracks and looks into her eyes. "Aside from family, have you ever held a man's hand?"

"No," she says and laughs.

"Good." He grabs her hands and intertwines his fingers with hers. "Now neither one of us will forget this. Whether we get nowhere or see everywhere, we're making a memory." She's never heard anything so outrageous yet astonishing in her life. The butterflies multiply in her belly and her heart begins to pound. And all of the horrible things that have happened, if only for that moment, seem worlds away.

What happens next is fragmented. The sounds of bones crack-ing. Gabriel screaming her name. Tasting dirt in her mouth on the ground. Her most cogent memory is when she lands on her back in the trunk of a car, her hands zip-tied in front of her. She sees the vastness of the trunk come down, like a tidal wave crashing over her. She brings her knees to her chin and uses the soles of her feet to keep it from closing. But it works only the first time. And after that, she remembers the panic that consumes her in the trunk. And the brightness of the red taillights from the inside when the car brakes.

Lord, be with me.

7

HIGH SCHOOL SWEETHEART

Dear Mason and Rebekah, though once upon a time, you were Ethan and Layla,

To pick up where I left off last: ah, prom, yes. 1989. If you recall from my last letter, I think I was still floating on cloud nine after Mark Delaney had asked me, that bad boy of William Floyd High School I was assigned to tutor in English in the after-school program. It wasn't that he wasn't smart—quite the opposite, in fact—but he spent too much time smoking under the bleachers instead of actually in class. I remember my mother laughing at me because I sat, perched on the kitchen stool next to the phone, just waiting for Mark to call and cancel. I wish you guys could have known my mother; there was nothing not to love about her. Except cancer. You can't love cancer.

Anyway. Oh, God, I'd nearly forgotten about that dress, something with pink silk and black lace; I think I was going for Madonna's "Material Girl" meets *Desperately Seeking Susan*. I wish I still had that old thing. It was the last dress my mother made for me. Consider yourselves lucky, to have missed the biggest embarrassment of our generation: fashion trends of the '80s. I still cringe at the thought.

When Mark came to my door, my mother didn't like him right away. He wore one of those tuxedos printed on a black tee with a leather jacket, smelling like an ashtray. His naturally dirty-blond hair was dyed black. *What kind of respectable man wears eyeliner?* Mother would shake her head and read her *Vogue* magazine, Estelle Lefébure was on the cover that month, I remember. Mother's sweet tooth was for fashion, a gene that'd skipped me, apparently. Believe me, I've been referred to as a lot of things, but fashionable was never one of them.

I sat in the front of the Dodge Colt, with Matthew, Luke, and John sardined in the backseat, ready to crash prom and spike the punch with Absolut. Depeche Mode's "Never Let Me Down Again" in the cassette player. It was a big deal back then, to still be in high school and have a car, that wasn't your mother's, with a cassette player.

Mother would worry that Mark only wanted to ride my coattails of good grades and being valedictorian into college, and would constantly warn me that if he ever knocked me up, she'd kill me, cut off his pecker, and then kill him too. This point was made quite often.

On the way to school, the brothers passed around a joint. I declined, earning the comments of being a priss, that I was probably glued at the knees, that Mark should have stayed with that easy bitch of a cheerleader named Donna. I can't smell marijuana or Love's Baby Soft today without thinking of that night. From the backseat, Matthew kept pulling at my curls (reminder: huge hair was the in thing). Matthew always pulled at my curls. He had that Billy Idol thing going on, the spikes, the leather, fingerless gloves. The bleached hair. He even practiced curling his lip in the rearview mirror and faking a British accent. Ah, to be seventeen again.

Between the comments, Mark would look over at me from the driver's seat with a particular look, a look that said he couldn't keep his eyes off me, a look that said he thought he was falling for me, a look that made me weak in the knees. My heart pounded so hard I literally thought I might get sick. And in that moment, I knew I was looking at the most beautiful person in the world.

When we arrived, Cheap Trick's "The Flame" echoed into the parking lot. The others disappeared somewhere into the side doors of the gymnasium, being that they weren't in our graduating class. Mark thought it'd be romantic if we stayed outside, always the outlaw. When he pulled me close and began to sway, my body felt weightless. Toward the end of the song, he made a hook of his finger and lifted my chin. It was my first kiss—yes, at seventeen, embarrassing and pathetic, I know. But the times were different then.

And while I'd love to tell you that we entered prom and danced the night away, we actually never made it inside.

8
THE SUICIDE JAR

My name is Freedom and I keep seeing images from twenty years ago, images of Mark's brains splattered on the kitchen wall back in Mastic Beach.

Anyway, I plan to kill myself soon. Not today, but soon. I'll wait until the jar is full to the brim with my pills. I pull my script out of a white paper bag. I never eat them. They make me nuttier than I already am. I can't even pronounce them, why would I take them? I live just fine with the voices. Well, at least until the jar's full with my pills. I hold it up and try to estimate how many are in there. Two hundred? Three hundred? I don't know. I've never been all that good with numbers. But when I do, when I'm good and ready, I'll send these letters to Goshen, Kentucky, to my children.

The sun hides behind the comforters I've tacked over the windows. The sounds of daytime television scream from behind the walls, from the apartment of Mimi Bruce. It sounds like The Weather Channel. What's the point in monitoring the weather? She never leaves the house anyway. I look at the clock. 9:13 a.m. Have I really been sitting at this same spot at the table in darkness this whole time? The tips of my nails are dull after tapping them in the same spot for the past six hours. I walk to the kitchen sink and splash water on my face and rub the sharp pieces of sleep from my eyes into the skin of my cheeks and the side of my nose. Near the sink are the remains of that one photo that survived, the one of my dead husband, Mark. If he were alive today, I'd kill him. Again. Or at least that's what I tell myself.

The smoke alarms go off and I already know why. Mimi. If one smoke alarm in the complex goes off, they all do. I run to the front door, the sun blinding me as I step outside and hurry down the shared balcony to Mimi Bruce's apartment next door. It's locked. I step back and kick it in, surprised by my own strength. It makes me feel like I'm in an episode of *Law & Order*. I see the smoke in the back of the apartment. Mimi continues to watch TV with a cup of coffee in the front living room. She smiles at me. Why smile at a person who has just kicked in your front door? Her dementia's getting worse. I run into the back where the kitchen is.

Eggs crushed in their shells burn in a frying pan with flames trying to pull the pan down. I grab a pot holder that hangs from the oven door. Black smoke collects on the walls and ceiling above the stovetop. I chuck the pan in the sink and run the water; not as bad as it could have been. But when will it be? is the question. In the corner of the sky-blue counter, coffee drips onto the hot plate, the pot not in its place.

"George Clooney called me." Mimi walks into the kitchen, oblivious. She says his name like she's a naughty little schoolgirl. But she's an eighty-something-year-old, abandoned by the government in this good-for-nothing place because she can't afford assisted living or anything of the sort. The economy ate her pension, along with her Social Security and medical benefits. Living the motherfucking American dream.

"What did he say to you?" I ask while I take a butter knife and scrape the blackened chicken fetuses from the pan into the sink.

"Who?" She forgets what she said ten seconds earlier.

"George Clooney. What did he say when he called you?"

Mimi stands, confused, in her underwear. She puts her hands in the air for no reason, the loose skin hangs from her arms and she starts to sing, of all songs in the world, she begins to sing "Somewhere Over the Rainbow." There's no song on this planet that I resent more. Sharp white hairs poke from her armpits, and liver spots dance with the beat. And even through the tune, I hear the battery of her hearing aid ring.

I give up on the pan and help her put her arms down. "Let's go get you dressed, Mimi." She follows me to her bedroom, neat with photos of her deceased husband and other family members, the ones who never come by to see her. I pick out clean clothes from her dresser and maneuver them around her paper-thin skin. She hums as the polyester covers her face.

"Is George Clooney the one who spins the wheel on *Wheel of Fortune?*" she asks.

"Yes." I line the buttons up right. "He's a hottie, isn't he?"

"I don't kiss and tell." She winks at me and I wink back. I decide not to explain to her the need to have the coffeepot in the coffeemaker when she turns it on. I decide not to explain to her the need to get dressed after she wakes up. I decide not to explain to her the need to not leave pans and pots burning on the stove. You can explain these things only so many times before you have to just give up. I'd complain to the super, but he's useless. And the calls to her snot-nosed daughter are even more useless, her business skirts so tight that they apparently choke off the blood to her conscience.

"Do I have kids, Freedom?" She remembers my name this time. This makes me sad. I think of her son and daughter, the ones who come by only to raid her medicine cabinets and pillage her jewelry boxes. I warned them once, trying to do Mimi a favor, but it backfired. And now they never come by.

"No, Mimi. You don't have kids." I envy her ignorance. There is a piano in her bedroom, the only room with the space in the apartment to hold it. And despite the dementia, she can always remember the right notes to play. I lead her to the bench, an attempt to put her chaotic mind at ease, before she starts talking like a porn star, before the demons of dementia possess her head.

"Do you have children, Nessa?" I never told her my name was Nessa. She flips through a songbook like it's written in hieroglyphics.

"Nessa . . . why did you call me Nessa?" I straddle the bench right next to her.

"Who is Nessa? You're Freedom." There's no use asking her anymore. She has the attention span of a tsetse fly, not her fault. But I thought I was more careful than that around her. When did I slip? Twenty bucks says it was some night when I was striding the apartment's balcony in a drunken stupor. *I'm Nessa Delaney!* I let it go. The ringing from her head catches my attention once more. I help the hearing aid out of the side of her skull and speak loudly to her.

"I'll pick up some batteries from the pharmacist this afternoon." I flip through the pages until we get to Beethoven's Moonlight Sonata. I put the book upside down on the music stand, for no other reason than selfish entertainment on my part. But Mimi impresses me. She plays it by ear, and I have to wonder how much of it she can actually hear. I take advantage of the somber melody and her deafness.

"You know, Mimi. There will be a day when I am gone, and that day will come before yours. And I'll not be here to clean the eggs from the stove and to get you new hearing-aid batteries. And it saddens me, to imagine you dying in this home because you won't know what the sound of the smoke alarm indicates." I watch her hands create perfect sounds. In my head, I ask God that Mimi takes the whole apartment complex with her. And then I turn to the side of her face. "And when I lie dying next door after swallowing my suicide jar, I promise to think of you. Because I believe you were a good person, a good person who deserved better than what you got in this life. A kind soul, you were. And in some ways, I think you should consider the dementia a blessing. What I wouldn't give not to remember anything about my life. And after the paramedics take me away, I take comfort in knowing that you will never think of me again, despite me being your only friend in this world." The music fades with a few of the same notes interrupting the silence. Her hands curl into weak fists down to her lap.

"Would you care to have a cup of coffee with me, Freedom?" Mimi smiles. I appreciate her charm. "We can find that George Clooney on The Weather Channel, if we watch closely."

"I'd like that."

9
FREEDOM AND PASSION

My name is Freedom and there's barely room at the Whammy Bar to stick out my chest. Long, gray beards spotted with beer foam protrude from black leather biker jackets. Jailhouse tattoos with the Indian ink that fades to green. Pints of ale spill from the brims. Teeth rotted by crystal meth decorate the bar as they shout over the All-man Brothers Band and Pantera. A cloud of Pall Mall smoke inflates within the walls. And to my left, at the end of the bar, is Passion, though rare is the prostitute who uses her Christian name.

Passion gets stares from the bikers, and not because she's a pro, but because she's black; too many of the bikers don't like black people. But Passion frequented the place long before it was a biker bar. She came with the HOT PIE, where she sets up shop in room number 12. And it's that time of year when the air gets too cold and the hookers stroll in for a few minutes of warmth. They hide in the corners of the bar, though not for long after the men have a few rounds. They shiver in their fishnets and hover over pots of French onion soup and cups of coffee.

Passion is good people. She's ripe at fifty, the mother hen to the other runaways and coke-addicted pros. A gold tooth at the front of her smile always catches my attention from the corner of my eye.

Her short curly hair and long blue nails emerge from a long and old white faux-fur coat. And even above the loud music, and I mean decibels hardly within the human threshold of volume, I swear I can hear her lick and smack that gold tooth with her tongue. She always smiles. She always looks like she has a secret you're dying to know. She's great company, smart and up-to-date on all the politics and science and literature and such, and so I love having her around, someone in Painter I can have an intelligent conversation with. Yes, the only sensible person in the state of Oregon is a whore. Life's funny like that.

I have a minute to rest. I lean near Passion from my side of the bar. She stares into a newspaper and uses a plastic spoon to stir her bowl. She smells like spearmint gum, latex, and onion soup. There's a chewed-up wad of gum on the tip of her nail as she eats.

"Obama this, Obama that." She folds the newspaper away. She must be the only black person in America who hates Obama. For some reason this makes me like her more, because she's not a conformist. I wipe down the same patch of bar over and over again as we discuss politics.

"Sure, put all the gun crimes in the headlines to back a gun ban. But what good will it do? The guns aren't the problem." She blows on her soup from silver lipstick and raises her voice to get a rise. "It's these crazy-ass cracker white boys who are allowed to have them." Anyone else might take offense to such a statement. I know she means nothing prejudicial about it.

"I tell you what," she says as a fat biker named Gunsmoke with a blond receding hairline slams his glass on the bar.

"That nigger Obama ain't taking my rights from me."

"Relax, shugga, I didn't vote for him neither." She raises her glass to Gunsmoke, but he looks away. Passion and I share a smile. I go to the blond and take his mug to the draft taps. Foam falls from the Pabst Blue Ribbon faucet.

"Passion, would you watch the register?" Passion's practically management here. "Gotta go switch cans in the basement."

"You got it, honey."

I slip my way through the crowd with a few iron elbows to the door beside the restrooms where it says "Employees Only." The hallway smells like urine after a few courses of antibiotics and crack, the smell of sweet hay. Not that I've ever tried crack, but let's not be naive.

I hold my breath. Beyond the door, a hallway in darkness. Overhead are caged lamps that flicker, dim graves to fruit flies that failed to follow the sweet fumes of liquor into the bar. The sound of the music from inside is muffled behind the walls. I walk slowly. I hate hallways, I've always hated hallways, especially dark ones. I focus on these lamps, and I'm reminded of an interrogation room back in New York. The hall expands. The space grows darker. The music becomes distant. And suddenly I'm back in that interrogation room twenty years ago. Before I was Freedom Oliver. Before I met the whippersnappers. Before I went crazy. Back when my name was Nessa Delaney.

■ ■ ■

"Nessa, be smart," said one officer. He and his partner circled around me like buzzards. Their eyebrows formed V's, faces a shade of ruby with frustration. With each hour that passed, their shirt cuffs moved an inch higher on their arms. "Now, I know you don't want to end up having this baby in prison, do you?"

"Go to hell," I grunted, cuffed in a steel chair with the short leg, the one that makes the suspects uncomfortable and antsy. I'd seen enough NYPD Blue on TV to know the trick. The officer slapped me across the face. It stung more and more with each backhand, until it actually burned my ears.

But worse was the smile from the second cop in the corner of the room, his arms crossed. "Hell will be a lot better than where you'll end up."

■ ■ ■

"Freedom." I jump when Carrie shakes me from the flashback. "You all right?" I focus on a nude woman tattooed on her forearm. I focus on anything that can rip me from my memories.

"Yeah, sorry." I put my hands down in my cleavage and scoop out the sweat. I gulp at air polluted with crack and try to shake it off. I try to tell myself that it was years ago, that it's over now. "Gotta go to the basement and switch the PBR kegs."

"I'll take care of it." She squeezes my shoulder to put me at ease. If only it worked. "Take the night off. I'll watch the bar."

"You sure?"

"Yeah." She waves me off. "I got it. Go home."

10

THE DELANEY HOUSE

Dear Mason and Rebekah, though once upon a time, you were Ethan and Layla,

To pick up where I left off last: I was giving my mother a pedicure on her deathbed. It was the August after I'd graduated high school, top of the class, I might add. It was the day a pregnancy test came back positive in the restroom of a Roy Rogers. It was the day my mother died.

"Vanessa, I'm scared." Before that, I wasn't sure if she knew I was there. There were a lot of things that weren't there. Her voluminous hair wasn't there. The meat on her bones wasn't there. Her will to live wasn't there. But I was there. I was there until the very end.

"Don't be scared, Ma." I tried not to drown in my own words, tried to be strong. "I won't forget the cuticle cutter this time."

And that was it. Poof, she was gone. She never got to learn I was pregnant. Perhaps that was a good thing. She never did approve of those Delaney boys.

That was around the time your father decided to join the NYPD. I was suspicious at the sudden transition from lifting cars and sipping 40s to being a cop.

"Imagine the dope you could score in arrests," Lynn would push. Oh, yes, your grandmother was a fucking gem. Lynn, this stocky woman with bad teeth and a huge fucking mouth . . . never mind. I shouldn't talk bad about your grandmother. That's for you guys to assess without my editorializing. Maybe one day you guys will see for yourself if she's still around.

The apple didn't fall too far from the tree. I think that was Mark's plan all along: become a copper to score dope, to demand respect. He was always one who felt he deserved respect, even if he didn't earn it.

After Mom died, we spent a few months with the Delaneys until we'd gotten our own place, a house we bought on Huntington Drive with the money I'd inherited from my mother, an inheritance that turned all of the Delaneys into my best friends overnight. But on one particular night at the Delaney house, I was about four months pregnant, Mark didn't come home.

See, your father and I were kids at the time, excited at the thought of playing mom and dad at such a young age without knowing what parenthood really meant. Lynn Delaney was the only parent Mark was familiar with, so the recipe was already toxic. I was just too young to see it at the time.

It was the night before his graduation from the NYPD academy, and the neighborhood was already preparing the party. Not a bad idea to know a cop on the inside, the delinquents around the block would say. The rest of the Delaneys were fast asleep, but for your uncle Peter, the only one of your father's brothers that I ever cared for. Peter was this brilliant and kind man confined to a wheelchair, and probably the best friend I ever had in all my life. I miss him from time to time, think about calling him once in a while. But that would breach my contract with the whippersnappers. Peter and I talked about anything and everything, from our disagreements with the Delaneys to the unpleasant changes of pregnancy, from politics and science to movies and comics.

But anyway, it was close to 4:00 a.m., and in walked a stumbling Mark, a nightclub stamp on the back of his hand, the smell of peppermint schnapps and cologne seeping from his skin. I should note that while at the academy the past few months, the eyeliner and leather was traded in for CK One body spray and button-downs. He toppled a side table on the way in, ash and cigarette butts scattering on the floor.

"Mark, where the hell have you been?" I shushed. "Your graduation is in a few hours."

"Why don't you mind your own fucking business, you slut," he said, his mouth wet from drink and eyes glassed over. "Whose baby is that, anyways?"

"You sh-sh-shouldn't talk to her like that," said Peter.

"Oh, yeah?" And there, for the first time, I saw your father with this particular look, one that turned his eyes to black, one that sent a chill through my bones. He leaned over and reached under Peter's wheelchair. He wanted to humiliate Peter, and he succeeded when he pulled a black pouch from under his chair, a pouch full of Texas catheters. He took his car keys and began to stab the bag that held Peter's urine. The bag burst on Peter's lap. Your father burst out in laughter.

"What the hell are you doing?" I slapped his shoulder.

"Get away from me." He pushed me hard enough that I fell backward.

I should have left right then. Rebekah, take this advice. The second a man touches you like that, run as far as you can. But I was a stupid kid, a stupid kid who stayed. With my mother dead, I had nowhere to go. And in my head at that time, I'd thought that staying with an asshole was a better alternative than raising my child without a father.

After he stumbled back to his bedroom, I helped Peter in the dark, but I could feel his face burn red in the night. "How could you be with a monster like that?" He tried not to cry. "How could you let a man like that father your own flesh and blood?"

11
COPPER

My name is Freedom and my blood is sand. That's what it feels like when I get overhyped, when my head spins and I can't stop it. It's a side effect of trying to keep up with Earth as it spins on its axis, is all. Docs pass it off as mental illness. I call it eccentricity. There is nothing wrong with eccentricity. And I don't need to take the stupid meds. I keep the pills. I go to the leftmost cabinet in my kitchen and grab my suicide jar.

"Almost at the top." I swallow hard and bite my lip until I taste pennies. "Maybe another day or two." I screw the lid back on to the old mayo jar and hide it between the cans of peas and tuna fish.

I force myself back down. I'm still too hungover from last night to drink right now, so instead I listen to Judy Garland's "Somewhere Over the Rainbow." That song makes my skin crawl and my stomach drop. It was my son's favorite. I listen to it until I am on the brink of suicide. When my mind is there and I'm ready to grab a dull kitchen knife and trace the veins in my wrist, I'll call Cal for the distraction. He's used to it.

What time is it? Twelve? After Carrie said I could go home, I had a small run-in with the Viper Boys, a few regulars who think they're something to fear. All they did was suffocate everyone else in the establishment with Cuban cigar smoke and brag about their cars . . . Vipers. It's the only thing that probably ever gets them laid. One of them bear-hugged me from behind and burned the back of my shoulder with a cigar in his teeth. Douchebag. Passion tried to jump in, but she knows I can take care of myself. I head-butted him with the back of my skull, so all is now forgiven. He'll forget it by morning. I grab some Neosporin to put on the burn, but it's just out of reach between my shoulder blades. I use the end of a toothbrush. That works.

I'm back on the countertop with the phone still in the cabinet. *Why aren't you picking up, Cal?* After a long day's work I can smell myself. Cal's not answering his phone and Judy Garland fails to bring me down to suicidal levels. What a bitch. I'll just go for a stroll. Wait, can't leave Johnnie Walker Red behind.

I walk to my favorite spot, Sovereign Shore, for a bit of isolation and a chance to escape the carnival in my brain, as me and the voices in my head speak different languages. I walk under the streetlights and think of *The Exorcist,* and not even the "Tubular Bells" theme as I walk in the middle of the cold night is enough to bring my mind down to a more quiet and bearable level. Ha, look at the tree with the burned bark. Thank God it's a different mailman now, I'd hate to look at him again.

Anyway. The suicidal thoughts come and go as they please. I have no control over them I'll have you know, it's a full-time job. Mental illness, if that's what you want to call it. *I'm telling ya, Doc, I'm merely eccentric.* It's like constantly hosting a huge party for all these guests you really don't care for. Truly. Those unwanted guests who want to eat all your food and don't grasp the first million hints to get the hell out of your home. I think that's the best way to describe it. I have reached my destination.

The spray of the ocean is at its warmest this time of year, but the air is colder as I climb onto the craggy rocks in the pitch black underneath a moonless night. All that's to be heard are the sounds of oxygenated bubbles rising to the bottom of the bottle and the crashes of salt below. The scotch burns, and so I cough it out into the gusts that knot up my red hair.

■ ■ ■

I think back to the day I knew I'd never see my kids again. That was twenty years ago. The word *dismissed* ricocheted around in my skull for two weeks after I was released from prison. Dismiss: verb. To order or allow to leave; to send away. *Vanessa Delaney, the charge of second-degree murder against you is to be dismissed with prejudice.*

I sat in an office behind chambers in family court, not far from where I was charged with killing my husband two years prior. I waited for Sharon Goodwyn, a plump and pale woman with no nose, only holes in her face that made her look like a black-haired swine. She was the caseworker in charge of overseeing my children's adoption after I was charged. And I hadn't seen her since. But I remember her well, and I remember wishing that some homeless diseased freak would jump her in an alleyway for taking pride in a case that took away my children even though I was wrongfully accused.

Back when I was brought before the judge, I said not one word, not even when he asked me to speak. It was pointless. Even if I thought it would have made one lick of difference, which, trust me, it wouldn't have, I still kept my mouth shut as a big fat fuck-you to the system, leaving everyone in the court asking, "What goes on in that crazy woman's head?"

I had nothing nice to say. Not at all. My silence was perceived as an act of apathy, but it was more of a reaction to the constant voice in my head that said, *Don't do anything, because it will be stupid.* That voice was right. I was ready to snap my good-for-nothing attorney's neck and lick the blood off my fingers like I had just eaten the best southern fried chicken of my life. But no. Instead I stayed quiet. Quiet on the outside. People expected me to speak. My silence was a protest against them too, now that I think about it. Boy, do I remember the faces of my ex-in-laws, the Delaneys.

"Hello, Ms. Delaney," said Ms. Goodwyn when she entered, her briefcase bouncing off her gut. She didn't make eye contact with me. I wouldn't have either. Having to face the mother of the children you took knowing she's innocent? I had to give it to her, she had a set of brass balls, though she probably ate them too.

"I want my fucking children back," I demanded. She looked at me like she was seven shades of offended.

"Don't use that tone with me," she said as she opened her brief-case. I exhaled as deeply as I could and made sure she heard it. I wanted her to know my patience was as thin as paper. She started to jot notes in one of the hundred files.

"Would you be so kind"—I crossed my hands and brought them to my chin with puppy-dog eyes—"to give me my goddamn children back, Your Fucking Highness."

"Nessa, it's not that simple."

"Why the hell not?"

Sharon Goodwyn got short with me. "Because you gave up your parental rights." She pointed her pen in my face and it took all that I had not to take it and ram it through that pig nose of hers.

"They were taken from me because of the murder charge."

"There were other options . . ." She trailed off into her papers.

"Like what?"

"Like what?" She closed the file. "Let's say the Delaneys, for start-ers."

"Those crackheads?" I laughed as I lit a cigarette. "I guess you're not familiar with that family. Not a fucking chance in hell."

"You can't smoke in here."

"So arrest me."

"I'm going to be frank with you, Nessa." She sighed. "A lot of this is out of my hands." She slid a piece of paper over to me, one with my signature on the bottom. "The second you signed this, you made it damn near impossible to ever get those kids back, even if I had nothing to do with it." But I remembered the choice being taken out of my hands when I was facing a life term, the way they said that it was what was best for them since I'd be rotting the rest of my life away in prison. And if that were the case, they'd be right. But I wasn't rotting in prison, not anymore. "Nessa, this can take years. And even then, the chances are slim."

I put out my smoke because she was trying her best to be civil with me. I'm not saying I liked her any better, I'm only saying I put out a fucking cigarette. I hated the fact that she had to see it, but I couldn't control the tears that came. "Can I not even see them?" I cried.

"I can put in a request to the family they're with, but, ultimately, it will be up to them."

"They're together?"

"Yes. We do try our best to keep siblings together." I used my shirt to dry my face. She looked at me with pity, and there's nothing I hated more. "I've met them. I did the home study on them. I'm telling you, they're with a great family. Very loving."

I had a lot to consider, more than most people in their lifetimes ever have to consider. Maybe the swine was right. I mean, I knew the U.S. Marshals were waiting outside, since Witness Protection had already been offered to me. And what kind of life is that for children? And if I didn't go into Witness Protection, God knows what would happen if the Delaneys ever got to us now that Matthew Delaney was up on charges for Mark's murder.

Suddenly, I craved my son's skin. His laugh. I wanted to hear the breaths of my daughter, whom I hadn't seen since I gave birth to her in a prison hospital. I craved their small hands, their tiny fingers wrapped around mine. I craved the beating of their hearts against mine when they'd fall asleep on me. And more than ever, I craved their happiness.

"I assure you," Sharon Goodwyn continued. "They're happy there. And they will have a wonderful life with this family. I promise. It truly is the best thing you can do for them. It's the best thing that any loving mother can do."

But I had a plan.

I jumped up and flipped the table between us into the air and screamed something awful, something unintelligible. I kicked the walls, forcing the caseworker to her fat little feet and to hobble to the door. Two U.S. Marshals whom I'd never met tried to squeeze past Sharon in the doorway to get to me. But before they could, I'd already put my fist through the window. Glass severing my vein wasn't part of the plan, however. Blood squirted and poured; horror washed the color out of their faces.

"HIV-positive," I yelled to the men. It was the only thing that came to mind to keep them back. "I'm HIV-positive and if you come near me, I'll aim for your eyes and mouth, I swear on everything that is holy!" They didn't come any closer as I crouched down and shuffled through the files that Sharon had left on the floor. And the plan worked.

I memorized the details: Virgil and Carol Paul, Goshen, Kentucky.

And then I fainted from the blood loss.

▪ ▪ ▪

"*Mattley.*" *The voice sounds far away,* through what sounds like TV static and distant foghorns. "Help me out here. This woman is hurt."

"Whootha . . ." I try to ask, pretty pissed that this guy has a bright-ass flashlight in my face.

"She's not hurt, she's just drunk," says the all-too-familiar voice. *Fucking great.*

"Awwficer Matt . . . Lee . . . is that you?" I try to formulate sentences, words, anything. I struggle to sit up on the rocks.

"That's just Freedom. C'mon. Help me get her up," Officer Mattley sighs as he helps me up.

"Don't, you fuckin' raper . . . rapist . . . rape."

"She always says this," Mattley tells his new partner. "Always afraid cops have nothing better to do than comb the rocks for drunk women and rape them." They help me to my feet, but I can stand for only a few seconds at a time; my bones become rubber bands. They are relentless sexual predators. I can swear this when I'm drunk. Sober? I really respect Officer Mattley. In fact, I'm head-over-heels in love with the guy. But if you try to tell me while I'm drunk that you're not there to rape me? I'll just scream it louder. And Mattley knows how I am when I get drunk. He's one in a very few who knows how to deal with me in this state. "Yes, Freedom, I want to . . . you know." I see him cringe at the thought. "But only if you get in the car."

The rape that occurred twenty years ago never really left me. I don't talk about it, don't really think about it. But when alcohol livens up the darkest corners of my brain, those alleys where many of my skeletons dance, they just spew the most cringe-worthy parts of my mind, of that rape, right out of my mouth. The liquor dissolves any filters that I might have been born with. I don't mean for it. When I black out, those demons like to come out.

"OK," I say as I walk with them to the car. For the record, he'd never in a million years do such a thing. But for whatever reason, this works when I'm drunk.

"Matt . . . Lee," I dribble in the backseat of the cop car. "This new cop is newbie, new. Is he gonna rape me too?"

"What?" asks the new partner with shock. This amuses me. I see Mattley in the driver's seat nudge the new guy.

Mattley answers from behind the steering wheel. "He says he will, but only if you promise to go to sleep as soon as we get you home, OK?"

"Fan-fucking-tastic." Everything around me is distorted. "Tell him I like it rough," I slur.

"I will, Freedom." Mattley starts the car. "Just try and get to sleep fast, then, OK?"

"Sir, yes, sir." I begin to sing "Somewhere Over the Rainbow."

"Quick, turn around and grab her head," Mattley yells to the newbie.

"What?" he responds. Is that all this guy knows how to say? *What?* Mattley skids the car to a stop on the soft shoulder. He turns from the front seat and grabs my head, right as I'm about to head-butt the window. Don't ask me why I do the things I do when I am drunk, I just do. I hurt myself constantly, try to start fights so I get hurt, I feel I deserve to be raped, I'll sleep with anyone with hopes that they're sadistic just to feel the pain. This goes back to the glutton-for-punishment thing, I suppose.

After a small struggle, I give up on trying to break the window with my forehead. I think at one point I bite his hand. Probably. Mattley sighs with heaviness and turns to his partner.

"Next time I tell you to do something quick, do it quick and ask about it later." He's composed. See? That's what I love about Mattley. The coolest and most collected man you'd ever meet. "When Freedom starts singing 'Somewhere Over the Rainbow,' she's about to hurt herself."

"So, now what?" The kid asks. "We put her in the drunk tank for the night?"

"No." I scream bloody murder, as loud as I can, and throw myself around the backseat like a slug on a salt mine. I lie on my side to kick the shit out of the back of the front seat.

"No, Freedom, don't worry. I promise we won't take you to jail, got it?" Mattley has a way of calming me down, but it always takes a few attempts. He really should be canonized for his patience. Saint Mattley. "There's no point. She'll be like this the day after tomorrow too," he explains to the newbie. We pull up to my house. What a fucking depressing sight. Mattley pushes me up the steps to my shoddy apartment.

"Have I ever told you about Layla and Ethan?" I ask him. "Only now they're Rebekah and Mason, or some stupid shit like that. I mean, who names their kids Rebekah and Mason? Amiright?"

"Shush now, Freedom. No need for any of that. You just get some sleep," Mattley hushes as we reach the second story.

"Quakers! Quakers name their kids names like that." I begin to laugh. "Like that Quaker Oats man on the oatmeal cans with the white curly wig." Suddenly, I do my best impression of a Quaker. "Ho, ho, ho, I'm a fucking Quaker, and my Quaker offspring shall be called Rebekah and Mason Quaker Walton," as I mock in a Santa Claus voice. I actually don't know anything about Quakers.

He directs the conversation to Newbie, who stands behind in case I fall. Even I'm surprised I haven't yet. Mattley knows to never take me through the front entrance. I just can't stand the sight of the meth-head super, hate him telling me to keep it down. Sometimes it turns ugly, if I've had enough to drink. "Never mind what she's saying. Just grab her key from under that plant." He motions to the fake plant on the wooden fire escape at my front door on the second story of the building. And what fucking good are wooden fire escapes, anyway? Mattley carries me to my bed, kicking the mess in the dark with his toes.

"Try and go to sleep, Freedom." God, I love his plummy voice. It's audio Valium. I look up at Officer Mattley in the dark. He's a stern copper with most everyone else, but for whatever reason, gentle with me. He feels sorry for me and I hate it. I don't need anyone's pity. I'm no victim. Faint white light from the shades paints him into a recognizable being in the bedroom. I can smell his spearmint gum and see his bald head, but he's sexy. Good Lord, he is a sexy man.

Mattley helps my head onto the pillow and grabs a few blankets from the floor to drape over me. I pretend I'm dead. I pretend he wraps me in a sheet to take me to the morgue. I shut my eyes. I will have no recollection of any of this in the morning. Mattley is a good soul. I truly love his soul. Too bad he's a Goody Two-shoes, and too bad I'm the town drunk and too bad for a lot of things.

"Mattley, I need a huge favor."

"What's that, Freedom?"

"Those letters in the living room." I point to piles by the hundred. "If anything were to happen."

"We'll talk about it when you're sober, hon."

"Third-Day Adventists. Mason and Rebekah Paul, Goshen, Kentucky."

Mattley strokes my forehead for just a second. "Get some rest and forget all that."

12

THE FIRM AND THE ARCHANGEL

Glass flutes of gold ascend into the air with the cheers and salutations of the firm of Tyndall, Finn, and Moore, Esquire. Tight collars, crooked smiles, and ugly ties welcome Mason back to the office after this morning's high-profile victory, when an all-star college football player was found not guilty by a jury of his peers of sexually assaulting his eighteen-year-old one-night stand. Guilty as sin, innocent thanks to a few motions submitted, sprinkled with a few objections against the assistant district attorney and a flood of press releases and exposure of the defendant, a would-be valedictorian and prospective NFL star. The photo of the victim giving him a lap dance moments before the alleged rape was the golden ticket, the smoking gun. Mason tries not to remember the look of horror on the victim's face after the verdict was read out; he can't afford to. He clenches his jaw and fights the thought from his head; he's on a winning streak, so close to becoming a senior associate out of so many others clawing up for the position, the opportunity of a lifetime. Can't let something as petty as compassion ruin a good thing.

"Way to go, Mason."

"Mason the Caisson, full of ammunition and out on a mission."

"Thatta kid."

"Yeah, yeah, yeah," as Mason tolerates the discomfort of his shoulders being squeezed. "Piece of cake." Sylvester Moore, known as Sly, hands him a glass of champagne, but Mason takes it with disdain. He sees the way Sly looks at Violet every time she walks by, the way he touches her shoulder, her back at every opportunity. But Mason lets it slide and pretends not to notice. He raises his glass along with the others, "Here's to truth, justice, the American way. Oh, and standing next to your ugly mugs along the way." The men beam into the glasses, feet in the air. "I need this vacation." The words echo back from the glass. But Mason feels the weight on his shoulders, the burden that he's responsible for helping a rapist get away with it.

"You've earned it, kid," says Sly. Rhonda, the world's most dependable secretary, pulls Sly to the side.

Geoffrey Tyndall, the prehistoric attorney who started the firm back in the '60s, puts his arm around Mason. "You already know that you're only one of about ten of the fresh faces here just out of law school. Each one of you, all ambitious kids, all full of dreams. But the truth is, there's only one position available. The rest will go on and work on climbing the ladder elsewhere." Mason slows down so Tyndall's seasoned limbs can keep up while the others take the champagne back to their offices. Tyndall leans in, "Mason, are you ready to become the next senior associate attorney here at the firm?"

Mason swallows down the wrong pipe. "Really?"

"I've no doubt, if you keep up with how you're doing things around here that you'll become partner down the road." Geoffrey grins. "Go on and enjoy your trip, I'm tired of hearing about it. The offer will be here when you return." Mason shakes his hand for a long moment, clasping just enough so as not to dislocate the gnarled, arthritic bones. A part of him wants to scream. A part of him wants to cry. A part of him wants to curse with every profanity known to man.

"Thank you so much, Mr. Tyndall." Mason inhales the last sip.

Mason all but skips into his office, to where Violet sits, legs long, made longer by three-inch heels on top of his desk. "Is this a private party?" He smirks.

Her lips curl as she leans back in his chair. "If you'd like."

Mason rests his palms on the arms of the chair, leaning her seat farther back so her body arches under him. He puts his hand up her skirt and follows the warmth until he feels wet flesh, no underwear. Between tasting her lips he whispers, "I love you more than life, you dirty bitch."

A quick knock on the door before Sly walks in. "Listen, I'm sorry to interrupt—" Mason and Violet stumble to compose themselves behind the desk with an attempt to subdue their laughter. Sly turns his back but stands in the doorway with a fake cough. "There's a man who was assaulted, just waking from a coma. Asked for you."

"I'm on vacation," says Mason as he holds his hand up, still staring into Violet's eyes.

"I think you'll want to take this one."

"Damn it, Sly," Mason starts to reject him in the politest of ways. "Give the case to one of the ambulance chasers, it's not for me."

"This one is."

"Oh, yeah?" Mason continues to undress Violet with his eyes. "Why's that?"

"It's about your sister."

"What are you talking about?"

Sly walks to Mason's laptop behind his desk and Googles the name *Rebekah Paul*. After a few clicks, the screen goes to WKLY news, a press conference from Goshen, Kentucky. Mason recognizes his father right away and cringes as he sees him for the first time in six years. Beside him is his mother, Carol, as they hold each other in front of the cameras at the family's old church, the Third-Day Adventists, teary-eyed and looking twenty years older than what they used to. Behind them, Mason recognizes Sheriff Don Mannix, a deacon at the church for as long as he could remember. Mason sees the flashes from the cameras flickering on their faces, the microphones lining up in front of the desperate couple.

"We ask that anyone with information about the whereabouts

of our daughter please come forward." Virgil speaks like he's giving a sermon, a worn Bible held fast to his chest. Mason sees them squeeze each other's hands. "I will personally pay any price for Rebekah's safe return."

A female newscaster comes on the screen. "That was Virgil and Carol Paul, parents of Rebekah Paul, who was last seen on Sunday when leaving Mass at her family church, the Third-Day Adventists." A photo of Rebekah comes up on the screen. "She was last seen wearing a long, pale pink button-down shirt, a long khaki skirt, and white Keds sneakers. As you heard there, she is five feet, three inches tall and has a large birthmark on her right elbow. As of yet, no foul play has been suspected, but the family says that this is extremely out of character for their daughter not to return home. Anyone with information about Rebekah Paul can call 1-800-555-LOST. All calls will remain anonymous."

"Well, let's just hope she gets home safe," says the other broadcaster back at the studio.

Mason closes the laptop and draws a long sigh.

"I know the timing is bad," offers Sly, with his eyes looking through Mason at the doorway. "This doctor who called has this kid . . . Well, it's touch and go. His brain's bleeding out his ears and there isn't much time if he takes a turn for the worse."

"What about Turks and Caicos?" asks Violet.

"We can still go," Mason reassures her. "I'll just go and check it out real fast; we'll have plenty of time."

Violet sighs. "I'll be downstairs in the car."

When she leaves, Sly clears his throat. "Kid won't talk to the cops. Won't talk to anyone but you."

"He asked for me?" Mason rips his tie off and unbuttons the top of his shirt on his way to the desk.

Mason visibly breathes a little easier when Violet isn't there. Sly stands across the office, not sure what to say, watching Mason's face change to something serious. Mason picks up the phone and calls out. What person on the planet doesn't remember their childhood phone number?

"Thank you for calling Church of the Third-Day Adventists. This is Naomi. How may I direct your call?"

He wonders when the house number became the church's line. "Virgil or Carol Paul, please."

"May I ask who's calling?"

"Samuel," Mason lies. "Tell them this is Samuel." While on hold, the "God Bless the Little Children" tune, cracking like it's from an old record, borderline eerie. It's enough to make the hairs on the back of Mason's neck stand up.

It took Mason just as much effort to get through law school as it did to shed that image: a reverend's son, a son from Goshen. There were the rumors that surrounded Goshen, and many from the big city expected most from the place to have incomplete smiles, straw in the teeth.

"This is Carol Paul." It's the first time Mason hears his mother's voice in six years. She's crying.

"Mom, it's me. It's Mason. Don't hang up." There's no response. "Mom."

But then he hears his father's voice on the line. "We don't know no Masons. Never have." The phone clicks.

Mason sighs and pulls a pack of cigarettes from the drawer as he hangs up. A part of him wants to scream. A part of him wants to cry. A part of him wants to curse with every profanity known to man.

"Well, that was uneventful," he says, low enough so Sly doesn't hear. He looks for his lighter. "What's this kid's name?"

"Gabriel."

Like the archangel, he thinks to himself.

■ ■ ■

"I'll wait out here," says Violet, as Mason goes to talk with the doctor in charge of Gabriel's case.

"Mr. Paul, I recognize you from TV, with the case," says the doctor, who uses his arm to wipe the sweat from his brow. "He asked for you by name, and when I just heard about Rebekah Paul, I thought it'd be related."

"Were the police called?"

"They were and they took a statement as best they could." He hands Mason a card. "Told me to call them back when he's responsive. Left their card, if you want it."

"Has this guy said anything?"

"No, but not for lack of trying." The doctor removes his hospital cap and gloves as he leads Mason down the hall and into an empty room in triage. "I've stomached a lot of things in my day, but this one takes the cake." He takes his scrubs off and throws them in a soiled-linens bin in the corner. "Sounds cliché, doesn't it?"

"Is this kid going to make it?"

"Probably not." The doctor leans on the sink and crosses his arms, focusing on a fly buzzing around. "For his sake, I hope he doesn't. For your sake, I hope he does."

"But he's talking?"

"No, he can't. His jaw's wired tighter than Alcatraz." The doctor washes his hands. "Besides, somewhere along the line, he chewed half his tongue off before the paramedics brought him in. Perhaps from a seizure, I'm not sure." He splashes his face with water. "He can't write because he's had a stroke while here, but he can point to letters. He pointed the words *Maton Paul*. When I asked if he meant Mason Paul, he grunted. And then he went into cardiac arrest. We were able to stabilize him, and we're making him as comfortable as we can, but we can't get in touch with any of his family." He sighs and fetches new garbs from one of the cabinets. "I can bring you in, but I'm warning you, it's ugly. Real ugly. He's under as heavy sedation as we can get without inducing him back into a coma. If by some miracle he makes it, he's not leaving much smarter than a third-grader."

He walks Mason back to Gabriel's room, close to where Violet waits. The doctor seems to slide the white curtain that surrounds Gabriel in slow motion. Gabriel's face hardly looks human. One side looks like raw ground beef, an eye missing. His neck and torso are stitched like a Raggedy Andy doll. His heart rate croons slow on the monitors; the sounds of his trying breaths echo through the tubes.

It takes all that Mason has not to gag and turn away. "Any idea who or what did this to him?"

"No idea who," the doctor replies. "But my guess would be a tire iron or a Louisville Slugger or something of the like."

"A tire iron or a baseball bat could make tears like those?"

"A rolled newspaper can rip the flesh, if hit hard enough. Just makes the skin burst." A nurse enters with a board full of alphabet stickers. The doctor cuts off the liquids of an IV to Gabriel's arm and uses a syringe to inject the catheter with something else. "I'm waking him up. Make it quick. This is painful for him."

Gabriel wakes up, his eye squints at the lights. The nurse turns them off. Panic rises, the heart monitor goes berserk. He tries to scream, baring the razor-sharp shards of broken glass that are his teeth, unable to open his mouth from the silver wires that are stitched in and out of both sets of gums to hold his face together. The doctor and two nurses collectively try to calm him down. They breathe loud and slow so he can mimic. When he calms down enough, the doctor nods for Mason to speak.

"I'm Mason Paul." He leans in close, feeling like he's already paying his respects at a funeral to somebody he doesn't know.

"Blink once for 'No' and twice for 'Yes,'" the nurse says.

He blinks twice with understanding.

"Is this about my sister, Rebekah?"

Gabriel blinks twice.

"Do you know where she is now?"

He blinks once.

"Have you seen her in the past few days?"

He blinks twice. He raises his hand with all the strength he can muster and points to letters: R-U-N-A-X-A-Y.

The doctor writes it down. "Runaway?" he asks.

Gabriel blinks twice for yes.

"She was running away?" Mason asks.

He blinks twice.

"Do you know where she was going?"

He raises his arm once more, as if his bones are made of paper and his muscles made of lead: W-E-S-T-C-O-S-T. It takes him a whole ten seconds to point between letters with a shaky finger that pokes from bloody gauze, missing most of its fingernail. Defense wounds. "Westcott, as in the hotel?" Gabriel blinks once. "West Coast?" Gabriel blinks twice. Mason breathes a little easier. "So she's all right?" Gabriel blinks once. Once more, he brings his finger up: K-I-D-N-A. "She was kidnapped?" Mason interrupts. Gabriel blinks twice. "Did you get a look at who took her?" Two blinks. "Do you know who they are?"

Suddenly, the pain starts to return to Gabriel. His muscles contract and bones straighten like rods. His eye rolls up like he's trying to get a visual of the back of his skull.

"This interview has to end, Mason." The doctor hooks him back up to the IV.

"Tell me who did this," Mason screams. "Who took my sister?!" Mason is pushed out of the room, met by Violet. He goes into his phone and onto the Internet to find the number for Sheriff Don Mannix in Goshen. He grabs a pen and paper from the nurses' station and jots it down.

Minutes later, the doctor goes to his side. "We were able to stabilize him for now, but I don't think he'll make it through the night."

"Doctor, do you know where the paramedics picked him up from?"

"Let's have a look." He shifts through a bin for the records behind the nurses' station. "A place called the Bluegrass, outside the truck stop at La Grange." Mason knows where it is. He takes Violet's hand to let her know she's not completely invisible to him. He leaves for La Grange.

On the way, Mason can't help but think of his sister, his father, his mother, Gabriel. *Like the archangel.* And like riding a bike, he can't ever forget the exact words of scripture. And he hates it. He remembers Luke 1, the irony sends a pang to his gut.

And the angel answering said unto him, I am Gabriel, that stand in the presence of God; and am sent to speak unto thee, and to shew thee these glad tidings. And, behold, thou shalt be dumb, and not able to speak, until the day that these things shall be performed, because thou believest not my words, which shall be fulfilled in their season.

"You're smoking too much," remarks Violet from the passenger's seat.

Mason says nothing in return. It's supposed to be one of the most important days of his life, all the hard work was just seeming to pay off, a long-awaited vacation was just on the horizon. And as the rain begins to beat on the windshield in a traffic jam, Mason feels the inkling of fear grow in his chest. The harder he inhales the smoke, the more he hopes it can take away that feeling.

Hypnotized by the red lights before him, Mason remembers his last day in Goshen.

■ ■ ■

"Come with me, Rebekah. I can take you from here, I'll take care of you," Mason pleaded as he packed the last of his belongings into his suitcase on his bed.

"But this is where I'm supposed to be," she answered, unsure of why Mason was packing. *"And so are you, here in God's will."*

"This place is a fucking trap!"

Rebekah crossed her hands under her chin with a gasp, praying for the salvation of her brother. Mason often had to remind himself of his sister's handicap, that her IQ was low enough that it bordered retardation. He had to remind himself that she needed some extra help, extra kindness. Her whispers ran rampant: "Forgive him, Lord, for he knows not what he does."

Mason grabbed her shoulders and shook her from the prayer. "When you're ready to leave, you can come to me. Always. Anytime." He could see the blankness in her eyes. She couldn't even grasp at the concept of leaving home; it was inconceivable to her small mind. But Mason didn't feel sorry for her. He was envious of her ignorance, admired her innocence. "Just promise me that you'll always remember me if you do change your mind, if God tells you to move."

Things had been getting strange in their home. Their father seemed more interested in filling the pews than he was in his own family; he claimed he had these dreams where God would talk to him, would call him to lead people to the church before a certain date. It was supposedly the date that God told him Christ would return, a date that he could tell no one. And it went against what Mason was raised with in church, that not even the angels of heaven would know the date of Christ's return. As far as Virgil was concerned, Mason was deliberately disobeying God for questioning these visions. Finding a packet in the mail from the University of Louisville for prospective students was all that it took for Virgil to kick Mason out of the house.

Virgil was stern about it, claiming it was what God would have him do, which made no sense to Mason whatsoever. He warned Mason never to come back, forced Rebekah to amputate her brother from her life, like he was a cancerous mole. And Mason decided that, when it felt right to her, Rebekah would follow suit and try to find him, and that until then, Mason would never look back.

Rebekah's eyes filled with water as she looked up at him. "Will you at least wear your cross?"

Mason tucked his lips in and reached in the front pocket of his bag to retrieve it, just to make her feel better about the situation. He held it against her necklace, identical to the one in his hand. "Will you promise to visit me?"

Rebekah smiled like it was a sin, turning over her shoulder to make sure no one saw it. She stood on her tippy-toes to kiss him on his cheek before running off.

13
ON THE BREAST

Dear Mason and Rebekah, though once upon a time, you were Ethan and Layla,

Mason, for the first year of your life, I breast-fed you. You'd wake in the middle of the night often, hungry. I could hear Lynn in the living room, a late visit from one of her many regulars, a coke deal. I knew I had to get the hell out of there as soon as possible, I was just waiting for my inheritance to clear with the lawyers. I was still recovering from childbirth, still sore, hormones running rampant.

The room was dark when you woke. Sleep was hard to get, as hungry as you always were. I rolled over to turn on the lamp, not surprised to see that Mark wasn't there. I crawled toward the end of the bed, to where your bassinet was. In a chair at the corner of the room, I was startled to see your uncle, Matthew.

"Matthew, what the hell are you doing in here?"

"Just bored."

I felt like my privacy, our privacy, had just been invaded as he watched me sleep. "I need for you to leave." I picked you up to stop your cries of hunger.

"But I want to watch," Matthew said.

"No." And just as I said no, Lynn walked by the door.

"No, what?" she barked. I didn't say anything.

"Oh, Mommy," said Matthew, his eyelids heavy as if he were stoned, his words soft on the cigarette smoke. "Nessa here is telling me no. I hate it when cunts like this tell me no, don't you, Mother?"

Lynn marched to me, her finger in my face. "Now, you listen to me, you prissy little bitch. I'm sick of you going around *my* home, acting like you own the place, acting like you're better than us." I felt a tear of rage escape my eye. "No one says no to my boys, am I understood?"

I thought, in her last sentence, that that's why her boys were all little shits, with the exception of Peter, of course. I could tell Lynn was high; her agitation was worse than it was most days, her top lip tucking itself in by her teeth. But I just nodded. Lynn went back out of the hallway. "And shut that baby up, he's interfering with my work."

I'd grown afraid of Matthew. This fear would dissipate the older I got. I continued to feed you, in front of him, because what choice did I have?

A few days later, Mark and I were alone in the house. I cannot recall where everybody else was, but for Peter, who'd usually locked himself away in his room. "Ness," Mark called down to me from the hall. I was holding you in the living room, studying, with contempt, a box of illegal fireworks that your father had brought home after one of his busts. He was always bringing things like that home. Illegal fireworks, guns, drugs, even the odd boa constrictor.

"What is it?" I yelled back.

"Leave the baby for a minute and just come here." I walked up the hallway, Mark standing there in his uniform, leaning against Matthew's doorway, thumbs tucked behind his belt. He reminded me of some cowboy. "What is it?"

"I want you to stop leading my brother on," he said, his voice indifferent.

"But I'm not—"

Mark grabbed my upper arm and squeezed hard enough that in the days following, I could map out the bruises from where his fingertips were when I'd raise my arms in the mirror. He pulled me into Matthew's room, where, on a desk, were photos of me. Candles. Locks of my hair tied in bows. A shrine, in honor of me.

I felt sick; I felt violated. "I know you are," yelled Mark. "*My* wife will not be whoring herself around, especially to my own brother. Am I clear?"

I nodded.

He looked down at me and adjusted his shirt, like I was a piece of shit on the bottom of his shoe. "I'm leaving to go finish packing for the new house."

14
MATTLEY

Officer Mattley kisses his mother's cheek as he enters the house. "I hope he wasn't too much trouble for you."

"No, he was an angel. I was just fixing his breakfast." At the breakfast bar, seven-year-old Richie puts the heads of his rubber dinosaurs into the milk of his Lucky Charms. "You look tired. Let me make you some coffee."

"Thanks for coming over again, Mom. These night shifts are killing me." He takes off his uniform top, leaving a white tee that was underneath. He wraps his arm around his son's waist and kisses the back of his head. "Morning, Champ."

"I'm not Champ," he says as he holds the toys by the tails. "I'm Spider-Man!" Richie turns and pretends to shoot his father with projectile spiderwebs from his hands.

"You got me," Mattley says as he stumbles back into the wall. Richie goes back to his dinosaurs drinking marshmallow milk and makes slurping noises.

"How was your night, dear?"

"It's Painter, Mom." He smiles as he grabs a stool beside Richie. "Nothing exciting to report."

"You mean you didn't catch any bad guys?" His son doesn't take his attention away from his T-rex.

"Luckily, there were no bad guys to catch. The world was safe!"

"Just Painter, Dad. Just Painter was safe."

Mattley rubs his son's brown bowl cut. "You already packed for your mother's house?"

"Do I have to? I just saw her," he whines.

"Yeah, like a month ago. C'mon." He lifts Richie off the stool and pats his butt. "We don't wanna be late."

"But Mom yells too much," he says as he drags his feet down the hallway.

"Sounds about right." It was a nasty divorce. A wife of two years with some insane trust issues. A wife who fell out of love with a man who cared too much about his work. A wife who didn't adapt to the fact that she was a mother and no longer belonged at the club scene.

"Are you doing anything exciting with your day?" His mother asks, the smell of dark roast surrounding them.

"Gonna stop and see my friend at the Whammy Bar and maybe grab a drink before sleeping the rest of the day."

"You mean Freedom?" yells Richie from his bedroom.

Mattley's perplexed. "What do you know about it?"

"Remember, we ran into her not long ago at the line at the fair? You love her, I can tell. You couldn't stop flirting with her. At least she is pretty, though, not like that Jennifer next door who's in love with you."

"I was not flirting, and Jennifer next door is not in love with me." Mattley looks at his mother, his voice low. "Where the hell does this kid get his smarts from?"

"He gets his smarts from you." She smiles as she makes his coffee. "Accusing you of flirting with women? That he gets from his mother."

■■■

"*It's odd seeing you*, when there's only one of you to see." Freedom laughed, poking Mattley's side from behind. In all fairness, it was just as odd for Mattley, seeing her for the first time in daylight while she was sober. Away from the night, she was strikingly beautiful.

It was a few months ago, the Fourth of July. The fair smelled of sunblock and gunpowder and watermelon. Vendors' stations smoked with hot dogs and burgers, the kids had their faces painted. "Freedom, how have you been?" Mattley's cheeks were tinged pink, an insulated beer cup in hand.

"I didn't know you drank."

"This?" He raised the can. "This is maybe my first beer since Christmas."

"So, you're here for the fireworks?"

"I am, here with my son," he looked around. "He's around here somewhere. What about you? You here to share your patriotism with the rest of Painter?"

"Me? No." Freedom adjusted the red bandanna on her head. "I'm just walking through. I prefer to be drunk by myself."

"Well, all the cops are already here. Might as well save 'em a trip." He smiled. He lifted his sunglasses to his sunburned head. "You shouldn't drink, though."

Freedom looks at his beer. "Oh, really?"

"I'll make you a deal. I will, hand on heart, not drink one more sip if you don't." He tilts the beer, ready to pour it out.

Freedom smiled, perhaps for the first time in twenty years. "Why shouldn't I?"

"Because." He had to think. Freedom recognized the buzz in him and was amused by this unseen side of Officer Mattley. "Because you have beautiful skin, and alcohol is bad for your skin."

She rolled her eyes with a laugh. "You're not that smooth."

"Well, it's my day off." He leaned in to her ear. "And I kind of like being your knight in shining armor."

Richie ran up and grabbed his father's leg. "Daddy, Daddy, look at my face paint!"

"Last chance," he says as he tilts the beer once more.

"All right, fine, fine."

He put his arm around her shoulders as he spilled the beer onto the dried grass. "Thatta girl."

"That's alcohol abuse, ya know."

Throughout the evening they flirted until it was time for the fireworks to finish off a seemingly perfect night.

Moments after the grand finale, their ears and eyes sore from the blasts, and the sun long set, Richie fell asleep on Freedom's lap, melted ice cream pasted all over his face. Mattley took her hand.

Attendees from the show were packing their blankets and balloons and beer cans and lighting the last of their sparklers. Freedom buried her face in Richie's hair and remembered the softness of her own son's from twenty years ago. The smell of his kid's shampoo filled her heart with lead. She looked down at the boy from above his head, which rested on her chest, and swore it was Ethan. She placed her hand on his heart, feeling his chest rise. Mattley wondered what she was doing, caressing the top of her hand with his fingertips. He realized that in his son's hair, Freedom was crying.

"What's wrong, Freedom?" His touch moved up her arm.

She lifted her head, the lights of children's blinking toys reflecting off her flooded eyes. "I'm sorry, I can't—I just can't." Freedom cautiously handed a sleeping Richie to his father before running off to her home, where she proceeded to drink by herself until she could no longer function.

15

THE EMPTY WOMB

My name is Freedom and my womb is empty. I am reminded of this insult from God every time I'm on the rag. What a bitch Eve was. It's ten in the morning and I am alone at the Whammy Bar. I stretch out on top of one of the pool tables. The day's as gray as the cigarette smoke from a whore in Times Square on a frigid January morning, like most days are in this godforsaken state. Carrie did a swell ol' job of cleaning last night and so I use the next hour to stall. With my forearms at the end of each side of the table, my hands hang off the sides. I hold the cue ball in one hand and the eight ball in the other and try to discern a difference in weight between the two. I'm bored out of my fucking skull. But I feel the voices start to come. I use the remote to turn the bar's surround sound as loud as it can: Screamin' Jay Hawkins. "I Hear Voices" comes on.

I inhale a menthol cigarette through my nostrils to smoke the suicidal thoughts out of my head. It's the hangovers that make me this way, nothing more, nothing less. Lots of bad thoughts, lots of terrible voices. I don't know what they say; they're hard to hear over Sir Jay Hawkins's blues, one of the first shock-rockers who ever lived. I can't tell where my voices begin and where his drunken gurgling and grunts of his tunes begin. With the filter to my nose, I think of the voodoo bones Hawkins wore in his nose. Right, as if I really think snorting through the filter of a menthol Pall Mall will actually work. I bring the billiard balls to each temple and massage my head by swirling them, but nothing works. I'll ignore them, as always. I see a faint strip of light on the ceiling above the front door, but I don't move. Whoever it is tries to come in unnoticed and so I'll play along. Could be Carrie. Could be Cal. Could be worse.

"Whoever that is." I hold up the billiard balls. "I have balls that can prove fatal if I put enough force behind the blow into your frontal lobe."

"If that's the case, I'll never look at you the same way again." Mattley.

"I knew it was you."

"Oh, really? And how is that?" He walks closer to me.

"Bacon, donuts, you all smell the same." I rise up as best as I can, given the hangover. "How's the boy?" Not that I especially care.

"Getting at that age." Mattley removes his hat. "Any day he'll be bringing home the ladies." There's that smile I love. It aches to sit up. I think I might actually still be drunk from last night. "Listen, Freedom, I want to talk to you about something." He looks down and scrapes the toe of his shoe over a spot on the floor. "About your kids."

"What are you talking about?" I straighten my arms to my sides on the pool table. "I never had kids."

"I know that's what you say when you're dry." He plays with his Stetson hat. "But you do talk a lot when you're drunk."

"I get, um, creative when I'm drunk." I stare off. "Have I told you about the time the pope and I bungee-jumped off the Eiffel Tower?"

Mattley sighs with his chin to his chest. He taps the side of the table where the palms of his hands rest. "You don't have to fool me. I'm not asking for the truth, Freedom. But what I am asking is that you consider talking to someone."

"I'm already talking to someone." My anger makes its way to my voice.

"OK." He clears his throat. "That was suggestion number one." I roll my eyes. "Just a suggestion, is all." He smiles. *God, I love his smile.* "Have you considered getting help in other areas of your life? Like with the drinking?"

Only inches separate our faces from touching, and right now it takes all of what little decency I have left to stop me from throwing myself on him. He cares. He's the only one who cares and I hate it more than anything. I don't deserve it. But I want to tell him my feelings for him are strong, that I wished all the time that something terrible and freakish would happen to him so that I could go to his rescue and comfort him in the night. But I say nothing about it. "That's my business." I break away from him. "Now fuck off and leave me alone."

It's better this way, to nip it in the bud before anything might have a chance to flourish. He has a kid, a nice home. Can't let myself get anything near normal. Me and normal are like gunpowder and fire. The two things should never mix.

■ ■ ■

Back in the office before the regulars can ride in, I go back to the Internet. Still nothing on Rebekah's Facebook page. Nothing new from Louisa Horn. On Mason's page, a few random congratulations on his wall about some legal victory this morning and one from last night, a post he was tagged in from Violet about a trip to Turks and Caicos.

I don't know what makes me do it, but I do a quick Google search of their names. The legal case that Mason won this morning pops up first. Already knew about that. Then I type in Rebekah's name.

The room spins. The music outside fades further and further from my ears. I grab the nearest garbage can and dry-heave. I think I'm having a heart attack. I stand to go for the phone, to call for help. But my knees buckle. I panic. I fall. The lights fade to nothing, not anything that the name of a color can describe. Like I'm in slow motion, the floor comes closer and closer to my face. And that's the last thing I can remember.

16
PETER

TWO DAYS AGO

Peter feels the gusts of people rushing by. Loudspeakers announce inaudible messages about departure times and platform numbers. He zips his electric wheelchair through Penn Station in Manhattan; his coat hanging on the back to hide the lewd stickers his brothers have stuck on there over the years. Below him in the chair's compartment are the essentials: underwear, soap, a toothbrush, two pairs of jeans, three T-shirts, deodorant, the rest of Matthew's welcome-home cake in Tupperware, his laptop with its accessories, and a cell phone he lifted from his mother while she slept, her head practically inside a bucket of chicken bones. She was in a foul mood after this month's disability check from social welfare was late. Of course the government does this to her on purpose, and only her, those spiteful bastards. One big giant fucking conspiracy from the White House against Lynn Delaney. But Peter didn't mind, as long as he was able to lift what money she had from the drawer next to her underwear and sex toys. He'll do his best to forget he ever saw them. And as long as she forgot to put the lock on the refrigerator.

"I n-n-need uh Amtrak ticket to Loo-Loo-Louisville, Kent-t-tucky." Peter can barely see over the window; his cheekbones twitch and eyes squint with every consonant that doesn't want to come out.

"I'm gonna need a driver's license for ID."

"Does it luh-look like I can fucking jer-jer-drive?" He reaches in his pocket and slides his New York state-issued ID through the window.

An hour later, when the train just finishes boarding, Peter reaches for his mother's cell. *She must have been high as a kite if she forgot to lock the refrigerator and left the phone out of her reach.* He takes a few minutes, struggling to keep his hands still enough to scroll through the contacts. He scrolls to Matthew's number and sends him a text, phrasing it the way his mother would:

Matty, do me a favor and give me that cunt's phone number.

Minutes later, the phone buzzes and the number comes through. Peter calls her right away.

"*Yeah? Yellow? Hello? It was the wrong number. Those good-for-nothing salesmen or something.*" Peter hears one other voice: "*Your face says otherwise, Free-free.*" Peter hears her sneak off. "*I gotta shower. Please be gone by the time I'm out.*"

■ ■ ■

Lynn Delaney chews on her last Xanax, drinks the all-purpose wine right from the box, and wipes the cabernet from her chin onto the blouse closest within her reach. She glides down the hall on her scooter and kisses her hand and slaps Mark's photo as habit would have it. She finds this rage toward Peter within her that helps her, for the first time in several years, stand on her own two feet, but not without much difficulty. How could Peter do this to her? After all the years she's taken care of him? She has to lean on the counter to slam the refrigerator door that was left open before she grabs the nearest kitchen knife. The TV blares a Chia Pet commercial, ceramic Obamas and poodles with sprouts for hair. With a shriek that makes the pit bulls bark out back, she stabs the TV. *Ch-Ch-Ch-Chia.* The jingle makes her eardrums want to shatter. The blade of the knife breaks in half, no damage to the television. She pulls the TV from the entertainment center in hopes that the screen will smash into a million pieces, a swift pull fueled by grade-A adrenaline. Instead, the cords hooked up to the wall keep it inches from the ground. It's like her heart pumps gravel as she falls to the ground when her weight can't find some harmonious balance. She wails, and now the neighbors' dogs yap at the sounds. She doesn't know how she'll get up and starts to scream for help from her neighbors as the tears trickle down to her temples. *My babies, my boys, my Peter. How could you do this to me? After Mark, after my daughters, after the grandson I haven't seen in years and the granddaughter I've never met, how could you do this to me? You're a fucking monster, Peter. A fucking monster!*

From the floor, she chews her fingernails off and spits each one to her side. The Xanax shuts her tear ducts down and the sobs are reduced to childlike whimpers. The blood comes back to her, slow currents that feel good to her nerves.

Her laughter ricochets against the halls and doors, her abdomen contracts with the cackles. Above her is a photo of Peter, back when she sent him to that camp for retarded kids when he was eight. Lynn talks out loud to the picture: "It should have been you instead of Mark." Her eyelids become heavy with the pills, her laughs still present but subdued. "I should have aborted you when I had the chance."

PART II

17

THE BLUEGRASS

The Mercedes pulls into the dirt lot; a whirl of dust follows. The polished black paint job that Mason was so proud of sticks out like a sore thumb against the rust of the pickup trucks left here overnight. Eighteen-wheelers stand cold in rows, mechanic stations abandoned in light of the storm that's expected to hit any minute, like something out of an old Western. In the car, Mason has his phone on speaker while he calls Sheriff Don Mannix's office. He recognizes Don's voice when he answers.

"Hiya, Don. It's Mason." He puts the car in park.

"Who?"

"Mason—Mason Paul."

"I apologize, mister; I never met no Mason Paul a'fore."

Mason looks over at Violet in the passenger's seat. He feels the heat of his blood flood his face. "Cut the shit, Don, I need to talk to you." Mason knows sure as hell that Don knows who he is. "Goddamn it . . ."

"Sorry, but I don't know you. An' I don't appreciate you callin' me and using the Lord's name in vain." Don hangs up. A chill runs up Mason's spine; his shoulders shake.

"What the hell is going on, Mason?" Violet asks.

He stares off. "I guess that's what happens when you're shunned."

"What kind of church is your father running?"

Thunder cracks overhead; a cloud of purple inflates. The radio tuned low warns of a sudden storm, a tornado warning. As if God answers her question, a downpour beats down on the car. Ahead of him, Mason sees a "closed" sign on the window of the Bluegrass's front door. "Wait here. I'll be just a minute," he tells Violet. Before she can stop him, he runs for the front door and stands under the awning to stay dry. *Think, Mason. Think.* He cups his hands and peers inside: dark except the neon-lit jukebox. He looks around. No cameras, not that he expected the security on the outside of the seedy bar.

He wonders what in hell's name would bring Rebekah to a run-down, redneck place like this. The doors are locked. He looks back to Violet, who waves her arms to hurry him back to the car. Mason ignores her. Hailstones the size of Ping-Pong balls begin to crash to the ground, Mason uses his blazer to cover his face. Across the parking lot, steel garbage cans and debris fly around. There are always tornado warnings in Kentucky.

He gets an idea.

With his coat over his head, he runs from under the awning, takes a garbage can, and brings it back with him. *No one would think twice about a broken window during a storm like this. If there are cameras inside, I can take the tapes. A witness? I'm just a passerby trying to get out of the storm for my own safety, right? Show me some of that southern hospitality of yours, ma'am.* Violet honks the horn at him as he raises the can up and beats on one of the windows. He cracks it and a large shard of glass falls inside. He wraps his coat around his fist and breaks it the rest of the way. He uses the anger he harbors against his parents and Sheriff Don Mannix for pretending not to know who he is behind each punch to force his way in.

Inside, the place is eerily devoid of life. The winds of the storm whistle through the cracks of the wooden building; the drumming of hailstones on the floor follow him inside, the neon lights of the jukebox drone across the bar. He doesn't know what he's looking for. He only hopes to recognize something once he sees it. Staticky music plays upstairs, where he assumes there must be an apartment or an office. Johnny Cash, muffled behind closed doors. Mason goes behind the bar to find something to protect himself with. Leaning near the cash register is a baseball bat. He lets it rest on the palms of his hands and his stomach turns at the notion that it could have been used to beat Gabriel within inches of his life. He inspects it for blood: none that he can see.

Thoughts of his sister being beaten in the way Gabriel was mangled consume him. He imagines the photos of the rape victim from his court case being Rebekah. He feels sick and slaps his own face as hard as he can. He looks around before grabbing the first bottle of alcohol he sees from the cheap, rail rack and takes a swig. The door upstairs opens; the Johnny Cash record becomes clearer, a background to men's voices heading for the steps. Mason takes the bat and hides under the stairs.

The hurried paces of about half a dozen men scrape above him. Mason clenches the wood and holds his breath. "Get in the cellar," one says. A window breaks. Rubble from the outside slams on the doors and windows. The power goes out. Mason pokes his head out to see the men. Skinheads. Neo-Nazis, whatever you call them. Swastikas inked on their arms and skulls, wifebeaters and red suspenders, a way of saying that they've shed blood for what they believe. Mason knows this only from a case he had a couple years ago. They run behind the bar and open a trap door to a cellar under the pub. As soon as the last one disappears, Mason hears the sirens for the first time. Tornado warnings. *Violet!*

He runs to one of the broken windows to look at the car. She isn't there. *Fuck.* The window beside him breaks, a slice to his ear that starts to bleed down his face. And against his better judgment, he runs upstairs. A small hallway is dark as night. To his left, he sees a room with a large Confederate flag hanging above a table, scattered coffee cups and papers swirling about with the drafts from outside. On the other wall, a flag with a large swastika on it. Johnny Cash's "God's Gonna Cut You Down" still plays on a battery-operated record player.

Out the window, the skies resemble shifting leather on the back of some god rolling in excitement. He has to hurry up. From one of the seats, Mason grabs a pile of unlabeled CDs in hopes that one of them might be security footage, though he realizes it's unlikely. The bar shakes under his feet. He runs downstairs and avoids the windows. He darts for the kitchen and kneels near the stove when he sees Violet ducked down on the other side. He goes to her and covers her. She squeezes him as hard as she can, covering her ears from the deafening blows of the storm.

"We need to get the hell out of here," Mason yells to her, remembering the gang of neo-Nazis below them in the cellar.

He holds her tight, uses his coat to cover her skin, until minutes later, the storm passes. Above them, sand flies from the cooking vents. The whistling dies down. The rain settles. The calm of the storm is a presence, something heavy on a person's bones. "I'll explain later, just stay quiet," he says as he motions for the back exit. Something stuck tings in the kitchen vent; it sounds like change in the clothes dryer. He doesn't mention the Fascist party downstairs and guides Violet toward the Dumpsters, baseball bat still glued in his fists. But the rattling in the vent from the corners of his ears irks him. Something tells him to go back.

"Start the car, I'm right behind you." Mason goes back inside the kitchen and to the vent.

The daylight that breaks from the clouds and down to the alleyway reflects off of the object. It's just out of Mason's reach. He holds the baseball bat between his thighs and grabs a kitchen knife from a magnetic strip on the wall to shimmy the shiny object closer to him from the vent. He hears the men from below return to the bar.

Beads of sweat form at Mason's temples and trickle down his face, mixed with the blood from his ear. He hurries. He slides the object closer to him but loses his hold on it. *I'm probably doing all this for a fucking nickel stuck in a vent.* But it becomes a vendetta; something in his head won't let him give up. He tries once more, with success. He pulls a black string attached to the object. It gets caught. The voices of the neo-Nazis seem to get louder. Mason gives the string one firm yank and pulls it free.

He doesn't look at it right away, just runs out to the alleyway, where, unbeknownst to him, Rebekah was making a memory with Gabriel three days ago. Rebekah had experienced her first buzz of beer. She'd met a boy, for the first time in her twenty years, who gave her butterflies in her stomach. Mason's phone vibrates in his pocket. A voice mail. A doctor. Gabriel did not survive.

Mason opens his palm to see what the tornado swept up into the vent. He looks at the cross. He holds it next to his. They're identical.

Only Rebekah's is spattered with blood.

18

FREEDOM IN JESUS

My name is Freedom and if this bitch doesn't get that needle away from me, I'm going to shove it through her retina, I swear it. I rip an IV from my arm and toss it on the floor of the ambulance. Never mind the blood dripping down. "Everyone, out of my way." Around me are two paramedics, Passion, and about half a dozen bikers. One of the paramedics tries to get me to sit back in the ambulance, but I spit on him. "Don't you fucking touch me," I yell. Passion tries to calm the guys down. I look back to the bikers. "We'll open in fifteen, boys."

No one tries to dissuade me. It was just a panic attack. Not my first. Won't be my last. They're terrible. Imagine falling through the ice and not being able to find your way back up. The terror kicks you so hard that you don't have anything in you to tell you it's freezing. You know you're supposed to hold your breath, but a racing heart won't let you. You flail your arms, trying to break through the belly of a thick sheet of ice, hopelessly. Only now you've lost the ice, you don't know where it is. Up is somewhere, down is somewhere, but you can't grasp onto *where*. You gasp for air, only there's no air to gasp for. Drowning. Panic. Panic, in its rawest form. And as for these attacks? Exactly the fucking same.

I hear Passion's heels scuff on the gravel as she tries to keep up

with me back into work. I wouldn't want to try to run in those harpoons.

The Rolling Stones play low around us, the lights still off. Strips
of light whip across the wooden bar, beams of dust. I sit on the
patrons' side of the bar, reach over and grab the first bottle I can feel.
Tequila will do. Passion drapes her fur coat over one of the stools.
She smacks that gold tooth. "You gonna tell me what's going on?"

"Just going through some shit," I say as I take a swig. "Nothing I
can't handle."

I think about the letter I wrote reaching Rebekah, reaching the
Pauls. Suddenly, the horrifying notion that my letter is the reason for
my daughter's disappearance hits me. I take another sip, an attempt
to settle my heartbeat to a more bearable level.

Passion reaches into her purse and pulls out an orange prescription bottle. "This'll help." She shakes a pill out.

"I don't take pills."

"A low dosage of Xanax." She presses it into the palm of my
hand. "I'll get you some water."

"I don't drink water." I take half of one and put the other half in
my pocket for later. I'll add it to my suicide jar. "Fish fuck in it." Passion rubs my arm, but neither one of us say a word. There's no need
to. Words mean nothing now. I think about Rebekah once more. I
start to cry. But I don't want Passion seeing.

"It's OK." Her blue claws stroke my arm. She is comforting, a
calm presence to my fucked soul. "Tell me what's going on. Maybe
there's something I can do." I have the urge to tell her of my biological children, about Rebekah gone missing. But I don't.

"Passion," I start. I look up to her eyes, deep with concern, dark
with interest. "What's your real name?"

She rolls those eyes, sighs, and smiles. I'm surprised she takes
the Jose Cuervo from me and takes a sip of her own. It's the first time
I've ever seen her drink alcohol. "Ann."

"Ann?" I spin on my stool and wipe my tears while my back's to
her. "That was the last thing I ever expected you to be named."

"Tell me about it." Passion hands the liquor back. "What's yours?"

"My name?" I exhale something long and controlled. "Vanessa. But everyone just called me Nessa."

"A good white girl's name." She smiles.

"If you say so, *Ann*." I return the tequila to the rail and pat Passion's back before I head to the office. "I'll be out in just a minute. Gotta take care of something."

I lock the door behind me as I power up the computer with a twitch of the mouse. Rebekah's photo is still on the screen. I click on the contact page and pull out my cell.

"Thank you for calling Church of the Third-Day Adventists. This is Naomi. How can I direct your call?"

"This is FreedomInJesus from Oregon. I'm calling to speak with Reverend Virgil Paul, please."

"One moment." Naomi transfers my call.

"This is Reverend Virgil Paul," says the deep southern drawl. I already hate him.

"Reverend Paul, this is Freedom Oliver, FreedomInJesus from Oregon, we've spoken before."

"Of course, yes, Freedom." He doesn't sound like a man whose daughter's just gone missing. He's cheerful. "And to what do I owe this pleasure?"

"Well." I sit back down and let the Xanax swim its way through my blood. "You might think this sounds crazy, but I've been praying, praying hard. God spoke to me. He told me to go to Goshen. Am I crazy?" I have to seem like an amateur. I have to let him believe he's superior to me to avoid the chance of him thinking of me as a threat. *I'm just a naive zealot. I need someone divine, such as yourself, to guide me down the righteous path.*

"No, Freedom. That doesn't sound crazy at all. Sounds like God has a plan."

"Is that right?" I absentmindedly write on a stack of neon Post-its: *Find Rebekah.*

19

THE THIRD-DAY ADVENTISTS

Virgil Paul lifts his head from prayer to look down to the four hundred–plus parishioners. The women's eyes stare up to him from blue headscarves, the men are in pale yellow ties: the liturgical blue signifies heaven; the yellow represents divinity. Virgil's armpits and ribs itch with drops of sweat as his clammy hands close a red leather Bible. The congregation smiles. The congregation nods. The congregation faces forward, their backs to a camera on a tripod at the end of the aisle near the church's front doors.

"As we finish here today, I ask for a special prayer for the safe return of our sister in Christ. Our daughter, Rebekah. Go in peace." Virgil makes the sign of the cross with the edge of his hand. "And may the Lord bless you and protect you all." A uniform "Amen" fills the room. Virgil waits for a member to walk to the camera and give the nod, the nod that indicates that the podcast has ended, the filming is over.

An occasional clearing of the throat echoes from the corner. The noise of an infant crying from the back pulsates through the church.

"Let us prepare for our second sermon. Let us show our true colors to the Lord." The flock of worshipers reaches under their seats as Virgil disappears into the back. In his office behind the altar, he locks the door behind him. His long, rectangular office is eggshell white with a large poster of his face hanging over his mahogany desk. In it he grins, a set of pearly dentures from thick, ham-ish lips. A farmer's tan he acquired as a child out in the soybean fields seems to have permanently stained his skin. His mousy brown hair with impressively not one gray strand borders a pale tan line on his forehead from straw hats worn in the summer sun. The window-sill behind his desk holds several versions of the Crucifixion: some gold, some wood. Reverend Virgil Paul begins to masturbate.

It's the power trip he gets from a growing audience that submits to him. The thought of being chosen by God himself to be such a faithful servant so high in the ranks of Christianity. Virgil tries to stay quiet so no one can hear. He thinks of the young and blossom-ing Michelle Campbell who lives next to him on the compound, at the very end of the street.

He opens a wardrobe and takes out a makeshift whip made of an old belt now hot-glued with thumbtacks. As he nears his climax, he wraps the belt around his thigh and pulls, the sharp points mak-ing him bleed onto the floor. The closer he gets, the harder he pulls until he finally finishes. This mortification of the flesh is his pun-ishment for sin, his penance and atonement. He recites: *"For if ye live after the flesh, ye shall die: but if ye through the Spirit do mortify the deeds of the body, ye shall live."*

He removes his coat, rebuckles his pants, and grabs a long pur-ple robe from the wardrobe, the color signifying royalty. He steps into it, weak from the climax but ready as ever to save as many souls as he can, to prepare them for the Day of Freedom.

He remembers back to a time when he thought he knew so much about God. Virgil supposes many think that upon leaving seminary. And that was before Gabriel, the archangel and messenger of God, came to him in a dream and told him to recruit in preparation for the Day of Freedom. For God told him the exact minute of the day when Christ will return. And now he looks forward to the arrival of FreedomInJesus, Freedom Oliver. A sense of gratification rushes over him, that God allowed his reach to stretch across the country and all the way to Oregon. Time to carry out God's work, and God's work through him was amazing. Part of Virgil's mission was to send out volunteers to stand at the supermarkets, gather the people, make the masses grow. *Aim for the runaways, the drunkards, the whores.* People like this had nowhere to go, no one to turn to. What better people, then, to lead to Christ and to this very church.

But the recruiting had to stop; Gabriel the archangel even said so in one of his dreams. It was attracting too much attention from the townspeople. Besides, he couldn't just have his congregation come and go as they pleased, lacking that kind of discipline. But for the Pauls, Virgil had to put an end to the recruits out in public. And aside from the Paul family, no one was allowed out.

When he returns to the pulpit, the people have transformed. They all wear white robes. "For it says in Revelation chapter six, verse eleven," he shouts to the group. They continue together, "'... and white robes were given unto every one of them; and it was said unto them, that they should rest yet for a little season, until their fellow servants also and their brethren, that should be killed as they *were*, should be fulfilled.'"

Twenty-four deacons, including Goshen sheriff Don Mannix, sit in the front rows and continue reciting scripture with gold foil crowns on their heads: "Revelation chapter four, verse four: 'And round about the throne *were* four and twenty seats: and upon the seats I saw four and twenty elders sitting, clothed in white raiment; and they had on their heads crowns of gold.'"

Virgil continues: "Let us pray." The congregation goes to their knees. From the back, a man with a loud voice yells. He speaks in tongues, a language no man can understand. Halalas and tikabobs pour from his mouth and the people pray. They listen. They agree.

In the front, a woman who claims the gift to translate tongues.

She yells, "The Lord speaks this message to those who shall inherit the kingdom of God: The Rapture is upon us. We are the chosen ones, the fruits of the vine." The people utter their *amens* and *praise-the-Lords*. Two more members go to the aisle, where their bodies thrash and jerk on the ground. Praises follow as the woman continues: "The storms this week: they destroyed houses, homes of the people of the world, wicked people. It was God's way of showing He is coming back soon." Virgil shouts an amen, fist in the air. "And we were spared, because of all we've done for the Lord. But God warns us that we are on the brink of losing our seats in heaven." The man shouting in tongues ceases with the babbling.

"This is not the last of it!" Virgil shouts, eliciting cheers from the people. "Another storm is on its way, says the Lord. For He told me in a dream: a bigger storm, a more catastrophic storm, is on its way, a storm that none of us are yet prepared for."

■ ■ ■

The sermon is three hours in. Behind the row of deacons, in the second row, are two dozen visibly pregnant women who try to hide their squirms of impatience. Behind them sits Carol Paul, a tall woman with short, curly black hair and hands that no soap could wash the lemon scent from. In fact, calluses on her hands were tinged yellow from hours of making homemade lemonade day in and day out. The tie of her blue headscarf chafes under her chin from the sweat. The fluttering up and down of paper fans offers no respite from the foul-smelling sweat of people who are allowed to bathe only once every two weeks. But Carol, the obedient wife that she is, must be doing only one of three things: singing hymns, praying, or smiling. She has to urinate but continues to hold it. Leaving in the middle of one of her husband's sermons, well . . . she should know better than to show such disrespect toward Virgil.

She feels the air on the sweat of her lap as five-year-old Magdalene wakes from her nap. She rubs her eyes and stares off as her father continues with his sermon. Carol adjusts the blue headscarf on her daughter's head and fixes her light brown pigtails. "Did Rebekah make it to church today?" Magdalene asks as she rests her tired head on Carol's shoulder.

"Not today, sweetie." Carol lifts her hands in praise.

Magdalene does the same, waving her arms back and forth over her head. "She's in big, big trouble. Right, Mommy?" Carol looks down and smiles to Magdalene, peels the matted pieces of hair from her face.

Carol and Magdalene join the other parishioners in speaking in tongues as the row of expectant mothers slide their robes over to expose their bellies, tight and stretched, skin full of limbs and fluids and living tissue that swim in utter darkness. The reverend places his hands on the bellies as he walks past them, muttering blessings to the unborn in a language only God's chosen can understand. He anoints them, using oil to leave signs of the cross with his thumb, using the hand he just jerked off with. Some of the women convulse with praise; others faint. God has a way through Virgil, that's for sure. Michelle Campbell, one of the expectant mothers at fifteen, jumps to her feet.

"Look, Mommy." Magdalene pulls on her mother's robe and points to Michelle. In a loud whisper: "Sister Michelle went pee-pee in her pants!"

"A miracle is upon us," Virgil yells. The songs of praise become louder and louder until Magdalene has to cover her ears. Virgil instructs Carol to run back to the house and get what's needed to perform the birth. "A gift from God is on its way!" She grabs Magdalene's hand and races out of the church.

Carol and Magdalene's matching black loafers skid against the dirt road, their feet covered in dust. Carol squeezes her daughter's hand and hurries farther from the church, the sounds of praise becoming syrupy vapors in the day's humidity behind them. The lanes are lined with small white bungalows-turned-apartments, one-bedroom homes that sleep half a dozen, easily. At the end of the road, farthest from the compound's entrance, is the Paul house, an old double-story country house one would imagine being the topic of the *Southern Living* magazine dream. A copper rooster of a weather vane glows still in the autumn's anomalous heat wave.

The house smells of lemons and baked Dutch apple pie. "Do you remember where Mommy's doctor's bag is?" Magdalene's pigtails bounce in the sunlight. "Go on, I'll be right back." Carol runs down the hall and slams the bathroom door behind her, shimmying out of her underwear before she's halfway to the toilet, about to burst. She grunts with relief, a moment to herself so she can breathe; moments alone are few and far between. She hears Magdalene drag the doctor's bag down the hall before she knocks on the bathroom door. Carol pulls her clothes back together, damp with perspiration and tarnished with dirt. She opens the door and looks down to Magdalene, who smiles with pride on bringing the bag half her weight to her mother. She expects her mother's gratitude, but she doesn't get it. "Go wait outside, I'll be out in just a minute." A look of disappointment sweeps over Magdalene's face; her head hangs low. She drags her feet out to the porch.

Carol places the doctor's bag on the bathroom sink and unzips it. She traces a stethoscope with the tips of her fingers, remembers a time when she was at the top of her class at the College of Medicine at the University of Kentucky. She remembers the sin associated: the clubs when the bass of bands like INXS and the Smiths would move her. The boys she'd steal cigarettes from and make out with back in her dorm room. The marijuana she and her sister used to smoke behind their parents' backs. But that was nearly thirty years ago, many moons into the past. That was before she found God, who saved her from her evil ways. Before she found Virgil.

Carol looks in the mirror; she looks at an entirely different person. The crow's-feet plant themselves unkindly around her eyes these days. She thinks about how Virgil was right all those years ago, though she didn't see it right away: that doctors don't heal; only God has such power.

At the bottom of her doctor's bag is a faded, half-ripped sheet of lined paper.

Dear Carol,

I've only imagined that you still think of me, of your family, though we've had no contact in nearly three years. But I am alone these days, I've lost you to a man who only loves himself, a man who uses God as a tactic for evil. I just wish you could see this the way I saw it. And who can be expected to live with such loneliness? There's been so much that's happened, so much I wish I could tell you. But you're not here. And who knows if you'll be there to get this letter, to go to my funeral. I just miss my sister. I miss my best friend. Tell Ma and Pa that I love them, and that I'll always be with them.

Always,

Clare

Carol doesn't notice a tear that makes a streak on her cheeks through the dust she collected outside. She remembers when she first received the letter half a decade ago, when she could smell her twin sister's perfume on it. And while the smell disappeared only weeks later, Carol sniffs the note in a hope that she can detect a residual trace. But she doesn't. She never does.

"Mommy, come on," Magdalene yells from the porch through the screen door, breaking Carol from her trance. "Sister Michelle is still sitting in her own pee!"

Carol shoves the letter back to the bottom of her bag and zips it up. Under her breath, she says, "You're not with Ma and Pa. You're in hell with the rest of the suicides." She looks once more into the mirror and continues to speak to her dead twin sister; fury stirs within. "You're burning for eternity in a lake of fire, weeping and gnashing your teeth."

■ ■ ■

At the top of the altar is a sky-blue plastic kid's pool etched with cheaply designed tortoises and dolphins; underneath it, a large, opaque tarp. Michelle Campbell climbs into the pool, aided by Virgil. Everyone else is on their knees, arms stretched out and following Virgil in a way that reminds Carol of sunflowers following the sun; the people follow Virgil. The people follow the light. As Carol approaches the altar, Magdalene sits back in the pew; the reverend gets on his knees to help Michelle onto her back in the kiddie pool. He bounces back to his feet. "If you are between the ages of ten and twenty, please come forward." His bellows make people assume his lungs are made of iron.

Michelle becomes exposed; Carol immediately recognizes that the baby's crowning. Blood-tinged amniotic fluid flows from Michelle and into the pool, around Carol's knees. The teenagers cover their mouths with disgust as Virgil continues to preach. "To the youth: this is the result of Eve's sin." Virgil's nose, up as he shouts. "And this agony shall be yours if you lust for one another. And when one part of your body makes you sin, you're better to cut it off and throw it away. Better your right hand than your entire body go to hell!"

THE NOSE OF A VIPER

My name is Freedom and I'm getting the hell out of Painter. Shift's over. Act normal. I'll make a false call to the police station because I know Mattley's on duty tonight. I'll instruct him to go to my house and mail out my letters, in the event of something happening to me before I reach Kentucky. Time to go. I have to go find the daughter I've never known.

· A heaviness drags behind me as I go to clock out of work on this cold, rainy night. Everything's new in perspective. The things people say from here on out tonight will be meaningless, won't mean a thing when I'm burning miles across the country. The place is packed, but I look around with the knowledge that I'll never see it again. I'll never see Oregon again, thank Christ. Walking out, I feel like a prisoner on that fearful final journey from a cell to the lethal-injection chambers. Somehow, I get a bad feeling about Kentucky. And then I see the Viper boys. *Fucking great.* It scares me to death, the possibilities of what's happened to my daughter.

"Freedom," they all yell out to me. *Stay away from me. Don't ruin my last motherfucking walk, pricks.* I ignore them, but it doesn't matter. The fattest of them, the one who left a cigar burn on my shoulder the other night, knocks chairs over on his way to me.

"Whatta you want?" I ask, not that I give a flying fuck. And then it happens, of course, because why should my last walk be my one plan of perfection? He takes his fat fingers and grabs my snatch through my ripped jeans, full force. And suddenly, the world turns red, the blood boiling behind my eyes. All I hear is Carrie from behind scream for me to get off the guy. But I can't. I can't control the rage. I see the broken bottle of Corona in my hand, covered in blood. It's only after that that I realize what I've done. I look around. I'm surrounded by hardened criminals and bikers who back away in fear. And now I calm down and see I am feared.

I look down at the Viper; half his nose is sliced off. "You ruined my walk," I scream at him, not that he'll know what the hell I'm talking about. No one will. He whimpers like a baby. Pathetic. I look to Carrie and then over to Passion, who stands on the foot of her stool at the back of the bar. Not even Carrie knows what to say. Silence on top of something by David Bowie. I drop the bottle. It thuds to the ground. I have to go. I have to get out of here. I have to move. But then I hear sirens. "That was quick." I wipe the blood from my face and walk away. I look into Carrie's eyes. "I'm sorry." But really I'm not sorry for cutting that scumbag's face off. It's a future apology for when I don't show up to work tomorrow, or ever again. Who wouldn't do the same? I head for the rear exit, back down that same dark hall that smells of crack rocks and antibiotic piss. And I can feel the flashback, I can. Those hanging lamps of interrogational purgatory beckon me back to the '90s. *Not now, not fucking now.*

I run through the hall. I run to escape the flashbacks of my incarceration in New York. And now I see the police lights at the end of the hall, like a light at the end of the tunnel, something akin to the dying dream of a fugitive. On the walls around me lights flash red and blue, and still I run toward them to escape that hallway. The dark hall starts to close in around me and there's a figure at the end. I run faster to it. And I make it. I've run into the arms of Officer Mattley. I crack.

He catches me as I sob and fall to my knees on the dirt near the icebox. The rain surrounds us and Jimi Hendrix's "Hey Joe" bleeds from the pub to where we are. Between the tears and the rain, I feel the stickiness of the blood run away from my face. Mattley holds me tight in his arms, his mouth in my ear. He tells me everything is going to be OK. If only I can believe him. Still, I grab the front of his shirt and wipe the blood and tears all over his uniform.

"Take me home," I cry. "Just take me home."

"Freedom, what'd you do?" he asks as he holds me like the child that I feel like. I can't control the tears.

I show him the bloodied bottle. "Arrest me tomorrow. But tonight, just take me home. Take me home once more."

"You know I have to bring you in," he says and sighs.

"Tomorrow, I promise." I stay still, cradled in his arms. "Just one last time, take me home. There's one thing I have to do." I think about my suicide jar. Maybe that plan is better. I'll tell him I have to run into my apartment for just a minute. I'll take the pills. I'll let him arrest me and take me down to the station. I'll tell him everything I've always wanted to tell him. And then I can die. I can die close to Officer Mattley.

But a voice doesn't let me. *Shut your fucking face and find Rebekah!*

"Hurry." He stands and leads me to the patrol car. We rush in. "Before they call it in." He speeds away.

The weight of wet pine branches holds the long road in a wave of black. I sit in the front of the patrol car with the window open just a crack. I smell autumn encasing the branches and the salt of the Pacific not too far away. Aside from the headlights of a random car coming from the opposite direction, Mattley and I are enveloped in darkness. I tell him to pull over. He does. The windshield wipers whine in the rainfall on the side of this dead country road. He thinks I need to get sick.

"I'm a protected witness," I start.

He shakes his head. "Freedom, you can't tell me this." This puts him in a bad position, I know. But I don't want to hide it from him. What's the point, anyway? He puts his hands up to keep me quiet. *Right, as if that will work.*

"I was charged with killing my husband." I ignore his attempts to keep my mouth shut. "But the man who was later convicted, my brother-in-law Matthew, has all the means in the world, even from prison, to have me killed." I unbuckle my seat belt and lean closer to Mattley.

"What are you doing?"

I see he's nervous. "But now he's out of prison." I look around. We're still alone. "And I have to leave."

"Where are you going to go?"

"I don't know." We look into each other's eyes and I just can't get enough of it. "Someplace where I can't be bothered. Somewhere far. Somewhere where no one will find me."

"Why are you telling me this?" His words get faster and his vocal cords have just a little more pressure behind them. "You can't tell me these—" I don't let him finish. I kiss him. In the middle of bumble-fuck nowhere, I kiss him. My first and last kiss with this man. And just as my thoughts return to the suicide jar, he kisses me back. But I can feel him fight it. And it makes it all the more beautiful. His tongue passes my teeth and inside, my organs start to sing.

In his strong arms, I finally feel at home. Home, amid the sounds of the leather seats that shift below us. He tells me he shouldn't be doing this, and sure, I know that, because he ought to be arresting me. But no one has to know. I won't be around soon enough, and this is our last chance. Mattley will be the last person in Oregon who will ever feel the warmth of my lips. And the only person in the world who'd ever in the past twenty-something years taste them without Jack Daniel's between us. His attempts to push me off him are half-assed. He wants this too. And he gives up on resistance. I breathe in the air he exhales deep through his nostrils; his embrace tightens.

But then I remember my priorities here. I have to find Rebekah. I have to steer clear of Mattley, of normalcy. I pull my tongue from his mouth and back away.

"We can't do this," I say. I know this. He knows this. And despite these facts, the distance between us still continues to shrink and our breath makes the windows fog up. We kiss again. I slip my cold hands up his shirt to feel the tightness of his skin. I melt.

"Get over here," he manages to say through my teeth. I put my hands behind the buckle of his belt and pull myself closer to him. But leave it to a burst of static from the police radio to kill the mood. He winces.

"All units to Twenty-seven Wilson Drive, Painter."

"That's my apartment building."

"Yeah, what's going on over there?" He calls back.

"Firefighters en route. Blaze is out of control."

Shit, Mimi! The rest of the place can burn to the ground, for all I care. Mattley puts his sirens on and flies through the night.

21

A FAVOR

My name is Freedom and I'm helpless and small. We arrive at the apartment building, the flames boxing against the blackness of the sky. All the cars of the police department, and by "all" I mean both of them, are already there by the time Mattley and I arrive. I can make out the silhouette of the super screaming with his hands in the air, shouting at the officers, but his cries are not audible against the bellows of the blaze. I run to him, leaving the dust of what should be a yard behind my Doc Martens.

"Where the hell is she?" I roar. I rip at the super's T-shirt and pull his face close to mine, giving a stare that says that I can and will kill him if he's not helped her out. The pockmarks and scabs of tweeking on crank pepper his face, his bones full of homemade tattoo ink. "Where the fuck is Mimi?" I really thought I'd be more concerned about my suicide jar or the hundreds of letters to my children. To my surprise, I am not.

I wish I took the broken bottle with me from the Whammy Bar so I could make this super suck on it. But I've already drawn too much attention to myself. "Mimi who?" he yells. *Yeah, go back to your meth pipe, you sleazy bastard.*

"Mimi Bruce. Where the fuck is she?" I feel Mattley pull me back.

I accidentally elbow him in his nose behind me and feel it crack in half. The sound gives me a chill, despite the heat of the burning home. *God, me and noses, right? What the hell is wrong with me?* I take off my Sex Pistols shirt so I'm exposed in my black tank top and try to stop the bleeding. When I hear the cracking and crashing of what I can only assume is the second floor of the building, the floor that Mimi and I live on, falling, I run toward the house. Mattley screams my name after me. Everybody screams after me. I get as close as I can to the complex before the heat wants to melt my clothes onto my body. I scream Mimi's name.

I can feel a fire stirring within me in the same way it stirs in my building, craving oxygen so it can explode into something fierce. That's called a back draft. For me, it's called fury. I go to kick in the door least engulfed in flames, just the way I've kicked down Mimi's door so many times before. Doesn't matter that it's not the floor we live on, I just have to get in. But just as the sole of my Doc Marten is about to plant itself beside the doorknob, I feel an arm around my waist and I'm carried away from the blaze like a sack of potatoes, upside down over his shoulder. Suddenly, I'm facing Mattley's police-issued Glock on his waist. I can practically taste it. *Hope you don't mind if I borrow this.* I'm able to unbutton his holster and slip the gun in my underwear between my jeans and pubic bone as I squirm and scream at him to let me the hell go. And when I take a minute to look around, I see probably about a hundred bystanders, too blinded and enthralled by the fire to notice a cop getting his piece stolen by the crazy town drunk. At least I hope so.

Mattley lets me go and I disappear somewhere into the crowd. And then I see Newbie, the new officer that assisted Mattley the other night. He is at the back of an ambulance with Mimi, who wears the same shirt I helped her into the other day. *Jesus Christ.* I walk to check up on her. She's slapping Newbie as he tries to get a report out of her, and somehow I feel like a proud mother. "What are you hoping to get out of her?" I ask Newbie; I don't know what his real name is.

"She'll tell you George Clooney started the fire in a fucking leotard, if you ask her long enough."

I go to hug Mimi, relieved. "What?" she asks. She's having a moment of lucidity. Let's see how long it lasts this time. I send Newbie away so I can get a minute alone with Mimi.

"Mimi, what happened? What did I say about leaving the stove on?" I make it a point not to sound angry, but instead like a person who cares. I spit in my hand and wipe some of the soot from her forehead around a large but shallow gash that already starts to turn black and blue on the sides.

"But Freedom." She's starting to get upset. I have to keep her calm. I have to keep her lucid. "I wasn't cooking anything! I thought you were cooking. I mean, that's where the flames came from. From your apartment, not mine." Her voice gets louder. I can feel the demons of dementia on their way. "You did this! You did this, Nessa Delaney! That's who they were looking for! Nessa Delaney. You're not Freedom. You're Nessa Delaney!" I realize she's not losing it. And before anyone from the crowd a few yards away can hear anything, I close the ambulance doors and close the small, blue draperies to keep anyone from seeing in.

"Who, Mimi? Who was looking for me? Who was looking for Nessa Delaney?"

"Three men, I think. I heard them making all sorts of racket next door. And they came to mine." She points to her forehead. "How do you think I got this? Thugs, they were."

I think about the other day with Cal the cockroach.

■ ■ ■

As Cal was getting ready to leave, I untangled the cord and took the phone with me from the kitchen counter into the bathroom. I recognized Peter's voice in an instant, that deep stutter and the way he called me Nessa. I was at a loss for words. I really had no control over what came out of my mouth. "How the hell did you find me?"

"I'm on my way to Kentucky, but the guys have a head start. Not sure

*if they're going to you in Oregon first or to the kids in Kentucky . . . you
remember my mother."*

"Of course I fucking remember," I whispered so Cal couldn't hear, covering my knees with the extra-large tee.

"They won't hurt the kids," he reassures me. "You, on the other hand . . ."

"Nah, they'll never find me. These Feds have me hid good." And Mason
and Rebekah aren't babies anymore. They're not going to just kidnap grown
adults and bring them to New York. And let them come for me. Probably
just a bunch of talk, anyway. I doubt they'd even know how to read a map.
"I've missed the shit out of you, Peter." I hear him smile with me.

■ ■ ■

I call Passion. "Passion, I need your help. I'm in a lot of trouble."

"I think that same trouble just walked in. Three men. New York
accents. Showing your picture around."

"I don't have a lot of time. I need a huge favor."

"What kind?"

"You remember Gunsmoke, right? The one from the other day
calling Obama a nigger and such?"

"Yeah, sure."

"Could you give him a hand job and I'll pay you double when I
can?"

She's about to ask why, but I tell her to hold on. Mimi yells for
my help, scared of the officers who bang the shit out of the ambulance doors. But I can hear that voice, that fucking voice of Matthew
Delaney on the phone. And I wish I'd saved my energies with that
Corona bottle to slice his face off. Mattley and Newbie finally pry
the doors open.

With my hands up, I say, "I was just coming out, boys."

"I'm not decent!" yells a fully clothed Mimi. *Thanks for the effort,
you crazy bat.*

"Freedom, what the hell are you doing?" Mattley yells, a nasal
shout with a newly shaped nose.

"Your stupid partner was scaring the shit out of her." I point at

Newbie. "I was just trying to calm her down." I start to walk away. "She left the oven on, *again*." I ramble so he can roll his eyes at me and let me walk away. "I can't help it if you pigs don't do your job. The lady in the muumuu, sure. Leaves the oven on. Sic the rent-a-cop on her. What, y'all fucking graduated the police academy with Big Bird and Rain Man?"

I go back to Passion on the phone. "Can you get him off before I get there?"

"Yes, but why? And what about those men?"

I tell her my plans and then find my car, where upon inspection, I see a knife in my front driver's-side tire. I pretend to drop something on the ground, my back to the cops. I look around to make sure there's no copper breathing down my neck and yank the knife from my tire. I walk toward the only two cop cars there, the fire behind me. Dozens of bystanders with their backs to me stand between me and the cops. "They won't even look my way."

"They're busy with their faces in some hot pie, anyway," says Passion.

I bend down behind car numero uno. With my back to it so I can see who's coming, I reach behind me and stab the rear tire. I poke my head out.

I steal the car next to it. I steal Officer Mattley's patrol car and make my way.

■ ■ ■

My name is Freedom and this is a rush. I park at the base of the HOTEL PAINTER/HOT PIE neon-lit sign in the middle of the parking lot, where the cops usually park to scare off fresh pussy renters when they're not inhaling their warm Krispy Kreme donuts. The neon tubes buzz overhead like the electricity created between pros and customers alike. I switch on the spotlight near the driver's-side mirror so people turn their heads, scatter like cockroaches. At the Whammy Bar I can spot Luke at the entrance. He must have been the one that Matthew put on lookout detail. *Bitch.* Passion sees me and walks across the dirt.

"You got some nasty people looking for you, Freedom." She shakes her head, her elbow resting on the roof of the car.

"They're not looking for me." I examine the buttons and switches on the inside of the patrol car, playing with them. *This one's the siren, whoops. This one's for the lights. This knob's for AM radio. I need something like this.* "They're looking for Nessa."

"I figured . . ." Passion trails off.

"You do that favor I asked?"

She looks down at me and smirks. "You know I did, you ain't gotta ask." She dangles the keys to Gunsmoke's motorcycle from her finger. "Hand jobs can be so distracting."

"I would have gotten them myself, but the second I do and those men see me, I get a bullet in the brain as an early Christmas present."

"Sovereign Shore?"

"Sovereign Shore. Take the back roads."

22

THE LAND OF FREEDOM

Officer Mattley can't stop staring at the dirt ring of sweat on Captain Banks's collar and the white that collects in the corners of his mouth; they're hypnotizing. His blond hair whips across his lazy eyes; it moves even after his head stops. Mattley doesn't have to listen to his actual words to know what he says as he paces the office. Barking. Sweating. Mattley's already watched his face burn through sixty shades of red. *I fucked up, I know,* Mattley thinks. *I fucked up bigtime, Cap'n.* He feels like a child being reprimanded in elementary school over a careless mistake.

"And Freedom Oliver, no less," Banks yells in the closed office with the blinds down, not that they stop the other officers and staff from trying to get a glimpse of the golden child that is Mattley having his ass handed to him. "Leave it to the town drunk to steal your firearm and car." Banks takes a deep breath as he plants his ass in his desk chair.

"Sir—"

"I can't listen to it, Mattley." Banks lowers his head and raises his hands. "You're suspended until further notice."

Mattley thinks about Freedom and what the hell might be going on in her mind, and he finds himself wondering why he cares about her so much, what makes her different from anyone else he's ever known. He thinks about the eyes that will burn a hole through him once he leaves this room. But more than anything, he thinks of racing right to the Whammy Bar, because chances are, that's where she'll be. *What a friggin' mess.* But he bites his tongue: doesn't say a thing.

"Hand me your badge," says Banks.

Mattley reaches for it only to find it's gone. "Fuck."

"Goddamnit, Mattley."

He wants to keep his nose to the floor but forces his head upright as he leaves the office. The others pretend to be busy at nothing at all, the rumors coming to a quick halt the second he steps out. And he knows they'll resume as soon as he leaves.

Mattley kicks himself in the ass, curses as his shoes tap on the asphalt toward his pickup truck. He grips the leather of the steering wheel and rattles it with bellows that draft from the crevices of his teeth. And yet he's not angry with her, with Freedom. No, he's mad at himself for being so stupid, for letting his feelings for her interfere with his duties.

Even though Mattley quit smoking years ago, back before Richie was born, he always kept a spare in his center console, in the event of one of those hard days that come once in a while—the random rape victim, the dead child—but now seems just as good a time as any. And he hates that he loves the way he can still smell her hair on his skin, that his tongue still twitches in excitement at the thought of kissing her. He closes his eyes, rests his forehead on the steering wheel, and blows the smoke into his lap as the truck warms up. And then the taps on his window.

"Officer Mattley?"

"Not anymore." He lifts his head and steps out to two men in suits. "Smells like something federal to me."

The two men pull their badges from their coats. "I'm U.S. Marshal Lenny Gumm and this is Marshal Raymond Howe from Portland."

Mattley slams the car door and plays stupid. "And to what do I owe the pleasure?"

Howe, with his permanent half-smile, nods toward the precinct. "Why don't we take this inside? Need to talk to the boss, anyhow."

Mattley stretches his arm and does a curtsy for the sake of theatrics. "After you."

Mattley knows that nothing about the night is the fault of Captain Banks, but he can't wait to see his face when the Feds knock on his door, especially given his mood. It's common knowledge that small-time police departments clash with Feds. And like Mattley, Banks can smell who they are before they can even say "Good evening."

"What the hell is this all about?" Banks curls his lip.

"Department of Justice," Mattley interrupts with a smile over the ludicrousness of the night. "U.S. Marshals."

Banks grunts as he closes the door behind the Feds and offers them a seat. "What does the Department of Justice have anything to do with a fire?"

"Anything you can tell us about it?" Gumm narrows his brow.

"Nothing, until the fire chief can start an investigation," Banks says as he unbuttons the collar of his shirt. "Off the record? There's a woman who lives there, senile. Wouldn't be the first time she left the stove on; that's what's running through the rumor mill so far."

"Yeah, well, we don't go by what runs through the rumor mill where we come from, with all due respect, sir."

Banks's nostrils flare out as he clears his throat. Mattley can almost see the outburst rise to his lips before one occurs. "I'm sorry, I still don't see how this would involve DOJ."

"We don't care about the fire, Captain Banks." Howe shimmies to the edge of his seat and leans forward. "We're interested in Freedom Oliver."

"That lush?" Banks scoffs. "You don't think she had something to do with causing that fire, do you?"

"No, but we think she may have been a target."

"A target for what?" Mattley asks from the file cabinets behind the Feds.

As if previously rehearsed, Gumm and Howe simultaneously pull out their notepads. They notice Mattley's interest. "Has Freedom ever said anything that might raise a red flag? Something about her past, perhaps?"

Mattley raises an eyebrow. "The only things she ever says are the incoherent babblings of someone who wants to drink herself to death."

"Nothing? Nothing at all?"

Mattley clenches his jaw at their skepticism and cuts his answers short. "Nope."

Gumm pulls out a folder with a pile of mug shots, grabs the attention of Banks and Mattley alike. "Tell us if you've seen any of these upstanding citizens around here." One by one, Gumm places the faces of the Delaneys, including Lynn and Peter, on Banks's desk. But neither one can identify them. "We need to find Freedom before these guys do."

Banks looks up to Mattley as if what's about to come out of his mouth is going to be painful. "I have to say it." Banks rubs his brow. "Freedom just stole a patrol car and a cop's firearm." He swallows hard. "She's in the wind."

"Not surprising," Howe says and pulls out a phone. "Can't you just track the GPS in the car?"

Again, as if the words were small knives that slice at the corners of his lips, "We don't use them here."

Mattley can read the Feds' thoughts: *Stupid small-town cops.* Howe looks up to Mattley. "I take it it was yours?" He smirks as Mattley turns his head away. "Don't be too hard on yourself. It's not the first time. Not for Freedom. She can charm anyone she wants. She's been doing it for years."

"I assure you, there's nothing charming about that woman," Mattley reacts. *But I can still taste her,* he thinks to himself.

Howe rises from his seat and paces the office on his cell. He commands, "We need an APB on a stolen patrol car, calling for backup from Portland on a fugitive who is armed and considered extremely dangerous."

"Freedom's not dangerous," Mattley says and tries to get in front of Howe to stop him from making the call. "I mean, if she's going to hurt anyone, she's only going to hurt herself. There's no need to get the Feds here, you'll just scare her off."

"Who? Freedom?" Gumm laughs from the chair. "Nothing scares that woman off. She's a cold-blooded cop killer."

"What." Mattley's surprise comes out completely deadpan. "She's no killer." They can barely hear him. He knows he'll be caught in his own lie. "She was falsely accused, she never killed her husband."

Banks's jaw hits the ground. And now Mattley wants to rip the smirks clean off their chins.

"So she *has* talked to you?" Gumm smiles. Mattley shakes his head and grinds his teeth. "So you know all about Nessa Delaney?"

"Never heard the name," Mattley growls.

Howe pulls out an old mug shot of Freedom. The arrest plate reads DELANEY, NESSA. Mattley has to squint and study the eyes to realize that it's her, from decades ago when she was in her early twenties. Gumm begins, "Once upon a time, Freedom Oliver was sweet little Nessa Delaney of Mastic Beach, New York." Banks examines the photo after Mattley. She's hardly recognizable. Gumm speaks like he's reading from an instruction manual. Most Feds do. "And then Nessa Delaney gunned down a well-respected cop of the NYPD."

Howe pulls out a police academy portrait. Gumm continues, "This is Mark Delaney, husband of Nessa Delaney. And these?" He waves his hands over the montage of criminals like he's some federal wizard in Hogwarts, Oregon. "These are the rest of the Delaneys, the ones that want her dead more than anything else in this world."

"She's a protected witness . . ." Banks trails off.

"That's right."

"Then why are you telling us?" Mattley asks. "No one's supposed to know that."

"Because the second she committed a federal crime, like, let's say, stealing a patrol car and police-issued firearm"—Gumm takes Freedom's file and tears it in half—"she left the program."

"She said that the guy who did it was released from prison just the other day."

"The guy who did it, this cop's brother Matthew, just served *her* time. Just like your little girlfriend planned."

"What the hell does that mean?"

"It means she killed a man and got away with it," Howe yells. "And not only did she get away with it, but she had the wrong man locked away for it for nearly two decades." Howe goes on. "*That's* who you're dealing with. This Freedom nonsense? She's dangerous. She's cunning and calculating, and she's always, I mean *always*, two steps ahead of you." His words hang in the air. "Dismissed with prejudice . . . means she can't be charged for it again."

"Only in the good ol' U.S. of A.," Gumm offers. "Land of Freedom." The Feds begin to leave. "It's like Jesus once said. *Freedom* is just another word for nothing left to lose." He smiles. "Didn't Jesus coin that phrase, Howe?"

"Think so."

"You guys can think about that. We'll let you know if we find her." Gumm gives Mattley their card, a not-so-subtle hint for Banks and Mattley to stay out of their way. In truth, Gumm and Howe were more than happy to have her expelled from the Witness Protection Program. They were sick of having to come all the way down there from Portland, constantly giving her warnings, through one ear and out the other. There were people out there more deserving of such relocation, waiting for ages, when ungrateful people like Freedom had it handed to her.

"Where are you guys going?" Mattley follows.

"To the Whammy Bar." Howe tucks the files in his jacket. "If she's not there, the Delaneys should be."

23

FREEDOM AND SACRIFICE

The moon tries to break through a smoky canopy that covers the picturesque view of the ocean. Pinpoints of silver light shoot through the pine branches and over Passion's body as she winds down the roads that line the cliff's edges, on her way to Sovereign Shore. Her white fur coat follows behind her; Passion's chased by rabbits. The chill of autumn bites at her cheekbones, makes her eyes tear. Gunsmoke's bike vibrates under her, her nose close to the gas cap as she hums "(Sittin' on) The Dock of the Bay" to keep her nerves at ease. The glow of a speedometer shines off her sequined suit that looks more like a bikini as the Harley bawls through the night. With the ocean to her left and the cliff side to her right, she focuses on a double yellow line.

Meanwhile, with the knowledge that the Feds are on their way there, Mattley races through the back roads to beat them to the Whammy Bar. He flicks another cigarette out the window. Trying not to make a habit of it again, he unwraps three sticks of spearmint gum at seventy miles per hour and chews. And at the Bend of Beelzebub, the notorious strip of road that swallows the lives of speeding teenagers and buzzed bikers, he falls back to second gear. But wait . . . *Did I just see Passion pass me in a bikini on a fucking bike?* He merges onto the next soft shoulder and makes a U-turn to follow, and while he's already lost her through the knots and turns, he has an idea of where she's going: to Freedom's favorite place in the world to get drunk. Sovereign Shore.

Passion makes the right onto a dirt lot lined with driftwood fence posts. The lot opens up to the cliff top roped off with signs of danger. Passion parks the stolen bike near the stolen police car, and on the other side of the ropes, near the edge that stands a good hundred feet above sharp boulders and the shore, is Freedom.

***

My name is Freedom and I hear the exhaust of Gunsmoke's motorcycle from down the road; the headlight dances with the curves of the cliff's edge and beckons my attention, my focus. And suddenly, I hold my breath. Because I really don't have a plan since my original one turned to shit. All I know is that I have to stay in motion; I have to move. If I don't, I'll jump. I'll crash. I'll die. Even if it's just a few inches, a few minutes, I have to get closer to finding my daughter.

Passion parks the bike near the police car. I see her shadow and hear those harpoons as she walks toward me. "I hope you're not thinking what I think you're thinking," she calls out.

I smile and step a few feet back from the edge. My voice is low, I'm not sure she hears me through the wind. "I'm not going to jump." Our footsteps wring rainwater from a blanket of reds and yellows and browns of fallen leaves as I meet her. "The car's still warm, if you're cold," I offer. Her fingers feel like frozen bones wrapped in leather as she hands me the keys to Gunsmoke's bike. "I don't have a lot of time. I'm gonna have to get out of here."

"Any idea where you're going?" she asks, her voice soft through the fog that surrounds us.

"East," I tell her. "East, to the ends of the Earth." And somehow, I think the ends of the Earth are exactly where I'm going to end up. I walk to the bike and she follows. I peek inside a leather pouch on the side of the seat, one bolted on with silver studs reflecting in the moonlight. Inside, a burned spoon and a stack of ten thousand dollars, give or take. *Shit.* I zip it back up before Passion can see.

"To me, that's only Sallins Street." She tries to laugh. I pull a smoke from my bra. Passion lights it for me. The spark lights up the shadows around us, illuminates the demons in our eyes. Then the slews of a truck race on the parking lot behind Passion. *Who the fuck is this?* Mattley jumps out, practically before the vehicle stops. He marches toward us before I can even get the first drag of my cig. He looks pissed. I take Passion's arm and step in front of her. I reach down my underwear and grab the coldness that is Mattley's piece and point it toward his head.

He stops dead in his tracks and puts his hands in the air. And I hate having to do this, really, I do. But I see no choice. Like I said, I just have to be moving. I will keep going. I will not be stopped. "Is this what it is, Freedom?" he snaps, in a way I'd have never imagined coming from the placid copper. "You're gonna kill another fucking cop?"

And there I was, feeling bad. But this? This sloppy accusation, this fucking assumption, this topic he knows nothing about? Who the hell does he think he is? Gumm and Howe must be around here, because I only told Mattley I was charged with killing my husband, never mentioned him being a cop. The fire would have surely brought the whippersnappers out this way, anyway. "Only if you stand in my fucking way, James." It's the first time I ever use his first name, and it feels so foreign on my tongue. I take a shot, but I don't actually aim for him. I miss his head by a few inches, just to show him I'm not fucking around.

Passion screeches behind me and pulls at the back of my shirt. "What the fuck are you doing?"

"You're out of your goddamn mind," Mattley roars from the pit of his lungs.

"Old news, James. Old news." I step sideways toward the bike. "Now, I'm going to need for you to get out of my way."

"Freedom," his silhouette cries. A tear runs down my cheek. It could be anger, it could be sadness, I'm not sure. Either way, it brings a pang to my gut. Pieces of my heart seem to rise to my throat, but I swallow them. I can't let anyone see that all I want to do is tell him I love him, but what's the point? I won't because as a glutton for punishment, I can't let a good thing like Mattley happen. There are no happy endings, not in any of my stories, not in real life. Life doesn't want to see two people like us together in each other's arms. And it never will. Such is life.

"I'm sorry." I point the gun toward his truck and shoot out the tire. I reach in my pocket and throw him the keys to the cop car. "This way you can't cross state lines, not in a cop car and not in a truck with flat tires. Take Passion home." I turn around, hop on Gunsmoke's Harley, and turn the ignition.

Just as I'm about to leave, he walks to me. "At least take this." He worms out of his black bomber jacket and drapes it over the handlebar. I look up at him and he turns his head away. My stares hurt him. His avoidance hurts me. And as I give Passion a little nod of gratitude, I leave.

With my back to Painter, Oregon, I ride east into the night.

"I'm coming, Rebekah. I'm coming."

24

FREEDOM AND THE ROAD LESS TRAVELED

My name is Freedom and I'm eight hours out of Painter, in the darkest part before the dawn. I think I've passed Hell's Canyon back at the Oregon-Idaho border, so that would make this Snake River Plain, Idaho, I suppose. Unless I went south, then I'm somewhere in the Great Basin like the Sierras, maybe Nevada or Utah, as long as I avoid Death Valley, Christ Almighty. Eight hours of riding this bike and I have no more sensation in my clit from the vibrations. My knuckles are frozen stiff. My legs feel like a wishbone being pulled at either side. Between the tears and the wind, my eyeballs feel like they've been removed, dipped in salt, and put back in my sockets. I'm thirstier than I've ever known, to the point where I'm weak and my tongue's stuck to the roof of my mouth. Perhaps I should have planned this better, because I haven't seen a single sign of life in four hours, since the general store and gas station, if you call that toothless redneck drinking Mylanta a sign of life, I'm not sure. I pass the signs too fast to know where I'm going. I can't turn around, there's nothing to turn back to. Just rocks and cacti, cacti and rocks. And Rebekah isn't there.

The open road gives you ample opportunity to think; in fact, the road forces reflection on a man . . . or woman, in my case. And it's a terrifying thing, my thoughts. With each thought, each idea, each regret that makes my blood curdle, I accelerate. I race fast enough on the motorcycle so my demons can't catch me, but they always seem just a step ahead of the game, always there to entertain my sin.

I stop the bike at the top of this hill, one of about a thousand hills I've rolled over so far. I light a smoke to curb the hunger and crack my back and neck to relieve some of the stiffness. I'm still, unfathomable darkness, nothing but black against black. But up ahead in the not-too-far distance is a lightning storm, a dangerous place to be in the desert. It's as if I'm standing in nothingness, something I imagine before life and after death. And if God exists, this was what it was before he created the Earth and life. Black. Nothing. And I try to wrap my head around the concept of no time, no feelings to feel, just nothing. It's a mind-boggling thing if you have the desire to imagine it. And rides like this through nothing make you try to grasp just that concept.

At the bottom of the hills, clouds flicker with purple and white and orange electricity that rips through the sky. The distant growls of the storm sound like something biblical. But where else can I go? What else can I do? I'm not going to make it out here alone in the desert for much longer. And it's a risk, but it's a risk I'm just going to have to take, because on the other side, the daughter I've never known is waiting to be found. On the other side is freedom from the authorities who are surely looking for me. On the other side is survival. I race down the straight-and-narrow roads. I try to get these fucking demons off my goddamn back. I try to survive.

I'm a liar if I say I'm not terrified. The closer I get to the electric storm, the faster it seems to move my way, and before I know it, I'm in the thick of it, the belly of the monster. I count. *One. Two. Five. Holy shit.* And I scream as I watch the bolts strike just a few feet from me. I keep screaming, but don't panic. *Just get through this, and everything else will be smooth sailing from here on out. Do this for Rebekah. Do this for your sins, for your mistakes. Do this because you deserve this fear after*

all the awful things you've done with your life, Freedom. Each bolt lights
up the Earth around me brighter than the sun, and it's blinding. The
purple flashes of land around me make me feel like I have new eyes,
like those of an animal that can see everything. In this way, I can see
the horizons of the desert in the middle of the night, in the middle
of the nothingness. Like I'm seeing this world in a way that no man's
allowed to. Forty strikes per minute. I am going to die.

The thunder is deafening and I wonder if my eardrums are rup-
tured because I can't hear myself scream anymore. The electricity runs through my spine, through my blood, and suddenly, I am
unstoppable. Insatiable. Immortal. I crouch down on the bike and
go faster and faster. I am the lightning. And then. . . .

My bike stalls in the middle of the electrical storm. I'm a dead
woman.

I try to restart the bike; I beg it like it can hear me to turn back on.
I begin to roar something violent, something vicious. In the middle
of the desert, where no one can hear me, I scream and scream. My
heart breaks. Because I can't do one fucking thing for the daughter
I'll never know. As I scream, I see a yellow, dim light about a half-
mile into the barren plains. I turn my bike so it faces the house and
wave my hand in front of the headlight. In turn, someone in the
house flicks the porch light on and off. And with what little energy I
have left in me, I leave the bike and try to run across the desert.

I seem to be in rhythm with the lightning all around me, this
song and dance. I run blindly; blindness in the dark when the lightning settles, blindness in the brilliance of light when it crashes into
the soft and dry dirt that I jog on. I have an idea that hell might be
above us after all. But there's no telling what I'm running into here.
For all I know, I could be running to the home of Leatherface, who
wants to make wind chimes out of my severed limbs and eat my
skin with his oatmeal.

And then lightning comes up from the ground.

I've been shot in the leg. I fall to the dirt in unimaginable pain.

■ ■ ■

I don't know if I've been followed, maybe the Feds or State Police
or the Delaneys. I don't know if I've been shot by the person who
owns this home in the desert. I don't know if I'm going to make it
out of here alive. I can't stand. I turn around and start to crawl back,
but what the hell is there to crawl back to? I summon everything
in me to use my arms to pull my legs behind me back toward the
road. I grunt and cry with each inch, each haul of my body. It starts
to downpour. I fall on my back with my mouth open to drink. I'm
desperate and dying of thirst. And then I'm shot again in the arm,
through Mattley's jacket that he gave me. "Stop, please," I yell.

When the lightning strikes, I catch a glimpse of movement from
the corner of my eye. Someone walks toward me. But as I try to continue to crawl, I can't breathe. My heart races. It feels like something
in me has exploded and my blood cells are made of fire and razor
blades, trying to rip through my skin and out of my body. I can feel
my throat close up. Everything gets blurry and I can't move a damn
muscle.

The figure stands over me, but my brain isn't working right. I
can't make sense out of anything. I'm delirious, confused. Through
the lightning, I see a man. He looks down at me, a sideways look. He
shakes something over my head, but I can't see what. "Hy-ya, Hy-
ya," he barks, but his voice is soft and smooth. "Hy-ya, Hy-ya," he
almost sings. In his other hand, a lantern that squeaks, yellow light
painting the right side of my body.

"Please," I try to tell him, but I don't think the words ever make it
from my mouth. "Don't kill me." I can't move one damn muscle, no
matter how hard I try. Not one fucking finger. I'm paralyzed. "Help
me," I try to plead. He says something, but I can't understand. It's a
language I've never heard. It's not English, it's not Spanish, it's not
anything I can figure out.

The man takes my ankle and starts to drag me toward his house.
I wheeze to breathe, my back scrapes against the dirt while I still try

to get the rainwater in my mouth, but I can't even open it all the way. The man's slow in his steps and there's quite a way to go. I fear I'll be dead by the time I reach the house, and perhaps this is a good thing.

I start to panic. While my insides thrash in me because I can't breathe, I only show so much of this on the outside. I feel the man drop my leg, here, in the middle of the desert. Is he abandoning me? Is he going to shoot me in the head and leave me for the birds? He kneels down beside me. With the lightning, I can see two long, silver braids.

He takes off my jacket. He's going to rob me.

He takes of my pants. He's going to rape me.

He rattles an object over my head again. He waves it over my body as he speaks some lyrical language, like he's singing a soft lullaby as I lie here dying. This man is fucking insane. The glint of a knife that he pulls from his side catches the lightning, catches my eye. He slices my leg with the blade, the pain making the muscles in my neck constrict even more. I find myself praying to a god I hardly believe in. He lifts my leg close to his mouth. I think he's drinking my blood. I want to beg him to stop, to not do this. But I am powerless. I am more dead than alive. I am defeated.

I'm so sorry that I couldn't save you, Rebekah, I think to myself as I fade out of consciousness. *I'm so sorry for everything I did and didn't do.*

25

CAT'S CRADLE

Rays of sunshine warm the large bedroom full of handmade quilts and lace doilies. The smell of banana bread fills the house, a reminder to any southerner of their childhood. In the corner of the room, Carol Paul sits in a rocking chair, waiting for Michelle Campbell to wake up. She hums "God Bless America" as she double-knits a pink cap for the new baby. She thinks, *It's almost hard to remember when Magdalene was this small.* She checks the clock on the shelf so that she's not late for Virgil's dumplings and fresh-squeezed lemonade after he returns from the grounds with some of the other guys who are cleaning up what the storm left behind.

Michelle stirs in her sleep, heavy-eyed and heart racing. The light that turns the room of the Pauls' home into gold seems to make Michelle nauseated. The shadows stretch farther across the room with the passing of the afternoon. Her throat and chest burn like fire and her vision is blurry. Carol rises from the rocking chair and takes the ceramic bowl from the side of the bed, where Michelle vomits. Carol rests the bowl on her lap and holds her hair up. "Let it out, there you go."

"How long will this last?" Michelle cries.

"Not long now," says Carol in her most comforting tone as she inspects the Cesarean incision right above her pubic bone. "This is common after childbirth. Especially a rough one, like you had."

"Every time I throw up, it feels like the wound's opening back up."

"It's not, but it'll be sore for a bit. It's healing nicely."

"Can I see my baby now?"

"Let her sleep." Carol helps Michelle back to the pillows. "It's been a long few days for her too."

"Her name is Rebekah." Michelle's words are tired and faint.

"What's that you say?"

"I want to name her Rebekah," Michelle pants. "Rebekah was my best friend."

Carol says nothing about it. She tucks the blankets around Michelle's sides. "I'm going to go and make you soup. You need the strength."

"Please, no," she tries to protest. "I can't even think about food right now, Sister Carol." But Carol leaves anyway.

As Michelle hears her footsteps go out to the kitchen and the fresh breeze that carries from the window, young Magdalene sneaks into the bedroom, talkative, as she always has been, just looking for a friend. She jumps up to the foot of the bed, her legs dangling off the edge.

"Theresa sure is pretty, Sister Michelle." Magdalene practices the cat's cradle with a black piece of string tangled around her fingers. "She looks like a porcelain doll, only a real porcelain doll, ya know?"

"Theresa?" but she's almost too weak to speak.

Magdalene glows. "Your new baby, you goose!"

Tears of frustration and confusion escape her eyes and trickle down to her temples. "Her name is Rebekah."

"Like my big sister?!" But Magdalene doesn't see her distress.

Michelle starts to sob. "I just want to go home."

"You don't have to cry, your home's just out the window here." Magdalene zips to the window and opens the lace curtains. "See? I can see it from here. Just lift your head!" She becomes disappointed when she sees that Michelle won't even try to look up. "Are you sick or something, Sister Michelle?"

"Magdalene, now, what did Mommy say about bothering Sister Michelle?" Carol says as she returns.

"Sorry, Ma," she offers. "I was just going to show her my cat's cradle."

"Maybe later, dear." Carol brings a tray with soup and water on it. "You can help me feed the baby in a few minutes. I'll be right out."

Magdalene starts to leave but stops at the door. "Can I lay hands on Sister Michelle and say a prayer for her first, Mommy?"

"A quick one, but then you have to leave."

"Very quick, I promise." Magdalene runs up to the side of Michelle and places both hands on the top of her sweaty head.

"Dear Jesus, I say a special prayer for Sister Michelle during these trials from Satan. Please help her to feel better so I can show her the cat's cradle and so she can see her baby again. And make sure she eats all her soup so she doesn't go hungry. In Jesus's name, Amen." She starts to run off, but halfway to the door she turns around and resumes her praying position. "Also, Jesus. Please bring my sister, Rebekah, back home because I miss her very, very much."

Carol walks over and quietly shuts the door behind Magdalene. She looks at Michelle once more. "Now we're going to eat as much of this soup as we can so we can get you better, right?"

But Michelle doesn't answer.

Carol goes to her and checks her pulse through her neck. It's faint. She's more dead than alive. She looks at her medical bag; she contemplates helping Michelle. Instead, Carol goes back to humming her hymn. And waits for her to die.

26

THE END OF AUTUMN

The scent of Lysol is enough to burn Mattley's eyes. As he signs in, a man in the corner eats square, wooden Scrabble tiles. "He thinks the vowels have nutritional value," says the nurse at the sign-in desk. Officer James Mattley can't imagine any place being more depressing. He waits near a window and looks down to the courtyard where nurses suck nicotine through wrinkled lips and gnaw on their cell phones. None of them seem to mind the sleet and rain on this nasty morning, as long as they get their caffeine fixes for the day.

Mattley's eyes water from a mix of the Lysol lingering thick in the back of his throat and too much yawning, his body sluggish from overexhaustion and barely any sleep last night. He pinches the palms of his hands for any kind of stimulation that can keep him awake right now. A parade of elderly patients in full diapers drag on into the common room, waking from sedated trances and hangovers of sleeping meds and antianxiety candy. *This is more like the fucking loony bin.* Mattley observes yet doesn't stare. He watches them line up for an orderly, take a pill, and begin to assemble around *Wheel of Fortune* and chew their medicinal potpourri.

"She's in room number twelve, right over here," the nurse points. He's on his toes, cautious around the woman's room he walks into. "I'll be right over here if you need me."

"I know you," Mimi exalts. "You're my son!"

"No, no," Mattley shushes her. "I'm Officer James Mattley. I met you the other night at the fire." The room is painted a shocking yellow, an eyesore to visitors who don't have the luxury of being medicated like these fine folks.

"Fire?" She looks around. "What fire?"

"The other night, remember? There was a fire that started in your home. We took you in an ambulance. Remember now?"

"The fire didn't start in my house." She stands from her bed and adjusts a pink fleece robe over her. "It started in Freedom's house, from those men who were looking for her."

"What men?" Mattley suddenly wakes up. "Who was looking for Freedom?"

"The crazy-eyed kind," she says as she looks in a handheld mirror tacked to the wall as if she doesn't recognize her own face. "Three of them. They hit me. They started the fire."

"Why didn't you tell this to the police?"

"I told Freedom in the ambulance. I figured she would."

Mattley pulls out his phone and scrolls through his contacts until he reaches Newbie. He sends a text:

Get report from fire chief, should have been ready by now. What was cause of fire? Don't tell Cap'n I'm asking.

"What can you tell me about these guys?"

"What guys?" She forgets already. "Where's Freedom? Where am I?" She begins to panic.

"Just take it easy, Mimi." He tries to assure her and direct her back to her cot. "Freedom's close by. You're safe."

"I don't want to be here," she screams. "I want to go home. I want to go home!" The scene is heartbreaking as she curls up at the head of her bed and sobs into her hands. A syringe-happy nurse runs in, with white leather loafers and a red curly Afro, like something cartoonish.

"Give me a minute," Mattley shouts as he stops the nurse. He grabs Mimi's arms and looks her in the eyes, stays quiet so the nurse can't hear. "Mom," he calls her. "Mom, it's me." And Mattley feels terrible at having to do this, having to resort to such cruelty.

"Son?"

"Yes, Mom, it's me."

Mimi smiles through the tears and falls into his arms. "It's about time you came to see me."

"I know, Mom, I'm sorry." He nods at the nurse to leave. She sighs with disappointment. With Mimi's head in his chest as he rocks her, he looks over to various pieces of mail scattered at the foot of the bed. One envelope is addressed to Nessa Delaney. Mattley softly pulls back from Mimi while she calms down and reaches for the envelope. "Nessa Delaney?" he asks her.

"I never heard the name."

Mattley notices it's addressed to Freedom's apartment number. He opens it.

Dear Nessa, or should I call you Mom?

There is so much to say; there's so much to take in. I've so much to tell you, but so little time, as I hide here in the shed of my church. I look back at my life. I wonder how'd I not see it, and looking here at your photo, I can see it, I can see it all.

For ages, I've been praying for a way out. Praying God takes me far from here. But in all this time, I've had nowhere to turn. There's Mason, but I need to be farther. I have to get away from here, I can't tell you why. Please, trust me. Trust in God. Because he sent your letter to me.

I will contact you in a few days when I reach Oregon.

Rebekah

Mattley reads the postmark and sees it's from Goshen, Kentucky. He itches while he waits for Mimi to go with a nurse out to the lounge.

Five minutes later, the frozen sleet stings his cheeks, the biting wind sounds like the sharpening of steel. In Oregon, while early, autumn seems to have ended. He lets his truck warm up; the ice tings on the windshield when his phone vibrates from his back pocket.

He reads a text from Newbie:

Report came in yesterday. Came from Freedom's apartment. Arson.

With the weather report on AM low in the background, Mattley whispers out loud, "I shouldn't be doing this." He thinks about his son, still at his mother's for the week, thinks about what good could possibly come of it. But who the hell else was there to look out for Freedom? Mattley shivers in his red flannel shirt. He rubs his hands together and sees his own breath. To his right on the passenger's seat is a duffel bag full of his belongings. On top is his personal gun.

Mattley drives to the Amtrak station to save him a good fifteen hours of traveling. His destination: Kentucky.

27

AMERICA THE BEAUTIFUL

After waiting forty-five minutes for a handicapped-accessible taxi to arrive, having sent two regular four-doors away, Peter finally checks into a Louisville motel. It takes him two hours to do his best with bathing himself and changing his clothes. He finds his muscle spasms are more severe today, as he attempts nearly half a dozen times to call Freedom. But the phone keeps jumping out of his hands. There's no answer, anyway.

Peter sets up his laptop and connects to the motel's Wi-Fi. What Peter lacks in motor skills he compensates for in technology, as it's all that occupies him as he hides in his bedroom back at home. Playing stupid lets him get away with so much more than he should.

It takes longer than usual to maneuver the computer in spite of his hands, but he opens up several windows and starts his research. He starts with the Pauls.

A person can compile almost anything that's left a digital trail if the person they're looking into has an account on any social media outlet. And such is the case for Mason and Rebekah Paul. And it takes only a quick Google search to learn that Mason is some hot-shot defense attorney and that Rebekah has been missing for a good part of a week.

He continues with Virgil. It goes into his seminary training, his church's website and podcast. Peter even watches a past sermon, one that would make his eyebrows raise, if he had such control over his facial expressions. And then he looks into Carol Paul, who once upon a time was named Carol Custis.

Carol Custis, unlike the rest of the Pauls, has a rich history. Peter learns of Carol's twin sister, Clare, who made the news as a minister's daughter who hung herself in her home one morning back in 2009.

"Clare Custis," Peter says out loud as he searches the name on the Internet. And through that, he finds Adelaide Custis, the mother of Carol and Clare, who's been missing the past four years. "No wonder this bitch turned to Jesus," he says in regard to Carol and her messy family.

According to Mr. Gerald "Ger" Custis in all the local news programs' archives, his wife left one afternoon to go to the local post office and was simply never seen again. Her car was found a week later in the Ohio River.

Peter clicks away, stores all this information on a USB drive that he keeps tucked away in one of the leather pockets on the inside of the wheelchair's arm. Crumbs from his brother's welcome-home cake fall on the keyboard. The neighbors in the next room are arguing about something. The daylight heats the room; it's warmer in Kentucky than it is up in New York.

He tries to turn the television on with the remote, but his hands just don't want to work. It takes him fifteen minutes to put it on. Of course, it's the local news. Virgil and Carol Paul plead for any information regarding the whereabouts of their daughter. And when they show Rebekah's picture on the screen, Peter is amazed at how much she looks like Nessa.

▪ ▪ ▪

"*I appreciate this,*" Peter tells a Good Samaritan who offers to help him grab a few things from a nearby Walmart.

"Not a bother," says the morbidly obese woman in a ride-on electric cart. That's always pissed Peter off. Fat fucks like his mother who get dibs on handicap parking spaces and ride-on carts because they're lazy. Meanwhile, Peter's the one with the real disability, a congenital condition he would do anything to get rid of. But these people? They did it to themselves, and whose tax dollars do you think pay for these lard buckets to sit at home and watch *Jerry Springer* instead of working because they're eating deep-fried everything in a fucking trough?

"I feel your pain, I know what it's like." She uses a cane to hit the wheels on her ride-on. *Are you fucking kidding me?* "Got the diabetes and a bum foot." The Samaritan uses a long-reach gripper to pull a bottle of Diet Coke from a shelf. Her muumuu exposes a ton of underarm fat that swings with her wheezing. He feels sick. *Oh, my fucking God.* But Peter plays nice, pretends not to notice.

After Peter pays for a large bottle of water, granola bars, apples, and a Salisbury steak TV dinner, he waits near the entrance next to the gumball machines and Halloween display table. From there, he can see her buy a carton of Pall Malls and pay for her junk food with food stamps. On days like this, Peter regrets being an American.

While waiting, he studies the wall: fliers for babysitters, car stereo installation, churches, firewood, you name it. And on the top is a row of black-and-white pictures of missing people.

He immediately recognizes Adelaide Custis, mother to Carol Paul and Clare Custis.

And to the right is one that he doesn't recognize, but Peter studies it anyway. It's of a fifteen-year-old female who went missing two months ago.

Her name is Michelle Campbell.

28

CHARMED

Back at the office with Violet, the whispers of his colleagues behind the door about the disappearance of Mason's sister rips at his insides and ties them in knots. *This is the charmed life,* he thinks as he looks around the large office, crystal decanters and silver teapots shimmering in the autumn sunlight. A successful man, guts twisting with rage behind a designer suit. *I'm the most insufferable son of a bitch I know.* But for the first time in his life, Mason snaps a little. He opens the bottom drawer and slugs at his emergency stash of Maker's Mark bourbon, knuckles tight enough that he might break the neck.

"I don't care if he's having his lunch in fucking Guam," Violet yells into the phone, waking circles around Mason's desk. "Just get the sheriff on the damn line!" She raises an eyebrow at him, motioning as if she's about to throw the phone across the room. She stretches out her arm for the bottle, double-checking that the blinds are closed. "Gimme that," she whispers. Covering the receiver with her hand, "A police department run by rednecks. I'm just waiting for one of them to tell me I have a purdy mouth."

"It wouldn't surprise me in the least," Mason says as he stares at the screen of the computer, head in his hands. He slightly tugs at fistfuls of his own hair with frustration.

"So much for that vacation," she says to herself. The bottle tings her teeth.

Mason pretends he didn't hear her. He turns to her while waiting for an upload to complete. "Why don't you head on home, in case Rebekah shows up there?"

She rolls her eyes at the phone and hangs up. "Yeah, OK."

He reaches for her hands. "Listen, hon," he begins, about to apologize.

Violet knows what he's about to say. "Don't worry about it," she says and sighs, failing to hide her disappointment. "You just find her." She leans in and kisses his forehead. She goes for the bottom drawer to return the liquor.

"I got that." He takes the bottle from her and grabs her blazer from behind him on the back of the chair. "Just get on home safe and I'll call you in a little bit."

"Keep me posted." She starts for the door. "And don't drink too much, you're going to need your wits about you."

He smiles as she closes the door behind her. When he's sure she's gone, he takes a good two or three shots. He opens the bottom drawer, the one he stopped Violet from going into. In it is a velvet box with an engagement ring inside.

The computer beeps with a pop-up saying an upload is complete; the CDs he lifted from the Bluegrass. He slams his mouse and opens the folder, face hot when he sees the files are encrypted. He can't sit, can't stand the thought of living in his own skin for a second longer.

"Mason, there's someone here to see you," says his secretary over the intercom.

"Gimme a minute." He looks in the mirror and tucks in his shirt, realizing that the glass that cut his ear at the Bluegrass the day before left a perfect slice. He searches his inside pockets for a pack of gum to help conceal the booze on his breath. "Send him in."

"I hope I'm not disturbing you." A man in a wheelchair enters the office. Mason looks at the stranger, his curly black hair and thick lips.

Mason shuts off the television and closes the laptop. "Forgive me, I'm actually on vacation. Can I help you?"

"It's about your sister, Rebekah. I'm here on behalf of a friend." He squints against the sun that cuts through the blinds as he looks up at Mason. It's remarkable how much Mason looks like Mark, Peter thinks.

Mason furrows his brow. "How is that?"

Without a word, Peter nods toward the bottle of Maker's Mark on Mason's desk. Mason doesn't quite know what to think of it at first, this stranger, this guy who claims to know something about Rebekah, here on behalf of yet another stranger. But Mason doesn't see many other options that might get him closer to finding Rebekah. He puts the mouth of the bottle to the man's lips. "What's your name?"

"Peter." He breathes out the fire.

"And you said this is about Rebekah?" Mason sits behind his desk and crosses his arms.

"That's right." Peter swallows. "I may know who took her."

Mason suddenly jolts from his buzz, still unsure about this guy. He twirls the bottle between his knees. "All right, then. Who took my sister?"

"Well, I should rephrase." He reaches into the chair's pocket and pulls out a USB drive. "I *thought* I knew who took her. It may be she has more than just a few people out there who are looking for her, and not for her best interest." Mason gives a red-wheat-flavored smile because he doesn't quite believe him yet, waits for Peter to continue. "What do you know about your maternal grandmother?"

"She and my grandfather died when I was a teenager." Mason wonders if he was all the smarter for entertaining this stranger with answers, but it's too late to take it back. "What does she have to do with anything?"

"Under my chair." Peter jerks his head. "Grab my laptop."

At first, Mason doesn't believe what he sees in the local news archives on the computer, chalks it up to too much to drink. "All right." He paces the room with the laptop in his arm. "Let's say this is my mother's mother, my grandmother." He lets the last few drops of the bourbon trickle down the back of his tongue. "I still don't see what this has to do with Rebekah."

"Go to the photo gallery of the Third-Day Adventists' webpage." Peter directs Mason to a group photo of the tweens' youth group in someone's living room, the awkward kind: teeth they have yet to grow into, acne, the works.

"The Mickey Mouse Club, so what?"

"Look at the two girls in the back."

Mason recognizes Rebekah, smiling, hugging another girl who's facing the opposite direction. "What about it?"

"That girl Rebekah's hugging . . ."

"I can't see her face."

"There's a mirror on the wall, her reflection is in it."

Mason has to peer through the pixels of the computer screen. "How the hell did you even notice that?"

"I'm observant." He adjusts himself in the chair and his bones stiffen under his skin. "The girl in the mirror is Michelle Campbell, a teenager who went missing two months ago."

Mason recognizes her face from the news, but to confirm the wild notion, he opens a new page and Googles the name. To his disbelief, there's no denying. The girl in the photo with her back to the camera and face in the mirror is none other than Michelle Campbell. Mason grabs the laptop and slowly drags his feet back to his chair, deaf to the whirrs of the electric wheelchair trailing behind.

"That's three missing people who can be tied to your family's church: Adelaide Custis, Michelle Campbell, and . . ."

"My sister," Mason finishes. "How did you figure all this out? I mean, why the interest in Rebekah's disappearance? In the other disappearances?"

"Because before I pieced it together, I thought someone else might be responsible." His stutter was a little more subtle. "In fact, it can't be ruled out. We must look into both possibilities."

"Which are?"

"It's either my family or yours."

"Your family." He sits up straight. "What do you mean your family?"

"My brothers: Matthew, Luke, and John." He glances over at a childhood photo of Mason and Rebekah that sits on a bookshelf behind the desk. It takes all that he has not to tell Mason of the *whys* and the *whos* of his brothers, who they are to him, why they might have something to do with Rebekah. He can't tell him that his father's mother, that sick bitch, is on the hunt for her grandchildren. He can't tell him that his biological mother is too. "I didn't piece this connection until after I got here. But you must look at my brothers as suspects."

Mason's afraid to ask, wondering a million terrible things: Are these brothers waiting downstairs in the parking lot? Was Peter sent as a distraction? "Where do you stand with them?"

Peter straightens his head and pierces Mason's eyes with his. "I can't stand at all." Mason laughs, despite himself. Peter says, seriously, "I don't stand with monsters."

Mason swallows hard. "And what might your brothers want with my sister?"

Peter rolls forward so his face is close to his nephew's. "Mason, there are two types of men in this world. There are the common, and then there are the all-too-common monsters. Men like you and I would fall under the category of common. Then there are men who crave disaster; they suck the souls out of anyone they can. Those are the all-too-common, too many walking on this earth. And my brothers? Well, they fall into the latter category."

"And this friend that sent you. Where does he stand?"

"*She.* Her name's Freedom." Peter leans back. "Freedom stands somewhere in the middle. Her interest in your sister is nothing but good intentions." Peter tries several times to lift his pant leg. "Do me a favor. There's a flask in my sock. Would you grab it for me?" He hopes this will avert him from the subject of Freedom.

Mason obliges; his head swims with the liquor when he bends over. "Why should I trust you to help me?"

"Because who else do you have?" The response lingers thick in the air, so strong that Mason can almost feel it with his bare hands. While the words are sharp, he knows Peter's right. His thoughts are interrupted by Peter sucking through a straw from the flask.

"And you won't tell me who Freedom is? Why she's involved?"

"That's her story to tell, not mine. But somehow, she knows your sister." Peter accidentally drools when he pulls away from the straw. "You'll meet her soon, don't worry."

"I don't suppose your brothers are skinheads, are they?"

"No, why?"

"Hmm." Mason remembers the CDs he lifted from the Bluegrass. "I got my hands on these CDs, but they're encrypted files, I can't read them. They could be security from the night she was taken."

"What makes you so sure she was taken, anyway? I mean, who's to say she didn't just run away?"

"She did." Mason gets up and paces. "But she was taken before she could reach wherever it was she was trying to get to. There was a witness who was with her that night. Beaten to a pulp. I got a text saying he didn't make it."

"Pull up the CDs," Peter demands. "We'll get the fuckers."

▪ ▪ ▪

Twenty minutes later, Mason sits in the back corner of the office, texting Violet to tell her he loves her. While he's distracted, Peter sneaks into one of his desktop files labeled "Bills" and memorizes Mason's home address.

He'll text it to Freedom later. Peter calls out, "I got s-s-something."

Mason runs to him at his desk. "What is it?"

"Interesting, to say the least." Peter uses the back of his wrists to rub his eyes, strained from the screen. They see a blond woman walk in wearing a Jack Daniel's shirt and tight jeans. They see some redneck rubbing on her. They see the cook come to her rescue. "Recognize anyone?"

"I don't know." Mason studies the black-and-white but clear footage. "Any one of them could be Gabriel; he was unrecognizable when I saw him."

"And the out-of-place blonde?"

"Rebekah has long red hair."

"Could have cut and dyed it, especially if she were running away." Mason knows Peter could be right.

"Any way to zoom in?"

Click. Blur. Pixelated. Focus. Repeat. As clear as day, Rebekah is in the video, in disguise, but there's no question about it. It's her. Mason can see her necklace.

"Who the hell is that guy rubbing up on her?" Mason asks under his breath.

"One way to find out," Peter offers. "Let's print his face and head to the Bluegrass. Show his photo around."

THE LEGEND OF FREEDOM

My name is Freedom and I don't know where I am. I'm lying on my back in a large bed with what feels like the worst hangover a person could possibly imagine. The throbbing pushes itself toward the front of my skull when I sit up. It's afternoon. I am naked, wrapped in those stringy white blankets that usually sit for years in the back of every linen closet in America. *Where the fuck am I?* I try to recall last night's events.

The sound of static in my brain turns into the drumming of heavy rain on the aluminum roof. To my left, a fireplace crackles; dream catchers of red feathers ornate my blurry vision. I look around the wood cabin and no one's here with me. Out the window is a view of a back porch with rocking chairs and wooden wind chimes, screened off from the desert that stretches farther than the aches of my head and heavy rainfall will allow me to see.

I wrap the white blanket around my body and get up from the bed as quietly as I can, but as soon as I put my weight on my right leg, I fall like a deer that's been shot, the way I fell last night, I think. I'm starting to remember. All the blood in my body seems to rush to my calf, a pain that feels like my leg's being impaled by a hot poker. I hear footsteps from the other side of the house. *I have to get the hell out of here.* Naked or not, I go to leave the sheet behind and head for the window.

But I'm not fast enough.

With one impressive sweep, a man lifts me like a child and lays me back on the bed. "You're going to hurt yourself, miss. You need to lie down."

I squirm, I try to snap my teeth at the man. "Put me down!" His long, black hair brushes over my face. His shoulders bulge from a wifebeater, his skin tight and sun-tinged. *Shit, my gun. My money. My stolen motorcycle.* "I have to get out of here. You have to let me out. You can't do this to me."

"Ma'am, I need you to stay calm."

"Don't tell me to stay fucking calm," I bark at him from the bed, pulling the sheet tighter around my body. "What the hell is going on?"

In his hand is an orange bottle of prescription pills. He walks to my side and puts a tablet in my hand. "Take one of these. It's amoxicillin for the infection."

"Infection?" I sniff the pill and discern that it is an antibiotic, that foul smell. "Wait a minute," I say as flashes of last night form in my mind like a broken ornament being pieced back together. The bike stalling, the lightning storm, the old man with silver braids rattling something over my head and singing something velvety and ritualistic. "I was shot."

"Stay here, I'll grab you something to drink." In his absence, the harmony created between fire and rain constructs an atmospheric milieu. A voice outside breaks my trance from the fire licking the walls of the fireplace, black with years' worth of silt and soot. It's the voice from last night. The wood of the porch groans with age under the chair; it sounds like a record player spinning over and over again after the music stops. I suddenly realize the kind of people I'm with.

"You're Indians," I tell the man as he returns with a mug, steam rising.

"We prefer *Native Americans*." He sets the cup on the nightstand.

"So you're politically correct Indians?"

He gives half a smirk, something childlike and innocent. He's one of the most beautiful men I've ever seen in my life. His jaw is strong, his dark eyes gentle. The fire paints him into something sculpted, muscle you can see through his shirt. "Drink up."

"What the fuck is this, some Indian twig-and-berry poison crap?"

"Starbucks." He takes a band from his wrist and ties his long hair back into a ponytail. Black-rimmed glasses fall from his head and land on his nose.

"Why the fuck am I naked?" I snap.

"Anyone ever tell you that you curse like a sailor?"

"Go fuck yourself, Dances with Wolves."

He sits at the foot of the bed and lifts the sheet from my leg and looks under the bandage. "My father had to strip you naked. Your body was beginning to swell up." He focuses on my leg while I reach for the coffee and blow into it. "He's old-fashioned, cut the wound right off of you. The antibiotics will fix the infection. It did save your life, though."

"I don't understand . . ."

"Rattlesnake bite. Caught you twice, once in the leg, once in the arm."

"So I wasn't shot?"

He raises his eyebrows. "Were you expecting to be shot?"

"Well, I certainly wasn't expecting to be attacked by a rattlesnake and dragged across the desert by an old Indian man."

"Native American," he corrects me, not that I don't already know the difference. "Shoshone. We were called the Snake Indians many years ago." He has a warm touch, places one ankle next to the other. "I'll clean it in a little bit." He moves up the bed and closer to my face while he inspects the bite on my right arm. He smells like that bright, orange Dial soap that pediatricians of my childhood would use. Above his upper lip is a faint scar.

"You found my gun and my money?"

"Mmhmm." His breath touches my upper arm. "We'll give them back."

"And you won't say anything?"

He covers my arm back up. "Say what to whom?"

I clear my throat. This has to be one of the best cups of coffee I've had in my entire life. "Are you a doctor?"

"I'm a surgeon at Saint Michael's."

"And what's your dad, the backyard butcher witch doctor?"

"A shaman." A trace of a giggle from his nose. "You're a real feisty one, aren't ya? My father always warned me about crazy white women."

"Did that ever stop you?"

"Ask my white ex-wife." He starts for the door. "I've cooked up some breakfast out here."

"What's your name?"

He stops. "Chuck."

"You didn't strike me as a Chuck," I say as I watch the flames on the other side of the room.

"Chanteyukan." He leans his shoulder in the frame of the door. "It means 'benevolence.'"

"I thought you were going to say Dances with Wolves for a moment there."

"What's yours?"

"Freedom."

"You're lying to me, aren't you?"

"Just a little."

He smiles. "I'll grab some breakfast. You'll need it. Just stay there." If there's one thing that can be said by any doctor who has ever treated me, it's that I don't stay down. More than once, I've opened stitches, and even found it worthwhile, just to keep from not moving. Hell, nothing's going to keep me down. I get up.

Chanteyukan doesn't see me, his back facing me as he prepares breakfast. It's a one-room space, the living room shared with the kitchen and eating area. Dozens of pieces of white twine stretch from one side of the room to the other. Clothespinned on each line are individual hundred-dollar bills, approximately one hundred of them, drying in the heat from the wood-burning stove. On top of it, a small, silver percolator where Chuck made the coffee.

"You ought to be resting," he says without turning around.

I pay no mind to him. I suppose there are still good people in the world. I can't say I would have done the same, salvage ten grand from a complete stranger when pocketing it seems so much more pragmatic. Life likes to throw curveballs at you once in a while. "Breakfast smells swell."

"Venison steak and quail eggs. Your clothes are hung over there." He points.

"So, you live here?"

"No. I live in a condo about an hour from here, in town." He sets the table made of twisted tree bark. "I come by to check in on him every few days. He shouldn't be on his own. But he's the most stubborn man on the planet." Sounds like a challenge to me. Still wrapped in a sheet, I walk to the back screen door and see the man who saved me for the first time in the light. I only pretend to ignore Chanteyukan as I step out to the porch. "Or we can eat outside . . ." he mumbles behind me.

The old man looks at me for just a second from the rocking chair before he resumes his stare back into the vastness of the wilderness, a far-reaching view of both desert and prairie. Sporadic trees protrude from the earth to look like upside-down paintbrushes dipped in reds and yellows and oranges. Rain cascades from the eaves of the home. The air tastes cleaner in this part of the world. Chanteyukan follows me with the plate of breakfast and a medical bag.

"Hello," I offer the old man. He doesn't answer. I take a seat when I notice a wolf resting beside the man's chair. "A wolf? Really?"

"A coyote. Her name is Aleshanee. She's an old pup," Chuck tells me. "Can't see or hear anymore."

"Does your father know English?"

Chanteyukan goes to put the meal on my lap, but I take it from him first. "He knows it." He squats down, takes my leg, and puts it on his lap. "He just refuses to speak it." The old man says something in his native tongue of Shoshone. He speaks straight ahead to the rain from a gray flannel and black jeans, feathers hanging from two braids. Chanteyukan translates, "He says last week he dreamt of a white woman with hair like that of a cardinal." Chuck pulls out gauze, surgical tape, and Neosporin. The old man laughs, a full set of pipe-tarnished teeth. His son repeats, "Crazy white women."

"He didn't say that." I smile down to Chuck, but his father laughs. Apparently it wasn't lost in translation. The father's voice rattles like that of an old smoker. The laughter dies and he recommences with the gravity of what he has to say.

"Last night, I was certain you were the woman in my dream. But it wasn't you." As he unwraps my bandages it feels as if the muscle is rotting from the inside out.

So not to interrupt the shaman's words, I whisper to Chanteyukan, "You have a drink or something for the pain?"

"No drinking while on antibiotics."

"C'mon, man," I whine.

"No, and I mean it." He cuts a piece of gauze. "Besides, something tells me that that's the last thing you need."

"But it's killing me." But Chuck isn't stupid, doesn't buy my excuses of pain. I sigh with frustration when his father says something like *ta ta ka* and hands me a pipe. "What is it?"

"Nothing legal, I'm afraid," says Chuck. The old man raises his eyebrows and nods toward the pipe. The smoke is sweet, smells like flowers cooking in a wok. It starts warm at my toes and rises up. For a moment, I think I urinate on myself. And then the warmth hits my head, something that can be compared only to some orgasm of the soul. The pain is gone. The anxiety withers to nothing. Peace. Peace, unlike anything I've ever experienced. In this moment, I swear I can feel God. Wherever he is.

I light a cigarette. Chanteyukan squeezes a small plastic bottle of antiseptic on the carved X that the old man crafted on my calf with a knife. He continues to translate for his father, who doesn't realize he's just become my new best friend. "The girl in my dream was young. She has an understanding with the spirits. She is innocent. She is not like you, in these ways. But, like you, is a tortured soul."

"Is it that obvious?"

Chanteyukan pats my leg gently and answers for himself in English: "Yes." In each droplet of rain that beads off the eaves is a panoramic view of the landscape, as if each drip of the sky carries the entire world inside. "This girl wanders the Earth, she searches for somebody she doesn't know. But wherever she walks, there is no one."

"What happens to the girl?" I ask.

"That's not my story to tell." I wonder if he's talking about Rebekah. I wonder if he's talking about a younger version of me.

"Where am I, anyway?" I ask Chanteyukan.

"Where do you think you are?"

"Nevada?"

"You're about five hours from the Nevada border." He moves to the bite on my arm. "You're in Idaho, right near the Wyoming and Utah borders in the Snake River Plain."

I give the cherry-flavored wooden pipe back to the old man. "I've made better time than I thought."

"Where are you heading?"

"Kentucky."

"Kentucky," the old man repeats, a wave of his arm forming a curve across the land.

"In Shoshone, Kentucky is translated into 'Land of Tomorrow.'" It's fitting.

"What's your name?" I ask the shaman.

For the first time he looks at me. "Deseronto." His eyes have a permanent squint to them.

Chanteyukan finishes with the cleaning of the wound on my

arm. "It means 'lightning has struck.'" Also fitting, I think. "Try and eat your steak and eggs." I rip a piece off and hang my arm and wave the piece of deer so Aleshanee the coyote will detect it and come.

"What's Alesh, or whatever her name is, mean?" I ask.

"She who plays."

Deseronto says something in Shoshone and Chuck translates. "My father wants to tell this story":

"It wasn't far from here, during the Snake War of 1864, when the white man came and invaded our tribes. They killed our children, they raped our wives. This was a war forgotten over time, though it killed more than the ill-famed and superior Battle of the Little Bighorn. Nearly two thousand Shoshones were murdered by the white devil. Soon after, the Europeans settled on the land they stole from us. But there lived a man named Freedom, once the strongest warrior around, but he acquired blindness from an outbreak of influenza. When his family died at the hands of the Europeans, he spent his days brokenhearted and alone.

"Years before the white man took his home and murdered his wife and children, Freedom was famous in the village for this tree behind his home. This was a tree of knots, a tree that stood for thousands of years before him. It was big and beautiful and unlike any other tree of its kind. People would pass it and say, 'I've never seen such a strong and beautiful tree in all my life.' They would say, 'This tree knows the hearts of men and has witnessed generations before us.'

"When the homes of the village were demolished, Freedom was left with nothing, the only survivor of his tribe. He retreated to the woods where his wife and children were buried while big houses were built where he once lived, fences, and roads. And believing the woods were haunted, no white man ventured their establishments past Freedom's old tree.

"Freedom, in all his years, loved that tree. As a child, he'd tell this tree all his thoughts and dreams and worries. He cared for it more than any other tree or crop. But after he moved to the woods, the tree belonged to a white man named Colonel Woolworth, who built his home so that the

tree was in the center of his backyard. Colonel Woolworth hated that tree and more than once did he try to chop it down; he found it ugly and it obstructed his view. But the tree was too big, too strong for the likes of Woolworth's strength and ax. He hated how it still seemed to grow even in the cold season; the branches grew out, nearly touching his house. And so every morning, Woolworth went out there with his axes and saws and would cut the branches off. He would try to dig it out, but the roots were too deep. By night, in fear of the forest and tired from trying to destroy this tree, Woolworth would retire.

"*This would break Freedom's heart. Though blind, Freedom could hear Woolworth's actions and feel the branches being chopped down. By night, when the whites had retired and he couldn't be seen, Freedom would sneak from the forest with a bucket of water for the tree. He would water it and sing to it and pray with it. And while he was never able to see this tree, he loved it and cared for it, despite Woolworth's attempts to take over the tree and destroy it.*"

▪▪▪

My name is Freedom and I follow this story very closely. Chanteyukan finishes his mending. Aleshanee rests her head on my lap and looks for more venison steak. I take this story as something symbolic, my children and I, I being the blind Freedom who cares for something while not being able to see it, while the world tries to destroy it.

"What happens to Freedom and the tree and Colonel Woolworth?" I ask.

Chanteyukan translates once more: "The dance between Freedom and Woolworth lasted for many years, until both were old men. The colonel's defeat against the tree made him even more bitter than before. But the tree that Freedom cared for with all he had gave Freedom a reason to live, something to love.

"Because he didn't cease in his love, no matter all he had already lost, Freedom won the war he never knew he was fighting. But do we say that Freedom won because the man gave up and turned bitter? The answer is no."

"So then what made Freedom win the battle?"

"Because Freedom, with a good heart and good intentions, kept the tree growing and strong. And because of this, the roots of the tree grew under Woolworth's home, right where Freedom and his family lived first. The roots lifted the house from underneath and destroyed it. Woolworth was forced to uproot and move elsewhere. Not only was Woolworth driven away, but the roots grew under the entire town and forced everyone to leave the homes they built on the raped land of the Shoshones.

"This, in your language, might be called karma. But where we are from, it's all part of the circle of life. And Freedom completed that circle, as everything in life happens in a circle." The old man draws a circle in the sky with his finger. The rocking chair continues to creak under him. "And to this day, that very tree continues to grow."

■■■

I wash up and get dressed in the bathroom. The rain is dying, the pain is easing. I wrap my money back in rubber bands and splash my face with cold water to get rid of the fuzzy edges of this high before I'm on my way. On the windowsill are magazines: a Native American newspaper, a *Reader's Digest*, a *TV Guide*. Sticking out of the newspaper, probably hiding, next to a Shoshone crossword puzzle, is the corner of an envelope addressed to Deseronto. My nosy ass opens it and reads it. Inside is a letter from the county: a final notice from Margefield Properties that because of the 2011 border shift, his property is no longer part of a federal Indian reservation. He owes back taxes of nearly twenty thousand dollars to the state or he will be forced to vacate the premises. I get the feeling that his son doesn't know.

I look into the mirror and make a decision.

Outside, I start my recently repaired bike and get ready to leave. I dry-swallow another antibiotic and put the bottle back in my coat. Deseronto and Chanteyukan see me off. On the side of the house is an old, abandoned motorcycle with Utah plates.

"How much to switch plates?" I ask. No doubt there's an all-points bulletin out on this bike. The father and son look at each other.

Chanteyukan walks to the old motorcycle and uses his hands to unscrew the plates and hands them to me. "Whatever's chasing you, I hope you make it." I smile to him, and with no response I head for the road.

I drive eighteen hours straight, with five-minute breaks every hour to fuel up on nicotine, Red Bull, and the occasional glazed donut to keep my sugars up against the alcohol withdrawals. It makes the ride long; seems I've been riding for weeks. I can't tell where the tremors end and the shakes of the bike begin. The wind doesn't stop the sweat. And even I'm surprised I don't end up pulling over to vomit on the sides of the interstates. My tendons feel like lead and my skin of glass. But I have to get Rebekah. I have to find her. Because like the story of Freedom, what the fuck else do I have to live for?

I wonder how long it will take Deseronto and Chanteyukan to find the money I left for them, dried and neatly wrapped in rolls, under their bathroom sink. Deseronto needs it more than I do, so I gave him all of it, minus just enough to get me where I have to be. You're welcome, Reds.

I am now entering Louisville, Kentucky.

30

CUCKOO

"I don't want to see that at the dinner table, you understand?"

"Yes, Mama." Magdalene takes her cat's-cradle string and puts it under her.

Carol Paul's leg shakes. A bowl of baked chicken sits in the center of the table. She sees a piece of skin and pulls it off before Virgil comes home and sees it. A bird springs from the hole of the cuckoo clock and sings nine times, for 9:00 p.m. Magdalene rests her head on her arm across the table. "But I'm so hungry and tired," she whines.

"You know the rules. We don't eat until your father arrives to the table."

"But it's so late."

"I know, dear." Carol wraps her own hair around her finger, a nervous habit she's acquired over the years. Magdalene mimics her. Carol offers her a little smile to boost her spirits.

"Where's Michelle and Baby Theresa?"

"Well," Carol says as she folds her hands and tucks them between her thighs. "Theresa is asleep upstairs. And Michelle is resting back at her house. She'll be asleep for a while."

The two of them sit straight when Virgil comes through the

front door. The chicken, mashed potatoes, biscuits and gravy, and sugar snap peas are cold enough that they look like wax artifacts on the dining room table for display. Carol wipes the sweat from the pitchers of hand-squeezed lemonade to look like she's doing something when Virgil arrives.

"Yay, Daddy. You're home," Magdalene squeals with delight, her stomach growling like a monster. And while this is the part where Virgil usually pats her on the head or kisses her cheek, he brushes her off. And even the five-year-old knows when a room becomes heavy.

He sits down without washing up. His knuckles cracked and bleeding, his palms calloused to stiffness. Magdalene recognizes that look on her mother, the one that says it's best not to say a word or even point an eye in Virgil's direction. She can feel her father's hands tremble when he reaches out to hold the girls' hands to say grace.

They try not to seem too eager to eat. The one time Magdalene did that, he denied her strawberry ice cream, and she wouldn't want that, now, would she?

"I suppose my punishment for being late is cold dinner," he says as he shoots Carol a cold stare, a ball of anger in his throat he subdues to hide from their daughter.

"I can reheat it if you'd like, dear," Carol gushes.

He puts his hand up. "No, no. I'm far too hungry to wait another second longer."

Carol avoids eye contact with Virgil, always looking off to the side, hiding her half-smiles like they warrant punishment. And for supper being cold, she knows she'll suffer. Over the years the punishments got worse, but who is she to second-guess her husband, who was appointed by Christ himself to be a leader? She entertains the thought of pointing out to him that he could have called to let her know he'd be four hours late so she could have prepared the meal a little better, but it will make things worse for her. After all, he's usually never later than five for dinner. And for this, what will their God deem deserving? Sleeping in the closet? In the backyard on this cold night without a blanket? Kneeling on rice with buckets of water? A whipping with the belt would be easy, but she knows Virgil wouldn't be so gracious, not this time. The more God speaks to him and uses him as a soldier for God's army, the more heavy-handed he's become.

And yet he's never so much as raised a voice near or at Magdalene; she's the apple of his eye, the joy of the household, the innocent. God told Virgil in a dream that Magdalene was divine like he, but it's to remain a secret until the Lord approves that the divinity be exposed.

Magdalene shovels mashed potatoes into her mouth. She gazes at her father's pink button-down shirt with blood on it. Carol clears her throat and gets her attention, glancing at Magdalene's plate so she stops staring.

But Virgil catches her. "I hit a deer on the way home tonight," he says as he gulps his first glass of lemonade, Carol quick to refill it before the glass hits the table.

"Oh, no. Did the deer die, Daddy?"

"Unfortunately, yes. So I had to bury him in the woods, that's why the blood on my shirt. But I said a prayer over him. He's in heaven with all the other deer that've died."

Virgil eats the meat off the bone of a thigh with bloodied knuckles and a dirty face, making him look primitive, masculine. Carol sees this. And she also knows the story of the deer is a lie. But it's a white lie, a righteous one. After all, who could expose such a cruel truth to a five-year-old who cannot understand?

In her eyes, Virgil did what he had to do.

31

SUNSET

The mosquitoes seem attracted to Mattley's body odor. And while he'd love nothing more than a hot shower after the fifteen-hour train ride from Oregon, he can't sit still in his skin knowing that Freedom might be in trouble. Between the Delaney brothers and the authorities back in Painter, Mattley hopes to get to her before anybody else does. What he'll do when he *does* finally get to her, he doesn't know.

On his night shifts, when he'd practically carry Freedom up the stairs to her apartment, all the drunken ramblings about her children, the constant reminders of the letters to her children that she'd show him ... Mattley knew who Mason was and it only took a little asking around to find out where he lives, since Freedom's letters were addressed to some church in Goshen.

The yellow light of the porch hums when he rings the doorbell. His stomach growls, his lower back aching from sitting in both the train and the hired car. He swears he's lost ten pounds just between Painter and Louisville. The sun sets beyond the trees behind him, just enough so his shadow grows on the front steps of the house. A woman answers the door.

"I'm sorry to be bothering you, ma'am," Mattley says, keeping his mouth as closed as possible, as he hasn't brushed his teeth in more than a day. "Is Mason Paul around?"

"No, I'm sorry," says the woman. "Can I help you?"

"My name is James Mattley. You'll have to forgive me, I've come a long way." He reaches in the duffel bag that hangs on his shoulder. He pulls out a photo, a mug shot. "I was wondering if you could tell me whether you've seen this woman?"

Violet inspects the photo of Freedom, puzzled by the unexpected visit. "I'm sorry, I haven't." She hands the picture back him.

Mattley sighs, frustrated after a long trip and no answers waiting for him at the other end. "Well, I'm sorry to have bothered you, miss." He turns to leave.

She calls after him, "Is this about Rebekah's disappearance?"

He stops dead in his tracks. "Disappearance?" It's news to Mattley, and he figures that it would soon be news to Gumm and Howe as well.

"Well, sure." She crosses her arms and leans against the frame of the front door. "Mason's sister. He's all torn up about it."

"In Louisville?"

"Goshen." Violet turns off the lights and steps out to the porch, activating the alarm system and locking the door behind her. "Don't y'all talk to one another? You're the third cop here in the past couple of hours."

"Sure," he lies. "In fact, I'm on my way back to Goshen now." *But if I don't get something in my belly soon, I'm going to faint,* he thinks to himself.

"Please let us know if you hear anything," she says as she walks toward her car. "I'm on my way to meet my friends at Metro Police to see if they've got anything yet."

"Here, let me walk you." He stares off at a dying sun, thinking of how he'd like to leave there as soon as possible to see what he could find out, in reference to the discovery of Rebekah's disappearance. *But play it cool. Don't alarm the woman. Keep the urge to kick a lawn ornament to yourself.*

This couldn't have been Freedom. Could it? The Delaneys? The same men who are after Freedom? The thoughts run rampant in his head.

"Shit, I forgot my phone," Violet says as she hurries back to the house.

Mattley waves as he rushes to the rental car. "Have a good evening."

32

RUN, REBEKAH, RUN

Two women scream outside through the arms of juiced-up bounc-ers, drunken slurs about home-wrecking and baby-mama drama. The cold night doesn't stop them from wearing skirts that hug their cellulite-filled legs and stiletto sandals that squeeze their old toes to kingdom come. Too much lipstick, too much cake face. Mason can't help but smile as they cross the dirt lot together toward the entrance. Not much recovery has been done to the Bluegrass since the storm, except a little duct tape and cardboard over the windows, already graffitied with those tribal *S*'s junior-high-schoolers draw on their notebooks. Ah, the twelve-year-old vandal.

Mason holds the door for Peter and a million stares shoot in their direction. Beer guts held fastened by suspenders, the smell of hot wings in the air. Mason blows into his hands to warm the chill of October from outside while "Lay Down Sally" reverberates through the alligator-skin boots and denims and wools.

They spot the man right away, the one from the surveillance tapes who was seen rubbing all over Rebekah the night she went missing. He wears the same New Orleans Saints football cap, black with a gold fleur-de-lis, and leans on the side of a pool table. He chalks his pool cue and holds a lump of tobacco in the side of his cheek. Peter sees him first and points him out. The man makes eye contact with Mason as they approach him. He picks up a coffee can from a makeshift shelf on the column beside him and spits out his tobacco. He leans his cue as his game ends and pulls a can of menthol Skoal from his jeans. "Why you eyeing me like that?" he says as he pulls the fresh tobacco apart and tucks it under his lip, not looking at either one of them.

"Actually," Mason says, suddenly feeling out of place for the first time since he strolled in, "I was hoping you might help me with something."

"Well, I don't know what it is you all are looking for, but my help doesn't come without a price." The man looks up from his can and eyeballs Peter as if he's never seen a man in a wheelchair before.

"I'm looking for a young woman named Rebekah Paul. Do you know of her?"

"You mean that spicy redheaded firecracker they've been showing all over the news?" He grins. "I never saw her before. And even if I did, what's it to ya?"

"She was in here a few nights ago, but we think she might have cut her hair and dyed it blond." Mason steps closer to him. "A little birdie in my ear said you might have seen her."

The man hocks a wad of phlegm and swallows it. "Yeah, I saw her, so what?"

Mason grabs his shirt and pulls him near. "Listen, you inbred pig-fucking redneck, I'm not kidding. That girl is my sister and I swear to God, if you don't help me out here, I'm going to drag you out back and take this nice, shiny pool stick of yours and . . ." Peter grabs Mason's arm. Everyone at the bar watches. Mason smooths out his white button-down and clears his throat.

"You don't gotta make a goddamn scene about it." The man raises his arms to assure the witnesses that everything's under control. "Follow me to my truck; we can talk there if you like."

"I'm not going anywhere with you. You can say whatever you have to say right here."

But the man leans in to Mason's ear. His voice an octave deeper. His southern twang gone. His words no longer sound like those of a stupid hillbilly. "Not here. Shut up and just follow me."

They pass the bouncers and cross the parking lot to where dozens of freight trucks cool down in the light of a full moon. With the stranger ahead, Mason puts his hand on Peter's chest to stop them as the man goes to walk through a long aisle of trucks alone in the dark. They both give each other that look that says *Maybe this ain't such a good idea.* When the man hears them stop he turns to them. "I'm not up to anything sneaky. Do you want to know about your sister or not?" His steps echo between the eighteen-wheelers, giving the truckyard a haunted feeling.

Mason's spine is replaced with a rod of ice, sending slivers of frost to each one of his nerve endings. Every cell in his body tells him to turn around, but this is the closest he's been so far to finding Rebekah. The thought that this man was the one responsible for beating Gabriel and taking Rebekah comes to him as a terrifying possibility. But he keeps his focus on the back of the man's head to avoid letting the fear consume him. Peter's electric wheelchair whirrs beside him when the man fuddles with his keys and uses them to poke around in a lock on the back of a truck labeled REDIN-DELLY'S PRODUCE with plates from Virginia.

"You never saw this, you understand?" the stranger says, to which Mason nods. The door of the cargo trailer clatters as it rolls up, a strip of faint light coming from the opening. Peter has to sit as erect as he can to see inside, Mason poking his head so the light whips across his eyes. At the far wall are several screens with black-and-white pictures on them, too far away to make out from outside the truck. There are several men inside, including a skinhead with a large swastika tattooed on his arm who shaves with an electric razor and paces, while the others look at Mason and Peter with headphones on their heads. "It'll be tough to bring him in too." He points to Peter.

"I'm fine out here," Peter assures Mason.

The bang of the door slamming behind Mason travels up his spinal cord.

"What the hell is this?" asks the skinhead as he holds up a handheld mirror to examine his shaved head.

"He's looking for his sister," says the man that Mason followed. "The name's Joe." With his back toward Mason and Joe, the skinhead uses his mirror to give the man a cold look. In the reflection, the light tinges his skin silver and blue; his eyes look like solid black marbles.

"Well, I'll be," says the skinhead without turning around, tilting the mirror so he can see Mason. "If it isn't the Virgin Mary's big brother."

"Sorry?" Mason is as confused as ever.

The skinhead smirks. "Yeah, I know all about you, Mister Hot-Shot Attorney."

"Do I know you?" Mason wishes he were still a little drunk, a current of red wheat to wash through his guts and flush with it the fear that makes his voice tremble. The skinhead turns his razor off and calls out to one of the others, "Sammy, you have the one for the chest?" A man near one of the computers at the back wall of the truck reaches in his drawer and pulls out a long piece of paper and walks over to the skinhead with a bottle of water. "Almost forgot this one." Sammy grabs a rag off the floor and wets it, before lining the fake tattoo across the skinhead's collarbones. He looks right at Mason. "We were just as shocked to hear about your sister as you."

"What are you guys, Feds?"

"Bureau of Alcohol, Tobacco, and Firearms, Department of Justice," says the stranger who brought Mason here.

"So how do you know who I am?"

"Mr. Paul, you wouldn't pass us off as a few inbred pig-fucking rednecks who don't know anything about the direct kinships associated with our targets, would you?"

Mason can't help a breath of half a laugh. "Rebekah? There's no way she could have been a target for anything you guys are working on. She's never so much as cussed her whole life, let alone . . . wait, what the hell are we talking about here? A skinhead operation?"

The skinhead laughs. "Not quite." Sammy peels off the paper to reveal wet, fake ink with symbols sporting pride of the Aryan race.

"Somebody tell me what the hell is going on, or I swear I'm marching back into the bar and telling all your bigot friends that you're an undercover pig, I swear to Christ. Where is Rebekah?"

"Sadly, that had nothing to do with us," answers the stranger who was trying to take her home. "No one knew anything was wrong until it was too late. That was when I found that kid Gabriel in the back."

"C'mon, tell me something that can help," Mason pleads. "No offense, but someone like Rebekah just doesn't chop and bleach their hair and wind up in a place like this."

"Ha!" the skinhead barks. "Virgin Mary was here every Sunday, like clockwork."

"Will you stop calling her that?" Mason shouts. "Just tell me why she's on your radar."

The skinhead's shoulders straighten. His jaw barely moves when he says the words. "Virgin Mary is one of the most proficient gunrunners in the God-fearing South."

It's the kind of silence that people allow when facts can't settle comfortably in thick air. Mason's grin twitches with nerves. "Well, that's a relief. You guys have the wrong girl."

"The daughter of Reverend Virgil Paul of the Third-Day Adventists, whose face is plastered on every news channel in Kentucky?" asks the stranger. "No, Mason. We don't."

"OK, not sure if any of you guys have actually met Rebekah in person." It pains Mason to say this. "But her intelligence quotient borderlines on mental retardation; I really don't think she's capable of something like gunrunning."

"How else you think your church is getting all those guns?" says the stranger.

"What church?" Mason is more convinced that they're talking about someone else.

"When was the last time you went home?" Mason doesn't answer. "Oh, I guess that twenty-acre property was still rolling hills and bluegrass when you were there last." The stranger stuffs his hands in his pockets and keeps his voice low, eyes aimed at one of the screens across the space. "That was before Daddy the reverend had the church members build their own little commune there and seal themselves off from the rest of the world."

"You're talking about a cult," says Mason, not realizing the severity of it until the words are said out loud.

"And they're not getting their guns from Jesus."

"Wait a minute, wait a minute." Mason squeezes his head between the palms of his hands. "Guns for what?"

The skinhead jumps to answer, but the stranger makes it a point to interrupt him. "We have our suspicions that your father's leading some radical movement, maybe one that's leaning toward something antigovernment."

"You're talking domestic terrorism?" asks Mason, to which the stranger looks down and nods. He continues: "Why are you telling me this? How do you know I'm not a part of it?"

"We've been watching you," says the skinhead as he puts on his bomber jacket.

"What you mean is that you have me bugged, don't you?"

"We know you're not a part of any of it, that's the main thing."

"I believe you when you say you only want to find your sister," says the stranger. "And I really wish we knew more."

"Where were you guys when she went missing?" Mason paces with a knot of apprehension that forms between his shoulder blades.

"We don't have surveillance in the back alley," answers the stranger. "Like I said, it was too late. She was already gone by the time we realized anything amiss was happening."

"Well, then who sells her guns?"

"That'd be me and my boys," says the skinhead. "It's compli-
cated, but we had a strong case against your father and his oper-
ations when she was buying from another undercover. Only now
he's in some private rehab for meth and so anything he claims is
inadmissible. He was too messed up to even compile a simple profile
on her. It all turned to shit." He stomps and huffs to the back door
of the truck. "We had to start from scratch last week. It was going
to be my first meeting with her. But she disappeared before I could
even meet her."

"Wouldn't one of the other skinheads look good for her disappearance?"

"You'd think so, but they were all accounted for. They were with
me in the cellar where they manufacture the guns. Still building a
case against them too, but I can tell you straight in the eye, they're
not the ones who took your sister and did that to the cook."

The stranger finishes, "We had this information relayed to the
sheriff of Goshen when we realized she'd been missing. But you
know small-town cops . . ."

"What was his name?" Mason asks, although he already knows
the answer.

The skinhead and stranger both look to Sammy, who looks it up
on his laptop and answers, "Don Mannix. Still waiting to hear back
from him. The guy keeps ignoring us."

"I'm afraid that's all we have about your sister." The stranger spits
the chewing tobacco into his can. "God, I really hate this Skoal shit."

"And no one has any idea what they're going to do with these
guns? I mean, are we talking a lot?"

"Not sure." The skinhead zips up his jacket and cracks his neck.
"Could be aiming for a mosque, a synagogue. Perhaps something as
sinister as what we saw in Oklahoma City. We're talking hundreds
of firearms this year alone."

"You guys have to stop them," Mason orders.

"Legally, we can't." The stranger removes his hat and shakes his hair. "We'd have better luck getting inside Mother Teresa's panties than we do getting into the Third-Day Adventists. Rebekah was really our only shot. They won't even have anything to do with you, their own son, let alone us. They stopped recruiting last year, right when we caught wind of the guns."

Mason sighs with frustration. He slowly walks back toward the doors, only just remembering that outside, Peter waits. "Please, I beg you. Please let me know if you all hear anything?"

For the first time, the stranger seems sincerely sympathetic. "Same for you. Listen, we know the kind of person Rebekah is; we don't think anything in a court of law could even be held against her. But someone's got the reins on her, and finding out who is all we're really after." He holds his hand out and shakes Mason's before he leaves. Mason already knows they mean his father, Virgil.

He jumps down to Peter as the skinhead slams the rolling door after him. He's fast in his pace, Peter rolling the best he can to keep up toward the Bluegrass.

"You find anything out?" Peter stutters.

"I'll tell you on the way."

"On the way to where?"

"To Goshen." Mason stops to light a cigarette. "We're going to visit the sheriff."

33

SPEAK UDDA DEBBLE

In Goshen, Officer James Mattley puts a quarter in the old jukebox at the end of the table and presses F11 to hear a staticky rendition of Patsy Cline's "Crazy" play throughout the roadside diner. If he hadn't stopped for food, he'd have been useless. He plans on shoveling it down as fast as he can before continuing with his investigation. He blows into his third cup of black coffee, the tar-like substance left at the bottom of the pot, and pokes at his chocolate chess pie. "Homemade," the waitress said. Only Mattley can taste the plastic from it sitting too long in the store-bought box, but he says nothing about it.

Between finding the letter from Rebekah Paul to Freedom with Mimi at the nursing home and the brief visit with Violet, the disappearance of Rebekah comes front and center, the mysterious link that holds it all together. But Freedom was still in Oregon when that happened the other day. And it didn't take long to learn the reputation of the Third-Day Adventists. Captain Banks may have taken him off active duty, but Mattley can't just ignore this whole bizarre situation. Moreover, he can't *not* help the woman and forget the fact that there are men after her who burned down her entire apartment complex.

"Why, I almost forgot." The twenty-something-year-old waitress squeezes Reddi-wip topping on his pie. "You just passin' through? Ain't ever seen yer face around here."

"Something like that," Mattley answers as he fakes the enjoyment of his pie. He can't pretend she's not as cute as a button, long brunette hair pulled back, bright blue eyes, and a full set of lips. With no one around except the cooks behind the kitchen window, the waitress sits in the booth opposite Mattley and removes her shoes halfway.

"It's as dead as doornails 'round here this past week."

"Seems so." The cop side of Mattley kicks in. "I passed a property this afternoon with these huge black gates with signs on the outside that said HELL AWAITS YOU and all kinds of weird things. I tried to peek through the gates and trees and saw a bunch of little white houses. What's that all about?"

The waitress laughs as she applies lipstick in the reflection of the jukebox, a shade too red for her face. "That's the old Paul farm, the Church of the Third-Day Adventists." The two of them look up when Sheriff Don Mannix walks in; the jingles of the door ring. "Speak udda debble."

"Heya, Shirley," he says as he removes his Stetson hat and takes a seat at the table right across from Mattley. "Pumpkin pie and coffee, darlin'." As the waitress leaves, he steals a newspaper from the table behind him. He shakes his head and tsks.

"The news nowadays can depress any man," he says, but it doesn't stop the sheriff from flipping through the pages. There's just something about this guy that Mattley doesn't like, but he can't put his finger on what.

"So," Mattley changes the subject. "Shirley was just filling me in about this church I passed on my way through here this afternoon."

"I see." The sheriff raises an eyebrow.

"Being as I might be here a few days, perhaps I can attend a Mass there."

"It ain't open to the public, I'm afraid," the sheriff says as he suddenly pretends to be nose-deep interested in the paper.

"Since when is a church not open to the public?"

The sheriff slams the newspaper on the table. "What the hell, you some kind of reporter or something?"

Mattley puts his hands up. The song comes to an end. You can hear cockroaches fucking if you listen hard enough. "Was just curious, is all."

"We don't need no outsiders nosin' around here with curiosity." Shirley serves the sheriff his pumpkin pie and cup of joe. "Thank ya, darlin'," he says as he immerses himself back in the news.

"Here's your check." She taps her finger on the bill in front of Mattley. "Sir."

"I guess I can take a hint." Mattley tosses a ten on the table and leaves the diner.

By the highway, an eighteen-wheeler labeled REDINDELLY'S PRODUCE with Virginia plates thunders down the road as Mattley returns to his car and reads the check:

Corrupt sheriff, part of cult. If you're here about Rebekah, start with Michelle Campbell. Xo Shirley.

But Mattley waits in his car to see the sheriff's next move.

A car pulls up beside him in the dirt lot. Mattley recognizes him from the Internet after playing around with research about the Third-Day Adventists. Virgil nods to Mattley with a smile, and he nods back. A moment later, the sheriff comes out of the diner and gets into Virgil's car, making sure that Mattley sees his dirty looks before they leave.

But Mattley will give them a head start. He isn't stupid enough to trail them on these country roads; he'd be spotted in no time.

He types "Michelle Campbell" into his phone to see what the Internet will bring up. And for the next half hour, Mattley will dig deeper into the bizarre history of Goshen: the Paul farm, the disappearing girls . . .

34

THE WHIPPING POST

About forty minutes after leaving the Bluegrass, Mason and Peter enter the Goshen Police Department, a one-room jail that dates back to the 1800s with a pillory and whipping post on the small patch of grass in front of the building, a reminder that Goshen held fast to outdated diligence and iron-fisted penalties to criminals and sinners alike, as far as modern law would allow.

A dais faces them, a long desk as soon as they walk in, where a uniformed officer sits: face beet red, beads of sweat around his temples. He sits up and rearranges papers on his desk at a feverish rate, pounds his hand on the wood, and calls attention to a second officer unseen behind a partial wall to the right where they might keep the rare criminal in one of the two cells.

From one of the cells comes the second officer. Mason recognizes him right away: Darian Cooke.

Back in high school, Darian Cooke was the six-foot-seven football jock who would laugh from his keg of a belly in the back row of biology with invitations for sexual exploration under his breath for every girl in class who dared to raise her hand. God, how Mason hated him. The typical popular jockstrap in a varsity letter jacket who'd torture Mason about being the son of a reverend. Always stabbing the backs of his ears with pencils, spitballs to the back of the neck. And here he is, a cop. *Of course he is. As if his head wasn't big enough seven years ago.*

"Well, well, well. Mason Paul. Holy shit," Darian calls out as he tucks his light blue shirt into his trousers. "What brings a celebrity lawyer like you back to this neck of the woods?"

"Hey, Darian, long time no see." Mason tries to stomach his presence and pretend to like the guy. He goes to shake his hand; Darian wipes his on the side of his pants before taking Mason's.

His blond hair is already thinning, his freckles turned to red splotches. "Sorry to hear about your sister. She was a good girl."

"You talk about her like she's dead," Peter says.

Darian Cooke gives him what southerners call the stank-eye, an expression to appropriately reflect his arrogance. As he eyeballs the wheelchair, he asks Mason, "So what can I do you for, anyway?"

"Just doing the best I can to find my kid sister, is all," Mason says, his smile not genuine. "Was hoping you guys can help me out, anything on the investigation. Preferably the police report."

"*Psh*, you're better off asking your folks. They're the ones who gone'n filed it."

"I know, I know," he lies. "I just wanted to have a look for it myself."

"What, you insinuatin' that us small-time folk don't know how to do our jobs?" Darian suddenly gets defensive.

"No, I'm not insinuating that at all. Just covering my tracks, you know."

"No, I don't know," he says, his voice getting louder. "Now I suggest you two be on your way and don't come back unless you have a warrant, you understand? A big-shot lawyer oughtta know that."

"C'mon, Darian," Mason pleads. "You and me, we go a long way back. Can't you just throw me a bone, here?"

"'Fraid not. And I know Sheriff Mannix doesn't have a likin' for you neither, so don't let the door hit you in the ass on yer way out." He joins the second officer behind the desk.

Mason goes to storm out, a mutter under his breath about

cousin-marrying douchebags from Goshen. He curses, resents being here after years of convincing himself that he'd never come back to this hole of a hometown. The faster he can find Rebekah, the faster he can get out of this place. A place where wheat fields as far as the eye can see represent how far away they are from a big, bad world that had Mason's name written all over it when he was young. A place so backward that the pursuit of justice became its own version of injustice, as seen in the occasional lynch mob that seeks their own righteousness by back-alley vigilantism like beatings and chasings out of town. A place where God's grace became a weapon of suppression and acquiescence used by men in authority, big fish in small ponds who have nothing better to do than sit at home, boost their own egos, and jerk off to their own power trips. Darian Cooke is no exception.

Mason stops at the door when he realizes Peter's not by his side. He looks back at him, but he refuses to leave. "Peter, what are you doing?" Mason hisses. Peter says nothing until Mason goes to him.

"I smell pussy," Peter shouts.

"What did you just say?" asks Darian with a narrowed brow, marching back from the dais to look into Peter's eyes.

Peter jolts his head forward to show Darian he won't back down. "I said, I. Smell. Motherfucking. Pussy."

"He's right." Mason jumps to his defense. "Is that why you were sweating when you were coming back from the cell?" He skips to where the cage behind the wall is, only to see a young woman leaning against the wall, shirt unbuttoned and skirt crooked, clearly drunk out of her skull. Peter's right. It does smell like sex. "Oh, just you wait until I call my friend, the state attorney general. He's going to have a field day with this." Mason feels satisfied with this version of revenge.

"Darian, just give him what he wants," frets the second officer, whose badge reads DIX.

"Turn around," Darian demands of Mason.

"Or what? You going to shoot me, Darian?" Mason puts his face close to Darian's, fighting the urge to stand on his toes to better do so. "Go ahead and shoot me if you're so tough."

Darian grabs his upper arm with force and spins Mason around; Peter tries to kick Darian in the shins from his chair, but fails. All four men yell at one another, the scene getting out of control. Peter spits in Dix's face. Darian slaps handcuffs on Mason's wrists. Dix manually pushes Peter's chair out of the building. "Get the fuck out of here." He rolls him out. "Consider it a favor."

"What, no parting gift?" Peter yells back.

Dix pulls a Taser from his belt. "You want a parting gift?"

"I'd think twice before Tasering a retarded man in a metal wheel-chair," Peter shouts.

Dix has to think about this for a moment. Feeling like a bigger idiot for not realizing it first, he spits in Peter's face. "There's your fucking parting gift, you gimp."

Peter whizzes to the corner of the cobblestone street under an old-fashioned gaslight and calls Freedom.

"Where are you?" she asks.

"Stuck in Goshen. Mason just got arrested by some bully cops for sniffing around."

"Jesus Chr—" she starts on the other end. "Sniffing around what?"

"Trying to find Rebekah. It brought us knee-deep into this ATF investigation with skinheads and gunrunning. Looks like the Pauls are involved in some pretty heavy shit."

"Like what?"

"I'll explain it all when I see you. I need to follow up on something right now. Where are you?"

"I'm at a motel in Louisville. I'll think of something to get him out. What about you? Want me to grab you?"

"No, I'm going to take a cab over to someone who might be able to help. Where you staying?"

"Some Motel 6 in the Highlands section."

Peter hears a motorcycle revving in the background on her end of the conversation. "There's a club right next door to where I'm staying, called the Phoenix. Meet there at midnight?"

"I'll see you then. Just get Mason out of there."

"I'll do my best."

"Cops here are all fucking insane. Don't trust them."

"I hadn't planned on it." They hang up.

Peter, who shivers in the cold, looks through his phone at the local yellow pages. He calls a cab first. "And where are you going?"

"I'll know once you're here," he tells the dispatcher. When he hangs up he looks up the phone number and address of Ger Custis, the father of Carol Paul. The clock says 9:30, should be there by 10:00, as long as the taxi dispatcher heeds his *many* requests for a wheelchair-accessible transport this time. He sends a text to Mason with a hope in hell that he gets it:

Meet me at the Phoenix at 12. Still fighting the good fight on this end. We'll find her together.

■ ■ ■

Back inside the Goshen police station, Dix helps Darian Cooke drag an already bloodied Mason into the cell with the girl passed out drunk. Darian handcuffs him to the bars of the cage and pulls his head back by his hair.

"You're not going to get away with this, Darian. You can bet your ass on that," says Mason with a grin full of blood.

The two officers empty his pockets. They mock Mason, with his expensive-looking monogrammed cuff links and his fountain pens, and scatter his business cards on the floor. Darian and Dix take turns hitting Mason. Knuckles are turned raw; adrenal glands detonate. Mason hears a rib or two crack, the occasional sock to the gut that takes his breath away. But he doesn't beg them to stop. He doesn't make a noise in pain. He won't give them the satisfaction of seeing him suffer, they can forget about it. And after a little while of this, what feels like hours of abuse, the officers stop what they're doing when Sheriff Don Mannix walks into the station. At his side, Virgil Paul.

"What in the hell is going on here?" Virgil demands.

Thank God, Mason thinks to himself as he looks up through eyes blurred with tears. He can barely make out his father. "Dad, you can't let these animals do this to me." The men un-cuff him and Mason falls to the floor. On his hip, he uses the bars to pull himself forward toward Sheriff Mannix, who squats to become eye level with Mason.

"These boys wouldn't have done this 'less you gave 'em a damn good reason to."

"Don, you know me."

"I don't know you." The words linger for a few seconds as Mason tries to catch his breath. The sheriff rises while Darian Cooke and Dix leave the cell. "What are we charging him with, anyway?"

"Blackmail," answers Darian. "That's illegal, ain't it?"

"I don't know, Officer Cooke," answers the sheriff. "Is it?" But Cooke doesn't answer. "We can hold him here for the next few days if we have to. Now get back to your paperwork." Don and the officers disappear.

Virgil stares down at his son on the floor. "This is God's doing, for your blatant defiance against the Lord."

Even through the walls of tears glassing over his eyes, Mason sees that his father's wrinkles have paved deeper into his face in the past six years. An inkling of hope sparks in his chest, the hope that after all this time, his father will change his heart, will help Mason, see him as the son that Mason always wanted to be. But it takes all of three seconds to see that this isn't about to happen. Mason sees it in the twisting of his lips, the growing blackness in his eyes that represents his father's soul, if there's even one left: his father is even more adamant in his beliefs, more firm-footed in his corrupted delusions of martyrdom than ever before. His inkling of hope turns into this hardening rage. "I just want to find my sister," he says, the rage boiling behind his face. "I want to know what kind of bullshit you had her involved in, with the guns. What the hell was she doing?"

Virgil locks the door to the cell with a sneer. "Boy, where are you getting these wild ideas from?"

"From the ATF, that's who." A wave of concern sweeps across Virgil's face, and Mason sees him try to subdue it. Mason already regrets telling him.

"You let God handle this family's affairs," says his father. He tosses the keys up in the air and catches them before walking away. "Till then, you can just sit here and mull it over." He and Don Mannix leave together.

Mason tries not to imagine Darian Cooke's semen on the floor he's sitting on. It hurts him to breathe; every inflation of his lungs makes it feel like his ribs are stretching and ready to snap inside of him like twigs being stepped on. It takes all that he has to collect his belongings from the ground.

He stuffs everything back into his coat and feels the phone in his back pocket. *Idiots forgot that.* He reads Peter's text to meet him at the Phoenix. *Wish I could, buddy.* He takes a seat on the bench bolted to the wall, next to the girl, still passed out. He takes his pen and writes on one of the business cards:

Contact me soon. I will help you.

He slips the business card in the pocket of her shirt.

FREEDOM AND DISCOVERY

My name is Freedom and I wander through the dark in my son's home, the son I haven't seen in twenty years. *Thank you, Peter, the one man I can count on to get Mason's address for me.* I learned a time or two in the past, always losing my house keys in a drunken state, that a good pair of earrings can pick almost any lock if you know what you're doing. The alarm system was easy: white rubber buttons with black numbers, faded from being pressed too many times. The numbers were 1, 6, 9, and 0. Mason's birthday is June 19, so I tried 0619. But that didn't work. I entered his birthday backward: 9160. *Bingo.*

In the kitchen, I turn on a lamp that hangs over the center island. In the middle is a glass of merlot. His girlfriend Violet, who I'm always seeing on his Facebook page must have been here; there's lipstick on the rim. The light through the glass of merlot decorates the countertop with red beams, and I wonder if maybe the man who discovered the laser was just a guy with some wine and a lightbulb. I walk into the dark.

I see the suitcases full of clothes on his bed. *Vacation?* I see a backpack. I empty it. I figure I might need some clothes if we're meeting at a club tonight. *Sorry, Violet.* Mason's pillows smell like Head &

Shoulders shampoo. Back in the fridge, I see he likes hummus and healthy snacks. And Heineken, just like his good-for-nothing father. On the door, a note from Violet that reads

With metro police, be back later xoxo V.

I've learned more about my son in five minutes of walking through his house than I have in all these years that stand between now and my last moments with him.

My poor Mason. The way he cried when they arrested me. The way he screamed "Mommy, don't leave me" still stretches out that black cavity in my chest where my heart was ripped out. It turns my guts in knots, that sweet voice of his, so young yet so full of desperation. Feelings like those know no age limit. Children feel desperation, pain, sadness, just the same as adults. And I told him I'd be right back, that I wouldn't be long. And it grinded my insides to mince, trying not to cry in front of him, trying to keep a smile. It felt like I was drowning in my tears from the inside out. I can't take the thought, twenty years later. I take the merlot from the counter and chug it in one, easy swallow.

What the hell am I doing? I don't want my child's first impression of me to be a terrible drunken mess. *Hello, I'm your mother. Watch me piss myself and uppercut a few innocent bystanders and tell you how much I hate you because I have no earthly idea what in hell I'm saying when I'm blackout drunk! Oh, what a glorious fucking reunion this is!* I run to the sink and shove my fingers as far back in my neck as I can to make myself throw up. My nails scratch my throat, my bowels clench with the heaves. I need to get the hell out of here. I need to get him out of jail. I need to find my daughter. I need to move.

But then my cell phone vibrates in my back pocket. Should I answer it? Should I let it ring? The caller ID reads "Mobile Number," with a 631 area code. That's Suffolk County, Long Island, New York. Mastic Beach. That's the Delaneys. It's not Peter's cell number, at least.

"Hello," I answer. My heart feels like it's about to burst its way out of my sternum.

"Hello, my love."

My first words to the Delaneys. I've thought about this a lot over the past two or so decades, what I'd say to them. But words fail me; I freeze.

My heart stops as he continues. "What's the matter? Things getting a little too hot for you back in Oregon?"

Play it cool, Freedom. Play it cool. "Well, a little birdie came to me and told me that you delinquent simpletons were making rounds to see my children." There's a short silence. "Delinquent. D-E-L . . ."

"Fuck you."

"Lovely."

"You know, Nessa. Eighteen years gave me a lot of time to think. A lot of time to paint pictures in my head."

"They let you finger-paint in there too?" I pull Mattley's gun from my boot and place it on the counter on the off chance that he's keeping me on the line to stall me, to corner me. I mean, I know he's not that smart of a man, but any idiot could plan something like it.

Matthew ignores me, his voice as smooth as ever. "It can get awfully lonely in a place like that. And a sweet, innocent thing like Rebekah? With all that fun we had years ago, that time we made love, I suppose your daughter could make a close second."

"When you fucking raped me?"

"You say potato, I say potato," he says. "Either way, you remember when we made love. That was the night you killed my brother."

"My two years in Sing Sing was worth killing your shithead brother. And Matthew, I promise you this. Touch one hair on my daughter's head and I will stick the needle in my own arm and save the state a few tax dollars if it means watching you die right in front of my eyes."

"But Nessa, she even looks like you! Do you not find that romantic? How I still want you after all these years?"

"It's fucking terrible, how you can think of your own flesh and blood like that."

"I guess it is weird. Perhaps illegal in some states, though I don't know about here in Kentucky." He laughs. "But I've had a twenty-year hard-on for you, Nessa."

"Let her go, Matthew." I make sure he can hear the rage burn holes through my vocal cords. "I'll fuck you till the cows come home, if that's what you want. Just let Rebekah go!"

"You know what?" Matthew asks with urgency. "Here's an idea! Why don't you join us?"

"Here's another idea, scumbag. Me for her. A fair trade. You let her go, you can do whatever you want with me, *capisce*?"

"That works for me. La Grange. There's an abandoned warehouse on a lot past the closed-down power plant."

"Let me talk to her."

"She's a little tied up at the moment."

"Then no deal."

Matthew grunts. "For you."

A short silence, then a cough, a woman's cough. "Where am I?" she cries.

And for the first time since she wriggled out of my body twenty years ago, I hear Rebekah. I bury the phone in the heel of my hand so they can't hear my emotions burst out of me uncontrollably, a shriek of relief, of pain, of rage, of longing. Her voice changes everything. This isn't about the Delaneys. I have to get her. Rebekah isn't just a concept, something to move toward. She is real, and I swear I can feel her as if she's standing right next to me.

It's not until I try to speak that I realize all my emotions have complete control over my voice. *Compose yourself. Be strong. Get her.* "And how do you know I won't call the cops?"

"Because you're a fugitive now." He inhales. "And because you want me to keep my beautiful niece Rebekah alive until you get here."

"She's not your—" I start. But he hangs up on me before I can finish the sentence. I punch one of the cabinets and let out a roar.

Stay cool. Don't blow your lid, Freedom. Stop looking at that bottle. Pour it down the sink. Good girl. Now map it out on your GPS. The warehouse is only twenty minutes away. Make sure you have Mattley's gun. Now move. Fucking move. Go get Rebekah.

36

RETIRED

One perk about being confined to a wheelchair is that it's easy to gain a person's trust. "I really ap-ap-appreciate you seeing me, especially th-th-this late," Peter stutters.

"I'm actually happy to see someone's going out of their way to help Rebekah. I, of all people, realize how corrupt the police here really are," Ger Custis says as he pours tea from the kettle into a cup for Peter. "And, like you asked," he says and puts a straw in it.

"You do?"

"Sure," says Ger as he mutes the television in the living room with a remote. The two of them sit around a folding tray stand with their teacups. The heating vents drone from the ceiling, the room full of antique tapestries in the old Colonial two-story home. In a small garbage pail beside his recliner are a couple empty boxes of TV dinners. "My wife went missing four years ago. Took the police around here all but a week to give up on investigating what had happened." He puts his hand in the air.

Peter stares up at a plaque on the wall that reads AS FOR ME AND MY HOME, WE WILL SERVE THE LORD. "It's nothing that the police are looking into, unfortunately. But I'm wondering if they can be related. That's why I'm here. Maybe you wouldn't mind telling me about your wife's disappearance."

"You really want my opinion?" He helps Peter with his straw and pushes a small plate of cheap cookies toward him. "Virgil Paul. I saw him and my little Carol on the news channel. And it's the first time I've seen my Carol in twelve years. I nearly dropped dead at the sight of her. And goodness me, how big Rebekah looked in those pictures they showed. I haven't seen her since she was a tiny thing."

"And what makes you think Virgil had something to do with your wife's disappearance?"

"My wife didn't disappear, she was murdered." He sits back in his recliner in his red flannel pajamas and with a full head of white hair. "I know it. Fifty years of marriage, I knew my wife enough to know she didn't just disappear."

The singing of a mechanical wooden bird interrupts them at half past. "That's some clock you have there," Peter comments.

"Thank you." He crosses his hands over his chest. "Was a hobby of mine until a few years back."

"So, what about Reverend Paul were you saying, Mr. Custis?" Peter says as he chews a stale oatmeal cookie.

"*Psh*, that man has the audacity to call himself a reverend."

"That's right, you were a reverend too, weren't you?"

"Yes, a Methodist." He shakes a cigarette out of a soft pack. "I'm retired, it's OK to smoke. Anyway." He sits up. "I've known Virgil since he was a yuppie in seminary. Was a good kid. I was one of his professors when I taught history. Was a helluva preacher too. But, as it happens with the rare preacher, he lost sight of God and set his focuses on other things. On money, on himself. I suppose people forget that we're only human too." He flicks the ashes into an empty teacup and continues: "Virgil and Carol seemed happy for a long time. Especially when they adopted Mason and Rebekah, they were the happiest family you'd ever seen, or so we thought." Peter sips through his straw and listens with intent. "They became more isolated, his views becoming less and less aligned with what the Bible says about love and humility. He started to become convinced that God spoke to him, that he told him the exact hour of his return. He found ways to take scripture out of context for his own advantage. It was as if overnight the gates went up and that was it. And believe me, we tried our hearts out to reach them. We called the police and everything. But there was nothing we could do. He had Carol under his spell, along with a good-size congregation who stayed with him during this transition. Many had left, stories here and there about what happened with the Third-Day Adventists. But you know rumors in small towns, like playing the game telephone. And that was it." He rubs his brow. "Peter, do you believe in God?"

"No, but I get it," he answers honestly. "As a believer in God, what do you think of the dreams Virgil claimed to be having?"

"I'd say it was one of two things. Virgil is either psychotic or evil."

"Is there a difference between the two?"

"Psychotic people will do bad things because they can't help themselves, they don't understand it's wrong. Evil men do bad things because they *know* they're wrong and *can* help themselves."

"Do you think he could be capable of murdering your wife or granddaughter?"

"I couldn't even pretend to know the man enough to answer. But let me tell you about Adelaide, my wife." He cracks open a can of beer. "I'm retired, it's OK to have one a night," he justifies. "Adelaide was the stern one between us. I was the softie, the one the girls would talk to about personal things. But Adelaide was a strong woman, in body and in spirit. As a Christian, she never questioned God when Carol went into isolation. She never questioned God when Clare hung herself a few years after that. I can't say it was the same for me, but Adelaide was what got me through it.

"But I think in many ways, Adelaide only appeared to be as strong as she was. Between Carol and Clare, I think a good part of her died. But she stayed strong, if only for me." Ger pulls at the Budweiser can. "And four years ago, I don't know what encouraged the choice, but she was dead set on getting into the Third-Day Adventists." He smiles at the thought. "She was ready to put up a tent in front of those gates, I tell ya. And I insisted I go with her. But she said no. Said she needed the drive to herself so she could think. She always liked to think when she drove, liked to pray behind the steering wheel of a car, for whatever reason." He becomes distracted. "God, she was the most beautiful woman you'd ever lay eyes on, I mean a knockout."

"Was that when she disappeared?"

"When she didn't return that night, I knew something happened. I reported it to the police, but they said I had to wait twenty-four hours, and I waited. It was the longest twenty-four hours of my life."

"And that was it?"

"That was it. Except they found her car a week later in the Ohio River. But there was no sign of Adelaide. Police said she probably drowned outside the vehicle." He uses his sleeve to wipe away a tear from his face. "Carol and those kids are the only living family I have left. And Virgil has stolen that from me."

"I'm really sorry."

"Not as sorry as me." Ger coughs. "All those souls wasted on that evil man and his cult."

Trying to distract the old man from thoughts of his wife and daughters, Peter says, "You know, I never got into history, myself. I was always bored by the subject."

Ger smiles at Peter. "Think of your favorite movie, or your favorite book." The subject seems to put a gleam in Ger's eye. "Now imagine only ever seeing the last scene, or reading the last chapter. You'd have no earthly idea what the heck was going on, would you?"

"I see."

"The same thing as now. We can't understand anything about this world without knowing what led to here, what happened before us."

Peter finds this a good point, but he has to get something off his chest. "Mr. Custis, did you not know that Mason isn't a part of that cult anymore?"

Suddenly, the sorrow in Ger's eyes is replaced with something that might be hope. "He's not?"

"No, and I hate to say it, but he thinks you're dead." Peter starts to head for the door. "And I know he'd love to see you. He's turned out to be a good man."

"Why, that'd be wonderful." He stutters, can't seem to catch all the words trying to escape him at once. "Would you tell him for me? Nothing in this world would make me happier." Ger opens the door and holds it for Peter. He shakes his head in disbelief.

"By the way, why did you stop making these? They're amazing." Peter points to the cuckoo clock on the wall.

"The last one I made my wife took with her to bring to Carol in hopes that she'd get to see her. After that, it only became a reminder of my dead wife."

Peter looks down at the cell phone he stole from his mother. Eleven missed calls. A text:

Smile! We finally have the bitch! :D

37

FREEDOM AND SURRENDER

My name is Freedom and I stop the motorcycle beside a car with New York plates. When I turn it off, the silence is deafening. I can just about hear the burning of the stars above me. Ahead, a building of loose siding, rotting in isolation. Behind it, a silhouette formed by moonlight, the steel of an old power plant etched against an icy sky, a long and distant curtain of steel and hazardous waste. I think about letting the air out of the Delaneys' tires; that's what instinct tells me to do. But then they might have to take me to her. Things might not end well if I do that. Actually, I don't see them ending well at all.

I stand in front of their car and my bike. I force my shoulders upright, leave the fear behind. I build up the rage, the determination I have for getting my daughter out of here. It all collects into a ball in the pit of my lungs and rises to my throat.

"Matthew!" I scream with all the power I have in my windpipe. "Here I am." An animal scurries in the tall grass beside the warehouse. There's no other response but for the high-pitched squeaks of bats that zip from a few trees. "Matthew!"

I breathe it in. The night. The cold. The darkness. God help anyone who stands in the way between me and my daughter. *Remember, you are not a sad case anymore, you are not Nessa Delaney. And don't revert back to Nessa when in their company. You are Freedom. You are strong, unbreakable. You are the monster they fear, their worst motherfucking nightmare.*

But still, there is no answer.

My phone vibrates with a text:

Come inside.

I have to use all my might to push open a sliding wooden door; I grunt with the force. Bundles of hay and farming equipment decorate the abandoned space, the smell of years-old gasoline seeped into the ground. The door slamming open sends an echo through the warehouse, a gust of wind blowing back. Stillness.

My steps make the floorboards creak; moonlight pierces the spaces between the wooden planks that make up the walls. I listen for any kind of life, but instead I'm met with the wind hissing through the space. Somehow, though, I can feel Rebekah here, like a sweet breath that stands out from such a bleak place. I smell the trace of cigarette smoke when I hear the steps above me. A loft, Matthew front and center, looking down on me.

"Nessa, Nessa, Nessa." His voice calm.

I look up at him. Don't let him see me sweat, see me tremble. "I'm here."

His smile slices through the shadows; I feel it in the roots of my hair. "So you are."

"And Rebekah?"

"But of course, love." He looks over his shoulder. Luke and John join Matthew at the edge of the loft, a landing with no railing. The brothers manhandle Rebekah by the elbows, her hands tied behind her back, a hood over her face. She screams, but there must be something in her mouth. I think my heart stops beating. This is my daughter. This is her, in the flesh, at the hands of the most psychotic people to have ever walked the planet.

"We have a deal?" I call up. "I'm unarmed, alone. Just let me have her, and I'm all yours. You have my word."

"Your word?" He laughs. "Sure."

"Don't—" I start to scream. But before I can, the men push her from the loft. She screams. I run. It's natural, perhaps my first push of maternal instinct. Like a ton of bricks, she falls on top of me, but I break her fall. I can't catch my breath on the impact, but hearing the men's footsteps run down to me does the trick.

I lift Rebekah up by the back of her pants. "I need you to stand, honey." I whisper to her. The men charge us like a wall, shadows becoming more recognizable the closer they get. I push her in front of me, but she falls; one of her legs is not working. I reach for the gun. It's not there. *Where the fuck is it?!*

There's nothing to defend myself with: no wooden beams, no crowbar, nothing convenient like you see in the movies. *Think, Freedom.* But there's no time to think. I get in front of her and try to gently shove her with my back.

I unbuckle my belt and yank it through the denim loops of my pants. A line of rope burn bites my hips. As soon as Matthew's face is close enough to see, I use the buckle's end to whip him across the face. I can feel the sting from here. Luke and John try to tackle me, but I rip through the darkness with the leather strip, my aim impressive, even to me. "You stay the fuck away from her!" I scrape the floor with my boot, hoping to find the gun with my foot. In the corner of my eye, I see Rebekah feel her way out with her shoulders, head covered and hands still tied. She finds her way out the door.

Matthew raises his hands. "This is my revenge, boys." He brings his hand to his face. "Go get our niece." They follow her.

We're alone. When he looks back at me, I feel nothing but the abyss that replaces his soul. My heel shifts the gun on the ground. Only felt like forever to find it. I whip him again, hard enough that it sends pins all the way up to my elbow, this time across his chest, just to keep him back for a second while I fetch the pistol off the ground. He grunts, but I can't tell if it's in pain or pleasure.

"Looks like it's just the two of us," he pants.

"Why couldn't you just leave her alone?" With my finger on the trigger, it takes everything in me not to let it move.

"It wasn't her I wanted to begin with. I only wanted you." In the shadows, I can see his grin curl upward. "It was all a means to get to you."

"Yeah, well, here I am."

"So I see." It could have been romantic, given any other place. At any other time. With any other person. Under any other circumstances. I swear I can feel the welts start to rise on his skin. Instead of words, our minds race to twenty years ago, the same memories but different experiences, different perspectives. The silence gets under my skin, I can't take it. Not only do I want to break it, I want to shatter it so it can never be repaired again.

"Rebekah isn't your niece." I let the gun down and take a step closer to him. "She is your daughter." I put the gun in my jeans to show him I have no intention of shooting him. I reach over and take his hand. Mine fits perfectly in his. My words seem to have stopped his breath.

"That night ..." His voice raspy, choking at the attempt to whisper.

"Yes, that night." I put my palm on his chest, feel his heart race. I imagine myself ripping inside of him and squeezing the blood from his heart until it simply stops. I kiss his collarbone and press my body against his. I think about the oils of his skin staining my lips and the thought makes me want to gag. *Move slow. Don't be too jumpy around him. Gain his trust, even if it's for this second. As much as you hate him, gain his fucking trust.*

"When we made love ..." His voice is unchanging.

I kiss a trail from his shoulder to his back, fight the urge to pull his spine out with my teeth from the base of his neck. *Get behind him, that's the plan. Keep him enthralled. I'm holding the cards. Seduce him. Stay calm.* "I think about that night all the time," I say. In this, I tell the truth. I caress his torso from behind him.

He can't finish his sentences, just lets them trail off into the hollowness of this place. "Our daughter . . ."

"*My* daughter." In a rapid sweep, I put the belt around his neck and pull hard enough that we both fall down. Lying on my back, he wriggles on top of me, his back on my chest. I wrap my legs around him and pull until his kicking and thrashing becomes random jerks and spasms. When I let go of the belt, I feel the life return to my face, to my airways.

It drains me for a moment; my attempts to push him off me are weak. He's not dead. Only because killing him wasn't my intention. Matthew isn't worth it, isn't worth the spit on my shoe. I press my fingertips onto the artery in his neck to confirm he's alive. His pulse is faint but present. That's what counts.

I check the gun in the back of my pants. Not putting the belt back on. *No, that can stay around Matthew's neck, a leash for the dog that he is. I'm not going to leave him here. I'll use him as ammo, use him as bait. Pull.*

His backside scrapes against the sawdust and hay. It's not as simple as dragging him across the ground; I have to give a few firm yanks to pull him forward. Dead weight. I remember this heaviness from when I dragged his own brother, my husband's corpse, across our home. When I leave the warehouse, the chill of autumn dries the sweat of my brow. Luke and John can't see me yet, not from the trunk of the Delaneys' car. I pause for half a minute to catch my breath. The distance between us is short, but the darkness is deep. They taunt and push Rebekah around like dogs fighting over scraps. Two words dominate the millions of thoughts that ricochet inside my skull: *Get Rebekah.*

I become fixed at the concept, unstoppable. I find that I cannot plan my next move, don't really think about it. I run on autopilot, like my mind can't think of what to do next but my body does. I'm going to have to just let my body lead the way. Because all I can think about is getting Rebekah the fuck out of here.

"Well, well," they call out when they see me, all whistles and hollers. But what they don't see is their brother's unconscious body dragging behind me, his neck at the other end of my belt. When they do, they freeze; Rebekah falls to her knees, sobbing.

"Open the trunk," I tell them. I put the toe of my boot on the buckle of the belt to hold it on his neck, make them see me give a good tug with my right hand. With my left, I aim the gun at their faces and scream, "I said open the fucking trunk."

They look at each other. Right, like either of them know what to do in a situation like this. Luke is the one to open the trunk. "Get in." They don't seem angry. They don't seem scared. They only seem to be taking me seriously. They crawl in, stiff in the fetal position. I take the keys. "And your phones."

"You're not going to get away with this, you stupid—"

I interrupt John's sentence by slamming the trunk door down on them. I shoot out the tires, then throw the car keys into the tall grass as far as I can. Rebekah leans against the car, her cries stifled by a burlap hood. "Rebekah." I help her up. There's no time for introductions; Matthew's starting to wake up and the boys are making quite the racket.

"Follow my voice." I get on and start the bike before helping her on behind me by keeping my arm on her so she feels my fingertips at the top of her chest. I pinch her clothes and pull her closer. "We need to hurry. Use the good leg and get behind me on the bike. I'm getting you out of here."

I haul ass. With her hands still behind her back, Rebekah squeezes me with the insides of her thighs to maintain her balance as I speed out of there. She screams in pain through the bandanna tied around her mouth, her cries coming out of her ears. "Hang tight!"

I breathe for the first time leaving La Grange, a gulp at the air where I never felt more alive. But I'm not in the clear yet. I'll have to stop soon.

I turn when I see a grassed-over trail that leads through the forest, maybe five miles from the warehouse. I go in as deep as the path takes me until I'm sure we're safe. When I turn the bike off, I listen to hear if anyone's following. So far, we've made it. I use my heel to put the kickstand down and help Rebekah off the bike. She cannot walk after the fall. I carry her and lean her against a tree. "You're OK. You're safe now."

I sit beside her in the pitch black and lean my back against the same tree as her. I can't even see my hand in front of me. I take off the hood and I feel my back pockets until I find a lighter. I use it to untie the knots on Rebekah's wrists. And so this is it. This is my first meeting with my daughter. *My daughter.* While circumstances of the reunion are far from ideal, thank God she's safe. Thank God she's OK. She frees her hands, rips the bandanna from her mouth. She pants and swallows the fresh air, coughing to catch her breath. It's too dark to see her face.

"Relax, now. You're fine," I tell her.

She forces steady breaths, her gasps wet with spit and snot. "Who the hell are you?" she demands.

"My name is Freedom." I don't know what to say yet. This wasn't how I planned it. But I'm OK with this. As long as she's away from the Delaneys. It takes all that I have not to grab her, to hold her tight, to run my hands through her hair. It takes all that I have not to sob like a baby into her neck, to breathe her in.

"They thought I was Rebekah."

Why the fuck did you just refer to yourself in the third person?

I hadn't before gotten a good look at her face. I put the flame between us. My heart sinks. If I wasn't already sitting down, my knees might buckle below me. "You're not Rebekah."

"No," she wheezes. "I'm her brother's girlfriend. I'm Violet."

Fuck. The blood from my heart pools in my stomach. I try to swallow hard, but I can't manage to. It feels like my ribs have sharpened themselves to daggers and are stabbing my heart to bloody shreds. Over and over I hear my head say *You're not Rebekah, you're not Rebekah, you're not . . .*

"I know your face," she says. "A man visited me today, looking for you."

I lean my head against the bark. My face scrunches with a sob, but I hide it in the dark and try to force something, something that I might say if I wasn't so consumed by devastation. "I've no doubt about it."

"Does Mason know you?"

I sigh with a forced groan. "Once upon a time."

▪ ▪ ▪

My name is Freedom and I help Violet's broken body limp into the waiting room of a hospital. I think it's the fact that she dresses like a rich little girl that she's taken in before the drunks and the vagrants looking for a warm spot to stay. That's fine by me.

I close the curtain around us as the nurses become busy and leave us. I inspect the bruises on her wrists from being tied up, see the swelling of her leg even through her skirt.

"There was a cop who came by to see me while I was on my way out," she starts. "After he left, I ran back in the house. When I came back out, they were there. They asked me if I was Rebekah. I guess they hadn't heard the news of her being missing. And that was the last thing I remember." She feels under her hair, winces when she finds a knot.

"You're OK now." I try to comfort her. But I think she can sense my disappointment, no matter how hard I try to hide it. With the nurses away for the time being, I go through the backpack that I took from Mason's house and change into the clothes I stole from Violet. I'm sure she realizes they're hers. That's OK. Gotta get to the club. I'll keep my boots on for the ride and slip on her heels once I'm there. I let her watch me leave Mattley's gun in the backpack. Yep. I can tell in her face she recognizes the stuff. She gives me a nod. I thought she'd be a little more objecting about it and was ready to tell her to shut the fuck up and take the gun anyway.

"I heard those men talking," she says. "You're Mason and Rebekah's mother. . . ."

What am I supposed to say to that? I just stare at her without a word. What's the point?

A nurse appears from behind the curtain. "Ma'am, are you family?" she asks me.

"I was just leaving." And off I go. I can't get distracted. I have to remember that Rebekah is still out there. Somewhere. I'm caught in this medium: between dragging my feet with disappointment over Violet not being my daughter and racing to actually find Rebekah. In this brief state, I must catch my breath. Think. Swallow all that has happened.

Out in the parking lot of the hospital, I skim through John's cell phone until I reach "Mom."

"This is Lynn. Leave me a message and I'll get back to you soon."

"Hello, Lynn," I start. "I suppose I don't need to make the introduction, you'll know who this is. Your sons failed. You're never going to find me. You're never going to find my children. It's a shame. Pathetic, really. All these years, you've been driven by your own hatred toward me. But I have no shame in the fact that without any effort, I could still keep you from happiness, keep you bitter." I swallow; I think about how the same was reciprocated. "Unhappy you will stay. Bitter you will be. And as for me? I will stay free."

Meanwhile, Peter, who still had the phone he stole from Lynn the day he left New York, listens to Freedom's message on Lynn's voice mail. He can't help but smile.

Now that I no longer have to worry about the Delaneys, I can focus. Break time's over. Now. Go get Rebekah.

■ ■ ■

In Mastic Beach, Lynn Delaney still can't get herself up from the floor. It took all the strength she had to pull one knee forward, push an arm past it. This could be called crawling. But with Lynn, it's a project. Over a period of several hours, she finally made some headway over the carpet. And while she had the option to crawl to the front door and call for help, a choice that might very well save her life, she passed the door and went to the adjacent kitchen.

The chilled box of wine on the bottom shelf of the refrigerator will ease her distress. The water is a close second. *How long are they going to fucking be?! Not even one visitor to help!*

She rolls up fistfuls of Boar's Head ham and dunks them into the jar of mayonnaise before stuffing them into her face. *I raised a bunch of good-for-nothing bastards.* In the bottom drawer, a carton of Newports, chilled to keep them from going stale. She opens a pack and pulls out a cigarette. She's able to reach above her and pull the cord to the toaster. She pulls it down to her side and lights her smoke off the blazing red zigzags inside. *Good-for-nothing bastards.*

38

FREEDOM McFLY

I am a boy, back in the arms of this redheaded stranger in the ocean. The people back on the shore are small, faceless. I use my hand to wipe the hair from her face, her smile brighter than the sun that warms my shoulders. A sky, clearer than glass, is interrupted by a banner trailing a small yellow airplane that buzzes through the summer. "Look, an airplane with a flag!" I squeal.

The redheaded stranger looks up, her hand over her forehead to shield her eyes from the sun. "Look, Ethan," she says in my ear. But I don't know why she calls me Ethan. "It's a superhero plane with a cape."

"Wow, a superhero plane! What does that flag say?"

The woman points to the plane's banner and replies, "Freedom."

"That's the superhero plane's name?"

"That's right," she smiles. "We can call him Freedom McFly."

"Go, go, Freedom McFly," I yell with my hands up as the plane soars over our heads.

"Now." Her face close to mine. "Where is your sister?"

Mason jumps up to the sound of a man shouting, "Get him the fuck out of there, right now." The short nap makes his head pound. The beating he's just endured doesn't help. A stranger marches toward him on the other side of the cell. His accent's not local.

"You guys can expect to be hearing from the attorney general in regards to this," he says as he walks toward Mason to examine his wounds. "C'mon, Mason. We need to get you the hell out of here."

"Who are you?" Mason asks him.

Mattley ignores him and directs his words toward Darian Cooke and Dix. "Whatever bogus charge you have him on better disappear, you understand? Tell your sheriff once he gets back that he should start looking for a new job." He helps Mason up and leaves the cell, stopping right in front of the officers. "The same goes for you two."

After hearing of Rebekah's disappearance and the peculiar circumstances back at the diner, Mattley thought it best to head to Goshen Police Department to try to get to the bottom of things. He had to suppress his surprise at finding Mason locked up in there, after recognizing him from his research on the Internet. In seeing him heavy-eyed and waking from a dream, he imagines Freedom in a different way. It takes him seeing Mason in the flesh and blood to view her as more than this woman he has a crush on from back in Oregon, more than a woman with a severe drinking problem, more than the bartender at the Whammy Bar, more than a woman who lives in a shitty apartment. It takes seeing him in person to realize that she has a history far richer than anyone could imagine. She is a grieving mother. She is a woman stopping at nothing to find the children she never knew, a woman who had sacrificed everything at the risk of suffering more than he can imagine. He finds himself wondering, *Who ever thinks about the birth parents of adopted children? Adopted children everywhere, adoptive parents everywhere, even celebrities. But who the hell ever thinks what's behind the curtain? What the context was? Who thinks of the suffering on the other end when all we see is the one side, the face value?*

Through the bars, Mattley studies Mason, looking at exactly what she had sacrificed. Flesh and blood. Freedom's own flesh, her own blood, stretched from coast to coast. And Mattley can finally see exactly what she's fighting for, striving for, running to. It makes sense only when he sees him. And Mattley sees no other way than helping Freedom, even without her knowing.

They say nothing as he and Mason leave the police station. Only Mason, pretending to accidentally trip into Darian Cooke, lifts his police badge from his belt and sneaks it under his shirt.

Mattley helps him to his car, Mason's grunts echoing through the stillness of the night, their breath visible in the cold. "Where's Peter?" he moans as he sits behind the wheel of his Mercedes with Mattley's assistance. "Who the hell are you?"

Mattley closes the door after him as Mason opens the driver's-side window. "I'm a police officer from Oregon; I'm helping with the disappearance of your sister," he answers.

"Oregon . . ." He trails off. "I'd heard Rebekah was trying to get to the West Coast," he says, remembering the information he received from Gabriel back at the hospital. Mason leans his head on the steering wheel, frustrated. He suddenly remembers that he's supposed to meet Peter at the Phoenix back in Louisville. "Listen, I'm sorry, I can't stay and talk." He starts the car. "Send the bill for my bail to my office. I promise to repay you."

"It's not about the—" Mattley starts.

"Listen, if you really want to help"—he reaches into his pocket and grabs another business card from his firm, just like the one he handed the drunk girl in the jail, a sense of urgency making his joints twitch as he jots something on the back—"find Joe. He's with the ATF. He'll be a helluva lot more help than me. Tell him what's going on, that the sheriff is behind something." Mason hands him the card and drives off in a hurry. Mattley's face heats up when not able to get a word in edgewise. There's so much to be said, so much to explain.

But Mattley, seeing Mason's rush, wakes to the grasp of solving Rebekah's disappearance not just as a priority, but as a time-sensitive matter. He reads Mason's words and gets a move on to find Joe, who should be at, according to Mason, the Bluegrass bar.

Mason leaves Mattley alone in the parking lot, and as he fades away from sight, Mason drives down the roads where the streetlights stop burning. He feels more alone than ever. Stillness, unlike anything. He pulls over and cries.

"God, if You're there, and if You give a shit about me, help me. Help me, Lord. Hear my prayer in my hour of need." He goes on to recite the Twenty-Third Psalm of David. *"Yea, though I walk through the valley of the shadow of death, I will fear no evil: for thou art with me . . ."* The desperation feels new to him, his cries to God almost regretful as he'd just about convinced himself that God did not exist. But left this vulnerable, in praying, Mason doesn't know what else to do.

Get a grip, Mason. He swallows the wariness of what the future might hold, a new wave of determination, like he can, and just might, take the world head-on. He wipes away the tears, almost feeling embarrassed by them, though there is no one around to be embarrassed in front of. *Let's do this.*

Forty minutes later, Mason enters the Highlands section of Louisville, a lively part of the city full of faux-Tudor buildings and old Victorian homes turned into apartments. A big sign stands high in the heart of the district, all black with white typewriter font that reads KEEP LOUISVILLE WEIRD.

The sidewalks swarm with women with shaved heads, colored hair, and steel protruding from their faces. A lot of hippie types, a lot of gothic. The corners are decked with local musicians with tin cups and open instrument cases, lots of indie rock. Mason looks at the clock when he parks in an alley. 11:45. The smell from the nearby Vietnamese restaurant fills his nostrils, scabbed over on the inside with dried blood. Parked behind a Dumpster, he grabs some spare clothes in the back, ones he keeps for the days when he wants to head to the pool hall with the guys straight after work without going home to change. He walks through the back door of a tattoo parlor, but meets with a sign: RESTROOM FOR CUSTOMERS ONLY.

Mason pulls out a hundred-dollar bill and holds it up to the lone tattooist as he works on the calf of another man. "In the back." The man jerks his head. "Wash your hands. This is a sterile crib." Mason leaves the bill on a glass countertop.

Death metal plays from the parlor, something that sounds akin to James Earl Jones belching underwater.

Under the sink in the small bathroom painted black, Mason grabs one of the small garbage bags they use for the bathroom pail. He peels off his sweaty and bloodied clothes and puts them in the bag. He takes a birdbath in the sink, scrubs the dirt and dried blood down the drain. He pulls out a wad of paper towels from the dispenser and pats himself dry before he slips into a pair of light blue denims and a fresh, white undershirt and a brown leather jacket.

On his way out, as the tattooist isn't paying attention, Mason takes his hundred-dollar bill back and heads for the Phoenix nightclub just a couple blocks over. He hopes that there, he will find Peter. Answers. Explanations. If anyone can shed some light on any of this, it might be Peter, if he can convince him. And if he leaves now, he can just make it on time.

39

THE SHADOWS OF THE PHOENIX

My name is Freedom and I'm glad Peter picked a place like this, a place where we could easily hide and grab a few drinks. I have to hang on to the hope that Rebekah is still alive. Hope. Without hope, a person is as good as dead.

People's faces are shadows in the red lights that thrash all over the Phoenix. The bass of the trance music rattles my body. Drinks sparkle when brought to the lips of those around me. The strobe lights blaze and I am reminded of my youth, when my tits were perkier, ass tighter, tattoos more vibrant. Nothing ages a person faster than grief.

In my mind, the music fades. The people disappear to the back of my perception. The bass of the trance music is replaced with the pounding of my heart, someone with a hammer beating on my chest bone to shatter my skeletal structure from the inside out. My knees become rubber, my mouth full of sand. All this, when Mason enters the club. And in this moment, he is the only one here. We are the only two people on the planet.

I am too consumed with awe to remind myself that I might kill Peter for arranging this. I wasn't prepared to meet Rebekah, though it turned out not to be her, anyway. And I'm certainly not prepared to meet Mason. I retreat to the shadows of the Phoenix, curtains of darkness I can hide behind. But I never take my eyes off my son. My son. The concept is dreamlike; it feels foreign on my tongue when I say it out loud.

My fingers trace a gold banister as I walk along the edges of the floor. It's not until I feel light in the head that I realize I haven't breathed for minutes. But I have to get out, I can't let Mason see me. He can't know I'm here. No, I can't do the whole confrontation thing, I can't turn his world even more upside down than it already is. It's bad enough I let a letter to Rebekah already slip through my fingers. It's worse that I was left to show myself to Violet. But I have to pass Mason to get the hell out of this fucking place.

I elbow through the ravers, shouts that no one can hear anyway. I take a red Cardinals baseball cap from a girl in a slutty baseball uniform, blacklight paint in her hair, and a pair of glow sticks, a long stretch of my arm through a huddle so she can put the blame on someone else. But a panic attack starts to rear its ugly head, and suddenly I'm drowning in hundreds of college kids howling at the colored lights and gyrating against one another. I become lost, suffocated in lust bastardized by kids who can't even see straight, but who the hell am I to talk?

I fall, surrounded by legs dancing across the floor, and no one can see me. If there is a special place in hell for dancers, this must be the place. Toes slide across the dark floor; above me is what looks like a million glow sticks creating an ecstasy addict's sky. I try to get up, I try not to get trampled on this dirty ground, but the dancers, blissfully unaware, keep me from rising. I pinch people's knees, I reach above me and pull on their shirts, I scream for someone, anyone, to let me the fuck up.

I try to crawl on my hands and knees when I feel someone's arm around my stomach to jolt me to my feet. I am faced by a million masks, angels and devils and vampires and the dead. My heart races, everything around me spins. And when I turn around to see who'd helped me, I am faced with Mason. But it's not Mason I see. It's Mark. Mason's father. My dead husband.

He's the same height as Mark at a good six feet; his eyes just as intense, like they stretch inward for miles. But where are the fireworks? Where are the open fields of flowers where we run in slow motion into each other's arms? Where is the part where we pick up from where we started and I miraculously know everything about my son that I've missed for twenty years? And I realize, despite the fact that this child swam in my own blood for nine months, I am looking into the eyes of a stranger. He mouths words, but I can't hear what he's saying. And what do I do?

I turn around and leave. *Consider this a favor, Mason.*

But Mason follows. I walk faster. Now he walks faster. I slam the back door of the club hard behind me when I leave. Mason slams it open. The music behind us becomes sunken compositions buried behind walls, and the scraping of our shoes on the grass grows louder as the ringing in my ears fades. "Wait a second," Mason yells behind me.

This isn't how it's supposed to be; you're not supposed to recognize me. Go back to your Bible bullshit and stay out of my way. If I wanted you to know who I am, I would have made sure you knew. You don't want to meet me; you deserve to have someone better as a mother. You deserve to carry on living in ignorant bliss. Now, these are the things I mean to say. But it's not exactly what spews out from my mouth. "You stay the fuck away from me, Mason, you understand? You don't know me." I run for the lights of the city, the noises of street performers.

"Will you just wait a fucking second?" he yells after me.

And say what you will about women my age, but I can haul ass. I flip off my heels. They fly away and land somewhere in the wet grass. I move, knees to chest. But this guy just won't fucking give up! The glares of woodwinds, the lights that bleed from the hazy flea markets, the headlights and whores of Bardstown Road. Some reunion this shit is turning out to be.

I crash my elbows through a glass door as a man's about to lock up and close for the night. I figure it will be dark. I figure it will be quiet. I figure I can lock the door behind me and tell the owner that a man is after me.

"What the hell are you doing?" the dark-skinned shopkeeper yells with a Middle Eastern accent as he holds the door shut with his body.

"You have to let me in," I say as I shove the other side of the door with my shoulder. "I'm being chased by a madman. Let me the fuck in!" I slap the glass until my palms are sore. And as the shopkeeper and I play this game of tug-of-war with a glass door and scream profanities at each other, the blow of Mason running behind me and pushing the door open knocks the shopkeeper down on his ass. With the sudden thrust from Mason, we nearly fall into the store together. This is it. This is the reunion I pictured time and time again in my head turning into one giant, disastrous clusterfuck. Twenty years of yearning and heartbreak finally crashing through a cheap pane of glass.

I look around and realize we're in an empty Arabic restaurant and hookah bar. I avoid eye contact with Mason, but I feel him staring. "We'll take an order of falafel and one order of baklava," I say, and I don't know why I'd say something so stupid, perhaps panic.

"You crazy woman, we're closed! You get out! You get out or I call police!" he yells from the floor.

"I am the police," Mason responds as he pulls a police badge from his back pocket. "Feel free to call Goshen PD to confirm it. The name's Deputy Sheriff Darian Cooke; want me to spell it out for you?" The Arab looks at the two of us with wide eyes. "Now I believe the lady asked for some fluffa and block something-or-other." The shopkeeper turns and walks fast for the back room. Mason turns to me, "And you," he demands. "You can sit your ass over in that booth there."

In the otherwise dark restaurant, a glass counter glows with wrapped platters of grape leaves and olives, cheeses, and breads. The hum echoes against the linoleum of the floor; the smell of vanilla-flavored tobacco resin in cold hookahs and rotisserie lamb encases us. The leather of the burgundy booth shifts as I slide over. Mason sits across from me.

"You realize the owner is calling the police right now," I say.

"I know."

"You're not Darian Cooke."

He slides the police badge across the table. "I know."

I pull out Mattley's badge from my back pocket and do the same. "Birds of a feather."

He takes my pack of smokes, holds them up, and raises an eyebrow. "I take it you're not James Mattley?"

"Do you know who I am?" I ask him.

"Freedom McFly," he says, his voice soft, still raspy, the way it was when he was a young child.

"Those were the terms I made with the whippersnappers; I would only go to Or-ree-gan if that was what they called me. Freedom McFly, though I never got to keep the McFly part. They said it sounded too Burger King–ish. Too '80s. Fucking whippersnappers."

"What whippersnappers?" But I don't give an answer, to which he tilts his head with confusion and changes the subject. "I remember the beach, the ocean. I remember Freedom McFly, the plane."

"I'm surprised you remember so much." I try to keep my hands out of his sight so he can't see them tremble. The nerves make my lips twitch. *Take a deep breath. Don't fuck this up any more than it already is.*

"It makes sense." He blows smoke and flicks ashes to the floor. The lights from the streets reflect onto his face with streaks of red as he gazes out the window. "I just don't know how I didn't see it sooner," he says, his voice surprisingly calm.

"Hindsight's a bitch." I clear my throat. "I, of all people, would know."

Mason speaks to his own reflection like he isn't listening to me. "You'd call me Ethan and would ask me where my sister is."

"Once upon a time, you were named Ethan Delaney." I rub my palms together between my thighs. "And your sister was Layla Delaney." I show a flicker of a smile. "That was my favorite song . . ." I trail off.

"Just to confirm . . . you are my mother, aren't you?"

I sigh. "Once upon a time." I swear I hear his brain spinning from here. He looks around, as if somewhere in a Middle Eastern hookah bar in the middle of Louisville, Kentucky, are the answers to a million questions, questions he can't seem to grab. I break some of the ice that holds his emotions, frozen. "You had a birthmark on your left knee. Your first word was 'get,' after hearing me say it so many times to a chocolate Lab named Mickey we used to own. Your favorite food used to be macaroni and cheese and you had a blanket with dinosaurs on it and a tan couch pillow you'd never part with. You wouldn't even let me wash them, so I'd have to wash them while you'd sleep." Mason listens while I put out my smoke on the windowsill and continue. "You have brown eyes like your father and your right one has a tiny speck of yellow at the top. You were born on June nineteenth at eleven forty three p.m., but the doctors wrote eleven forty five p.m. because the midwife who delivered you was a dunce with an ugly shade of lipstick and a mustache."

"And Peter?"

"Your uncle."

"Where was I born?" he asks, and I'm not sure if he's genuinely curious or just testing me. After all, he is my own blood, so the latter's likely.

"Stony Brook University Hospital, Long Island, New York."

Mason looks up at the corner of the room. I can see different waves of emotion wash over his face, the ebb and flow of anger, confusion, frustration, realization, the works. "And Rebekah?"

"I wish I knew more of her." The rattles of the antibiotics in my pocket remind me to take the pill. "I'd only known her for two minutes and seventeen seconds. Yes, I counted." I inspect the one half of Mason's face that isn't concealed by the shadows. Under his eyes looks dark with exhaustion, his skin stamped with cuts and shiners.

"But now. What about her now?"

"There was the concept that your uncles, as I'm sure Peter has told you, had something to do with her disappearance. But I know that that's not the case."

"How do you know?" His palms press into the table as he leans forward, his non-swollen eye widening.

"They mistook your girlfriend for Rebekah." I look down. "She's fine, though, I promise. I just saw her."

"Wh—" He jumps up, fumbling to get his cell from his back pocket. "Is she OK? Is she hurt—I mean . . . Fuck!" he screams as the battery of his phone beeps its way to the grave.

I'd love to sit here and explain it to him. Really, I would. But the shopkeeper returns from the back of the restaurant, chin up and eyes at the front door, like he's expecting someone. I lean in and whisper to Mason, "We need to go, like now." He slams his phone closed with a rumble of exasperation.

As we leave the restaurant, we are met by Peter. *God, Peter. It really has been too long, you son of a bitch.* I rest my hands on the arms of his wheelchair and give him a long peck on his lips. But Peter and I know just how platonic such a gesture can be. It's where we're from; everybody kisses everybody on the lips.

"Glad you guys could sort y-y-your shit," he says. "I'm not about to chase you all over this city anymore."

"Mason, meet the only decent person from your father's side of the family."

Mason looks at him with a new set of eyes, now knowing that this man who came to help Mason with his search is in fact his biological uncle.

"Well, what do we do next?" Peter asks.

From not too far away, the growing sounds of police sirens. "Let's get out of here, first," I say as I lead the way to anywhere that isn't here. When Mason follows, I stop short and turn to him in front of a storefront window full of flat-screen televisions. "I need you to understand that one way or another, I'm going to find her."

His eyes narrow with curiosity. "How?"

"I go first thing in the morning to the Third-Day Adventists."

"But they don't let anybody in there, even the ATF's tried," says Mason.

"I promise you, I have a way in. Virgil's already expecting me."

"It's as good a place as any to hide," Peter calls out from behind Mason. When I look over his shoulder, there's my face in the window of an electronics store on several TVs.

I tuck in my hair under the baseball cap I stole from the club, stand close enough to fog up the glass, and watch an old mug shot of mine from an old drunk-in-public charge on the flat screen. "Let's hope they don't have cable."

■ ■ ■

We walk through the fog in the darkness, our backs to the living and breathing creature called Louisville, Kentucky. Peter joins us but maintains his distance, a gesture to show that he appreciates the privacy I so desire. Each step away from the urban lights is a step further into silence, until we find a gap at the bottom of otherwise locked wired gates that seal off a baseball field, Peter parking his chair near the bleachers and reaching for his sock. I remember it's where he keeps his flask. Some things will never change with that guy.

Grounded in the fact that I did once live in the slums of Mastic Beach, New York, I recognize that what smells like Alpo dog food is the smell of a crematorium. The engines of the furnaces seem to growl through the smog, but Mason doesn't seem to mind. I don't mind.

Despite numerous refusals, Mason insists I wear his brown leather jacket. I wonder if he notices that I'm wearing his girlfriend's clothes. I pull the jacket tighter around me, and I'm not sure where to stand. *Is this too close? Is this too far? Does this facial expression show my guilt accurately? My sadness? How about my self-hatred? My pain, my suffering, my regret, my shortcomings, my anger, my fear. Do you see me, Mason? Can you see me, son?* In stillness that he probably deems awkward, he walks to home base as I walk toward the center of the diamond.

"In the last few months that I knew you, you had your little heart set on joining the big leagues and being a New York Yankee," I say.

Mason smiles for the first time tonight, stuffs his hands in his pockets, and scrapes the dirt off home plate. "I wanted to be major league until I was seventeen," he says, his gaze lost in the ground. "Even played in college."

As I step onto the pitcher's mound about twenty feet from home plate, I call out, "I always knew you would."

"Are you really going to make me ask?" he yells, making a stance ready to batter up.

"Ask what?" I throw an imaginary baseball.

Mason swings the invisible bat, holds his hand over his eyes, and watches a home run, his finger following the fake ball across the field. "Why did you do it? Why were Rebekah and I put up for adoption?"

"Depends." I pretend to throw the baseball over and over into a catcher's mitt. "Which version do you want?"

"I have options?"

"Well, there's the one where I tell you a bunch of bullshit to soften the blow for you, what I call the candy-coated version." I throw the ball and he swings. His eyes show it's a strike. "And then there's the truth, which will probably piss you off and keep you from ever talking to me."

"We haven't talked in twenty years." He hits the bat off the plate. "So it sounds like you really have nothing to lose by telling me the truth."

But I still don't know which version to tell him. Both I've rehearscd for the past twenty years, but both sound pretty incredible. Mason walks over to me. "If I promise not to stop talking to you, will you tell me the truth?"

Mason sits at my feet, rests his forearms on his knees in front of him, ass in the dirt. He reaches up and pulls out a flask from the pocket of his leather jacket that I'm wearing. He offers me a sip.

"I gave it up," I say as I plant down next to him. "But drink up. There's not much time until sunrise. Then we should go on our way and get Rebekah."

40

THE SKIN OF BUTTERFLY WINGS

My name used to be Nessa Delaney and I used to know what happiness tasted like, what it felt like, what it looked like. Well, at least I understood what it was supposed to resemble. But I had a family. I had a home. I had high hopes and great expectations. I was what the American dream looked like.

It was the winter of 1994. Black ice covered Mastic Beach, making streets look like polished onyx with the occasional tumbleweed of garbage blowing across it. There was the constant drip from the faucets to keep the pipes from freezing, the kind that irritates you if there's no noise to cover it up.

It was 10:00 p.m. on Black Friday, the night after Thanksgiving. The house still smelled of turkey and pumpkin pie from the night before and left-overs. Mason. That was what your adoptive parents named you. But you were named Ethan at birth. Anyway, you were snuggled between me and the back of the couch. The way your eyelids would flutter like the skin of butterfly wings as you snored turned you into something more than mere flesh and blood, something more precious. I stroked your hair and watched you sleep for what felt like days on end between chapters of L. Frank Baum's The Wonderful Wizard of Oz, after you'd fallen asleep at the part where Dorothy and the Scarecrow oil the Tin Woodman. I counted each freckle on the bridge of your tiny nose and rubbed the palm of your sweaty hand with the pad of my thumb. And if ever I believed in God, it was because of you. Because of moments like those.

Seventy-two. You had seventy-two freckles.

At the top of the pages I would squint my eyes at the lights of the Christmas tree that you and I spent the whole day putting up and decorating with your uncle Peter while your father, Mark, spent the day working. The bleary reds and greens and yellows seemed like glitter on a curtain of darkness.

"I wouldn't mind a glass of eggnog right about now," said Peter, from the middle of the living room. Back in Mastic Beach, your father and I had one of the nicer houses on the block: a well-kept one-story, newly remodeled and furnished with all the best things one could buy from Flanigan's furniture store up at the King Kullen plaza. In the living room, cream leather couches, cream carpeting, decorated for the holidays with red ribbons and faux-greenery.

"Let me put him down first." I took you to your room, kissed you on your cheek, and closed the door behind me.

In those days, I'd have only the occasional celebratory cocktail on a holiday. I added a pinch of nutmeg and cinnamon to our mugs on the kitchen counter that opened into the living room. And all I could think was that your father should have been home hours ago, and how I was so sick and tired of the all-night "work shifts," waking every morning to a cold bed, smelling the perfume on his clothes when I'd do his laundry. Sometimes I could even smell another woman's cunt when he'd get out of his clothes for the night.

"Ya know, Nessa," Peter said as he turned his chair to face me, the Christmas tree blinking behind him. "I like to downplay my intelligence too."

"Would you stop reading my mind?" I smiled as I added a shot of Southern Comfort into our drinks and walked to the living room. "It's better he stays out late. Less aggravation for me." But Mark's infidelity ripped at me, kept me from sleeping, from eating. I didn't let it show, but Peter was too sharp for my weak charades.

"Shoulda just married me and rolled off into the sunset," he joked into the eggnog. What the hell was I supposed to say to remarks like those? I mean, I knew Peter liked me and all, and sure, I liked him. He was my best friend, then. But I made it a point to never lead him on.

"I'll wheel you off a cliff if you don't shut it." I smiled and arranged the throw on the couch. Radiohead's "Creep" played in the background, a nice break from the Christmas carols I was already sick and tired of, despite it still only being November. "Before I get too comfortable," I said as I scurried off to take a piss.

The mug of eggnog warmed the top of my thigh as I sat on the toilet. It was a race, then: Could I gulp the whole drink before I stopped peeing? How easily bored I used to become. With my face at the edge of the mug, the winter's cold draft whispered through the cracks of the window. I put my cup on the windowsill to grab some toilet paper when I heard the all-too-familiar sounds of heavy footsteps on the front porch. Damn it, as I hurried to wipe before going to meet Mark in the living room. Somewhere as the warm buzz began in my chest, the mug fell to the floor into a million white shards of ceramic. Damn it, again. I went out to the living room, not realizing I was trailing blood behind me from my heel.

"Oh, it's just you," I said as Matthew poked his head in from the front door.

"Is that any way to greet your guests, Ness?"

He waited for me to invite him in. Sure, he had no problem opening the door, but he always waited for an invitation, like motherfucking Dracula or something. "Come in," I called out as I lifted my foot and placed it on the counter, reaching for a kitchen towel that had a snowman sewn into it.

"Here, let me." Matthew walked over to me with a cigarette in his teeth. He came to me like a cautious man who walks to a wounded animal. He looked me up and down and smiled.

"It's OK, I got it," I told him, careful not to look him in the eyes. You never looked Matthew in the eyes because with him came an uneasy feeling, a cloud that would follow him wherever he would go. I hated the way he'd peel my clothes off with his eyes, I hated the way he always smelled of barroom floor, like stale smoke and vodka hangover. But the more I tried to get a grasp on the sliver of ceramic, the more I seemed to push it into my foot.

"Jesus Christ." Peter rolled up to see the blood. There was more than I would have thought.

"Here," Matthew grabbed my ankle as gingerly as a strong man like him could.

"Wait a sec." I reached across the counter and grabbed the bottle of Southern Comfort and took a long swig from the neck. "OK, go."

"I think this is the first time I've ever seen you drink, Ness," he said, his words low and aimed at my foot. I cringed when he called me Ness.

"I hate blood."

The fact was, Matthew was incredibly handsome, very easy on the eyes. It was his personality that made my stomach turn. I suspected bipolar or something of the sort, like his mother. When he was nice, he was nice, gentle as he helped me take the ceramic from my foot. But when he was mean, he was a fucking nightmarish sonuvabitch. His hands were strong and calloused, stained with nicotine and oil. And while I didn't allow smoking in the house, on account of you and the fact that I never smoked back then, making such a suggestion to Matthew could warrant a loss of temper. Being around Matthew was like walking on glass. Well, ceramic, in my case.

"It's pushed far in there," he said as he leaned over the counter. "Hang tight." I wanted to smack him upside the head when he leaned over and started sucking ceramic from my heel. It was fucking gross, my brother-in-law's mouth sucking my blood.

Matthew, as he sucked on the hole in my heel, looked up and made sure to make eye contact with me. I assumed this was an attempt to make me think of how he might look up at me if he were going down on a woman. I noticed his effort to be seductive, and I'd be lying if I said that in that moment it didn't cross my mind, because it did. It may have even turned me on once upon a time, but I couldn't forget that this was Matthew, Mark's brother, an obsessive psycho. Plus, he was sucking my dirty fucking foot.

As I stood, leg up, at the counter, he placed one arm under my thigh and the other around my back. He carried me over to the sink, turned on the faucet, and spit out the long sliver of bloody ceramic from his mouth. Over his shoulder, I saw Peter raise his eyebrows, to which I rolled my eyes, a gesture to show we both knew Matthew's weaselly intentions.

"Deep breath, Ness." Matthew poured some of the Southern Comfort onto the wound before putting it to my lips.

I screamed. "What are you doing here, anyway?" I asked as the booze stung my heel.

"Mark didn't tell you?" Matthew put his lips under the faucet and rinsed my blood from his mouth. Clearly not. "Spending a few days here. I don't mind the couch."

Would have been good to know. Fuck.

■ ■ ■

Peter went home for the night. My foot throbbed. I tossed and turned in the bed, waiting for Mark to return from work. I heard Matthew rummaging around the living room, stumbling drunk. No, there are no pills for you in the utensil drawers, so shut the fuck up out there. I might have fallen asleep, but if I did, it was only for a minute. I rubbed my eyes, but didn't even have the chance to yawn. I could smell him before I saw his figure walk in, and before I could even comprehend what was happening, I was suffocating under the weight of his body.

I wanted to scream, I really did. But I had you in the next room, and what kind of mother would want their child walking in on their mother being raped?

I wanted to breathe, I really did. But his grip around my throat closed tighter and tighter; I swore I felt the skin on my neck tear.

I wanted to push, I really did. But his weight deflated the life from my lungs.

His huffs made from the vapors of cheap vodka were loud in my ears, his belt chiming against the bed frame. His sweat fell right on my lips. And with each grunt, with each thrust, with each dry pain between my legs, I felt my soul slip an inch away farther from my body. And no matter how hard I would try to reach them, those pieces would be gone forever.

The seconds lasted for hours, the minutes, days. I let my body go limp;

I gave up. I fixed my eyes to a mark on the ceiling, a dot of spackle. And when he was about finished, he released my throat. But I still didn't breathe. Matthew pulled up his pants, each sigh of relief from his climax turning my blood into bile, like his semen was made of this poison that would turn me into who I'd become, turn me bitter, turn me lost, turn me cold. I didn't move a muscle, I didn't make one noise, as he leaned over and gently grabbed my jaw, his face on mine. "You were great." He kissed my still lips and left the room.

Minutes later, he was snoring on the couch.

I walked into your room, still fast asleep in your toddler bed. My steps were soft on the carpet; I had trouble walking from the pain down below. Looking down, your lips puckered like you were drinking from a straw in a dream. My elbows and shoulders felt like they'd turned to rust as I lifted you, your body warm through the polyester pajamas.

Mason, you could sleep through anything, I swear, even after I struggled to the floor and hit a toy robot, sending sirens and incomprehensible, staticky phrases through the house. I feared Matthew would wake up. I cupped one of your ears and held the other tight against my chest, as I sat Indian-style on the floor and cradled you on my lap.

I buried my face in your hair and inhaled your shampoo. I placed my hand on your chest.

I cried, but I'm not so sure that I cried about the rape. Because as I looked down at you, I'd never felt so overcome with love and adoration. And in that moment, nothing felt realer than your chest expanding with each breath, your heart beating, the delicate pace of each snore. I tucked each whimper behind my lips, swallowing each shard of pain. In that moment, I knew I'd never cherish another moment quite like that one.

■ ■ ■

Time stopped working in the days following. Mornings remained dark and nights drew excruciating sunshine. I was a shell, a bruised one without any working organs, without any working emotions. Numbness, numbness in its rawest form is a terrifying notion. Because all of the emotions that you *are expecting to arrive: the pain, the sadness, the disgust, the rage . . . they just aren't there. And after a while, you'd do anything to feel something, anything, even the wreckage, the remnants of a broken soul.*

The weight of Matthew's fuck-fueled body pressed on my shoulders. When I looked in the mirror, the blueness of my eyes seemed to fade. A couple weeks had passed by. I didn't even take notice.

On the porch, I thanked Lynn several times, handing over the diaper bag, along with The Wonderful Wizard of Oz book. I was desperate, and I had no one else to call in that fucking town. "I'll be by in a day or two, just don't want to get him sick, is all."

"Well, of course not." She pinched your cheek as Peter wheeled up the ramp to our house. "White rum, that always does the trick." But I knew she didn't give one shit about the flu I was lying about.

She left. She left with you, Mason, the part where I watch you two drive off into the sunset.

But it's nothing but darkness from here on out.

∎ ∎ ∎

It must have been a couple weeks later; it was all such a blur. Time, that is. "Peter, please don't cry," I pleaded, resting my hands on his. I needed normalcy, not his tears.

"I'll kill him," he said, his bottom lip quivering. "I-I-I'll kill the fucking bastard my-my-myself." And together, Peter and I wept like children in the middle of the kitchen. Matthew was off on a construction job somewhere out east, though I'd made it a point to avoid leaving my room while he was still crashing at our house. Mark had been in and out, but he never noticed me, anyway. I made his dinner. I kept it warm. I somehow managed to keep the house tidy enough for his liking. Don't ask me how. I suppose autopilot is a powerful thing.

"I have to tell Mark," I whispered, my nose running for miles. I used my sleeve to wipe the tears from his face.

"But you know what he's like, Nessa."

"I do." I leaned my arm on the island counter in the middle of the

kitchen, where only some days before, Matthew had sucked pieces of broken mug from my foot. "Which is why, if anything happens to me . . ."

"Stop talking like that," Peter cried.

"I fucking have to," I said, and he knew I could have been right.

"You don't have to talk like that." He reversed his chair to turn his back to me. "You don't have to tell Mark."

And perhaps he was right. The thought of telling my husband made the chunks rise to my throat; it made my cheeks water something dreadfully sour. I inhaled hard through my nostrils, an attempt to keep the vomit down. I ran to the bathroom and embraced the porcelain bus, the force enough to make me pee myself a little.

When I finished, I blotted the tears and spit the last of the spleen from my mouth. The shower at my heels, I noticed a piece of ceramic from the other night when I shattered my mug, leaning against the tiles that ran under the shower door. Using one arm to wipe the sweat from my brow, I used the other to toss the shard into the bathroom pail. And when my hand slipped on the floor, I accidentally hit one of the tiles at the base of the shower, one already loose. I moved it, the ceramic cold on my fingertips. I caught it as it fell off, a small cavity in the base of the wall. Looking inside, I saw nothing.

And then, those heavy footsteps on the front porch once more. The sound of Mark greeting Peter. "What's the matter for ya?" he asked. I vomited once more. He banged on the door. "You almost finished in there Nessa? I gotta take a leak."

"I'll be right out," I yelled back. I put the tile back in its place and left the bathroom, passing Mark on the way out.

"What, you don't know how to kiss your husband after a long day's work no more?" I leaned up and kissed him on the cheek, the taste of vomit still on my breath. "Babe, where's dinner?" he asked as he unzipped to piss in front of me. I took a good long stare at him in his NYPD blues. I could smell the perfume of a whore, overbearing and cheap. I bet the whore was too. I could see the heaviness of his eyelids, that same heaviness he'd have after climaxing, back when we still made love.

"I'll warm it up."

Peter waited across the room. If looks could kill. "Where's Ethan?" Mark yelled from the bathroom.

"At your mother's for the night," I kept my eyes locked with Peter's. "Just until this hellish flu passes over."

"You mean some fucking peace and quiet, finally?"

I spoke so only Peter could hear. "Something like that." But perhaps out of habit, I turned the oven on, despite there being no dinner for probably the first time in our marriage. Nor was I expecting peace and quiet.

"You're throwing up?" Peter whispered from the couch, where Mark left his police duty belt on the arm.

I tilted my head, holding his gaze. Are you really going to make me say it?

He sighed, and I read his mind. That's why you're telling him . . .

"Where the hell is dinner?" he asked as he unbuttoned down to a wife-beater and dove into the fridge for a beer. "And no more Heineken?"

"Matthew drank it all," I said as I sat back on a stool. "Mark. We need to talk."

"C'mon, I'm not even in the door for five goddamn seconds."

"You have so. I just want to talk."

He opened the small cabinets above the stove and grabbed the emergency stash of Maker's Mark. He took a long, loud swig from the neck wrapped in red wax. He sat down on the stool across from me; the liquor made his cheeks start to blush. But for the dirty blond hair, he was the spitting image of Matthew, or rather Matthew was the spitting image of him. "Well, spit it the fuck out, will ya?" He spoke with his hands. And I did.

"I'm pregnant."

He crooked his head with a grin, that same grin as Matthew, the grin of their mother. And no wonder, they only crawled from the same swamp that was her vagina. I think I held my breath in the silence between the statement and his reaction.

Mark had barely touched me since the birth of our son, the last time a good six months ago. That's what this marriage had become: Mark getting his jollies off everywhere else, me staying home, embarrassed because every-

body knew and pretended it was a big secret to me. And he always had a temper, even since before we were married. Always the signature temper of the Delaney family, and in all honesty, I think it was also half the reason I found him so attractive all that time ago: the neighborhood badass, the respectable job as a cop, the one all the other wives wanted . . . and, well, they had.

The stools flew out from under us as he grabbed me by the back of my hair. And I'd have been a liar to say that I was surprised; he reacted more than once with his hands. A slap here, a sock to the gut there, a lot of broken furniture in between. It's hard to believe I was that woman, all those years ago. Weak. I never stood up for myself. Always the fucking victim. He pinned me to the kitchen floor, knee, with all his muscle behind it, pressed to my stomach. I pleaded, I begged. His eyes went black, his face filled with blood. He screamed through his teeth, but I couldn't hear anything with all the life I had pulsing in my face and ears. In the corner of my eye, the lights of the Christmas tree faded to black, my vision closing in on this monster. This is going to be the last thing I see of this earth, this fucking face.

He dragged me across the floor and toward the stove like a rag doll. God, did I scream bloody murder as he opened the oven door and pulled my head up by the hair. Mark was going to put my head in the oven.

And then the shot.

I pushed off the inside of the oven door just fast enough so as not to get burned. The room spun around me; my ears rang with the sound. Mark fell beside me. The blood. God, the blood. Nothing like you saw in Hollywood. It seemed to paint the walls from the exit wound at the side of his head. And when I finally caught my breath, I poked my head around the island counter.

Peter, the smoking gun in his hand, so to speak.

I raised my hand, my palm facing him, trembling in the air, "Just put it down, Peter." I hush. His eyes twitched and neck jerked, like it does when he gets nervous. He let his limp hands drop Mark's police-issued firearm and fall on his lap.

Don't ask me. To this day, I've no idea how Peter managed such a shot in that condition. It was chance. Pure fucking, brilliant chance.

I went to him and pressed his head to my stomach, stroking his hair. "It's

OK. It's going to be all right." But I got the feeling that he too knew it was bullshit. The jerking of his head on my gut was painful after Mark's knee. I grabbed the Glock from the top of his thighs. Suddenly, the thundering of Matthew's truck pulling up in the driveway. I heard him hit the garage door, a sure sign that he was already drunk, thank Christ. I had to think fast. I put the gun in the back of my pants and draped the police belt over my shoulder. "We don't have to make this any worse than it already is, Peter."

And with every ounce of emotion that had been nonexistent in me in the days prior, I acted. No time to think, just react, and at a pace that even surprised me. I ran back for the stove, where Mark's blood pooled in front of the sink. The island counter, the only thing that would block Matthew's view from the front door. The heaviness on the porch, the scuffs of his construction boots. "Keep him in the living room for two minutes; say anything you have to."

I grabbed Mark by his wrists and turned the corner to the hallway just as Matthew was stumbling in. Running on pure adrenaline, I dragged 190 pounds of dead weight all the way to the bathroom, a trail of blood following. I locked the door behind me. I heard Peter: "You hear about J-J-John's latest escapade down at Herkimer's?" One limb at a time, I managed to get all of Mark into the shower, throwing the duty belt in after him.

Before I reached the front of the hallway, I saw Peter sweating from a mile away. It was the first time Matthew had seen me since the rape. He sat on the couch, grabbing the remote to turn on the TV, elbows to his knees, chips of paint from his camouflage pants all over the carpet. "Jesus Christ, I need to piss," he said as he rose. He acted like the rape had never occurred, it just never happened.

Peter tried to speak, but the words couldn't make it to the surface.

I hurried past the kitchen, fetching the Maker's Mark off the counter, and to the living room, where we bumped into each other. "Whoa, what's your rush, sweetheart?"

Don't let him look to his left. Don't let him see the blood.

I waved the bottle under his nose, anything to keep him distracted from seeing his brother's brains splattered all over the kitchen. But he knew I barely drank, so I had to act drunk. "Just getting my drink on." I tried to maneuver him into the living room. But he pushed back, hard enough that I had to walk backward to keep from falling.

"All right, just let me drain the main vein, Ness."

He shoved me farther than I thought and before I knew it, we were at the bathroom door. He reached behind my back and twisted the doorknob. With all my might, I knocked him against the wall on the opposite side of the hallway, grabbing his crotch. "Allow me."

I kissed him, grabbed him by his belt buckle, and led him back down the hall. "You're killing me," he slurred. If only you knew.

I stopped in front of him, grinding my ass against his hard-on. "Tell me how fucking bad you want me," I said as I took one of his hands and put it up my shirt. With the other, I guided his fingers inside me. Anything to keep this fucker turned on. I took his fingers out and sucked on them. "Tell me how bad you want me."

"I fucking love you, Ness," he said as he kissed my neck, still throbbing from his brother. "I've loved you since I met you and I want you in every possible fucking way."

On the way to the bedroom, I avoided Peter's eyes. He'd suffered enough; he didn't have to see my face as I led his brother into the bedroom to let him have his way once more.

Behind closed doors, I faked ecstasy. We drank Maker's Mark. And I waited for him to fall asleep after drowning him in nearly a fifth of whiskey, enough that he was too limp to fuck anymore and fell into a coma.

■■■

It was an easy arrest for the cops. I had the bruises. I had the bloody clothes. I'd given my kid to my mother-in-law "because it was premeditated." And everybody knows that when an officer gets killed, especially murdered, the rest of them will stop at nothing to seek justice. Even if it's the wrong justice.

"I'm not the one you should be arresting, damn it!" I screamed at the cops. "The guy who did it is passed out drunk in the bedroom!"

Peter pleaded with officers. "I shot him! I shot the son of a bitch."

But the cops heard none of it. They wanted to get the guy who killed their fellow brother in arms, even if it was me, even if it was the wrong person.

But I wouldn't let Peter be charged for this crime. And in all honesty, I didn't think I would be either. "Oh, yeah?" I said before all the cops. "Then where's the gun, smart-ass?" But Peter didn't have an answer.

41

SUNRISE

My name is Freedom and I watch the sun rise on the lake. Behind me, a row of log cabins, nearly empty as tourist season fizzles out for winter. Adirondack chairs at the water's edge look lost without the bodies stained by summer. Sun umbrellas form a graveyard across the way. The sky, spectacular. But I wonder if it shines on Rebekah, if she's dead or alive. I can't help but think of the same sun shining on her rotting corpse somewhere. I don't mean to think this way.

I hate how still the water is, how beautiful the sky is. It's like God's rubbing it in my face, a reminder of how fucked-up everything is, how chaotic. *Why did this happen to me? Why did I have to be punished for being raped, for the death of my husband? More than anything, why did I have to be away from my children?* I rip at fistfuls of stones and dirt; I have to ruin this picture of still waters. I want to rip the sun from its sky. I roar with every piece of the earth I chuck into the lake, the mallards flying away. I try to rip an Adirondack chair to pieces, but I only end up with splinters in my hands.

The lights turn on in the cabin. The receptionist's dog barks. My screams tear the silence in half.

The men from my cabin come to the porch, I can feel them, even with my back to them. Mason. Peter. The ATF operation, which includes Joe and a scary-looking skinhead. As I stab the shallow water with a rusty umbrella pole, Mason runs up behind me. He pulls me into a bear hug and squeezes. He doesn't call me Freedom. He doesn't call me Nessa. He doesn't call me Mom. He just tells me that it's OK, that I have nothing to be sorry about. I realize that in my screams, in my cries, I've been saying "I'm sorry" the entire time.

My whimpers die out as he squeezes to hold me from collapsing. As I lean on his chest in his arms, he and I look out to the sunrise that I failed to single-handedly destroy. And like I did to him twenty years ago in the last time I was happy, he buries his face in my hair and holds me tight. "You're stronger than you think," he tells me, while the other men return to the rented cabin.

"We'll see."

▪ ▪ ▪

The cabin buzzes with intention; focus turns to static around me. I feel recharged, refreshed, reared, and ready.

"Quit being a perv." I smirk at Peter as I'm about to take my shirt off.

He smiles. "I'm no perv," he says as he turns his wheelchair around in the cramped cabin, joining Mason to face the wall. "I'm just human."

"I have to ask," says the skinhead, enjoying the sight of me in my bra a little too much. "How the hell did you manage to get access to this place?"

"FreedomInJesus," I tell them. "I've been following his sermons for as long as I can remember."

"I know that name," says Joe. "We all just thought you were some kinda crazy. Clever, I'll give you that. Clever."

Silence. "I just wanted to see my children."

Behind me, Joe speaks with a wire in his teeth, equipping me with a transmitter in the back of my jeans. "You remember the safe word?" he asks.

"I want immunity. If I'm doing this for you, I need any charges for me dropped: the cop's gun, stealing the cop car, the motorcycle, all of that."

"I told you you'll get it." Joe steps in front of me, pressing to secure the tape that holds the wire to my chest. "Now, what's the safe word?"

I chug on the last of my gas station coffee. "Get the fuck in here and save me from these assholes."

"Freedom . . ."

"All right, all right," I say as I put my shirt back on. "Looks like a storm's coming."

PART III

42

EGGSHELLS

My name is Freedom and I gear up to walk the crushed white clam-shells that make up the narrow roads in this corner of Goshen, Kentucky. The black metal gates of the Paul farm shelve frost. The ties that hold the posters and boards to the palisades shiver in the wind, the kind of wind that sounds like the sharpening of steel that might whistle through an arctic hell, the frostbiting kind that stings my cheeks and makes me tear.

Up ahead, a crowd made up of about a dime and a half protest against the cult, a chant that rolls over the hills, "Burn in hell, Burn in hell!" Tall picketers bounce up and down in the air, like they're poking heaven with a stick in the hope that their gods might react. Outside our car is a poster as tall as me that displays a list of four names in white, all with a line through them:

Manson. Koresh. Jones. Applewhite.

A fifth one, in bold red letters, reads:

Paul.

"Are you sure you're ready?" Mason asks from the passenger's seat of the ATF surveillance van pulled over at the side of the road and out of sight from the protesters.

"I'm our only shot." I stare at myself in the side-view mirror. "What's with the fucking lynch mob?"

"Don't worry about them," says Joe of the ATF, the undercover who last saw Rebekah, as he taps the microphone through my shirt. "They're nothing but Bible thumpers. Crazies, but harmless."

The sweat makes my armpits itch; it pools to a tarn at the sides of my snatch. On the other side of this gate is my only shot at redemption, my only shot at giving my life just a mustard seed of purpose, my one shot at finding the daughter I only knew for two minutes and seventeen seconds. "There's no turning back," I say under my breath.

"Just have a little faith, Mom," says Mason, the first time I hear the word fall from his lips since he was a child. But I have to wonder if it is only to encourage me as I ready myself into foreign farms of Jesus and quasi-forms of religion.

"Faith . . ." I trail off. "I don't need any more crutches." I press on the mic under my shirt to fasten the adhesive and turn to Joe. "If they make me sign over my car and milk cows or some shit, promise you'll get me the hell out of there."

"You'll be fine, just remember what we talked about. *Looks like a storm's coming.*" *Yeah, yeah, I know. Throw myself to the wolves, listen, find out what terrorist act they're planning to channel their zeal and self-righteous delusions of martyrdom. I get it, you redneck. Sub rosa.*

"Ready?" And I can see it in his eyes, the expectance of some emotional tell-my-kids-I-love-them bullshit good-bye. "Take this with ya," Joe says and hands me a Bible.

"Ah, the better to roll my cigarettes with, my dear." I leave the van.

"Yeah, good luck with that."

▐ ▌ ▐

The aftertaste of antibiotic flavors the watering of my cheeks and my upper lip carries the scent of a stale Pall Mall. And as I hold my breath and walk the half-mile stretch toward the front gates, I see a coyote, a coyote that looks identical to the deaf and domesticated one named Aleshanee back in the Snake River Plain of Idaho. He weaves through the woods, a dance with the birch trees. He walks with me from a distance.

The chants' subject changes from fire and brimstone into something about the Rapture, the Second Coming of Christ, and whatnot.

A pain to the side of my face, exacerbated by the cold. I bring my fingers to my right cheekbone, under my eye, pulling runny egg from my face. The voices of the crowd turn to white noise as it circles around me like a bunch of hunters surrounding wounded game. I see people's fangs, mouths shouting something pertaining to Jesus, something pertaining to love. In the front, I see a butch woman with dirty-blond hair with only one tooth on the bottom and one tooth on the top, a carton of eggs cradled in her arms. And while I'm outnumbered, I still act on instinct. I walk to her. And when she flashes her two remaining teeth in jest, I use all the rage inside to kick her in the kneecap. I hear something crack; a flutter of nausea ripples in my gut as she falls to the ground. I scrape against the shelly gravel when I straddle her, breaking every egg, even already-broken ones, over her face.

"Stupid fucking bitch." All these words come to the surface, not sure if any one of them makes sense. I'm too busy egging her to hear my own words, each syllable cried as I ram an egg on her face with the force of a punch behind it.

Shock, gasp, disgust, goes the crowd. *Sure, make me the bad guy now. Wasn't so bad when you were on the offensive, right? Hypocrite fucks.* A flashback to the Corona bottle and a Viper's nose back at the Whammy Bar. Behind me, a scream rings through the air, and when I turn back, a woman falls toward me. A man at her side grabs his own head and crouches to the ground. And like the event that took place at the Whammy Bar, leave it to a cop to save the day.

"Back off the lady." The man in light blue hits one more protester with his nightstick, causing him to fall to the ground. "Let her alone," he yells. He pulls me up by my arm with a jolt, off the top of the horse. I can feel the warmth of his body as he holds me close by the waist and uses the baton to strike gatherers out of the way, heading for the entrance of the gates. I look over my shoulder, past the crowd, to see Mason and Joe. They're reentering the van. I guess they were on their way to save the day, my capeless crusaders. Instead, I get this redneck with a receding hairline. I barely understand his accent, something about the reverend, something about expecting me, something about keeping this little incident to ourselves. With each word I pretend to understand, the smell of chewing tobacco emanates from his stuffed bottom lip.

He uses a Master Lock key to open the tall gate, rust flaking from hinges that whine. The chants subside as the officer and I start on a long dirt road that disappears ahead over a hill. He indicates toward a clunker of a pickup truck parked to the side at the edge of the forest. I climb in on the driver's side and slide over. He hands me a navy bandanna from his front pocket. I wipe egg from my face and hair. In the mirror, a welt develops; flesh begins to turn red raw before my eyes.

A Confederate flag sticker taped to the dashboard, a shotgun displayed right behind my head. *I'm in redneck hell*, I think. As we rattle up past several small white houses that resemble sugar cubes, the man, who said he was the sheriff, I think, spits his used tobacco into an old Chock full o'Nuts can he leaves on the side of his door.

"This here's the ol' Paul house." He puts the car in park beside a cop car, presumably his. As I look up at the porch from the truck, Carol and Reverend Virgil Paul step out from the house, a young girl running behind them to hide behind Carol's skirt. I think my heart stops beating.

I'm at the home where my children were raised, a place I've only conjured up in my dreams. And for a second, I swear I can feel them, as if they're right here, standing next to me at the foot of the porch.

The Pauls mean to be warm as they greet me. But their embraces are awkward, like they've only done it maybe once in their whole lives. Their dress, conservative: white turtlenecks and dirty Keds, a sight contradicting my ripped jeans and combat boots, wild, unbrushed hair that smells like smoke. They try to smile like they're happy to see me; their teeth show, but their cheeks hardly move. Not knowing what to say, I fix my attention to the young girl.

"And who might this princess be?" I hear the girl giggle through the cotton.

"Boo!" she yells out before nicking her head back. Out of everyone here, she looks like the only one truly happy. And I could only hope that that was the case for Mason and Rebekah, being raised here.

"This here is our daughter, Magdalene."

"Hi, there, Magdalene." I smile at her. "My name is Freedom."

"So what's your real name, anyway?" the reverend asks, more like an interrogation.

I shrug. "That's it. Freedom Oliver."

He curls his lip and looks at me like I have three heads. "So your parents were *those* kinds of people . . ." He trails off. Three minutes in, I already know I might end up biting my tongue right off through fake smiles that hurt my cheeks.

Virgil shakes hands with the sheriff before he takes off in his cop car. He stands close to me, like he's trying to remind me that he stands a good foot taller than I. "No luggage, I see?" I hold the jacket tighter around me, on the off chance that he can see the wire down my shirt.

"It's a funny story," I start, not really knowing where I'm going with the answer. And I'm glad it's not one I have to think up, as an old woman steps from the house to tow everyone's eyes. The soles of her leather sandals scrape against the peeling whitewash of the porch. Gray marbles peer from a black scarf that hangs on to lazy shoulders, eyes that look like they can tell a million stories but choose to keep them in their respective decades. She holds the door open for us.

Inside it smells like lemons and banana bread. A second hand ticks through the coziness of the living room. Old couches look like they've never been sat on, and balls of pink yarn and a pair of knitting needles rest on and near a black rocking chair in the corner of the room, near a small window that overlooks the driveway.

The house looks like something from the Colonial period: large wooden beams supporting the ceiling, a wood-burning stove, creaky hickory boards for floors, and about a dozen needlework frames around HOME SWEET HOME, HOME IS WHERE THE HEART IS, yadda, yadda, yadda.

"Well, let's get you settled, shall we?"

I jar with the entrance of a cuckoo bird. The bird sings, slightly out of tune. In fact, his words are my exact sentiment toward these people: cuckoo. *But be polite, Freedom. Act like one of them. Act human.* "I'd really love a shower more than anything, Reverend Paul."

"Plenty of time for that." He opens the front door. He gestures with his hand for me to follow. With a snap of his fingers he demands of the old lady, "Amalekite, come." The woman acts as his obedient lapdog. On instinct, I want to tell the man to go fuck himself. He continues to me, his voice matter-of-fact, "In this community, a man is not allowed alone with a woman without the presence of another female, I'm sure you understand." I've no fucking clue what he's talking about.

If ever there were an internal creep-o-meter instilled in humans, mine rings off the charts: the women walk on eggshells, eggshells on the tongue, like they're afraid to say or do anything unless it's confirming or in direct obedience to the reverend. Magdalene jumps to her stomach on the living room floor to resume with her coloring book of Christ's Resurrection, with only a purple crayon. "I'll start lunch," Carol says and disappears into the kitchen, probably an excuse to leave the awkward situation. "Magdalene, come with Mommy."

Magdalene goes to run past me and stops, stretching her head all the way back to see me. "You're awfully pretty for a grown-up, Sister Freedom."

For the first time in God knows how long, it's a compliment I cherish. "Why, thank you, Miss Magdalene."

She smiles a toothy grin. "But Sister Freedom is one funny name." Carol tries to pull the girl away with one of those *sorry-about-that* chuckles.

"It sure is."

43

THE GENERAL STORE

A fat man who looks like he hasn't bathed in weeks melts in a leather recliner that has no business being in a general store. Country music static drones in the background, Laffy Taffy products that expired years ago collect dust on the shelves, and outside are vintage gas pumps and a yellowed billboard that displays biblical scripture. On a cracked glass deli counter, a pig's head and chicken claws and cow's tongue, soul food of the like, attracting flies.

"Why, she was just on her way home from school. And no one's seen her since," the man answers, sweating in front of an aging fan while Mattley bundles up his new jacket.

"And this was the last place that anyone saw Michelle Campbell, is that correct?"

"I supposed so. She and her brother, Clayton. They usually walked home from the school together, only lived right here on this road, up at the yellow house on the end. Just Clayton lives there now. Don't see him too much no more, keeps to himself. Think he's drinking or sumpin'."

"And you didn't happen to notice anything peculiar about her that day, did you?"

"Peculiar?" He doesn't know the word.

"You know, like funny, or strange."

"Well," the general store owner recollects. "Looked like her 'n Clayton was arguing about sumpin'. Couldn't say what, though."

A butch woman with dirty-blond hair huffs through the door on old crutches. She goes for the back of the deli counter, trying to balance her weight on the sticks, and grabs a slab of steak to hold over her bruised face. The man raises his head but never leaves his recliner. "What's gone 'n happened to you there, Sue?"

"The Paul farm, that's what," she growls as she crosses the floor and grabs a bottle of Colt 45 from a fridge with no working lights. She uses the only two teeth she has to rip the bottle top off. "Some new woman, ain't from around here. Red hair, tats, a Yankee accent. Was just a peaceful protest, and she went all berserk and hit me for no reason at all! Think she broke my goddamn kneecap, the crazy bitch."

Mattley realizes this might very well be Freedom she's talking about.

"You mean you didn't show her that left hook of yours?" He chuckles.

"Was gonna, but then Sheriff showed up. Broke it up and took her inside the gates." Her gums make wet noises; her jowls ripple with each word.

"Why do people protest at the Paul farm, anyway?" Mattley asks.

"Because them people are going to hell, that's why," Sue barks. "Say they're the only ones getting into heaven, trying to recruit, stealing members from our churches to go and live with them. Real fucked-up in the head. Once you go in? You ain't never coming out."

■ ■ ■

The yellow house at the end of the road, home to the Campbells. A junk-yard of tractor and car parts scattered all over straw-like grass, empty beer bottles and old tires, the faint smell of gasoline. Shutters hang on their last rusty threads, the residual remains of yellow paint and plywood over the front windows of the first floor. The nearest neighbors are a good mile away. A mad pit bull tied with orange extension cord to a large oak tree with hundreds of dried-up wads of gum on it. The porch groans, decked with dozens of flypaper strips and a million cigarette butts.

"Hello?" Mattley's call echoes through the screen door and into the house, where something heavy metal plays from the back. But Mattley knows he doesn't have time to wait around, not if the woman the butch redneck mentioned was at the compound was Freedom. He walks in, tiptoeing through and calling out, "Clayton Campbell?"

Through the living room door, a pornographic film plays muted on the TV, the house full of smoke and an awful smell of chemicals. Through another door, a makeshift lab. The machinery is cold, the mechanical scent emanating from the room, windows boarded up with pentagrams spray-painted on the walls. On the floor, a still body with a gas mask on.

Mattley rips the mask off the young man, a glass pipe broken in half at his side.

The boy is recently dead, his face swollen with the telltale signs of an overdose, his body all bone, with signature scabs from picking at the skin while tweeking on drugs.

Mattley isn't sure if he should call the local cops just yet, not with him suspecting the town's sheriff in this mess of a cult and Michelle's possible ties to it. He sneaks upstairs, looking out every other window to make sure no one's followed. Up in Michelle's room, he finds nothing useful. Piles of clothes and old dolls, old test papers destroyed by dampness, the room stuffy, like it hasn't been entered since she disappeared. Everything about the room feels soggy.

Mattley sits on her musty bed among garbage bags full of clothes and old shoes, his head in his hands at the dead end. He finds nothing of significance and vents his anger by throwing books and bags of laundry across the room. He goes to leave, tripping over a pair of Converse sneakers that rattle.

He composes himself on the floor and looks inside the sneaker to find a bottle of prenatal vitamins. *Michelle Campbell was pregnant.* He opens the vitamins, a chalky smell. And inside, he notices what looks like a folded piece of paper. He pulls it out.

It is a pamphlet from the Third-Day Adventists, the header reading "Come to me, all who are weary and burdened." There's no doubt in his mind that it all comes back to this church in the hills of Kentucky. But first he decides to head to the Bluegrass, where Mason told him to go the night before and look for a man named Joe.

44

WITH PREJUDICE

Dear Mason and Rebekah, though once upon a time, you were Ethan and Layla,

My name was Nessa Delaney and I spent two years in prison for a crime I did not commit. There was this woman who I'd shared a cell with. I slept terribly because of her wailing in the night, unmoving air entombed around us, broken by her weeping. She'd curl up on her blanketless cot and play with the tears she'd cry on the mat by making piles out of them and swirling them around with the ends of her hair. "I have to get home," she'd say to herself. She'd chew her nails and pace like her steps might one day get her out of there.

Oh, wait. That woman was me.

Another plan, another thing I didn't think all the way through. No weapon, no charges, right? The Sixth Amendment says I shall enjoy the right to a speedy trial. Our forefathers were fucking idiots if they thought anyone could enjoy their trials. But what isn't afforded by most Americans is the right to a speedy holding process, that period between arrest and said trial.

I suppose I'd watched too many reruns of *Law & Order* to know better. You know, those episodes when the cops are standing right next to the forensic techs when they get a match on a set of prints, or when at trial, a suspect is still bruised from an assault when taking the stand. How about "no." Nothing is fast in the legal process. Nothing is simple. Nothing is easy. None of it is enjoyable either.

Between the rape and Mark's unexpected death, my brain wasn't working. The defense argued that I was in a "state of shock" when I called the police. It was the evening that Mark died, a few hours later.

Dispatcher: 911, what's your emergency?

Nessa: My husband (my voice calm).

Dispatcher: Yes ma'am, what about your husband?

Nessa: My husband is a cop and he's in the shower.

Dispatcher: Ma'am, do you or your husband need assistance?

Nessa: No. He's already dead. (I hang up.)

That transcript made headlines everywhere, nationwide. Overnight, I went from Nessa Delaney the homemaker into Nessa Delaney the cop killer. When the police showed up, they could smell the blood. Even I could, thick with iron, and I made no attempt at trying to scrub it from the floors and ceiling. I was sloppy. They saw my bruises; they saw his blood in my hair that I did not see.

I expected Suffolk County Police, that was where we lived. But because Mark worked at the NYPD, I was met by two counties. And news reporters. And sniffer dogs. And the bomb squad. (Why? I'll never know.) The gun was hidden right under his body, in that compartment at the bottom of the shower, the one I discovered on the night Mark died. The dogs couldn't detect it, not with its rightful owner resting in peace right above it. And I couldn't tell the cops, because how the hell would I know where my brother-in-law would have put the weapon after killing his brother in a drunken rage over me?

When they handcuffed me and led me out of the house, my heart sunk in my guts at the sight of Lynn Delaney holding you, Mason. My son. You saw me, and my mind raced with the notion that your last memory of me would be when the cops arrested me for killing your father. The way you screamed for me. The way you screamed . . .

On the way from paddy wagon to courthouse, the cameras burned my retinas. I thought, *Hey, I could spend a few days in the slammer until an anonymous call leads the cops to the gun, right?* Then they'd find Matthew's prints on it, which I planted there after getting him drunk, and I'd be good to go. I could live happily ever after with my son and the child I had growing inside of me. I thought of calling it my very own Mastic Beach fairy tale.

It took one year for someone to find the gun. One year! One year, even after the call I made my lawyer make to the cops to tell them where the gun was. I would have had Peter make the call, but his stutter would have been too easy to detect.

It took another six months to get the ballistics and fingerprints and such to point to Matthew.

It took another six months to be dismissed of the charges.

My defense waived the right to a speedy trial so they could build up a proper defense, in which I was urged to oblige, lest they take themselves off the case and offer disclaimers that could take months (I've heard even years) to process.

When he finally released me, the judge apologized for the mix-up and thanked me for doing my duty as a citizen. Really? Two years in prison and all I get is a half-assed "I'm sorry." I'm supposed to find some justification in it because my patience there is exactly what makes me a good law-abiding citizen. Twisting my arm to sign my parental rights over because you'd convinced me I'd spend my entire life here and because I had no one (but the Delaneys) to care for my children during my time here. Fuck that.

I didn't tell the judge out loud to go fuck himself. But I did express my fear of the Delaneys.

It was already in the news that my house had been vandalized, the death threats from them. People knew just how bad they wanted me dead. Could you believe Lynn and her sons (all but Peter) went onto *The Montel Williams Show*? Then the whole entire world knew how bad they wanted me dead, though they only made themselves look stupid. Doesn't take much. Lynn even hired a certain correctional officer named Jimmy Doyle to break my kneecaps, but a case couldn't be built from the rumors. Thankfully, there wasn't any follow-through to those threats.

Years later, I suspect this Jimmy Doyle was the same correctional officer who supplied Matthew with all the information about mine and my children's whereabouts during his incarceration. And so the idea of Witness Protection was offered to me. Nothing like a criminal family from hell wanting to kill you and/or shatter your kneecaps to get you an offer for relocation with the Witness Protection Program. Please, they gave Witness Protection to almost anyone in the 1990s. It was practically a trend.

When they went to arrest Matthew for Mark's murder, they found locks of my hair that he'd tied with bows. They found dozens of photos of me hanging on wire mobiles over his bed. He had notebooks with my name written thousands of times on each page, a good twenty notebooks full. Matthew's obsession with me made things very hard for him. And rightfully so.

45

STRIPPED

My name is Freedom, and in my paranoia, I wonder if they can tell I'm not the zealot I've claimed to be. "The storm we had last week brought quite the cold front," Virgil says to no one in particular as we cross a hill, the smell of fresh dirt and the bell of a nearby church ringing through the fog. With Virgil ahead of us, I try to make eye contact with the old woman to my right. But every time I try, she looks down, each grip of her hand tight on the other. At the top of the hill, the church just ahead, we follow Virgil toward a shed with a heavy Dutch door, surrounded by overgrown wildflowers.

"The church is impressive," I comment, if only for Mason and the ATF agent to hear me from the surveillance van. "Are we going to this shed to the side of it?" Play dumb, always a safe bet. This wouldn't be such a bad place to store guns.

"It is here that you will be prepared for baptism," Virgil tells me.

A wave in my stomach, the old woman's inability to look in my eyes, the fact that I'm being led to the middle of nowhere already in the middle of nowhere. The determination I carried for finding my daughter is being replaced by fear.

In the shed, shelves of nonperishable canned goods, linens, and worn hymnals and Bibles in bulk. The center of the room is bare but for a single wood stool. No guns. Virgil grabs folded clothes from one of the shelves. "You will be stripped and you will change into these." His stares down to me are cold. "It's all part of the cleansing process."

I swallow hard. "Have faith," I say, though the comment's directed to those at the other end of my wire. "I can do all things. . . ." That sounds like something a religious person might say, right?

The reverend smiles. "Go on." He shakes his head for me to strip.

"Sir, with all due respect"—I hold my breath, hoping it makes me look like I'm blushing—"I couldn't possibly get undressed in front of a man." Of course this is total bullshit, but it's what he expects to hear.

He raises an eyebrow as the old woman removes my jacket. When he sees the tattoos, he says, "I suppose that wasn't always a problem for you?" He eyes me up and down.

"That was before Christ changed me."

He nods approvingly. "I'll be just over here, then." His pace is slow to the Dutch door, leaning on the bottom half and staring off at the church, his back to us.

"What's your name?" I ask the old woman.

"You will refer to her as the Amalekite," Virgil shouts over his shoulder, his voice like the cracking of a whip in the room. "And she does not speak."

This is what's called being fucked. I can't hide the microphone, and I can't avoid getting naked before the mute. *Shit.* Why couldn't Feds around here be more tech-savvy and give me an earpiece or a pin like you see with nanny-cams? I turn, so my back is to Virgil. I shimmy out of my boots, the bottle of antibiotics rattling. Thinking Virgil is still at the entrance, I'm alarmed when he brushes to my side, reaching down. "Medicine has no place in the church," he says, his voice stern. "We rely on the power of God, not man, to heal. Understand?"

"Yes, sir," I respond. *Then did God not give us doctors? In fact, wasn't the apostle Luke a doctor? Fucking quack.* When he returns to the door and faces the other way, the Amalekite helps me get my pants off.

I wince when the jeans brush against the snakebite. The Amale-kite notices and takes her time, cautious around the bandages. She unfolds a thick white cotton skirt and struggles to crouch down. She takes my hand and puts it on her shoulder so I can lean on her as she slips on the skirt and a pair of matching grannie panties. Her bones feel arthritic under my hand, knots in her shoulders, her fingers cold as she dresses me. Last to come off, my shirt. My plain black tee that covers the wire.

I let her use my forearms to support herself, but I get the feeling I'm not allowed to help her. She goes to lift the shirt over my head. I pull it back down by the bottom seam. And for the first time, she makes eye contact with me. *Don't make me fucking do this, please, Lady, don't make me take it off.* I scream with my eyes. Hers, as gray as stones on the coldest of days.

Behind me, "Daddy, Daddy!" I hear Magdalene run toward the shed.

"Not now, sweetheart," Virgil answers back. "Go back and help your mother with lunch."

As Virgil leaves for just a moment, I seize the opportunity. I go to tell her to keep her fucking mouth shut. Sure, it's not like I'd enjoy being so blunt with an elderly lady, but what other hope do I have? But before I get the chance to hiss the words, she does first. "I'll say nothing to that bastard," she whispers, her nose up to mine as she glances over my shoulder to Virgil. I'm floored; I hold my breath as the Amalekite reaches under my shirt and pulls the wire down, rolling it up and putting it in her pocket, using my body to hide her. It stings, but not enough to make noise about it.

And if she can read my eyes, *What the fuck am I walking into?* She looks down as she removes my shirt; I unclasp my bra.

Virgil returns to my side, "We can't have this." His eyes narrow. He looks around until he grabs a pair of white gloves. He tosses them at the Amalekite. "Make sure none of that blasphemy is showing, not even on her hands," he says, regarding my sleeves of tattoos. "Sew em' on the sleeves."

I say nothing. I have to remind myself to keep my trap shut because of Rebekah . . . Rebekah. *Where the hell are you?*

❚ ❚ ❚

I need reasons to cry. I need to look like my conversion to the church is the most emotional one yet. I need to give an Oscar-worthy fucking performance. It's late afternoon, the day becoming chilly. Shadows grow taller on the ground. The entire "community" is here for my baptism. After Virgil and the Amalekite lead me to the church from the back door, I kneel on the altar, with Virgil's palm pushing down on my forehead.

"Do you renounce Satan in the presence of Jesus Christ?"

Back to crying. Think about the adoption. Think about the time Matthew raped me. Think about Mark's betrayal. Think about the arrest. Think about Mason's cries then. Think about the two minutes and seventeen seconds that I felt my daughter's breaths. Think about the redemption at the other end of this. Think about finding Rebekah alive with a happily-ever-after ending that one can only dream of. I cry my eyes out. "I do, in the name of Jesus Christ."

"Are you willing to suffer and die for your faith?"

With each *I do* that I utter, the crowd sings "Amen."

"Do you accept I, Reverend Virgil Paul, to carry an all-knowing gift from God? That God has indeed chosen me to relay to my people the exact hour of our freedom?"

"I do." *Amen.*

"Do you swear to this church never to forsake nor abandon the messages that I give to you, my faithful servant?"

"I do." *Amen.*

"Do you refuse the ways of the outside world, to never again associate with anyone beyond this family of disciples? To give your life to me, as Christ has done for you? To practice submission to me, as I am the chosen one of Christ, sent to this earth to gather the only holy people left of this earth, to lead them into heaven?"

"I do." *Amen.*

His shout forces the people to their feet. "Witness God's newest soldier, with God's perfect timing of bringing her here this very day!" A standing ovation, tongues, amens, seizures, convulsions, tambourines: it's a zoo. I didn't need to be a Christian to know that there was something not right about this. *But play along, Freedom, play along.* Because it's not about my beliefs. It's not about religion. It's not about these people. It's not about me. It's about finding my estranged daughter.

Whatever it takes, just help me find my daughter, I pray to a god I'm not even sure is listening. I guess it can't hurt. *God, if you exist, if you're up there, somewhere, hear my silent prayer. These people are backward, they're manipulators of you, they twist scripture. But who am I to talk, I suppose. But if for once you listen to me, please get me answers. No matter what's happened, help me find Rebekah.*

At the center of the altar, a large white cross. I sit in a blue plastic kiddie pool with the help of Virgil and the Amalekite. I have to lie on my back to be fully submerged. I fix my focus to the cross from under the water until I'm pulled back up, Virgil's strength effortless. My ears ring with the racket. And out of several hundred spectators, it's Magdalene who catches my eye.

Her pigtails bounce, as she smiles from ear to ear. Ah, childhood innocence blanketed with the brainwashing of adults, bastardized by evil men. The people empty their pockets, all their savings and possessions, including children's toys and corn-husk dolls, dumped into offering plates. Virgil runs down to the pregnant women, who expose their bellies. And every time I try to get just a fraction of the Amalekite's attention, there's always somebody there to make sure I can't get a moment alone with her.

I stand in the pool. Surrounded by hundreds of arms pointed at me. I'm soaked; the clothes weigh a ton when wet. I shiver. I fake a smile and pretend to pray. I've never felt more alone.

46

ALL DEBTS ARE PAID

"This should do it." Virgil's lip curls as he tosses the duffel bag full of cash between him and the skinheads in the basement of the Bluegrass. "Rebekah's debts are paid."

"Well, isn't this a surprise," says Joe, the undercover ATF agent who was with Rebekah on the night she disappeared. "We was waiting for the Virgin Mary to show up. She's much easier on the eyes." Joe smiles with sarcasm, knowing that everyone in and outside that room knew of Virgil's daughter's disappearance.

Virgil fears that Rebekah missing the meeting for the next pickup of guns will earn him a visit from these guys at his church. And who could fathom that? Lowlifes, raping your wife, your daughter, tearing your church upside down. He had to keep them at bay, ward their threats off by maintaining the weekly ritual. And with news that there might be some undercover operation against him, he has to lie. *Forgive me, Lord.*

A skinhead from the rear of the basement begins to carry guns from an arsenal in the back. "No, I don't need those," says Virgil. "I'm just here to pay Rebekah's debts, whatever she's involved in with you peckerwoods."

"Rebekah . . ." Joe trails off.

"Sure, Rebekah. I don't know how she got involved in all of this, but it's over. I'm paying her debts." The skinheads look around. *What the fuck is this guy talking about?* But Virgil realizes the risk of wires and taps. He has to keep up with the charade.

Joe starts, "You mean to tell me that that cute little retard willingly, on her own accord, with sound mind, just decided one day to waltz into a bar, locate the nearest skinhead, and start asking him to help her smuggle hundreds of weapons under her skirt and out of this bar?"

Virgil responds, "Do you mean to tell me that on your own accord, with sound mind, willingly, you just decided to waltz into a bar, locate the nearest cute little retard, and start helping her smuggle hundreds of weapons under her skirt and out of this bar?" Virgil waits for a response but is met by silence.

"You come here to pay her debts." Joe smiles, walking toward Virgil with his hands on his hips. "And not once do you ask if we had anything to do with her disappearance?"

"You know where she is!" Virgil growls.

Joe laughs and looks around at the others. "I guess he needed to be reminded."

"An ATF sting, eh?" Virgil smirks. Mason did him a real favor by letting the cat out of the bag back at the police department. Joe's eyes widen. *He fucking knows.* "Nah. I doubt you'd hurt the little retard."

"ATF?" Joe fakes a laugh. "Wouldn't that be just darling?"

Virgil kicks the bag closer. "We're done here." Virgil goes to leave.

"What are you going to do with all those guns, anyway?" Joe calls out. "Where are you targeting? When? When will we see that some inbred church from Bumblefuck, Kentucky, carried through with an act of domestic terrorism in the headlines?"

"Domestic terrorism?" he asks, his back to the skinheads. He breathes out a trace of a laugh. "I'm sure you've got it all figured out, Agent."

■ ■ ■

Upstairs at the Bluegrass bar, Mattley asks around, aiming for people who look like they're regulars, permanent ass prints on the bar stools, a constant haze about them. But none of them offer anything about Rebekah. After asking well over a dozen of them, Mattley gives up and asks for a beer.

The bartender notices him, his shaven head. She leans across the bar. "Your friends are already downstairs." Mattley takes his head back. "Looks like an important meeting too."

A small red light starts blinking behind the bar near the cash register. The bartender squats down, Mattley leaning over to see, when two skinheads climb up from the trap door. Behind them, Virgil steps up.

Mattley turns away, hoping Virgil doesn't recognize him from the diner parking lot. He hides his face with the pint glass. He waits until Virgil leaves with the group until turning back to the bartender.

"Say, ma'am, you know where I can find a guy named Joe?" Mattley asks.

"He was one of the ones who just walked out the door. If you hurry, you can still catch him."

But Mattley remembers that Mason said Joe was with the ATF. And now he's walking outside with Reverend Virgil Paul and a couple skinheads. There is no doubt in Mattley's mind that he just witnessed a knee-deep undercover operation just walk out the door. And, of course, Mattley couldn't jeopardize the case. He treads lightly, following outside as the men get in separate cars, the reverend in one, the undercovers in another. Mattley, too, gets in his car, ready to follow.

But when they begin to exit the parking lot, each car goes in the opposite direction. Mattley must make a choice: follow the reverend or follow Joe.

47

WHEN LIFE GIVES YOU LEMONS

The Amalekite sews new gloves to the sleeves of my dry outfit, identical to the last. I'm craving a cigarette. I'm craving a drink even more. But most of all, I crave to know my daughter's whereabouts. With the old woman to my side, and Carol across the dining room table, Magdalene goes to kiss Carol good night.

"Welcome to our family," she says to me as she jumps to kiss me on the cheek. "I made your bed all nice for you, Sister Freedom. For when you come to sleep."

"Thank you, sweetheart," I tell her as she runs off upstairs.

"You may leave us as soon as you're finished, Amalekite," says Carol, as the old woman stitches the last of the gloves to my sleeves. I mean, really, can I just not put the gloves on separately? Do they really have to be sewed on? *For fuck's sake.*

Spools of white thread and a thimble disappear with the old woman, who hurries off without a sound. I am alone with Carol. And I can't put my finger on why, but I hate her already.

"How do you find yourself adjusting to Third-Day Adventists?" she asks, her thumbnails digging into the peels of lemons at the table. The rest of the house is dark, and God knows where Virgil is, not that I care too much.

"Oh, I like it just fine," I lie. Above the silence, the ticking of the cuckoo clock pings through the room, the smell of lemon making my mouth water. Carol's head rocks like she has a song stuck in her head, or maybe she's too used to sitting in the rocking chair. "Can I help you with the lemons?" She lifts her head. Has she never been asked such a question before?

"Why, thank you," she says, her answer hesitant.

I switch seats and grab a lemon from a porcelain bowl. "That's sure a lot of lemons. What are you doing with all of them?"

"They're for Sunday," she says, her head still swaying. "I make fresh-squeezed lemonade for the whole congregation, a treat for everyone after service."

"The *whole* congregation?" I ask.

"That's right. All four hundred fifty-three members. Well, four hundred fifty-four, now that you're here."

"I'm sorry," I say as I fumble with a lemon. "I didn't think I could be so useless with these gloves." I think she's smiling. But upon a closer look, she's crying, turning her face away from me so I can't see. "Did I say something wrong?"

She shakes her head, covering her snout with her arm. "It's my daughter." She bites her lips shut to subdue the whimpers. "I just miss my daughter, and I feel like I'm the only one around here who cares. Virgil doesn't talk about it; no one does. It's like saying her name is a sin around here, and I just can't take it." I don't say anything, just let her talk. I put my arm around her shoulders. She grunts. "I'm sorry, I don't mean to be such a mess in front of you."

Act oblivious. "What's your daughter's name?"

"Rebekah." She wipes the tears. "Rebekah Jane."

"And where is she now?"

A baby's crying from upstairs breaks the bond between us. "Is that a baby?" I ask.

"Yes, a girl. Her name is Theresa." Carol rises and picks pieces of lemon peel off the table. "We just took her in. Her mother died during childbirth. Tragic."

"Rebekah, Magdalene, and Theresa. No sons?"

"No," she says as she shuts off the kitchen lights. "Thank you for being someone I can talk to." She disappears up the stairs, toward the room of a crying infant.

■ ■ ■

I look down to hundreds of parishioners at Third-Day Adventist Church. All of them, toppling over one another with fear, and I don't know why. I wave my hand. When I move my hand to the right, they run left and vice versa. I'm screaming at them, "Don't be afraid, don't be afraid." I don't understand why they're screaming at me in terror. I see Carol. I see Virgil. I see Magdalene. I see the Amalekite. I see Mason. I see Passion. I can see everyone. I wave my hand faster and faster, side to side, and they try to hide, they cannot leave the sanctuary. "Don't be afraid, I'm not going to hurt you."

"Eeny meeny miny moe." I laugh. I'm not sure why I say these words. And when I finally stop my hand, I'm pointing down the center, right down the aisle. I'm pointing at Rebekah.

That's when I see that in my hand, I'm holding a pistol. And that's why everyone is terrified. I aim it and I shoot. Rebekah falls dead, her head clean off. And I keep shooting, aiming for everyone, like shooting fish in a barrel, but Rebekah is the only one I kill. I keep waving my hand; click-click-click goes the now-empty pistol. But the clicking in my dream . . .

I jump from my sleep. For a moment I don't know where I am. The room's almost dark like the rest of the house, but for a night-light at the side of Magdalene's bed. As my eyes adjust to the dark, I see Magdalene jump back into bed and hide under the covers.

Breathe, Freedom. It was just a nightmare. I force a steady breath and sit up. I'm tangled in the heavy cloth I'm forced to wear; my legs can't find their way out. No wonder I'm having nightmares when sleeping in my missing daughter's bed. "Magdalene," I whisper. She doesn't answer, but I see her shift. I know what I heard. I might be crazy, but I know what I fucking heard.

I tiptoe to her and shake the lump under the covers. "Magdalene, I know you're awake," I say, making sure she can't mistake my voice as being angry.

She pokes her head out. "You were saying terrible, awful, shameful cuss words in your sleep, Sister Freedom."

I'm not sure what to say; I don't think I'm all that good around children. They make me uneasy these days. "Magdalene, what was that noise?"

"What noise?" But the kid's a bad liar.

"Honey." She slides over so I can sit at the side of her bed. "I promise I won't tell anyone if you were doing something that you don't want anyone to know about."

"It's not a secret I'm hiding from anyone around here. It's just a secret I have to hide from you."

"Says who?"

"Says Mommy and Daddy." She gasps at her own slipup, covering her mouth with her hands.

I smile at her. She's five, for God's sake. I can win this. "What if I make a pinkie promise not to tell?"

"On a stack of Bibles?"

"On ten stacks of Bibles."

She smiles.

I pick her up and off the bed, her hair wild and poking in every which direction, her eyes full of sleep crust. When I put her down, she goes to her knees and pulls out a shoebox. "This is called my secret box." She hands it up to me. On the top, a pistol. An honest-to-God, real-life pistol.

"Honey, where on earth did you get this?!"

"Everyone gets one. Didn't you? You can use mine if you want."

I'm at a loss of words. And before I ask, I fear I already know the answer. "Why does everyone have one, sweetheart?"

"For the Day of Freedom, silly." She grabs the pistol from my hand and goes to put it to her head, a fucked-up version of show-and-tell. I stop her. "When Jesus calls us home."

"Whatta ya say I take this for now, just until I get one of my own, is that OK?" I ask.

"Want me to show you how you're supposed to fill it with the confetti?" She holds up a bullet from the box. "We don't put it in until the Day of Freedom, and you can't see the confetti now. . . ."

They're aiming for a fucking mass suicide! Breathe. Don't panic in front of the kid.

"No need for that, I think I can figure it out." Five years old. She has no idea what she's doing. She has no idea of the consequences of a gun when it's loaded. Suddenly, I feel sick; my heart begins to race. But I have to hide it. "Go back to sleep, honey."

What the fuck have I gotten into? What have I let my children into?

I tuck her in, my mouth full of cotton, the sweat tickling my ribs under the heavy clothes, palms sweating through the gloves. As I go to put her secret box under the bed, tucking the pistol in the back of my underwear, I see a letter, a letter that I'd ignore at any other time. But this letter is singed at the edges.

And still smells of firecrackers.

I sneak it past Magdalene and take it to the window, where I can get some light between a full moon and a gaslight that illuminates the driveway below.

My dearest Rebekah,

I cannot imagine there being a right way to write this to you. My name is Nessa Delaney, and I met you twenty years ago and knew you a whole two minutes and seventeen seconds. I know this doesn't seem like a long time, but even eternity can last only a moment.

I've watched you, I watch you from afar. And you look so incredibly happy, my only qualm in writing this letter. And if you are happy and content with where you are today, then please disregard this. But if you ever seek truth, hard and heavy truth, then there is something you need to know.

Before those two minutes and seventeen seconds, I felt you grow in my body and swim in my blood for nine months. I felt your first hiccups. I felt you kick. And I held you for your first cries, your first gasps of air on this earth. I loved you before I knew you. I loved you every second since. And I love you tomorrow as well.

I trust that your family has raised you well, raised you in a happy and safe home that I could not provide for you all those years ago. And I could say "I'm sorry" from now until my last dying breath, but it could never actually express my full sorrow. If only you could see how I've suffered with such pain, penance for all the terrible things I felt for making that decision. But if you asked me, "Do I regret that choice?" my answer would still be no. Because from it, you grew in a place where you were loved, and what mother could ask for anything else? But do I regret the choices I made and didn't make that led up to that point? Well, the answer is yes, every day since. And for every day to come.

If you never want to see me or contact me, I will understand. But know this, above all else: I never loved anyone or anything in life more than you and your brother. You two were the only light I'd ever known in this dark world. And I never loved again, not since I loved you. I only wish that love was enough.

Be well,

Nessa Delaney

I look down at the driveway. All is silent but the resounding of the American flag flapping, the ropes hitting the pole in front of the house. I read the letter about a thousand times, maybe more, until daylight comes. I don't move from near the window. I'm too afraid to go back to sleep, at the risk of one of those horrible dreams again. I smell breakfast. The sun comes up. The dew glistens in the morning; people dressed in clothes identical to mine start pacing around their yards with a buzz.

I'd heard from somewhere, a long time ago, that killing a person in your dream meant that you are losing self-control.

I dreamt I killed my daughter. Can I really be losing control? Or is it already lost?

48

THE DEACONS

Reverend Virgil Paul hopes to breathe a little easier when his office door closes behind him and Sheriff Mannix.

"This is turning into one giant clusterfuck." The reverend shakes the light rain from his hair as he looks in the vanity mirror with worry. "This nonsense with the ATF. Something needs to happen."

"Sure does," the sheriff says as he removes his hat. "Lucky Mason spilled his guts when you saw him at the jail—my guys had no idea anyone was on to us 'bout the gunrunning."

"Rebekah . . ." Virgil trails off as he plops in his chair behind the desk. "Too bad they were too late. We already have all the guns we need for the Day of Freedom. She did a swell job." At the thought, Virgil stares out the window and looks down on the residents at their daily chores: the construction of a couple more homes, pruning the vines, chopping and collecting wood for the winter. He can smell that electricity in the air, the one that cautions winter is near. His thumbs play with each other on his lap.

"How'd you fare with Michelle Campbell the other night?" The sheriff leans his rear against the other side of the desk.

A lift of the lip shows his teeth. "I think I'm getting too old for this."

"You didn't bury her whole, did you?"

"Of course not, Don. What do you think I am?"

Virgil violently shakes his head at the thoughts: Whistler's Field, a neighboring meadow outside the compound's gates, where his secrets are chopped and buried. There was Michelle Campbell, the one who got the most media attention after she disappeared. There was Frannie Tish. There was Johanna Studebaker. There was Catherine Keller. There was Margot McDonald. There was Jenny Freemason. There were many.

The number of girls that the reverend and sheriff had buried in secret in Whistler's Field was bordering on too many to remember. Virgil can never forget their skin, like porcelain on a warm evening. Their lips, as sweet as the peaches that grow in Georgia. Their hair that caught all of Virgil's whispers when he came to them in the night. Their scents, fresh and brand-new, those scents of virgins.

Virgil has fathered a total of fifty-eight children within the past five years. Those girls' tender bodies starting to thaw from childhood were perfect breeding grounds for Virgil's seeds, the holy ones, the only holy ones that occupy this wretched and evil earth. And God deemed Virgil so worthy of the job that the young girls would welcome him with open arms, as they should. Who wouldn't want to breed holy in their wombs, after all?

But then there were those few who rebelled, the ones who let Satan get those seeds, in the forms of miscarriages or the mothers dying while giving birth, and God has no place for such people on this earth. With the sheriff's help, they were banished from the church, sent to Whistler's Field.

"No matter what you decide, Virgil, I'll back you up," says the sheriff. He was Virgil's most dependable friend; they had grown up right here in Goshen.

Sheriff Don Mannix had been part of the church since it began and remained loyal through all its transformations. He is a deacon of Third-Day Adventists, and that means he has one job and one job only: to kill off the survivors.

The Day of Freedom was upon them, when Virgil would lead

their souls into heaven, rid them from the sins of this world, make the transformation complete. But Satan will tempt some of them to cowardly actions, and it will be the deacons' jobs to complete their entrance into heaven, so that Satan cannot win.

■ ■ ■

"Where did you get such blasphemy?" Virgil screamed through his teeth at Rebekah, throwing the letter from Nessa in her face.

"This is wrong! This is all wrong!" Rebekah screamed back, at a volume that was foreign to her lungs. It made the skin of her throat raw; it turned her shades of red she'd never known. From the living room, the Amalekite took Magdalene upstairs to where Carol listened. "Why didn't you ever tell me?" she said, her words so loud that some syllables were absent of any sound at all.

Virgil backhanded her, her cheek tender, throbbing from his knuckles. She tasted the copper pennies, felt the newly formed groove of her bottom lip. "Your disobedience . . . You have the demonic blood of your biological mother. You and Mason both. You two were spawns of Satan! And I regret the day I ever let you enter this holy house! So go! Go, if that's what you want to do! Find the woman whose sewer of a womb you crawled out of!"

Virgil left because he could no longer stand Carol's whimpers while their daughter packed a suitcase. Rebekah barely said good-bye, but promised that she'd be back for Magdalene when no one was around to hear. Magdalene did not understand, but she cried at her big sister leaving. She followed her to the gates while the rest of the family remained at home. She squeezed the front of her face between the steel bars, yelled "I love you" to Rebekah, and waved her off.

Rebekah waved back, one last time before walking out of sight down the road. "I'm going to come back for you. I promise."

And that was the last time she was seen near the Paul farm.

■ ■ ■

Together, Virgil and Don stuff Virgil's wardrobe with stacks of cash, well over a million dollars: more than enough to get him and Carol and Magdalene over the Mexican border. It was the tithes he took from the residents, ninety percent of them for the past several years. It was their sacrifice, their keep; there were many things one could call these earnings. But they belonged to Virgil, they belonged to God's chosen master. He dreamed of starting a ministry on the white sands of the Mexican coast. In several years, Magdalene would be at that age where she could procreate.

The mass suicide of his congregation was a surefire way of escaping, an assurance so that while the rest would be sitting at the right throne of God, Virgil could continue with his work, sowing his seeds, spreading his reach to the south, maybe even as far as Central and South America. He couldn't let the laws of the earth, the ways of man, hinder this. Sure, they'd arrest him, saying he murdered all these girls. But Virgil didn't abide by man's law. He followed God's. And after all, that was all in God's plan, the girls and such.

Of course, little Magdalene had to believe in the Day of Freedom. If not, there was the risk of his escape plans falling through, the loss of his followers, had she told just one person that she'd not be entering the kingdom of God with the others.

The room smells like cash and anointing oil. He looks out the window, his sigh fogging the glass. In the distance, he thinks he sees Freedom, Magdalene trailing behind her. But Virgil thought he had more time. Between Mason's declaration back at the jail cell of the ATF being involved; the meeting with the skinheads; Rebekah's disappearance; their last arriving member, FreedomInJesus. Virgil thought there'd be more time before he had to say these words: "Prepare. The Day of Freedom is finally upon us."

49

THEIR BLOOD, YOUR HANDS

My name is Freedom and the heaviness of my skirt and robe slows me down. Men in construction trill their tools in the corners of my earshot as I shuffle into the dense forest, whipped by twigs, the scent of soil kind through my nostrils. Despite my lack of sense of direction, I aim for the protesters; I rip through the branches that catch the cotton like claws reaching out to stop me in my tracks. I rip, I roar, I bleed, but the pain only drives me faster.

In some way, I can feel it in my blood: the sense that I'm going in the right direction, the sense that I'm heading toward the clamshell roads that carry the crazies. But I'm slow, I'm out of shape. I wipe the snot with my sewn-on gloves. And I hear Magdalene trailing behind, but I pretend not to notice. I suppose it's better that she follows me than is at home with the fucking psychos.

"Sister Freedom, we're supposed to be washing floors! Why are we running through the forest?!" she squeals.

I see the black gates; I see the signs hung on them through the trees. Protesters' voices take shape the closer I get, their chants transforming from a thick purr into glass-like comprehension. "Stay where you are," I yell back to Magdalene, unsure of whether or not she hears me. I finally reach the gates. In a gesture of desperation, I pull myself up and stand on the lowest bar.

"You have to get us the fuck out of here," I plead with the activists. "You need to go get help!" But my words seem to drown in their clamor. "Will you fucking listen to me, for fuck's sake! Listen to me!"

I spit out words, words in no particular order: words like *Mass, Suicide, ATF, Fucking psychos.* And these are all attention-grabbing words. Yet their attention is elsewhere, settled somewhere between false gods and vehement indoctrination. The louder I get, the louder they become. I scream until my ribs ache and the walls of my throat might bleed.

And from the back, of fucking course, the short butch who egged me the day before makes her way to the front of the crowd. I reach through the gates and stare directly into her swollen eyes. "You need to get the ATF. There's about to be four hundred fifty corpses behind these walls." The woman seems to listen to me. Her shoulders rock from side to side as she walks to me at the gates. My heart rate drops down to a steadier pace when she shows signs of concern, when she listens. "You have to get help. There are children in here, for God's sake."

But her compassionate expression becomes a twist of the lips, there's a strange glimmer in her black eyes, and she pelts me with a hard-boiled egg. I just manage to catch her by the fringe of her hood and pull her back to the gates. I grab her, double-fisted, pushing the gates with my heels. With her back to me, I wrap my arm around her throat and squeeze with every drop of panic that swims through my muscles. I scream in her ear, "Their blood will be on your hands, then. Their blood will be on your hands!"

Then the strong arms of another around my own throat. I release the butch when I'm twisted around like a rag doll, a tornado of heavy cotton being pulled in a headlock back toward the compound. It's Reverend Virgil Paul, his pace faster than my thoughts. I cannot see Magdalene, but I hear her, her pleas for her father not to hurt me.

"Get on back home to your mother," he yells out to her. On the way out of the forest, the workers and residents stare, eyes cold and distant, lifeless marbles peering from blankets of cloth. The only sign of life, their breath in the cold front that sweeps over this place, this fucking place.

Ahead is the shed. That's where we're going. The people, the scenery, it all seems to disappear, fade away from me. It's only Virgil and I. The Dutch door slams behind us, the noise turning my spinal fluid into ice water. He grabs me by my hair, and in one effortless heave, I'm thrown to the floor. I remember the gun, still in the back of my skirt. I need to find out where Rebekah is.

He grabs a five-pound bag of uncooked rice and pours it around me on the floor. I try my best to keep facing toward him so he won't spot the gun.

"Kneel," he demands. "Kneel on the rice." It's uncomfortable at first, but I obey without one word. He kicks me, right in the kidney, enough that it takes the wind out of me. I'm sure to piss blood later on. The pain shoots up to my armpit, I can't make a sound through it. "For your iniquities, you do not deserve this Day of Freedom."

"You're a fucking murderer! This Day of Freedom is a lie. It's a mass suicide!"

He punches me in the face; I swear I hear my skull split in half. I taste blood almost immediately. Virgil seems to regain his composure, leaning down to face me. "Who are you, Freedom? Who are you really?" I hear his bones grind, I smell his sweat above me.

"I'm a fucking ATF agent." I'm not sure why this is the first thing to come out of my mouth—one of my most outlandish lies. But he doesn't gamble with it.

"ATF, huh?"

I grin, a mouthful of blood. "So you can forget your plans to kill me. They all know I'm here. And there's no way you'll get away with this horror." The rice begins to burn the skin of my knees.

From a standing faucet in the corner of the shed, Virgil fills two buckets with water. "I'm not going to kill you, Freedom. Because I'm not the murderer you think I am." His voice is alarmingly calm.

He places the handle of each bucket in one of my hands and makes me hold my arms up. He takes what looks like a broom handle and straps it on my shoulders, threading each end through the bucket handles. I am reminded of Christ's Crucifixion, carrying the weight of the world. The grains of rice start to feel like glass, and my knees bleed under the weight of the water. But I don't whine. I don't groan. I refuse to give this guy the satisfaction he so desires. "But you will stay in here. And you will listen to those around you ascend to heaven. And you will live the rest of your life with their blood on *your* hands."

The pain makes me impulsive. "Where is Rebekah?"

"Is that why you're here? Over her disappearance?"

"What does it matter if you tell me the truth now?"

"I loved Rebekah. What makes you think I had anything to do with her disappearance?"

"We know she was running guns for Third-Day Adventists."

His words become hisses. "Rebekah was the last one of this congregation to make me angry, to turn her back on this church." He walks around me. "So I'd choose my words wisely."

"Or what?"

Virgil gazes out the window. "What happened to Rebekah should be of no concern to you." He opens the top of the Dutch door and calls out to one of the nearby workers, demanding he fetch the Amalekite. "It had nothing to do with the guns."

"Just tell me where she is," I scream.

The Amalekite arrives with the other worker, head down, cotton dirty. "Stay here with the infidel," Virgil instructs them. The man with us is a thin one who looks like the offspring of a Holocaust victim and a scarecrow.

"Answer me, Virgil! Where the hell is she?"

He doesn't say anything at first. He just stares at me with cold, hard eyes. I'm shaking with rage. He leans down, close enough that I can feel his breath. "Which part?"

The blood rises up my neck to my bleeding face. I think I break a few teeth with my own jaw. The buckets of water shake with my hands, my body breaking under the weight, along with my heart. I want to chase the man down as he leaves; I want to rip him open with my bare hands. We listen to him lock the only door of the shed from the outside.

"Amalekite." It's hard to breathe. "Amalekite, you have to help me. You have to help me before it's too late." Her head doesn't move. She narrows her eyes toward the scarecrow. "You can't let this happen. You can't let all these people die like this!"

"We have a higher purpose," says Scarecrow. "We're gonna ascend to the thrones of the Lord."

"God's purpose has nothing to do with mass suicide, can't you see that?" The rice digs into my kneecaps. "What God wants this? You're not worshiping God, you're worshiping a monster who doesn't give two flying fucks about you!" The scarecrow scuffs his toes on the wood floor. I direct my attention to the Amalekite. "You can't let them hurt Magdalene. I know how much she means to you, I see it every time you look at her." There's sorrow in her eyes, the kind that begs to speak, the kind that's afraid to speak.

Suddenly, the sounds of a siren blaring through the compound. Everyone holds their breath. Everyone freezes. Everyone swallows their fear.

"What the hell is that?" I ask the Amalekite.

"The Day of Freedom has arrived."

I drop the buckets. I pull the grains of rice from my skin. I grab the Amalekite by the shoulders. But Scarecrow gets brave; he gets too brave for his own good. He tries to stop me. *Really? Your 140 pounds against a mother hearing the news of her daughter's death? I don't think so, buddy.* I'm insatiable, unstoppable, and I have this insane lust for violence right now.

I grab my empty pistol from behind me and whack the scarecrow on the side of the head with all the rage I have in me, every cell of this bag of blood you'd call a body. He falls to the ground, unconscious. *Consider it a favor, kid.*

"Do you know where they store the ammo?" I ask as I creep to the window. Outside, the people in white scatter home; they call out to one another. My rage turns to vitality. Hurt turns to ambition. It all turns into vengeance.

"I know who you are." Her pronouncement cuts through the air like a dull butter knife on dry meat. "She looked just like you."

"He's not going to get away with this."

"We're never going to make it out of here alive."

"Ye of little faith." I look around for a way out. "I just need the ammo."

"I know where it is."

"How much time do we have?" I ask.

"A matter of minutes."

I don't have a plan. I don't know where to start. There is no time to think. There is only just enough time to react. I find a spare pile of clothes in the shed, letting the bloody ones fall to the floor. The windows are painted shut, but no one seems to be paying attention from the outside. I wrap the soiled clothes around my fist and break the window opposite the church. I climb out, using my foot to kick the remaining shards from the pane. I help the Amalekite out after me.

"How fast can you get it?" I ask.

"It's up in Rebekah's room. Under her bed."

"Where will the Pauls be?"

"In the church," the Amalekite says. "They will all be there for the Day of Freedom."

"Shit." *React, Freedom. React.* "I'll get the ammo. I'll meet you back here."

50

CABIN FEVER

Mason and Peter take the tea that one of the ATF agents brings back from the Circle K. With the draperies of the cabin motel room drawn and the cloudy weather, it feels later than it is. Without asking, Mason reaches down to Peter's leg and pulls the flask from his sock. A shot in each one of their paper cups. "Bourbon's my poison of choice too," says Mason.

"You definitely have the Delaney blood in you."

"I shudder to think." Mason walks over to the radios that came from the Redindelly's eighteen-wheeler, the contents of which are now stationed in the one-room cabin only two minutes from the Paul farm. Closed-circuit screens show shots of different areas of the farm from the gates, but nothing beyond them. With the exception of the protesters huddling around the south end of the gate for reasons beyond the camera's vantage point nearly an hour ago, there hadn't been any movement on those screens since Freedom arrived. He stands shoulder to shoulder with the bald skinhead he met in the truck. "No word from the wire yet?"

"Not since she was with the Amalekite getting undressed yesterday."

Mason swallows hard. "How much longer are we going to have

to wait until we do something?" He takes a quick sip of the tea. "I don't know how much more of this I can stand."

"We're not going to jeopardize this case because you're having mommy issues," says the skinhead, without taking his eyes off the screens. "So just chill out and take a seat. Let us big boys do the work."

Mason rolls his eyes and walks back toward Peter, muttering the word "asshole" under his breath. He sits at the foot of the bed next to Peter when Joe pours another shot into Mason's mug for him. "Tell me about Rebekah," Mason says as he rubs his brow. "I've missed her. And I feel like I know absolutely nothing about her, given what I've just learned about her in recent days."

"She is kind." Joe moans as he slides his back against the wall and sits. "She would come in, every Sunday, like clockwork. She'd come in with her father's cash, by the hundreds, used to take the bus in."

Mason tries to imagine his sister on a bus.

"The guys would strap the guns to her, duct tape around the legs. It was easy. There's no security with the Greyhound buses, and the clothes from her church covered all of them. Hell, on a good day, we could strap her with up to sixteen at a time. Then she'd take the bus right back to Goshen." Joe looks over and sees in Mason's face that these aren't the kinds of things he wanted to know. He shifts the subject. "Her favorite food was biscuits 'n gravy." Joe stares off. "Before business, the kid always asked for biscuits 'n gravy and a Pepsi."

Necks turn, headphones land on the shoulders. "What the fuck is that?" says Peter.

The room freezes until one of the agents starts yelling into a radio, "We're going in, we have to go in now."

Mason runs outside and looks toward the direction of his family's home where the sirens come from. And suddenly it clicks. He turns back in and grabs the skinhead by the shirt. "You told me domestic terrorism, you sonuvabitch!" he screams in his face.

"They're about to kill themselves, aren't they? They're planning a fucking suicide. Tell me! Tell me, goddamn it!"

The skinhead's at a loss for words. The color of Joe's face goes white, his jaw dropping to the floor.

"Joe, we got something!" yells one of the agents by the radios. While the rest of them call for backup and storm out of the cabin, Joe turns up the radio.

On the other end: "Is there anybody there?" The voice comes from the wire they hooked onto Freedom. But the voice doesn't belong to her. "There are children in here, you have to get us out. Please, God. Somebody help us!"

As Mason and Peter go to follow the ATF team, Mason stops at the last second when he spots movement on one of the surveillance cameras: on it, three men scale the gates and break into the church of the Third-Day Adventists.

51

A PARADE OF WHITE

My name is Freedom and my mind races too fast for my hands. They tremble, I drop bullets, but I manage to load my gun. Magdalene's gun. *I'll get these bastards, Rebekah. I'll get them all, my only promise to you.*

The house practically shakes under me at the noise. It cracks through the cold air like the God they adore so much cracks his knuckles in the sky. Four hundred–plus pistols going off at the same time. It happens that fast.

I feel my knees give way. Magdalene. All those lost men, all those women, all those children. Magdalene.

Then, earth-shattering silence unlike anything I've ever experienced. An awful silence, a silence that would plague all my dreams to come. I fall on the bed, but it's not deliberate. I find myself inhaling the scent from Rebekah's pillowcase. I mourn for the daughter I never knew, and even more, I find my heart breaking over Magdalene. She's gone. Now they're both gone.

If anything could bring me back to life right now, it'd be Magdalene's voice. And here it is; as clear as a whistle, splitting through the house, I hear Magdalene cry. I hear her scream in terror, but it's not as terrible as hearing Virgil and Carol Paul accompanying her.

Suddenly, currents of electricity replace my blood and breath rushes through my airways. I've never felt more alive. I've never felt so alert. But I stay quiet. I listen. Not even they believed their own sermons. They never even had faith in their own twisted versions of God.

"Well, you shouldn't have gone public with Rebekah's disappearance," Carol barks.

"I didn't have a choice!" Virgil yells back. "Magdalene, get upstairs."

"Did you at least get the tithes? The money?"

"We'll get it now, just get your stuff! We have to leave right this second, before anyone catches on." I hear a cry from Carol, and Virgil, in a more reassuring voice, says, "The witnesses are taken care of; they're all dead. The deacons will take care of the rest. We just have to avoid them, and we'll be fine. We'll head to Mexico. But I'm not kidding, Carol, we have to leave now!"

As Magdalene cries on her way up the staircase, I crouch behind the door. When she comes in, I pull her down to my lap and cover her mouth, whispering in her ear, "Don't be afraid. Don't be afraid, I'm not going to hurt you," the same words from the dream where I gunned down my own daughter.

She turns and wraps her arms around my neck. "Stay as quiet as you can," I tell her.

The conversation between her parents downstairs continues. "You think it's the way I wanted? You think I wanted to hurt Rebekah?" he cries.

"You did what you had to do, Virgil," Carol reassures him.

That fucking cunt! Crying to me the other night because she missed Rebekah. She knew she was dead the entire time, the whole fucking time!

"She deserved better than the others chopped and buried in Whistler's Field. I couldn't help myself," he says. "I only meant to find her at the Bluegrass and take her back home. But things just got out of hand. Oh, Carol, if you only saw what I saw when I went to get her. She was dressed like some whore; bleached hair; getting in the car with some thug. The sight was horrible Carol, just god-awful."

"Stay right here," I whisper, as I carry Magdalene to her bed. I look out the window to see the Amalekite pacing on one side of the shed. A man approaches the other side of the building with a rifle, wearing a golden crown on his head. Magdalene pulls my arms, silently sobbing, begs me not to leave her.

But I have to. There's no way out of this. I can't prevent what I'm about to do. I can only prevent a five-year-old from watching me gun down her parents. And that is all.

If you think about it, it's a flawless scenario in which to murder two people: amid a massive suicide. If I can keep the angles right, it can be attributed simply to that. Plus, let's not forget the gloves sewn onto my sleeves. No fingerprints. It's almost perfect. And this perfection brings a smile to my face. *Does this make me an evil person? A sick one?* I creep down the stairs.

Perhaps it's only natural of a mother. I don't know the rules.

My hands are surprisingly still. My aim suddenly impeccable. Their faces freeze when I walk into the kitchen, gun raised.

"What's going on, Virgil?" Carol asks, the scent of her fear filling the room, lemons in the background. They're unarmed.

He puts up his hands. "She's ATF." And I'd love to sit here and deliver some speech to them, some Hollywood scene where I reveal who I really am, taking off the mask. *You're Rebekah and Mason's biological mother!* But none of that happens, because there isn't any time. I have to get to the Amalekite before the man with the crown does.

I point my finger left, toward the window. "Look, it's Rebekah!" I lie.

I shoot Carol first as she looks. One shot, in the side of the head. I can afford only one bullet per person to make it look like a suicide. Virgil's screams are interrupted by my second shot. He falls on top of her. They bleed. Bits of their faces and heads over one of their HOME SWEET HOME needlepoint works on the wall. And while I'd hoped that I'd find some relief in this, there isn't any.

The sight brings me back to my old kitchen twenty years ago

with Mark's body. A cuckoo clock chirps through the house, breaking the silence.

My heart races; my head fills with warm cream soda. A panic attack. The perfect fucking timing. The walls pulsate around me. My ears ring, but I'm not sure if it's from the attack or from shooting two shots indoors. I grab for something to hold on to, keep myself from falling off something that doesn't exist. But there's no time for this, I have to move, I have to keep moving.

Through the panic attack, my trip up the staircase feels more like a swim. *I'm coming, Magdalene.* And I'd forgotten. I'd forgotten until I hear the cries of an infant that Theresa is in the house. "Get the baby," I yell up to the girl. "Stay with the baby." I pull myself up by the railing and reach the top of the stairs just in time to see Magdalene hurry from her room and into a back one where the baby's cries rise, a tornado of cotton and pigtails up the hallway.

Through the sobs, Magdalene shushes the baby. "It's OK, Sister Theresa, there, there."

"Stay in there for just a minute," I call out to her when I enter Rebekah and Magdalene's bedroom. I sit on the windowsill, resting my sore ribs against pink lace curtains. I open the four-squared windows; chips of white paint and dead flies cocooned in dust fall to my thighs.

Now my hands tremble from the anxiety attack. But the deacon, by some act of God, has not yet spotted the Amalekite. A ray of sun pokes through the clouds and the light rain, it sparkles off his golden crown. A rifle rests like a beauty queen's sash across his chest. He's about to turn the corner to where the Amalekite is. I aim my piece; I inhale as slowly as I can to stop the tremors. I squint against an unforgiving but low, cold sun breaking through the leadenness of a waning autumn.

Then, like it has no business being in such a place, color appears from the corner of my eye, right when I'm about to put the pressure on the trigger. Three columns of color, crossing the browns and rotting yellows of a dying fall. I recognize them right away.

The Delaney brothers: Matthew, Luke, and John.

They walk around as if they're lost, wandering like children who can't find their mother, tourists who lost sight of the bus leaving for the hotel. Contrasting with those in white, like a blemish on the heaths of Kentucky.

"Stay in there, Magdalene," I call, quiet enough so no one can hear me through the silence outside, making sure she wouldn't do something as regretful as walking downstairs to the kitchen to see her parents, dead on top of each other on the floor.

"OK, Sister Freedom," she whispers back at me.

For a moment, I can picture myself sitting up here on the second floor, looking down, with one of those old-fashioned red-and-white striped popcorn bags, eating away, laughing at some comedy, hard enough that it aches my ribs. But in real life, I'm quiet as the deacon guarding the shed who sees the three men crossing the hill toward him. I fold the smile behind my lips. I have to stay in control.

I'll let the deacon do me this favor.

One. Two. Three. Three seconds to wipe out an entire family, each shot echoing like the sirens that called the rest into heaven . . . or somewhere.

Like puppets having the strings cut from above them, they fall to the ground. And in this moment, two decades of pain, of being tormented by my own memories, of self-hatred, seems to just dissipate. Like for the first time in twenty years, I take my first fresh breath. The memories of rape, no longer demons that come out when I drink enough to forget about them, seem to feel like something I've conquered, something I was pulled through. The weight of my husband's death no longer feels like a loss, but instead like a feat I braved. The loss of my children . . . well. Not sure if there's anything that can fix that. Not even watching the men I hate most in the world die right before my eyes can fix that.

The shooter is a virgin, gets sick all over the side of the shed, his crown falling disgracefully in his own vomit on the wildflowers that line the building's edges, color against white walls. Fragrant. Pleasing to the eyes. Abundant. Sprayed in vomit. Such is life.

The Amalekite hears the shots, hears him retch. *Don't worry, Amalekite. I got you.*

I aim, a shaky, imaginary line that vibrates on the side of his face while he wipes the puke with his sleeve. *I got you, Amalekite. Bang!* The hot shell casing stings my cheek, gives me a fright. I didn't get him where I wanted to; instead, I think I got him on the side of his ribs. But he's immobile. He's not going anywhere.

Beyond him, I see three more deacons, separated, but working in perfect unison, visiting house to house. Occasionally, the sound of a gunshot ringing in the air from one of the small sugar-cube homes. We have to get the fuck out of here. I reach under Rebekah's bed and help myself to two large handfuls of bullets, dropping them into deep pockets. I poke my head out into the hallway and whistle. "Bring the baby here." I take the front of my skirt and turn it into a sling for Theresa, fisting a bunch of cotton in front of me and putting it in my teeth to hold it together. I carry Magdalene on the other side of my body, mantled against my elbow, as I make my way down the stairs and through the kitchen. "You must close your eyes now, Magdalene," I say with the knot of cloth at the side of my mouth, held in my back teeth. "Keep them closed as tight as you can until I say so, all right?"

"OK, Sister Freedom." Her sobs have stopped, and the girl displays a level of bravery I could only envy. Truth be told, I'm scared to death. I'm not brave. I am not strong. I've only kept moving. That's all I've ever done in times of trouble, when shit hits the fan. I just moved. But I can't let it show. *Just move, just fucking move. React, Freedom. React.* "And don't make a peep, sweetie."

I carry the girls out the back door, stepping over Virgil's dead arm at one point, Magdalene's head buried in the crook of my neck. When we reach the back of the house and I peek around a corner, I put Magdalene down, maneuvering the makeshift sling to my side, holding Theresa like a football. "Magdalene, you can open your eyes, but keep them looking at the ground, all right? You gotta stay as quiet as you can, but hold on to my elbow and run as fast as I do; only stop if I stop. OK? And if anything happens to me, take Theresa and find the Amalekite behind the shed, understand? Do you understand everything I just said to you?" I take the bunch of cotton and put it back in my teeth, using my finger for the baby to suck on when she starts to move in her sleep, the same arm that Magdalene holds on to, as instructed.

"I'm so scared, Sister Freedom."

"So am I," I tell Magdalene, my words garbled with the fabric in the side of my teeth, high in my cheek. "But I believe in God. God's strength will get you through this. Do you believe that?" I'm not sure that I do. But the concept fills her face with determination, for which I am grateful. And out of desperation, I try. I ask the God that I hardly believe in to grant me strength, to help the girls make it out on the other end of this alive. He can take me, just save these girls. Because, while I may deserve what's in store for me, they don't.

We scuttle, dash like spiders across the lawn, the sun returning to the shadows. The rain's cold, cruel on my skin. I taste my heart; it pumps more blood than should be through my body. Terror moves me, once my enemy but now a friend that helps me go, go, go. And as I reach the shed, I realize I'm slower than the five-year-old, gripping the pistol with my other hand so hard that I can no longer feel my fingers.

The Amalekite puts her finger to her mouth to keep Magdalene quiet when she jumps at the sight of the old woman. We lean, backs to the side of the shed, the side that doesn't face the church. "I don't have a plan." I think I'm crying. I think I am. Because, once again, there's no hope, I've failed again.

"We've come this far; you can't give up now," says the Amalekite. She reaches into her pocket. "Not sure if it's working right, but I spoke, anyway. I told them, whoever's at the other end, to come and rescue us. That was only minutes ago." The wire I was wearing when I entered Third-Day Adventists uncoils at our feet. I hand the Amalekite the infant.

"Let us pray," says Magdalene, the childlike innocence almost comforting.

Our heads jump, noises from the forest that sound like lightning; *crack, roar, rev.* I look around the corner one last time. No deacons in sight. Weaving through the trees, red, white, and blue.

Red, white, and blue. The American fucking dream.

Sirens, bullhorns demanding the deacons to stand down. Military tanks with American flags flapping rapidly on top. The sun breaks through once more. We wait like impatient children, with impatient children. I squeeze Magdalene so she can hear my heart flutter. "We're going to be OK. It's over now. It's all over now," I weep.

It could have been another Waco, easily. It could have been a fifty-one-day standoff, history repeating itself. They could have set fire to the sugar-cube houses, turning them into burned candy, members of the congregation caramelized inside.

It takes an hour to feel safe enough to leave this side of the shed. The hills swarm with the ATF, the FBI, and I'm not sure if that's actually the military. The newspapers will tell me in a few days. We're led out by men who resemble insects, black shells for faces, armed to the teeth.

A parade of white. Myself, Magdalene, Theresa, and the Amalekite. Back to the clamshell roads we march.

The protesters are gone, but we're met by hundreds of cops, reporters, cameras. Stuck in the crowd, I see Mason with his uncle Peter. I nod to them. And aside from the suicide, I remember Rebekah. But I stifle the cries. Afternoon creeps closer toward the night. The masses ask for our names. To my left, a good few feet away, I hear the Amalekite. "My name is Adelaide. My name is Adelaide Custis." The crowd gasps. I guess the world already knows who she is.

"The wife of Ger Custis?" asks one reporter.

"Yes," she cries. "Carol Paul was my daughter. I was held here against my will."

The lights and flashes make my retinas crackle. The liberation of the surviving Third-Day Adventists brings only temporary relief. Because after all of this, Rebekah is still dead. She was dead this entire time.

It's been twenty years since I felt this: numbness. All the emotions I should have, all the emotions anyone else would have, just aren't there. I'm not angry. I'm not sad. I'm not anything. Just numb. I need to get away. I need the air. I need one goddamn moment to breathe. I turn from the crowds and sneak away.

"What's your name, ma'am?" asks one of the reporters, a blonde with too much makeup on, heels too high for the clamshells.

It's the only question I answer. And then I move. I just move.

"My name is Freedom."

52

WHISTLER'S FIELD

My name is Freedom Oliver and I killed my daughter. Perhaps not directly, but I think I'll always blame myself. It's surreal, honestly, and I'm not sure what feels more like a dream, her death or her existence. In so many ways, and maybe it's self-inflicted, I'm guilty of both.

I couldn't stand the thought of hanging around outside the compound near God knows how many dead bodies just on the other side, and certainly not to answer the press's questions. I let Mason and Peter know I was fine before I snuck off. I was still in *keep moving* mode, I just had to get the hell out of there. So I walked aimlessly down the road, away from town. And then I saw the sign for Whistler's Field. Whistler's Field, where a couple hours before at the Paul house, Virgil confessed that here, Rebekah was chopped and buried. *"Which part?"*

I tried to imagine it in my head. It wasn't that long ago when this field would ripple and rustle with a warm breeze, gold dancing under the blazes of a high noon sun. The Thoroughbreds, a staple of Goshen, would canter along the edges of Whistler's Field. If you listen close enough, you can almost hear the laughter of farmers' children still lace through the grain, a harvest full of innocent secrets of the youthful who needed an escape but didn't have anywhere else to go. Like my Rebekah, my daughter. My God, she must have been beautiful.

But a couple weeks is a long time when you're on a journey like mine. It could almost constitute something magnificent. Almost.

I catch my breath when I remember. Somewhere in this field, my daughter is scattered in pieces.

Goshen, named after the biblical Land of Goshen, somewhere between Kentucky's famous bourbon trails in America's Bible Belt. The gallops of Thoroughbreds that haunt this dead pasture are replaced with the hammering in my rib cage. The mud cracks below me as I cross the frostbitten field, my footsteps ripping the earth with each fleeting memory. The skies are that certain shade of silver you see right before a snowstorm; now, the color of my filthy, fucking soul.

But I've been followed. From the corner of my eye, I see a deacon. I see Sheriff Don Mannix behind me with an itchy finger and a Remington aimed between my shoulder blades. He, too, got away. I am reminded of my own white-knuckled grip on my pistol, the pistol I still had from the compound, a grip insulated with the gloves sewn to my sleeves. *The deacon who made it out alive and uncaptured.* It sounds like some western if I've heard one before. But he's here with his job. He's here to kill me.

Call me what you will: a murderer, a cop killer, a fugitive, a drunk. You think that means anything to me now? In this moment? The frost pangs my lungs in such a way that I think I might vomit. I don't. Still out of breath, I use the dirty robe to wipe blood from my face. I don't even know if it's mine. There's enough adrenaline surging through my veins that I can't feel pain if it is.

"This is it, Freedom," the sheriff calls out in his familiar southern drawl. The tears make warm streaks over my cold skin. The cries numb my face, my lips made of pins and needles. There's a lump in my throat I can't breathe past. *What have I done? How the hell did I end up here? What did I do so wrong in life that God deemed me so fucking unworthy of anything good?* I'm not sure. I've always been the one with the questions, never the answers.

Perhaps it was those prayers I made only an hour or two ago that let me make it this far. I'm not sure. But I'm sure I hear him cock his gun. And somehow, I'm accepting of this. What choice do I have, really? Do I cry like a little bitch about it? No, I've lived my life. I even had that agreement with God, that He could take my life for the lives of those girls. It's a good trade, one the world can benefit from. So how can I cry about it? Why should I whine when God keeps His end of a bargain?

Then, the sound of the shot. It's the scariest sound I've ever heard. It's the sweetest fucking sound I've ever heard.

With my back still to the sheriff, a murder of crows bark away from the field, a ribbon of black across my vision.

But I don't fall. I don't feel the pain. I'm not hit. And it's not me who pulls the trigger. I hear the sound of Sheriff Don Mannix falling, a hard crash to the earth, a pile of skin, bone, and Remington steel. When I turn, a harsh wind on my face, I see Mattley. I see mother-fucking Officer James Mattley.

I'm spent, I don't even have the energy to stand. So he comes to me, this guardian angel from the West Coast, eyes curious and head tilted. From his back pocket, he pulls out a letter. I can barely hear him over the breeze. "I got this from Mimi. It's how I found you."

In the midst of such grief, is a person capable of love? I get the urge to tell him that perhaps it's possible. But now isn't the time. I can't find the words to tell him how thankful I am for him. I can't find the words to tell him that I *can't* find it in me to say such a thing. I can barely speak at all.

I handle the paper he hands me like it's dust in danger of floating away. "Can I have a moment, please?" My voice cracks. He squeezes my shoulder and walks away behind me.

Dear Nessa, or should I call you Mom?

There is so much to say; there's so much to take in. I've so much to tell you, but so little time, as I hide here in the shed of my church. I look back at my life. I wonder how'd I not see it, and looking here at your photo, I can see it, I can see it all.

For ages, I've been praying for a way out. Praying God takes me far from here. But in all this time, I've had nowhere to turn. There's Mason, but I need to be farther. I have to get away from here. I can't tell you why. Please, trust me. Trust in God. Because he sent your letter to me.

I will contact you in a few days when I reach Oregon.

Rebekah

Have you ever heard your soul snap in two? Have you ever cried for so long that you find yourself on the verge of fainting? Have you ever clawed at the frozen earth so hard that your fingernails break off? Have you ever screamed so loud that there was no noise at all, your windpipes simply failing you under the pressure? The reaction of a woman kneeling on the several graves of her one daughter.

I scare away the ghosts of Thoroughbreds. I scare away anything that dares to haunt this field. And in a way that I cannot explain, I've never felt more alive. In my own daughter's death, I never felt so much more alive than this. Because on the other side of such tragedy, of such turmoil, of such a long journey, something waits for me.

53
A PARADE OF BLACK

NINE MONTHS LATER

"My name is Freedom and I'm an alcoholic." The group greets me. In a church library with cheap coffee rings and stale rum cake, and I'm sure there were a few who rolled their eyes at that, it's my nine-month anniversary of sobriety. It feels like years. But time's tricky like that; it'll make you think you've acquired control when really you haven't.

I've even lost some weight over these past few months. Could be from not drinking, could be that I've lost much of my appetite since that dreadful day. That day. I tried to avoid the news and the Internet in the days following, but hearing about it was inevitable. I heard about the leaked photos, the tormenting ones of dead children sprawled along the pews of the church. The crosses and Bibles splattered in blood. The parade of little black body bags leaving the gates and traveling up the crushed clamshell roads. The headlines said on that day 345 men, women, and children committed suicide in the name of God. I also heard that several of the survivors killed themselves in the days and months following. It was the largest cult suicide to occur on American soil.

In Alcoholics Anonymous, we're encouraged to "find" a higher power, a power greater than ourselves that can restore us back to sanity. Not sure if *find* is the right word; I can't imagine God hiding behind a tree. I'm not so sure what that is, today . . . God. But as opposed to the days that preceded my short stay with the Third-Day Adventists, I believe something is there. I know I wasn't alone, and I know something or someone heard me when I pleaded to God back in Kentucky. So I'm giving the Bible a try. Don't get your hopes up too much. I didn't say I was born-again or anything like that, I only said I'm giving the Bible a try.

The news of the Delaney brothers who were killed on the Day of Freedom traveled fast to the topmost of the headlines, a sensational story in New York: a Mastic Beach fairy tale, in its own tragic way. Peter was even asked to write a book about them. He respectfully declined. And by *respectfully,* I mean he spit on the ground and proceeded to tell the journalist who'd suggested the idea to go fuck himself.

Peter lives with me now, and I wouldn't have it any other way. He and Mason even Skype every Sunday over a beer. I even got him a job at the Whammy Bar. They love him there, and there's no wonder. Needless to say, I don't visit my old place of work anymore. Gotta change my people, places, and things, just like we're told in the groups. *Because if nothing changes, nothing changes. Hear, hear.* But I still keep close to Carrie, my old boss, and Passion. Life would be boring without those two.

From what little I've heard, correctional officer Jimmy Doyle, the one rumored to have been hired by Lynn to break my kneecaps, went over to the Delaney house after hearing the news about her sons. It was Halloween.

I suppose the door was open, and when he let himself in, a massive pile of gray grease lay in the middle of the living room floor. It was Lynn Delaney, literally melting the floorboards of the house with decomposition: six hundred pounds of rancid decay. I'm sure Jimmy threw up at the stench, an odor strong enough that it woke the curiosity of the neighbors and probably stuck to the back of his skull for hours. The medical examiner would place the time of death at five days before: the day Peter ventured off for God's country. The Land of Tomorrow. The Unbridled Spirit. Kentucky.

Nosy neighbors from all over watched, dressed in their Halloween costumes, as the fire department had to tear down the walls because she couldn't fit through the door. From there on out, the biggest legacy Lynn left behind: the neighbor who had to be taken away by a moving truck because she couldn't fit in an ambulance.

Natural causes. Well, as natural as can be with such an unnatural weight. She fell. And she was never able to get herself back up.

54

SUNDAY

After a Sunday beer with Peter, a couple months after the Day of Freedom, Mason closes the laptop and observes his new office. He uses his fingertips to trace the edges of his name on a plaque: Assistant District Attorney Mason P. Paul. No more defending criminals for him. On his desk, a gift box wrapped in red and gold for his mother. Inside, Rebekah's cross, the one he'd found at the Bluegrass.

"Heya, Mason, got something for you." His new assistant, a young brunette named Bobby Jo, hands him an A4 envelope, postmarked from Frankfort, Kentucky, the capital city.

"Wow, my very first piece of mail to the office." Mason smiles, sitting in his brand-new leather office chair.

"You should frame it," she squeals.

"You know what? I should." He tears into it, delighted, and pulls out the contents.

"Well?" She holds her hands to her mouth like a giddy child. "What are we framing?" But he doesn't answer her right away. "What's the matter?"

"Nothing," he says as the assistant watches him sink in his seat. "It's nothing. Say, Bobby Jo, can I have a minute?"

"Of course." She closes the door after her. He rubs the back of his neck, heartbeat getting faster, debating whether or not he should read all the details of his sister's autopsy report. He decides it'd be best that he doesn't. He doesn't want his last memories of Rebekah like that; he already knows too much: how she was dispersed shamefully in a field like fertilizer for the animals. That was enough for him. He tossed the papers behind him, having no intention of ever reading them.

He sifts through another box of his belongings and continues to spend the Sunday making his office feel more personal. He pulls out a framed photo of him and Violet from their trip to Turks and Caicos.

"I'm sorry to bother you again," says Bobby Jo from the speaker-phone. "There's someone here to see you."

"Send 'em in," he responded.

Mason studies the young woman who walks in, a visibly pregnant woman in jeans and a purple cardigan, eyes hiding behind thick bangs and nerdy glasses. "Can I help you?" he asked.

The woman says nothing, instead handing Mason a business card. His own card, his own handwriting. On the back:

Contact me soon. I will help you.

It is the woman from the Goshen Police Department, the drunken girl passed out. Darian Cooke raped this woman. And once she gives birth, it'll be impossible to deny.

55

PAINTER

My name is Freedom and I'm working on a crossword puzzle in bed. I like puzzles when I can't sleep. I'm too excited about my son arriving tomorrow. Twelve across, "Painter James McNeill _____." The answer is Whistler. Fucking Whistler. Goshen.

The only story coming out of Goshen that I really followed in the weeks after was Ger and Adelaide Custis, the Amalekite. We speak often, weekly. And in the four years that she was held against her will, her faith never subsided, no matter how bastardized it was in that group. I suppose they have the best happily-ever-after ending they could have, considering the circumstances. Mason visits his grandparents regularly.

I never knew what became of Baby Theresa. Those records were closed. But I can only hope that she was taken in by some nice family. I can only hope that her brief stay with the Third-Day Adventists will never haunt her. I can only hope she grows into a beautiful young lady.

The media painted Virgil and Carol in a terrible light upon the discovery of the corpses of the twelve young females in Whistler's Field, along with the fact of Virgil having fathered nearly sixty children within the cult. One of the bodies in the field was a decade old;

the rest had been killed within the last four or so years. They weren't all local, one being from Louisiana, another from Indiana, one more from Tennessee. But the most recent one was a local. And Rebekah Jane Paul, once known as Layla Delaney and later known as the Virgin Mary, was never documented as having been originally from a New York state prison. But she was. My Layla. My Rebekah. That said, I guess she was never mine to begin with.

But she carried my blood, she had that passion ... and she wanted to move.

Well, as for me, what can I say? I guess it was too much work for them, or maybe nobody cared about the monsters, but it was never publicly reported that the Pauls were murdered. That will remain a secret I will take to the grave. Mason will never know that skeleton. I suppose the Amalekite had her suspicions, but she never said a word. Like Rebekah, she was a victim.

"Are you crying?" Mattley comes from the bathroom, shirtless, smelling of toothpaste and shaving cream.

"I guess so."

He comes across the bed on his knees and leans down to me. "Don't cry, Freedom." He tucks my hair behind my ears and wipes a tear away.

"I don't know if I'm crying because I'm sad or because I'm happy."

"I know," he whispers. He pulls the drawer from the bedside table and pulls out my prescription, placing the Monday pill in my hand. No more jars. No more Gumm and Howe. "Freedom, I want you to do something for me."

I look up at him.

"I want you to marry me."

I lean in to kiss him, but I'm interrupted. "Daddy, I can't sleep," says his son, Richie.

"Me neither," trails Magdalene in the doorway. "Uncle Peter snores too loud."

I smile. "Get on up here, then." Mattley and I sit Indian-style, facing each other, Richie sitting on his lap and Magdalene on mine. The kids thumb-wrestle. I look at Mattley and nod to him.

Magdalene has been enrolled in several counseling groups since she came home with us. All the therapists say she's making great progress, that she didn't see as much at the Third-Day Adventists as she could have, and that, to *everyone's* relief, she'd missed her father's attentions by a matter of a few years. Every night, she insists on praying over dinner, and I'll never stop her. The kid's faith is admirable.

"Now," I begin. "Once upon a time, there was an Indian named Freedom."

56

SOVEREIGN SHORE

The sand between Mason's toes, a nonalcoholic beer from the cooler out of respect for his mother's sobriety. Sovereign Shore.

"Do you really have to work while we're here at the beach?" Freedom asks him, his briefcase half planted in the sand. The Pacific Ocean on the Oregon shore rocks gentler than he imagined.

"I promise, it won't take me long."

"Suit yourself," Freedom sings. "And we're off!" She lifts Magdalene in one graceful sweep and runs into the ocean. The girl squeals in delight, yells that echo off the surf, fading the farther out in the water Freedom takes her.

Mason looks out to his mother and his little sister. Suddenly he is reminded of his visions, his dreams of Freedom before he knew who she was. The more he sees of them now, the more vivid his memories become. Her tropical smell, her perfect teeth, her tattoos, and hair tangled with sand and salt. He watches, hypnotized, Freedom tossing Magdalene up and down, the sun behind them fading away to warm other nations, the sky turning to shades of gold and pink. It warms his face as the shadows grow longer around them, the evening still warm enough to sun-kiss his cheeks. And in his mind, he can imagine the airplane and banner from his youth. Freedom McFly.

He looks over at Violet and mouths the words *I love you*, and he's never meant it more. He smiles when she says it back. He thinks how he could not possibly understand what his mother had to sacrifice, never having known about being a parent. Looking at Violet, he imagines he might have an idea. In, give or take, seven months. And he can't wait to tell the rest of the family.

He returns to his work with a smile, papers now smudged with coconut tanning oil in the margins. He flips through them, a knot in his Adam's apple when he sees Rebekah's autopsy report mixed in there by accident. He inhales sharply, but he doesn't let the apprehension show on his face. He scans through it, with the knowledge that he'll probably regret it shortly after. His eyes stop at certain words: words like *serrated, bludgeoned, blunt-force trauma*. But one word makes Mason stop breathing. One word makes him nearly swallow his own tongue. One word makes him rise to his feet and stare out at his mother and Magdalene: *Cesarean*. It was noted on her, could still be detected by the ME. Though Virgil had cut off her arms, legs, and head and piled the pieces in a single grave, her torso and groin were still intact.

Magdalene was the daughter of Rebekah Jane Paul. She is the biological granddaughter of Freedom Oliver.

Mason looks out as Freedom dances with Magdalene in the breaks of the slow-rocking waves under one of the most unforgettable sunsets he's ever seen. Freedom stops to look right back at her son, cradling Magdalene like the daughter she held only once. And she holds her longer than two minutes and seventeen seconds. And in that moment, in the way she carries the girl, in the way she looks back at Mason, in the way she's changed her life for that child, Mason knows. He just knows: Freedom knew from the get-go that Magdalene was her granddaughter. She knew it the second she arrived in Goshen, Kentucky.

■■■

My name is Freedom and I look down at Magdalene's joy-filled eyes, the waves crashing around us. Magdalene reaches up to caress my cheeks.

"Finish the story, Sister Freedom," Magdalene asks.

And I think back, to a porch in the Snake River Plain, as I retell it to Magdalene.

"This, in your language, might be called karma. But where we are from, it's all part of the circle of life. And Freedom completed that circle, as everything in life happens in a circle." The old man drew a circle in the sky with his finger. The rocking chair continued to creak under him. "And to this day, that very tree continues to grow."

I hold Magdalene so hard that I could squeeze the life out of her. It doesn't matter that she was a product of violence, attacks, and evil. Because she isn't a product. She isn't a result. She is Rebekah's flesh and blood. She is my flesh and blood. She is mine.

ACKNOWLEDGMENTS

I have to start by thanking my husband, John, who is just crazy enough to actually tolerate me and my work on a daily basis. Without his support, this book would have long been burned and the hard drives still lost at sea . . . or the bathtub (remember that, John?). But all kidding aside, John has been one of the few people who took a chance on me and had faith in my writing when no one else did. And for that, I'll be forever thankful.

Next, my lead researcher, Miss Sarah Cailean, my favorite cop from Philly, whose invaluable advice and quick responses have been lifesavers throughout the writing of this book. In my very small circle of friends whom I continually share my work with, Sarah is my go-to girl, especially for help in legal and police procedure. Thanks, chica. You're the bestest.

Also in this circle are three gentlemen I've known for many years. Jason Marano from the Bronx, whose encouragement and excitement over my writing has lit fires under my ass on many days when I doubted myself. And Stephen Perry Quesada, my favorite psychologist in New York, whose help in understanding hard-to-understand people was a great help in this book and will continue to be a great help in the next one. Last in the circle, but certainly not least, James Cashman, who is literally one of the most beautiful writers I've ever known. I thank you guys for all your patience. And, of course, Heather Jackson, my home slice from Long Island. Thanks for always reminding me why I had to write this book and for being one of the greatest friends a girl could ask for.

Jessica Bonati, my sister: the only person in this world who *really* knows me. I love you with all my heart. Your pep talks and answering my calls in the middle of the night have proven to be absolutely necessary in order for me to want to achieve something in life, especially this book.

To Vik Usack, my father, a man who somehow knew since the day I was born that I was destined for something. Thank you for seeing things in me that I never could and for having faith in me when I gave you every reason not to. Without you seeing my potential, I may have never written this.

And now, we cross the pond. One of the most important people in helping me write this book is Helen Falconer, whom I refer to as St. Helen of Mayo, from the Inkwell consulting agency of Dublin. Thank you for editing the shit out of my book since the first page of the very first draft. Your help was more than I could ever ask for. Vanessa O'Loughlin, for leading the literary movement in Ireland with www.writing.ie and with The Inkwell Group. Many thanks for taking a chance on me and my writing. To everyone in the Irish Crime Group for their criticism and help as I was learning how to write. To Carousel Creates, for making available to me an outlet to work. And to my Irish family, the O'Donnells, whom I've come to love, for supporting me and for their continued support, especially Ber and Paddy, my in-laws.

Now last, not least, the guys behind the curtain . . . Oz, is what I call them. First, my literary agent at WME, Simon Trewin. It was you who single-handedly turned me from a writer at home to a real-life author. A million thank-yous and here's to a great literary marriage. And to my editors at HarperCollins UK Killer Reads, Sarah

Hodgson and Kate Elton, whose guidance continues to mold me as a writer and for helping me hone skills I never knew I had. And, finally, senior editor Zack Wagman of the Crown Publishing Group at Penguin Random House US, the literary genius god with a top hat and wings. Thank you, from one Yankee to another, for the bucket-loads of help you've poured my way.